A Jersey Kiss

Georgina Troy

Published by Accent Press Ltd 2016

ISBN 9781786150158

Acknowledgements:

There are so many people I'd like to thank I could go on for several pages, but I'm especially grateful to: everyone at Accent Press, especially Cat Camacho, Beth Jones, Stephanie Williams and Hazel Cushion;

Christina Jones for her cover quote; Kirsty Greenwood and Edward Jordan for their gorgeous cover and Bryan Hamiliton from eKindled for creating the paperback cover from their original artwork; the Novel Racers; CI Fiction Group; Jersey Writers Group; Romantic Novelists' Association; my non-writer friends, especially Rob, Andrea, Rachael, Kate, Jas, Andy, Fee, Tim, Lorenzo, Courtney, Trish and Beverley, as well as Sacha, Sharon, Tracey, Claire and Rach, who are always ready to open a bottle of champagne.

Most of all, my lovely, and slightly eccentric, extended family who are used to seeing my far-away look when I'm lost in a book.

Dedication

"To RC, JC, SC and MC"

One

June – Blowing Dandelion Clocks

'I'm coming, I'm coming,' Bea shouted breathlessly, stepping out of the shower and almost losing her balance as she slipped on the mat. She grabbed hold of the shower curtain in an attempt to stay upright, snapping it from its rings in the process before wrapping the nearest towel she could reach around her dripping body and running down the stairs.

'Bloody builders,' she cursed, stubbing her toe on the oak banister. Why did they choose today to arrive early, the one time she was running late? She pulled open the heavy front door.

'Sorry, love,' a man in paint-spattered overalls said, his eyes widening as he took in her lack of clothing. 'We, um, seem to have caught you on the 'op.'

'Yes, well, I'm in a bit of a rush.' She held the door open for the builder and his apprentice to enter the hallway. Making sure she held on tightly to the front of her towel with one hand, Bea pushed back a stray lock of her blonde hair with the other. 'I'll take you up to my bedroom.' The spotty-faced boy stifled a giggle, raising a pierced eyebrow at his boss until he was nudged sharply in the ribs. Bea cleared her throat. Realising what she'd just said, she added, 'So that I can show you the work I need you to quote for.'

'Right you are, love.'

She could hear the builder grumbling under his breath to his apprentice and led the two men up the carved oak staircase, trying not to think about how little her towel was covering and hoping they couldn't see her bottom. 'My bathroom is en-suite, or at least I hope it soon will be,' she explained, her face hot

1

and cheeks pink at the thought of what she'd just said. 'So I thought the best place to start would be my room.'

'Righty oh.'

'I'll need the wall from this room knocked through, and a doorway put in down that end.' She pointed across the room, noticing her knickers and bra had dropped off the chair and onto the floor. Kicking them under the bed, she took a breath to continue.

'Can't be done,' said a gruff voice from the hallway.

She took a backwards step out of her room to see who was talking. 'Why not?' she asked, her intended rant immediately catching in her throat when she came face-to-face with the owner of a pair of the most piercing blue eyes she'd ever seen. Bea was sure he must be handsome under all that facial hair and despite her annoyance with him couldn't help staring.

'This is a very old house, and that, young lady, is a load-bearing wall,' he said, his perfect lips drawing back into a slight smile she instinctively knew was more amusement than appreciation of her appearance. He cleared his throat before tapping the wall for emphasis. 'I wouldn't advise you to knock through it.'

Young lady? He couldn't be much older than her, she mused. Then again, thought Bea, he could almost be any age under all those whiskers. 'But I'd planned to,' Bea argued, not liking his condescending manner or his amused gaze. He may be used to women being stunned into submission by his overpowering presence, but she had just got rid of a bullying husband and wasn't about to replace him with a bossy builder.

'And you are?' she asked, wishing she wasn't in such a compromising position. Being late was one thing, but not being dressed in front of this scowling builder was another entirely.

'Luke Thornton,' he said studying the wall. 'I was a bit delayed so I asked Bill to come ahead.' He motioned for Bea to follow him and walked down the hallway to another bedroom the other side of hers. 'This would be a better option.' He narrowed his eyes, contemplating the wall in front of him. 'This box room would make a perfect en-suite.' He peered out of the window. 'Imagine soaking in your bath and staring across the

2

fields at that view of Corbiére lighthouse.' He stepped back, making room for Bea to have a look. She leant forward and gazed at the uninterrupted view across the fields to the white tower perched at the edge of the sea. He was right. She always enjoyed looking at this majestic building on the rocks at one end of St Ouen's Bay.

'Pretty spectacular, don't you think?' he said, coming to stand behind her.

Bea gripped her towel, wishing she'd at least taken the time to put on her underwear, and nodded. He was right of course.

'Then,' he continued without waiting for her to answer, 'you could keep the other as the house bathroom. It's bigger, after all, and closer to the rest of the bedrooms.'

She thought through his suggestion for a moment. 'I see what you're saying, but I'd got the whole set up planned out in detail,' she said, not wishing to give in to him too readily, but desperate to put on some clothes. 'It doesn't sound like I have much of a choice really, so I suppose I'll have to go with your suggestion.'

Luke shrugged. 'You can do as you like, it's your house.' He studied the clipboard Bill handed to him. 'According to my secretary, apart from replacing the house bathroom and creating an en-suite, you also need the downstairs cloakroom to be refitted, some plastering in the hall, and a bit of painting and decorating throughout the rest of the house.'

Bea nodded silently. It sounded as if this was going to be mammoth when he listed everything like that. Luke withdrew a biro from the top of the clipboard and began making notes. 'You two can get going if you like, I'll catch up with you later.' He walked slowly down the stairs, his hand grazing paint surfaces as he passed the walls.

'Don't mind him, love,' whispered Bill from behind her. 'He doesn't mean to be so abrasive, it's just his manner.'

'He's had a lot goin' on,' the apprentice added, before receiving another nudge in his bruised ribs. 'Ouch, what was that one for?'

'You can get in the van.' The builder shook his head and frowned. 'Bloody kid is too ready to give his opinion when it's not needed.' He tilted his head in Luke's direction. 'He's a grand chap though.'

Bea glanced at Luke's broad back as he stepped into the downstairs cloakroom. 'He hides it well, doesn't he?' she murmured before hurrying to her bedroom to dress. Once clothed, she slipped on her shoes and went to wait for him in the kitchen at the back of the house. What was his problem with her anyway? He made her earlier moodiness seem positively chirpy.

Bea checked the time and wished he would hurry up. She didn't have long and it would take at least fifteen minutes to get to her appointment, even if she took the open road all the way along St Ouen's Bay, past the sand dunes and over by the golf course to St Brelade's Bay. She took out a small mirror from her handbag and re-applied her cherry lip-gloss. Butterflies imitated kango-hammers in her stomach; she wasn't looking forward to this meeting. Business associates were one thing, but dealing with the spoilt wife of her biggest client was another entirely.

'Wow, this room's a shrine to orange Formica,' Luke announced from the doorway.

Bea frowned. He was right, but there was no need to be rude. 'It is a bit, but I can't afford to do everything I want with the house, unfortunately. It's functional, even if it is a little, um, orange, so it'll have to wait until I can find enough money to fit in a new one.'

Luke raked a hand through his messy brown fringe. 'It's not too bad.'

She noticed the glint of merriment in his eyes. 'I think that's a matter of opinion.' Bea raised her eyebrows, unable to help glancing up at the kitchen clock and checking the time once again.

'Right,' he said, smiling down at her. 'You obviously have to be somewhere and I've made all the notes I should need. I'll pass this on to my secretary in the morning, and she'll post a quote on to you.'

Bea couldn't help noticing how his smile seemed to light up his entire face, or what she could see of it through his stubble.

4

Her stomach did an involuntary flip when his dark blue eyes gave away his amusement, and looking away from him, she pushed her hand deep into her bag. She wished her aunt was still with her; they'd have laughed about his stunned expression on seeing the kitchen for the first time. 'I can never find anything in here,' she said, aware of him watching her as she rummaged around trying to locate her car keys.

'I know better than to comment on women's handbags.' He shrugged. 'Was there anything else you need me to add to this list before I go?'

Flea jumped out of his basket and started barking. He trotted over to the French doors and tapped the glass with his paw, frantic to be let out. 'Stop it,' Bea snapped, knowing the aging Miniature Schnauzer her aunt had adored wasn't listening to her.

'What's wrong with him? Did he see something, do you think?' He squinted out of the window in the same direction as the dog.

Bea bent to pick Flea up and put him down in his basket. 'Stay there. You know you can't catch the birds.' She looked over at Luke. 'He goes mad if a bird comes into the garden. He also does the same in the autumn if a leaf dares to blow past the window. It can get a little exhausting at times.'

Luke shook his head and smiled. 'Silly boy.' He stroked Flea's soft fur. 'He's a character though, I'll bet?'

Bea nodded. 'He can also be a pain in the bum, but I love him to bits.' She remembered the time and tried not to panic. 'Right, about that work?' Bea mulled over what she'd asked Luke to price for, and picking up her suit jacket from the back of her chair, she hesitated for a moment. 'This is a bit awkward,' she said. 'I'm not sure I'll be able to afford to have all the work done at once.' She chewed her lower lip. 'When I spoke to my sister about contacting you I'd hoped to be able to take out a loan for the work.'

His expression softened. 'Yes, I was sorry to hear about your aunt. I heard she was a remarkable lady.'

Bea swallowed. It was too soon to hope to be brave when talking about Aunt Annabel, but she needed to at least try. 'She was.' She cleared her throat, determined to draw her mind away from her heartache. She couldn't afford to mess up her mascara now; she didn't have time to fix her face before leaving. 'If you wouldn't mind only quoting for the bathrooms and plastering for now, I'll probably have to do the rest myself.'

Luke nodded and scribbled something in his notebook. 'Not a problem. Give me a call if you're happy with the quote. The guys should be able to start early next week.'

Bea was surprised they would be beginning the work so soon, but didn't like to say so. 'OK, thank you.' She walked through to the front door with him. He'd seemed so gentle, then, for a moment. 'Sorry to rush you, but I'm a little late for an appointment and need to get a move on.'

She waited for him to go out and step into his blue pickup truck and watched in silence as he disappeared down her long gravel driveway in a cloud of dust. It was like blowing a dandelion clock, she mused, you never knew where the seeds would end up. She sighed heavily. This was no time to start panicking about the massive responsibility she was taking on. How many people would swap places with her in a second if they could own a house and garden as grand as The Brae, she wondered. Bea glanced around the large panelled hallway. This house should be enjoyed by a family, though, not a solitary, newly separated, grieving thirty-year-old. Was she mad to try so hard to keep this place?

She walked back to the kitchen to check Flea was calmer and still in his bed. 'Good boy,' she soothed. 'I won't be long.'

As she walked through the hallway to the front door, Bea looked up at the assortment of paintings hanging from the panelling. 'Are any of you A Jersey Kiss?' she asked, doubting it very much. None of them looked like they could be. What was A Jersey Kiss, anyway and why hadn't her aunt left some sort of clue in her will?

Two

July – A Thorny Issue

'Have you discovered what A Jersey Kiss is supposed to be yet?' Mel asked. 'Do you think it could be a painting or something?'

Bea wished she knew. Ever since her aunt's lawyer had told her that she'd inherited something called A Jersey Kiss, she'd been trying to figure out what it was. 'I've no idea. I've never seen anything that looks as if it could be called that and I've checked all the paintings in the house.'

'Mum said it could possibly be a piece of jewellery. Didn't Antonio used to buy your aunt lovely pieces? She said they sometimes have names, if they're extra special?'

'Maybe,' Bea said, trying once again to picture the contents of her aunt's jewellery box and wondering why her stepmother, Mel's mum, who had never shown any interest in anything either she or aunt had ever done before, was now trying to unlock this mystery. 'Then again, the lawyer told me that Aunt Annabel made her will over twenty years ago. She's always needed money for her garden projects, so maybe she sold it during that time?'

'Probably,' Mel said, looking disappointed. 'Well, if it isn't the long-lost kiss thing that's making you look so thoughtful; I suppose something must have gone wrong with your visit to where?'

'Shoe shopping, to Heavenly in Heels, Paige's shop in De Greys where she sells her designs. I don't know why she couldn't go by herself, but I didn't like to argue. She's now the proud owner of four pairs of the most expensive designs. So, I suppose, Paige has had a good day.'

Mel pulled a face. 'Lucky cow, I'd kill for a pair of those

7

shoes. So what's up then? You look like a bulldog chewing a wasp.'

'You're so kind,' she said groaning. 'If you must know, I was thinking about Luke Thornton.' Bea dragged a black chiffon top over her chest, wishing, not for the first time, that her boobs were a couple of cup sizes smaller. Maybe she'd been a little over optimistic to think that she could fit into the clothes Mel had kindly brought to her house for her to try on.

'Oh yes, the famous Luke Thornton. I've never met him, but Grant tells me he's a pretty forceful guy.'

'Now why doesn't that surprise me?' Bea said raising an eyebrow. 'Although does your soon-to-be fiancé also explain why Luke's so moody?'

'Problems with his partner, I think.' Mel tilted her head to one side and studied Bea's torso thoughtfully.

'You mean she had the sense to leave him?' Bea couldn't help asking.

Mel shook her head. 'Not his girlfriend, a bloke, his business partner. I think he disappeared taking Luke's money, or something. Someone said he's been struggling a bit with it all.' Mel narrowed her eyes. 'You seem very interested in someone you said was horrible.'

'I'm only asking,' Bea said, pulling on a different top and scowling at her reflection in the cheval mirror. 'It's too tight. I knew this would be a waste of time. There's no way I can fit into any of your clothes and I've worn all mine to death.'

Mel tugged at the hem from behind her in an attempt to pull the top into shape. 'Will you hurry up and get ready?'

'I can't wear this.' Bea dragged off the offending article with a little difficulty and dropped it on her crumpled duvet cover with the ten or so other outfits lying in a heaped mess on the bed.

'We're going to have to think of something,' Mel said, folding the top angrily.

'This is my first time out since Aunt Annabel, well, you know.'

'She died, Bea. Yes, I know and I'm sorry, but you have to get a grip and move on.' Mel pulled back a few clothes hanging in Bea's wardrobe, checking for a suitable top. 'I know it was shit of Simon to leave so soon after, but tonight's my engagement party and I'm not going to let you mope at home.'

'You just don't want to have to deal with Joyce if I don't turn up.' Bea raised an eyebrow and grabbed hold of a purple silk peplum top that she seemed to wear to every smart occasion.

'Listen, we may not share the same mother, and I know she's a bit of a pain, but she only wants the best for me.'

Bea nodded. It wasn't Mel's fault her mother seemed so intent on pushing Mel forward in their father's affections. Poor man, how he coped with such determination, Bea could never understand.

'Anyway it's been months since Annabel told you about Simon getting all hot and heavy with that slutty assistant of his, slimy git.'

Aunt Annabel, thought Bea. She'd have known what to say to cheer her up. 'I think the hardest part is that Claire's already pregnant with his baby.' She took a deep breath and held her arms out. 'What do you think?' she asked, holding the top up over her chest. 'It's not perfect, but it'll have to do.'

'Great, now try this lipstick. It's a different shade to the cherry one you always wear. I think it'll suit you.'

Bea pouted in front of the mirror, concentrating on turning her full lips from their natural pale pink to a searing shade of fuchsia. Someone banged forcefully on her front door. Bea jumped, inadvertently rouging half her cheek. 'Shit.' She placed the lipstick down onto her dressing table and went downstairs.

'What the hell are you supposed to be?' Simon asked, looking her up and down as she opened the front door and stepped back as he made his way past her into the hall.

'Come in, Simon,' Mel invited sarcastically.

He ignored her and kept his attention focused on Bea. She grabbed an old Barbour jacket from behind the heavy door, dragging it on over her underwear. She really needed to stop answering the door wearing so little, she thought, annoyed for not thinking before doing so.

'I don't believe this.' He swung round, staring down at

Bea's chest encased in the new black satin push-up bra Mel had persuaded her to buy. 'You two are going out, together. Aunt Annabel would have been delighted.'

Bea crossed her arms to hold the coat in place and swallowed. 'You leave her out of this.'

'She never liked me, did she?' He peered down at Bea, his irritation at her barely hidden.

'Probably because your angelic looks and charm secretly hid the ugliness of a toad,' Mel said from the bottom of the stairs.

'What the hell is she on about?' He raised his eyebrows, ignoring Mel.

'You know perfectly well my godmother liked you, until she realised I wasn't the only woman you were sleeping with,' Bea snapped. 'She changed her mind then, of course.'

'We weren't getting on. It wasn't just my fault that our marriage broke down, you know. It takes two.'

Bea heard Mel's sharp intake of breath behind her, knowing instinctively her sister was seconds from exploding with indignation. 'Mel, why don't you go through to the kitchen and pour us both a drink?' Bea suggested, turning back to face Simon. His beautiful face contorted with spite. 'This won't take long.'

Mel for once did as she was asked, and stomped down the hallway towards the kitchen.

Bea narrowed her eyes. 'So you say, but I seemed to be the only who wasn't aware of that. Anyway, I suppose you're here about your letter?' Bea pulled out a crumpled tissue her hand had located in the jacket pocket, and spat on it before rubbing it against her cheek. 'I can't believe you want half of this house. You've always hated it here and you know Aunt Annabel left it to me.'

'Yes, she wanted to make sure you were looked after,' he said, repeating her aunt's often said words. 'It's not my fault your father has a scheming wife, or that your mother died. The fact remains that your aunt died when we were still married.' He lowered his face closer to hers. She could almost taste his minty breath. 'Technically, we still are. And as such, the house is considered a matrimonial asset, and I, as your husband, am

10

legally entitled to half of its value.'

The heat of her fury towards him almost gave her heartburn. How could he be so heartless to push for her to sell Aunt Annabel's house? 'Legally maybe, not morally though.' She recalled his letter. 'And what exactly did you mean by D-Day?'

Simon smiled, looking satisfied with himself. 'I thought that was rather clever, didn't you?' Bea glared at him. 'Suit yourself. D-Day, Debt Day. Get it?'

Bea closed her eyes slowly willing him to disappear. 'Right. Very funny.'

'I thought so. I don't want you forgetting the date.'

'I'm hardly likely to do that, am I?' She'd had enough. 'What did you want?'

'I've settled in to the apartment with Claire. Maybe, if we hadn't moved in to live with your aunt our relationship might not have fallen apart so rapidly,' he mused, then shrugged. 'Anyway, I thought I'd collect one or two things I forgot to take with me when you threw me out.' He straightened a picture on the wall before stopping to stare at it. 'This is mine, I believe,' he added, lifting the depiction of a bloody hunting scene Bea had always hated off the hook.

She took a deep breath and mentally braced herself. 'Take the painting, Simon and while you're at it, take yourself out of my house, and don't bang on the door demanding to be let in like that again.' Bea went to let him in.

'Well, the door was locked.' Simon put his hand out to stop her. 'When the hell did you change the locks anyway?'

Was he insane? 'As soon as you left. When do you think?' she asked, stunned by his ridiculous question.

'You've changed, Beatrice,' Simon said, lowering his voice. 'You used to be kind and decent.'

Bea took a deep breath to steady her voice, stunned at his sheer nerve. 'Really? I thought I still was.' She concentrated on remaining calm, unable to believe they were covering the same old ground yet again. 'Don't forget, it was you who moved on, not me, so I don't know why you're always so offended by everything I do.'

'Maybe if you were in a relationship too, you'd understand

how I feel about Claire. Anyway, you know as well as I do that the only reason I left was because your interfering aunt made such a fuss and wound you up.' He considered his next words and glared at her down his aquiline nose, the same nose she had not so long ago found very attractive, but now wanted desperately to hit, hard. 'I'd still be living here with you if she hadn't interfered.'

'You mean if she hadn't caught you with Claire. Don't you think I might have discovered your girlfriend was pregnant at some point?' She heard the catch in her voice and could have bitten her tongue. Pushing away the painful memory of her recent miscarriage, she narrowed her eyes. 'Aunt Annabel found you practically having sex in Claire's car. I think she had every right to be upset with you.'

'Look I am sorry about the baby; I know how that must hurt you.' He went to put a hand on her shoulder, but Bea stepped back before he could reach her. Simon shrugged and looked over her shoulder at the rundown hallway. 'Why can't you stop trying to punish me for being happy? The trouble with you is you spent far too much time with that old woman. Annabel might have been your godmother, and I understand how she took over when your mum died, but she's gone now and you need to stop hanging on to this heap of rubble. Then we can both move on.'

Bea didn't want to give him the satisfaction of seeing her lose her temper, or even worse, get upset. Her life had not worked out as she had planned and it hurt like hell, but she wasn't going to let him know how she felt. She clasped her hands together. 'I've already moved on, Simon; regardless of what you choose to believe.'

'Whatever you say.' He laughed, glancing at his latest Cartier watch. 'I couldn't care less, but I do want to know when you intend paying me my share of this mausoleum?'

Bea wondered if he was simply trying to punish her for not forgiving him for his affair when he'd asked her to. She felt the familiar nervous tingle expanding in her stomach. 'Simon, I don't know why you insist I buy you out of this place. You're a lawyer. You earn far more than I ever will and didn't need any extra money to buy your new apartment. The house was left to me, not you. Why don't we stop arguing and get this matter sorted, then we can have our *decree absolute* and neither of us have to bother with the other one again.'

Simon groaned. 'Yes, well, are you going to get a mortgage to pay me what I'm owed, or am I going to take you to court to get an Order for the damn money?'

Bea hesitated. She didn't have the money to fight him through the courts and he knew it. 'Simon, it's almost impossible to get a mortgage now, you know that as well as anyone. I'm going to need a little more time.'

'Time to find a way out of paying me, you mean.'

'No. I need to come up with a solution and you bullying me won't make it happen any sooner.'

'My lawyer explained everything in his letter to you. You have a year and a day from the date your aunt died, which will be when probate is concluded. That's 10th May next year. I think that's more than enough time to find a mortgage. You're the one insisting on keeping this crumbling 1920s dump, but Claire's given up work now she's pregnant and has decided she doesn't want to return when the baby's born. I need to get my finances sorted once and for all. We're going to get married as soon as the divorce is finalised and that can't happen until we've sorted the finances, so I'm not giving you any longer than I have to.'

'I'm not selling my house.' She clenched her fists.

He leant towards her, his eyes like steely flints. 'Be realistic, it's a mess.' He flung his arms wide, as if to encompass the cold hallway.

'That's my problem,' she said, knowing Aunt Annabel's legacy had been her magnificent garden with its endless species of plants she'd brought back over the decades from her travels.

Simon stepped back and made a point of looking her up and down for a final time. Shaking his head slowly, he sniggered before turning his back on her and marched outside towards his gleaming BMW.

Bea slammed the heavy oak door as hard as she could, realising too late, as a smattering of plaster cascaded like icing sugar on to the worn slate floor next to her, that it had not been a good idea.

She slumped down on to the Bishop's seat. It wasn't in keeping with the period of the property, but Bea had bought it at her first auction with her godmother when she was sixteen. The cool, familiar grain in the wood soothed her. 'What do you think, Flea?' she whispered to her aging Miniature Schnauzer as he ambled over to join her, resting his tatty grey head on her trembling lap. Petting him calmed her down a little, but it didn't solve the problem of her lack of money. It was all very well, this bravado, Bea mused, but how was she going to afford to sort out the house?

'Drink,' Mel insisted, handing her a double gin and tonic, and settling down next to her. 'That man is such a moron. It's bad enough he did the dirty on you, let alone he still feels he has control over every aspect of your life. He must earn so much more than you, too.'

Bea shrugged miserably. 'Unfortunately he does.' She took a mouthful of the refreshing liquid, and swallowed gratefully. 'Can you imagine he thought he could still use his key to get in?'

They sat silently in the hallway as her temper gradually subsided. Glancing at her newly French-manicured nails as they cupped the glass, she noticed for the first time the groove on her finger where her wedding ring used to be was finally fading. Soon there would be no trace of it at all. No trace of the Beatrice Porter, of old. 'Mel, I'm not sure I can face going out,' she admitted. 'I look a mess and ...'

'And nothing,' Mel interrupted standing up in front of her. 'It's my engagement party.' She held out her hands, displaying the brilliant diamond solitaire. 'When was the last time you were invited to celebrate something at Elizabeth Castle? You're not going to miss a second of it. It's not often we get on and I want tonight to be special. You're my sister, well half-sister, and you're going to enjoy yourself, whether you like it or not.'

Bea couldn't help laughing. 'Poor Grant, he doesn't have a clue what he's let himself in for does he?'

'No.' Mel nudged her sister and smiled conspiratorially. 'He

14

doesn't, and you're not going to tell him either.'

Bea stepped off the castle ferry that had taken her and other guests to the tiny island in the bay, wishing she'd thought to wear more sensible heels. She gazed up at the turrets from the small docking area, amused that Mel had chosen somewhere so romantic to hold her engagement party. Following the signpost inside to the party area, Bea spotted Shani and Paul by the bar. No surprise there then, Bea smiled, amused to see her two closest friends deep in conversation as usual. How they ever stopped talking long enough to fit in their jobs giving classes at the largest gym complex in town, she couldn't imagine.

'Hi, you two,' she said hugging them both. She looked down at Paul's blond head. 'These weren't the best idea,' she said lifting her leg to show off the shoes. 'I don't know why I thought they would be.'

'Only Mel could insist we all travel to somewhere that you have to get to by boat,' Shani said. 'I was hoping it'd be a little cooler in a castle, but these rooms are still hot for some reason.'

Bea nodded. She'd thought the same thing. She fanned her face with her bag. 'I love your hair though, Shan.'

'If she has it any shorter everyone will assume she's had it shaved off completely.' Paul laughed. 'If you didn't have such a girly face you could be mistaken for a bloke. Tall, no boobs, no hair.'

Shani laughed and elbowed him in the ribs. 'Don't start with me, we might be flatmates, but you know I'm tougher than you'll ever be.'

'You two act like an old married couple sometimes,' Bea said wincing at Paul's horrified expression.

'What a horrible thought.' He shuddered. 'Anyway, even if I was interested in women I can't imagine she'd be my type.'

Bea shook her head, used to their banter and constant bickering. 'If people didn't know you two were so fond of each other they might be concerned by the way you talk.' She pulled a face at Shani, so tall in her heels that she towered over them both.

'You're looking gorgeous,' Shani said. 'I can't believe

15

you're actually out tonight.'

Bea nodded towards where Mel was chatting to a group of her friends. 'Didn't have much choice, did I? I wasn't sure I would be much fun after Simon's appearance at the house when I was getting ready.'

Paul narrowed his dark blue eyes. 'Bea, sweetheart, tonight is a Simon-free zone.' He put an arm around her protectively. 'It's Mel's night and however annoying she may be, we're not going to let that spiteful prat ruin your fun. Bloody hell, it's a little warm in here, isn't it?'

'Agreed,' Bea smiled, feeling better already. 'We're going to have a great evening.' She glanced around the grand room full of her sister's guests. 'Have Dad and Joyce arrived yet?'

'Can't have done, we haven't heard a drumroll to announce her entrance.' Paul grimaced. 'I don't know how your dad copes with the two of them in that house. Poor man must be a saint.'

'Look, there they are. Oh my God, Joyce's hair looks like a mutation of Margaret Thatcher's hairdo and a dollop of candyfloss.' Shani giggled and shook her head.

'She does the mother-of-the-bride bit to perfection, doesn't she?' Paul said. Bea and Shani laughed. 'Behave yourself, girls. Now, on to lighter matters; have we all seen the ring?' He clapped his hands together. 'Assuming we have, what do we all think? Shani, you first.'

Shani mulled the question over for a second or two. 'It's pretty spectacular, that's all I know. It must have cost him a fortune.'

At the other side of the room Grant held up a glass and tapped it with a pen, calling for everyone's attention. 'Melanie and I,' Grant said, stepping nervously from one foot to the other, 'would like to thank you all for coming and sharing our celebrations with us on this steamy July evening.' Mel giggled and Bea ignored Paul's dig to her ribs. 'We've chosen our dream date and so that there are no excuses, we're going to let you all know exactly when our big day will be, tonight.' He winked at Mel. 'So, I want you all to keep Liberation Day free!'

'What did he say?' Shani hissed, her arched black eyebrows

knitting together in confusion. Bea could hardly form the words. 'They're setting her wedding date for ninth of May?'

Bea's heart pounded so much at the prospect, that she thought the others would hear it. 'It seems so,' she said, swallowing the lump in her throat.

'But that'll be the first anniversary of your Aunt Annabel's death.' Shani folded her tanned arms across her chest. 'Little bitch.'

Bea took a deep breath and slowly exhaled. She caught her stepmother's triumphant expression across the room as she dabbed her tear-filled eyes with a perfectly ironed, lace handkerchief and determined not to let Joyce see how upset this news had made her.

'Joyce is such a cow,' Paul said, a little too loudly for Bea's liking. 'I bet she's done it on purpose.'

Shani put her arm around Bea's shoulders and she didn't hear what else, if anything, Grant was saying. It was enough that she would have to face that dreadful day at all without having to look happy at her half-sister's wedding.

'Right, come on, I'm getting too irritated to carry on just standing here.' Paul cupped his ear. 'Do you hear that?' he asked, grabbing Shani's hand as the speech finished and the first strains of 'You're the One That I Want' began filling the room. 'Come along, girls, let's give it loads.'

Bea let them go to the dance floor and shook her head when they waved for her to join them. The room was far too hot. Bea needed some air and, relieved to have a quiet moment, picked up her bag and gingerly crossed the room out through the open sliding doors, trying her best not to wobble. She wondered if it was the sheer height of her shoes that was unbalancing her, or the overly polished parquet flooring that was the problem. She touched the cool granite castle wall before walking up to the metal railings and leaning against them, gazing across the bay where yachts moved gently in the calm sea. Bea sighed.

'You're not thinking of jumping are you?' a baritone voice asked from the other side of the Canary Palm next to her. 'Bit of a drastic way to make your escape, don't you think?'

Bea would recognise that brusque tone anywhere. She

leaned precariously over the balcony in a vain attempt to peer around the tree. 'Fancy seeing you again so soon, Mrs Potter.' He touched her shoulder lightly from behind.

Bea swung round, embarrassed to have been caught looking the wrong way, grabbed at the palm frond to move it away from her face and slipped on the floor, landing with a heavy slap on her bum. 'Ouch.'

'Sorry.' He unsuccessfully tried to stifle his laughter. 'I didn't mean to give you a fright. Here,' he held his hand out for her to take, 'let me help you up.'

She closed her eyes momentarily wishing he would disappear, and then opening them, looked up into those sparkly blue eyes as he waited patiently for her to take his hand. 'Thank you,' she mumbled, her heels not gripping enough to let her stand up.

Luke bent down. 'Put your arms around my neck,' he said, barely hiding a smile.

Unable to see any other way she'd manage to stand without taking off the damn shoes, Bea reached up and as he took hold of her, their faces millimetres apart, she breathed in the heady scent of his citrusy aftershave. Tingles shot to various parts of her anatomy she didn't want to think about right now, and as Luke placed her carefully back onto her feet, he stood upright and smiled. 'I hope you're not too sore.'

She could barely breathe as she looked up at him, so different now with his haircut slightly shorter and his beard trimmed. Bea rubbed her bottom to soothe the bruising pain. There was something very appealing about him, despite his enjoyment of her humiliation and she knew without a doubt that the self-assured Adonis in front of her was the very last man on Earth she should allow herself to fall for.

Three

Scorching Hot

Luke had to try hard not to let Bea see how amused he'd been by her confusion. Her eyes were the deepest jade he'd ever seen. They were so pretty, despite being narrowed in irritation, as she appeared to be stuck for words.

'My name's Beatrice.' She stepped forward, waving away the palm frond.

'Beatrix Potter,' he mused slowly, unable to help teasing her for a little longer.

The green eyes narrowed even further. 'No, it's Beatrice with a 'c' and Porter with an 'r' and I'll be changing my surname back to Philips first thing next week,' she said, straightening her short skirt and pulling her shoulders back so that she reached her full height, of, he estimated, about five feet four without those heels.

'It's not such a bad name, it could be worse,' said Luke, feeling a little guilty for annoying her so much.

'That's easy for you to say. The worst thing is everyone who makes up some joke about my name always assumes they're the first person to think of it.'

He tried to look a little serious. 'Annoying, to say the least, I should imagine.' He watched in silence as she studied his face, and wondered if he should explain that the bump in his nose was down to a particularly nasty rugby tackle several years earlier. If she wasn't so defensive, he would find it hard to resist kissing those pouting lips right now.

'When Mel gave me your business details,' she said, bringing him back to the present, 'she explained you were a friend of Grant's, though I've never heard him mention you before.'

Luke shrugged. 'School pals.' He didn't add that Grant was the one to break his nose so painfully. 'I only recently met up with him again and he invited me tonight.' He wished her eyes weren't quite so hypnotising. She was managing to stir up feelings he hadn't experienced since, well, since he'd decided that trusting people was a mug's game. 'I was going to make my excuses, I'm not sure this really is my thing,' he admitted, pleased to note she gave a momentary look of, what was it? Surprise? Disappointment? Stop it, he told himself, don't let her get under your skin. Pretty, she may be, and there's something a little too intriguing about her. 'I'm glad I came now though,' he admitted, immediately wondering why he'd said it out loud, when he hadn't intended doing so.

She flushed slightly, the colour enhancing her prettiness. He'd bet she had no idea how lovely she looked. 'They're getting married on Liberation Day too. That must have taken some arranging, don't you think?'

'Probably,' she said eventually. Luke frowned, had he somehow managed to say the wrong thing? 'That'll be something of an ordeal to sort out,' Bea added. 'Although my stepmother will no doubt be delighted at the prospect. She's been dying for the excuse to arrange a wedding for ages.'

'I thought you were sisters? Although to be honest you're so fair and Mel's very dark, you are very different to look at.' He wished he could stop talking nonsense, she'd think he was nuts.

'My mum died when I was four, Joyce was my dad's secretary and they got married a few months later.'

He wasn't sure what to say to such honesty, noticing for the first time the deep sadness in this beautiful girl's eyes. His problems had been different to hers, but he saw she knew what it was like to be hurt, betrayed. Luke wasn't sure what to say next. 'That must have been a little strange for you to come to terms with?'

Bea shrugged. 'I don't remember it very well, if I'm honest. They sent me to stay with my godmother when they left for their honeymoon and soon after that, Joyce became pregnant with Mel. I loved living at The Brae and it suited Dad and Joyce for me to be where I was happiest and so that's where I pretty

20

much grew up.'

'Was your aunt your mum's sister then?' he asked, wanting to make the most of her openness; he had the feeling she didn't often speak so readily about her past. She seemed a little detached as she spoke, as if she was recalling something.

Bea nodded. 'If I'm honest, Aunt Annabel is the only mother I truly remember.'

'You must miss her very much?' He couldn't help asking such an obvious question and the dark green pools of sadness in her eyes when she nodded made him want to take her in his arms and comfort her. He was about to change the subject when someone called her name from the doorway.

'Bea, there you are.'

Luke turned to see who had made her face light up so instantaneously and watched as a blond man, about the same height as Bea, entered the room.

'Sorry, sweets, I didn't realise you had company,' he said, looking Luke up and down before smiling. Luke glanced at Bea waving her friend over to join them.

'Paul,' she said. 'Come and meet Luke. He's a friend of Grant's.'

Luke could feel her watching them, as he shook Paul's hand. Then, when Paul didn't speak, but gawped silently up at him, Luke wondered if maybe they wanted to talk in private. He turned to Bea and smiled. 'Maybe I'll catch you later,' he said. 'Pleasure to meet you, Paul,' he added, shaking Paul's hand once more before walking away. He glanced over his shoulder at her talking animatedly to her friend, before returning to the party. She might be beautiful, but where did this compulsion to look after her come from? She seemed perfectly capable of taking care of herself. Luke sighed; he had enough to focus on with his own near bankruptcy and problems with Chris. He regretted ever meeting the man, let along agreeing to set up their building business together. Never mind, tonight wasn't the time for regrets. He forced a smile on his face and went back to join Grant and congratulate him on his forthcoming wedding.

'Well, you're a dark horse,' Paul teased her, once they had re-joined Shani. 'Fancy keeping such a magnificent specimen all to yourself!'

'He is drop-dead gorgeous, and so tall.' Shani sighed. 'How come I've never come across Luke Thornton before?'

'Do you know him?' Bea asked, unable to hide her interest.

'No, but I've seen his picture in the *Jersey Gazette* a few times. Something to do with a court case I think. He's very ambitious, and a bit of a one with the ladies, or so I'm told. Mind you, looking at him, it's hardly surprising.' She winked at Bea. 'Good for you.'

'Good for me, nothing.' Bea frowned and rubbed her bottom again. She was going to have to find that arnica cream she'd bought last year and put some on the bruising when she got home. 'I slipped over on these bloody shoes and he had to help me up. It was so embarrassing. If Paul had come to the conversation a little later he'd have probably heard us discussing the decoration his men will be doing on my house. I just hope Luke gives me a good price, that's all.'

'Maybe I could offer to help out?' Paul teased pursing his lips.

'I can't see you sanding down walls or being any good with a paintbrush,' Bea laughed.

'How do you know? I could be brilliant at it. Why don't I come along one day?'

'What, and embarrass me? I don't think so. He's a friend of Grant's, and I have a feeling he's doing him the favour, rather than me.' She looked at the two disappointed faces in front of her. 'I doubt he'll be the one actually doing the work at The Brae anyway. It'll more than likely be the two other guys who came to the house with him.'

'Er, excuse me,' interrupted Mel, from behind Shani. 'Grant said you were chatting to Luke, so now are you grateful to me for giving you his number?'

'Never mind that.' Bea glared at her sister, happy to finally be able to confront her out of earshot from the other guests. 'Why are you getting married on Liberation Day? You know that day is going to be horrific for me?

'It's not all about you, you know.' Mel ran her hands over

her shiny black bob.

'It is a little insensitive though, Mel,' Shani said.

'More than a little, if you ask me,' Paul snapped.

Mel stood with her hands on her hips and looked at each of them in turn. 'The entire island has a holiday on Liberation Day and there are flags decorating many of the houses, I don't see why I can't make the most of those decorations, good moods, and fun to hold my wedding.'

'But what about Bea?' Shani asked, resting a hand on Bea's shoulder.

'For pity's sake, surely it's a good thing to change the day from one of sad memories to one of celebration?'

Bea sighed. She'd like to think so, but it was too soon. 'Maybe in a year or two, but not for Annabel's first anniversary, Mel.'

'You're just being selfish, as usual. It's always got to be about you, hasn't it? Mum said you'd react like this.'

Paul glared at Mel and stepped forward. 'Leave it,' Bea said. She didn't need a full-scale row at this party. She took his arm and for a moment Bea thought Mel was about to slap him. 'Now isn't the time for this conversation.'

'Too bloody right it isn't. I'm sure you'll all excuse me,' Mel snapped. 'I think it's time I return to my friendlier guests.' She leant towards Bea. 'Once you've got over your sulking about my wedding date, remind me to talk to you about taking an injunction out against Simon. He can't be allowed to keep coming to your house and abusing you like he has been doing.'

Bea took a deep breath. She couldn't decide if Mel was really as unfeeling as she made out, or if she was merely influenced by her mother about the wedding.

'She really doesn't get it, does she?' Paul said, as soon as Mel had walked away.

'She's so odd. One minute she's giving you what for about the wedding date, the next she wants to help you against Simon. I think I'm the one that doesn't get it, Paul,' Shani said, bemused by the exchange between Bea and Mel. 'She does love being a legal assistant though, doesn't she?' Shani turned to face Bea. Thinking for a moment, she asked. 'So, what has

Simon been up to this time?'

Bea shook her head 'No, we're not going to talk about him, and I don't want you two getting involved in my rows with Mel. We've always been like this, so it's bound to be worse with the wedding coming up, those things always cause friction within families.'

'Especially yours, it seems,' Paul said, still red in the face with irritation. 'If her mother wasn't so desperate to push Mel forward in your dad's affections, there wouldn't be this problem between you both. You get along perfectly well when Joyce isn't pushing Mel to do things.'

Bea had to agree with him. She wasn't sure if it was because her mum had died so suddenly in that car crash that she'd become this mythical figure to them all. She recalled asking Aunt Annabel about it a few times years before and she'd always maintained that her father never stopped loving Bea's mum and just because he'd married his secretary so soon after didn't mean that he'd forgotten her. Bea supposed she was right.

'Getting back to more interesting topics.' Paul indicated to where Luke was talking to a group consisting mainly of fluttery-eyed females.

Bea looked over at him. Luke seemed to sense he had an audience, and turned his head to look straight into Bea's eyes. Paul sighed. Then, just before she managed to tear her gaze away from him, he turned back to his friends and continued with his conversation.

'He really is hot,' Shani groaned. 'Powerful looking, which is always preferable when you're as tall as me.'

'Shame he's not interested in you then, isn't it?' Paul teased, clutching his shoulder where she slapped him. 'Ouch.'

'Paul wasn't kidding, though, you're a lucky girl.'

'Will you both stop it,' Bea whispered. 'We're not teenagers any more, and he's only being polite. I'm a prospective client of his, nothing more. To be honest, I won't be able to use him for much of the work, because I've hardly got any money to spare for it. Anyway, I hate to disappoint you both, but I'm going on a date with Tom, probably next Saturday night. Mind you, he's got a lot on at the moment, so maybe some time after that.'

There was a heavy silence. Bea wished one of them would speak.

'Tom? Tom Brakespear?' Paul walked over to a nearby sofa and slumped back onto it, patting the seats either side of him. 'Sit, spill, I want to know everything. Wasn't he that beautiful boy from Jersey whose heart you broke when you dumped him to go out with Simon? The one you went to uni with?'

'He is.' Bea nodded, relieved to have so successfully drawn their attention away from Luke and remembering how amused her father had been that the boy she'd gone out with at university was also from Jersey.

'Where's he been all these years then?' Shani asked, sitting down next to them.

'London mainly, I believe. He moved back home to Jersey a couple of years ago with his wife and two kids, but he's getting divorced. Oddly enough his job is administering trust companies, like me, and he's my new line manager at work.' Bea enjoyed their wide-eyed surprise at her news.

'He's the new boss you were wondering about the other week?'

Bea nodded. 'I couldn't believe it when he was introduced to us all on Monday.'

'Won't that be a little awkward?' Paul asked thoughtfully. 'After all you didn't part on great terms.'

'He seems fine.' Bea shrugged. Meeting Tom again had been far easier than she'd ever hoped it would be.

'Are you sure it's a good idea to go out with him though?' Shani picked up her drink, stared at it for a moment and placed it back down on the table without drinking from the glass.

'He asked me, and I couldn't think of a reason to turn him down. I thought you both liked Tom, and let's face it you two have been desperate for me to go out with someone. You should be relieved.'

'We um, we are,' Shani said unconvincingly. 'But surely, if you have the chance of going out with someone new and exciting, like Luke, for example, then why bother with Tom?'

'Tom has asked me, Luke hasn't and it may not have

25

occurred to you, but I can't imagine I'd appeal to Luke in that way.'

'Why not?' they asked in unison.

'Because according to Mel, he has enough on his plate at the moment.' She checked he wasn't in earshot and leant forward, lowering her voice. 'And looking at him, you can see why. He's obviously a popular guy, and busy with his business.'

'I'd rugby tackle him to the ground if he came to my house,' Shani said.

Bea laughed. 'You probably would too, but I can't really see me flinging myself at a bloke. Anyway it's not a real date with Tom,' Bea changed the subject. 'We're only going out for a meal to catch up.'

'It'll do you good and should take your mind off Simon and that house for a bit. You're far too young to have been left with all these responsibilities,' Paul mumbled, taking a sip of his drink and gazing longingly in Luke's direction.

'Aunt Annabel expected to be here for years yet,' Bea said sadly. 'She was only seventy, poor thing.'

'Yes, well I'm glad you're going out with Tom. Is he still hot?' Shani asked, nudging Bea.

'He's not very different to how he used to look. In fact, I think he's better looking now. Not so much boy band, more rock band.' Bea laughed as she pictured Tom with his hair all ruffled while wearing a leather jacket and jeans.

'Rocker in a grey suit,' Shani teased. 'He was too immaculate to ever be in any band, apart from maybe a sixties crooner. At least you know him and knowing you, you'll want someone you feel relaxed with, at least to start off with.'

Bea smiled. 'We'll see. He might have changed, but he used to be good fun and didn't spend all our dates preening in front of other women, like Simon seems to do now. I have to admit I'm looking forward to Saturday.'

Bea slowly opened her eyes after an unsettling night dreaming that she had found a secret passage behind her wardrobe where she might find the mysterious legacy her aunt had left her. It was another hot day. She stretched, relishing the heat, then remembering her aunt's plants in the greenhouse, she threw back the sheet covering her legs and stood up. Staring at the antique wardrobe standing an inch or so away from the wall, it was obvious there were no hidden entrances behind it. She'd better go and water the plants before the temperature rose too much and the heat burnt their leaves. Bea pulled back the curtains and opened the window a little wider, looking out at the garden, wishing her aunt had given her a hint or clue as to what the Jersey Kiss could be. Pulling on a pair of denim shorts and a bikini top, she called out to Flea and went downstairs.

'Come on, you, don't be lazy.' She led the way outside towards to the walled garden. Flea stopped and looked up at the trees, obviously annoyed by the birds singing so near to him.

As she stepped back into the kitchen, Bea slipped on her bunny slippers just as someone rapped at the heavy doorknocker.

'Oh, hi.' She opened the front door surprised to see Luke standing on her doorstep so unexpectedly on a Sunday morning, wishing she'd thought to brush her cloud-like bed hair.

'I hope I didn't disturb you,' he asked, eyes twinkling, taking in her fluffy pink slippers.

She felt her cheeks heat up as she followed his gaze down to the bent pink rabbit ears she secretly loved. 'A fun birthday present from Paul.'

He shook his head. 'I know its Sunday, but I was on my way to my boat and thought I'd quickly check exactly what work you still want doing.'

'But I thought I told you?' Bea said, wondering if she'd missed anything.

'You did.' He glanced up at the plasterwork. 'But it's a big job and your sister hinted about a few issues with your ex-husband and this place.'

Bea clenched her teeth together in irritation. Why didn't Mel mind her business? 'I'll pay your bills, if that's what you're worried about.'

Luke frowned. 'No, of course not. I just didn't want to put added pressure on you with building work, if you weren't sure you wanted to carry it out.'

'I don't know exactly what you've heard, but if I change my mind about your men coming here, I'll tell you. OK?' It was too hot to be so angry, Bea decided. She hurriedly tied her hair into a ponytail.

'Yes. I'm sorry I upset you, it wasn't intentional.'

She watched as he looked around the large hallway with its wide staircase that wound around the walls to the first floor, and then to the original black-and-white tiles on the expanse of floor. 'Look, I'm sorry if I was rude. I'm not a morning person, as you've probably noticed,' Bea said, aware she wasn't being very welcoming. She stepped back. 'Please come in.' She pointed down the passage at the back of the hallway towards the kitchen. 'Would you like a coffee?'

Bea made them both a drink.

'You looked like you were having a lot of fun at the party.' Luke leant against the table appearing more relaxed than Bea felt.

'Yes, I did have a good time,' she said, the embarrassment of her fall making her toes curl. As Bea passed the mug to him, his fingers grazed her hand lightly, shooting miniscule electric currents throughout her entire body. 'I'm not usually that clumsy.'

'I think they'd polished the floor a little too highly,' he said. Bea wasn't so sure, but smiled, hoping that is what he'd thought. 'I'm looking forward to putting this place in order,' Luke said, leaning against the kitchen table. 'It's a beautiful twenties home and it still has so much of its character left. You're very lucky to own it.' He held the hot china mug in between his large hands. 'It's a big house for just one person. Wouldn't you prefer something a bit smaller?'

Bea shrugged. 'I would if this place didn't hold so many memories for me. It's more of a home to me than anywhere else has been.'

'It has a certain charm, I can see why you want to restore it.' Luke looked directly into her eyes. 'I couldn't help noticing the beautiful gardens as I drove up.'

Bea nodded. 'It is pretty amazing. My godmother planted the orchard herself when she first moved here years ago. She

28

sourced so many different plants and trees from her travels over the years. It's why I'd hate to move so much. All my memories are here, the important ones, that is, and I can't take her garden with me if I have to leave.'

'There aren't many people your age who are into gardening like you are.' He drank some of his coffee.

Bea enjoyed his questions. It helped her to think of things that usually only upset her, since Aunt Annabel had died. 'Maybe not, but it's a way of life for me. I can't imagine not spending time out there. My aunt adored her garden. She put years of her expertise as a garden designer into lovingly restoring it back to how the original owners had planned it, adding her own special extras as she went, of course.'

'She wasn't so interested in the house,' Luke smiled. 'Did she live here long?'

'Decades; it was bought for her by her second husband, Antonio. He was an Argentinian polo player. They loved each other very much, although she couldn't have children, which broke her heart, so he encouraged her in her love of gardening.'

'He died, too?'

'Ages ago; they'd only been married a few years. It was very sad for her. Then my mother died, my father remarried, and after a few years they sent me off to boarding school. I was really homesick, so my aunt insisted I came home to Jersey and pretty much took me on. I think it helped her to come to terms with the loss of the two most important people in her life. Well, that's what my dad seems to think and I have to agree with him.'

They stood in silence for a few minutes. Bea wondered why she'd been so open with this man about such personal and still painful issues. What was it about him, she wondered.

'Is that a walled kitchen garden through there?' he asked peering over her shoulder to the wooden French windows half way along the kitchen wall.

'That's my favourite place of all. I'll show you, if you like?' When he nodded, she got up and walked over to push them open, the creaky wooden doors reminding her of another job to add to her To Do list. 'These will definitely collapse on me one of these days,' she said, fully aware it wasn't a joke.

The heat of the morning sun warmed her face even further and she breathed in the sweet scent of rosemary. 'My herbs,' she pointed. 'The vegetables are along there, all organic of course, and the smaller fruit trees along that wall. Over there's my aunt's greenhouse,' she said, wondering why she had bothered stating the obvious to him. 'My greenhouse,' she corrected herself.

He surveyed the area in front of him, his eyebrows raised in what she presumed was an appreciation of what he saw. 'Impressive,' he said. 'And you look after all this by yourself?' Bea shrugged. 'I wouldn't think you'd have the time, what with holding down a job and doing up the house.'

'I'm not able to spend as much time as I'd like here, but I catch up on the most urgent things at the weekends. I'm dreading the winter when it'll get dark so much earlier. I hate the short days.'

'Maybe, but you've got more than enough to do inside this place to keep you going until the spring,' he said. 'You're very lucky having a home with such character.'

'I know,' she agreed, ridiculously thrilled he seemed to like the place so much. 'I just wish I still had Annabel around to enjoy everything with. She loved this place so much. I'm determined to bring it back to its former glory, even if I end up having to sell in the end.'

'Why would you sell it?' He picked up a small trowel she'd left on one of the brick pathways and placed it on the rickety metal table in the corner of the small patio. 'Is this what your sister meant when she referred to problems with your ex-husband?

Bea nodded. 'I might not have a choice about selling. My ex-husband wants me to buy him out, but I'm not sure I'll be able to raise enough money to do so.'

Luke looked up from the raised vegetable border and frowned. 'That would be a pity. I hope you can sort something out.'

'Me too.' She picked up her dented metal watering can and filled it at the tap, showering the bases of her plants. 'How about you, where do you live?'

'If you saw where I lived, you'd never believe I was in the building trade,' he laughed. 'It's a disgrace.'

'Why?' She straightened up, not sure why she was surprised. 'Surely you have all the know-how and contacts to do any work you need?'

'True, but I don't seem to have the time,' he admitted. He pushed his fringe back from his tanned face. 'I've got so much work lined up and,' he hesitated, 'I'm a bit snowed under, which is why I'm here calling in on you on a Sunday.'

So, that was why he decided to visit her at such an irregular time. 'Where do you live?'

'Near St Catherine's Wood.' He smiled thoughtfully. 'Mine is only a small granite cottage though, but it's in a leafy area, quite quirky from the outside, and almost uninhabitable. So I'm living on a boat for the time being.'

Bea could picture him on a boat and liked the idea. 'Sounds fun. I don't know how you manage to fit all your belongings into a boat though?' she asked, making him laugh.

'Probably because I don't have that many things to store; few shoes and no handbags.'

Bea liked the sound of his laugh. He seemed so carefree for once, and it suited him. Resisting a strong urge to lean forward and kiss him, she turned away and picked up their mugs to take them back inside.

Four

August – Sowing the Seed

'It's so hot out here,' complained Paul much later, fanning his face with an old notepad as Bea silently sowed tiny seeds into compost-filled trays in the small greenhouse. 'Do you have to do that now?'

'Stop moaning. You know I do. Why don't you go and wait for me in the house?' She looked over at him and smiled. 'Anyone would think you were going somewhere special in that outfit.'

'What, this old thing?' He winked, holding his arms out and turning around for her. 'I thought you'd like it.'

She loved his baby blue T-shirt, but it wasn't exactly the right sort of top for a dusty greenhouse. 'You know I can't wait to hear all about your visitor and you'll only forget the time like you always do when you come out here, then I won't end up hearing the more interesting details,' he moaned. Paul stepped outside and continued fanning himself. 'Hurry up, before I melt out here.'

'I told you, there isn't anything to tell. So be quiet and let me get on with this.'

'I thought we could go out for a quiet lunch, somewhere away from paint pots and peat bags.'

'Sorry, I can't,' she said, trying to concentrate as best she could on only placing one seed into each of the tiny sections of the black plastic container. 'Anyway where's Shani today? I didn't think she had any classes on a Sunday?'

'She's gone out with this new bloke of hers. Harry-someone-or-other. Besotted, she is. I offered to join them, but she told me to bugger off.'

'I don't blame her,' Bea said, throwing him a washed ice-

33

lolly stick and biro. 'Here, write 'Beetroot' on that for me, would you? Then you can come with me to buy paint for the house.' Paul grimaced. 'Choosing paint can be fun, you know?' Bea laughed. 'Although, I can see by your expression that you wouldn't be interested in helping me with the prep work I need to do on the bathroom and box room tonight then?'

'No, I wouldn't,' he said. 'I've got a good bottle of red waiting for me back at the flat and it's going to need my attention far more than your decorating.'

Bea almost fell through her front door the following day after work. She managed not to drop the shopping bags weighing her down, and kicked the door closed behind her with the heel of her court shoe. Immediately, she noticed a large white envelope in the wire basket attached to the back of the door and put the bags down on the floor. Taking a deep breath, Bea ripped open the envelope. Luke's quotation was lower than she had feared it may be. She suspected he was being a bit too charitable for his own good. After reading it through several times and debating for a little longer, she knew her conscience shouldn't let her accept the amount. She picked up the phone to give him a call. 'Luke, hi, it's Bea.'

'Bea,' he said. 'So you've received my quotation, then?'

'Yes, thank you, and I'd like to accept it. Although, I'm sure it's more reasonable than it probably should be.'

'Not at all. How soon can you have all the prep work done?' he asked, more business-like than she had expected. She felt a little foolish for being so casual on the phone in the first place.

'Um, well, your men can start on the bathroom as soon as they like.' She quickly tried to estimate how long it would take her to do the work needed on the box room. 'I can concentrate on the others in my free time, and will make sure I'm finished for whenever your men are ready to start work on them.'

'Great, I'll have two men up at your place tomorrow. Will eight o'clock be OK?'

'Perfect. Thank you.' She hurriedly rang off with the distinct feeling she had been dismissed. Bea stared at the phone for a moment. As she caught sight of the rickety banister, she was reminded of a pair of fiercely blue eyes and the hairs on the back of her neck instantly stood up. Whether this was from some sort of lust or embarrassment, she couldn't tell – she'd lost count of the years that had passed since her last real 'first date'. Dating was something in her hazy past, like bad perms and *Now!* compilation albums and maybe it should just be left there.

Bea carried her shopping bags into the kitchen and unpacked everything before going to get her hammer and chisel tool to begin removing the ugly chocolate-coloured tiles from the house bathroom. She found it hard to imagine her godmother ever thinking they were tasteful. With one wall finished, Bea brushed the dust from her hair and got into the shower. 'I must be clinically insane to attempt to do all this.'

Two men in a white van arrived at exactly eight o'clock the next morning. They followed Bea silently as she led them out to the disused stables at the back of the house. 'You'll find the bathroom suites in there,' she said. 'Sorry about the mess. I'll get round to clearing all the junk out one of these days.

'No problem, love,' the older of the two men assured her. 'You leave us to it. Luke has explained everything.'

'It's looking great,' she told Luke when he came to check the work later on, relieved that she'd showered and changed in to her favourite summer dress and sandals. 'I didn't expect for them to work on a Saturday, too.'

He stared at her for a few seconds. 'They're good blokes and both happy for the overtime. You need to get the house sorted and I thought it best if they came today, to get as much done as possible.'

'Thank you. Would you like a coffee or something cold?'

'Coffee for me, thanks.' He followed her down the stairs and through to the cool kitchen.

Luke tilted his head down to her level and kissed her, causing Bea's next thought to be extinguished from her consciousness.

'Sorry, I probably shouldn't have done that,' he apologised, looking anything but. 'You look so pretty with your hair up and those loose blonde strands over your cheeks.'

Bea attempted to tuck some of the hair behind her ears. 'My ex-husband always thought I looked better in suits and high heels,' she said, unable to think straight at this unexpected turn of events.

'Then he's a fool.' He leaned forward and kissed her once again. This time Bea responded instinctively.

'I come bearing gifts,' Shani shouted from the hallway. 'I thought you could do with some chocolate digestives. We'll put them in the fri …'

Shocked, Bea stiffened and stepped back. He walked to the other side of the kitchen as Shani entered the room.

'Hello, there.' Shani widened her eyes and pulled a face at Bea. 'I didn't realise you had company.' She strode purposefully into the kitchen. Dropping the Saturday papers onto the worn pine table and kicking off her flip-flops as she sat down, she crossed one long tanned leg over the other. Shani glanced from Luke and back to Bea, raising an eyebrow at her. She held out the packet of biscuits. 'These need to go in the fridge.'

'You remember Shani from the party, don't you?'

Luke smiled and nodded. 'Of course.'

'Phew, it's hot.' Shani smiled at him, her lips drawing back into a wide smile as she arched an eyebrow.

Bea thought she was enjoying their obvious discomfort a little too enthusiastically. 'Shani.'

'Well, it is,' she argued. 'It must be getting on for twenty-nine degrees out there.' She turned so Luke couldn't see her and winked at Bea. 'You look pretty today.'

'She does, doesn't she?' he said quietly, glancing at his watch, barely able to hide the hint of a smile. 'I'd better be off.' He placed his mug on the draining board. 'See you on Monday, Bea. Nice to see you again.' He nodded politely at Shani, who for once, Bea noted, didn't come out with a quick retort. 'Don't worry,' he told Bea, as she went to follow him, 'I'll see myself out.'

They listened to his footsteps until they heard the front door close heavily behind him.

'Oh. My. God.' Shani squeezed Bea's arm, causing her not a

36

little pain in her excitement. 'He's so,' Shani sighed. 'Well, big and impressive, and if you think you can make me believe there's nothing going on between you then you don't know me at all. The atmosphere was electric in this room when I came in.'

Bea turned to wash up the used mugs. 'He kissed me.' She almost breathed the words and touched her lips with her fingertips, unable to believe what had just happened.

'Halle-bloody-lujah,' cheered Shani. 'And before you start to justify this to yourself, I'm just relieved that maybe now you'll begin to see yourself as the gorgeous girl you are, and get back some of the self-esteem you used to have pre-Simon.'

'He's the opposite of Simon, which is probably why I find him so attractive, but I don't think what happened between Luke and I meant anything to him. I think it was a spur of the moment impulse, nothing more.'

'We'll see.' Shani's voice interrupted her thoughts. She picked up her jacket. 'Never mind biscuits, I'm taking you to the Bunker for a cup of tea and some of their delicious carrot cake.'

'OK, but I need to go to St Brelade's beach afterwards.'

'To the polo? I'd have thought you'd want to stay well away. Memories and all that.'

Bea had to agree, it was the last place she'd choose to be today. 'I'm not going by choice, but I received a phone call from one of the committee members reminding me that Aunt Annabel is one of the sponsors of the event. She donated a trophy and now she's not able to do so, someone else has to present it on the day.'

'Ah, I did wonder why you were wearing a dress and those gorgeous sandals.' Shani walked over and gave her a hug. 'I'm sorry, I don't suppose you can refuse to do this?'

'Not really.'

As they walked up to the large WW2 bunker built during the Occupation on St Aubin's beach front, Bea couldn't' help thinking how pleased she was to get out of the house. She'd been dreading going to the polo, but now at least she could keep her mind off it a little until it was time to be at the match. Shani went to the counter to give their order and Bea sat down at a table near the window that had, sixty-five years before, been the space where a large gun faced out towards the Channel, guarding the island from attack.

'You all right?' Shani asked, sitting down opposite Bea. 'I'll come with you this afternoon.'

'Thanks, I didn't think you'd miss an opportunity of staring at tight bums in jodhpurs.'

Shani laughed. 'Cheeky cow. You're right though, it'll perk up my mood no end.' She smiled at Bea. 'It's still very soon, you know. You mustn't expect too much of yourself. Losing Annabel is like losing a parent for you.'

'It is. I was remembering how she used to bring me here after school sometimes.'

Shani placed a hand on Bea's arm. 'I know it's hard for you, losing her, but I'm sure once you sort out this problem with Simon, you'll feel a little more settled.'

'You're right. When I can talk to Mel without wanting to row with her, I need to find out more about her suggestion about taking out an injunction against him. And as far as Luke is concerned, I'm not even going to let myself think about how gorgeous he is. I'd rather be alone than with someone who's going to end up breaking my heart. I might only be thirty, but I've got more responsibility than I'd expected, and I can't afford to go out to clubs with the rest of you all the time.'

'Well, whatever you say,' Shani added, as the waitress placed their plates of food down in front of them, 'I think it's going to be very interesting having him coming to your house each day. I can't wait to see how it all turns out after that kiss.'

'Just eat your cake.' Bea pushed a fork towards her friend and shook her head.

Shani dug her fork into her cake and took a mouthful. Bea did the same, surprised when Shani grimaced and pushed her plate away. 'What's wrong with it? You love this cake.'

'Nothing.' She forced a laugh. 'I just don't feel like it for some reason.'

'Is everything OK with you and Harry?'

Shani nodded. 'Yes, he's great. I adore him.'

'So why do you look so miserable whenever you think no one's watching?'

Shani narrowed her eyes at Bea. 'You don't miss much, do you?'

'Well?'

'Nothing. Eat yours and then we'd better get to the polo match. You can't be late if you're presenting a trophy, then you've got your date with Tom to look forward to later on.'

Bea popped a forkful of cake into her mouth and studied her friend. 'You're sure everything's OK?'

'Yes, too much sex has probably just turned my brain a little, that's all.'

Five

Sprinkling of Sand

Bea was glad she'd worn a sleeveless cotton dress and gladiator sandals; the heat was tremendous. She re-tied her ponytail, slid her sunglasses back over her eyes, and waited for the teams to come out. Grateful to be one of the VIPs for the day, she took a sip of her champagne cocktail and smiled at Shani. 'You glad you came?'

'Hell, yes.' She leant closer and lowered her voice. 'You didn't tell me we'd be getting free drinks and mixing with the nobs though, did you?'

'I didn't realise. I only checked the invitation they sent me on our way here to make sure we had the correct time.' Bea walked out onto the balcony reserved for the invited guests. 'Bloody hell.'

'What?' Shani looked out to the beach below. 'Luke Thornton. You never mentioned he played polo.'

Bea felt the familiar contraction in her stomach muscles. Aunt Annabel would have approved, she thought, smiling and feeling more cheerful than she had all day. 'I didn't know.'

She watched as the horses and riders moved into their teams and halted in front of the balcony to be introduced. Luke patted his horse's sleek neck. He looked up and his gaze immediately met Bea's. He smiled and gave her a nod.

'He's gorgeous,' Shani whispered, sounding as if she was in pain. 'I thought he had money worries, though? How can he afford polo ponies?'

'I was thinking the same thing,' Bea admitted, raising her glass to him slightly.

Watching the chukkas brought Bea back to when she'd been taken to England by her aunt a couple of times. This time though, with the waves lapping the beach behind the marked-off arena and the sand being thrown up by the horses' hooves as the players played one chukka after another, it was different.

Luke came on with a different pony for his third chukka and she watched him stroke the grey neck, slowly calming the agitated animal as best he could. The ball was rolled in and the players went after it. She stifled a cry when one of Luke's opponents bumped into his pony's shoulder a little harder than she thought acceptable, but watched as Luke chased after the ball, unfazed by the force. They swung their mallets and Luke's connected with the ball first. He scored. A horn sounded terminating the chukka.

'Yay, he's done it,' screamed Shani, jumping up and down with Bea, both forgetting where they were in their excitement.

Bea shook her hand to get rid of most of the drink she'd spilled on her arm.

'Wow, I didn't know it was such fun to watch. We'll have to come again next year.'

'You're not kidding.' Bea laughed. Maybe it had been the best thing to do, coming here, she mused. At least now she could think of polo without feeling miserable. 'Aunt Annabel would have been in her element here.'

'She's not the only one.'

An official came up behind Bea and cleared his throat. 'Mrs Porter, it's time for you to come and present the trophy to the winning team.'

Bea handed her drink to Shani and followed him down the steps to the beach. She waited as they announced the winners and was handed the heavy trophy just before the team captain's name was called out.

Luke stepped forward and Bea couldn't help smiling up at him. She held the trophy out and congratulated him. Luke lifted it up in the air and the crowds cheered for the local winning team.

'Please step this way for photos.' The photographer from the *Gazette* arranged them in position, and Bea and Luke smiled and shook hands once more for the camera.

Luke bent down and kissed her on the cheek. 'I didn't expect you to be here, but it was great to see you and your friend up on the balcony.'

Bea couldn't hide her happiness. 'I haven't been to a polo match for a few years and never one on a beach. I didn't know you played.'

'Shall we get a drink?' Luke turned to hand the trophy over to his teammates and accompanied her back into the hotel. 'They're not my ponies,' he said pulling a sad face. 'I wish they still were. I had to sell mine when my financial situation with my business became untenable. I couldn't owe people money and keep such a luxury for myself.'

'So, who do they belong to?'

'A friend of my father's. He'd seen me play on them and so knew they were good. He made me an offer and I wasn't in a position to refuse.'

'So, why didn't he ride them today then?'

Luke took two glasses of champagne from a tray held out by a waiter as they walked out onto the balcony. 'His son was supposed to, but he broke his wrist falling from one of them a week ago and when they asked me to step in, I was only too pleased to do so.'

'You were great,' Shani said, smiling widely. 'Where did you learn to ride like that?'

Luke laughed. 'When I was a kid at my dad's farm in South Africa. It's very popular over there and not such an elite sport as it seems to be in the UK. Would you ladies like to join me tonight? The team are going out for something to eat first and then on to a club.'

Bea chewed her lower lip, wishing she could accept his offer, but unable to let Tom down. 'I'd love to, but I'm already doing something, sorry.'

'I'm meeting Harry, so I won't be able to either,' Shani replied.

He shrugged. 'Never mind, maybe next time. I'd better go and catch up with the others.' He kissed Bea on the cheek once more and smiled at Shani. 'Have a lovely evening.'

Bea couldn't shake off the image of Luke playing polo and

wished she was looking forward to an evening with him rather than Tom., though she was pleased that Tom didn't still hold her decision to leave him for Simon against her.

'You look very glamorous.' Tom said, dabbing at his mouth with his napkin. 'I thought you'd enjoy the view here.'

Bea looked out of the large picture window across to Gorey Castle and the long stretch of Grouville beach beyond. 'It's fabulous. I haven't eaten here for a couple of years. It's good to be back.' Bea sighed heavily. 'I don't think I've eaten so much in years.' She took a sip of her wine. 'I can see now why they have such a good reputation here.'

'I'm glad you've enjoyed it. I used to bring my son and daughter here for the children's lunches on a Sunday when things were friendlier between me and Vanessa,' he said. 'Now, though, I seem to see them less and less.'

'That's so sad, Tom.' Bea reached out to touch his hand. 'I do hope things get sorted out with your ex-wife soon.'

Tom nodded. 'Me, too.' He sat quietly for a moment, only seeming to come back to the present when the waitress asked them if they wanted coffees or liqueurs. Bea nodded. 'Coffee for me, please.'

'Make that two,' he said before looking across at Bea. 'So, who have you got to do the work on your house?'

'He's someone Mel's fiancé suggested, Luke Thornton, Do you know him?'

'A friend of yours, is he?'

She was a little taken aback by the sudden change in the tone of his voice. 'An acquaintance rather than a friend,' Bea explained, aware she was doing her best to keep her voice light. She watched the waitress place her cup of coffee in front of her and stirred the muddy coloured liquid unnecessarily. 'He gave me a good price, which is a relief because I don't really have much money available for the work.'

Tom stared into the cup for several seconds.

'What is it?' Bea asked. 'Tell me.'

Tom looked around the room and then moved a little closer to her. 'I shouldn't really confide in you about this, but you're a trust officer, so you'll understand how these things work.' Bea nodded. It niggled a little that Tom was a director already even though their qualifications were the same and they had been in the business almost the same length of time.

'I look after a couple of companies for Luke's partner.'

Bea tried to steady her breathing. She could sense she wasn't going to like what was coming next. 'Go on,' she whispered.

'They're both under investigation.'

'For money laundering?' she whispered. It changed everything. Damn Tom for telling her this confidential information. Now she was aware Luke was under investigation she would have to watch every word she said to him.

'Sorry, Bea, but I couldn't let you, in your professional capacity, get close to someone who was being investigated. You obviously realise that if you let it slip that this is going on, you could get a maximum sentence of five years in prison. In fact any criminal record will make a difference to your career.'

'I'm well aware of my duties, thank you, Tom. Tipping off is one of the worst offences I could be caught doing.' She sighed, 'And if you hadn't told me, then I wouldn't have known, or been in the position where I could do so.'

Tom sat back in his chair and folded his arms. 'Ahh, yes, I see what you mean.'

'You shouldn't be discussing your clients with me. This matter is confidential, you know that.'

'Yes,' he took her hands in his, 'but what would you prefer; I kept this to myself and saw you in a position where if he were to discover he was being investigated, then you as an employee of the trust company would be an obvious suspect to have tipped him off, and we both know how difficult, if not impossible it would be to prove you didn't say anything.'

'True.'

'At the very least you'd probably stand to lose your job.'

And then how would I afford a mortgage for my house, Bea thought. 'What about him working at the house, though?'

'Just try to get him to finish what he's doing as soon as you can. It would be even more suspicious if you suddenly cancelled everything.'

'Do they really think he's capable of money laundering?'

'You know as well as I do that the first thing we're taught in anti-money laundering training is that money launderers don't look a certain way. They can be anyone, from any walk of life. So, who knows?' Tom shrugged. 'He and his partner have made huge amounts of money through real estate and development over the past few years. They made a lot of money very quickly.'

The waitress placed a silver tray on their table with their bill and a couple of dark chocolates. Tom picked up the bill thoughtfully. 'They were school friends and although Luke is probably less likely to be involved in this, the fact that they are partners means he's connected in some way.' He frowned and looked across at her. 'I'm sorry, Bea, but I thought you should know.'

Bea nodded. 'You're right, thanks. It just makes things a little awkward, that's all.' She still wished she hadn't been told. It changed everything.

'Don't just sit there, pedal. Faster.'

'Shut up, Paul, I'm only here because you wouldn't stop nagging.'

'You haven't been to the gym for over a year now and you can't keep making excuses.'

'I think you'll find I can,' Bea grumbled, deciding that as soon as she was out of Paul's studio she would not be returning.

'So how was the date?' asked Paul, running on a treadmill that looked to Bea as if it should be on a *Star Trek* set.

'It wasn't really a date, more like two old friends catching up on their news.'

'Sounds a bit more like a date to me.' He pressed a few buttons and the treadmill speeded up. 'Come on you, keep going.'

'Bloody hell, Paul, I'm going to die here.'

'You're not. Now pedal.' She sat up for a moment and wiped her sweaty forehead with her T-shirt. 'Do you think there's something odd going on with Shani?'

Paul frowned, but carried on running. 'No, what do you mean?'

Bea thought for a moment, then leaning down picked up her bottle of water and took a sip. 'I don't know, I thought she was acting a little odd the other day when we met for lunch.'

'Nah, she's fine, I'd have noticed if she wasn't.' He shook his head at Bea. 'Stop trying to distract me. You're going to do at least three miles. Get on with it.'

Bea groaned; this was so boring, no wonder she hadn't been to the gym in so long. 'I didn't tell you about my visit to Mr Peters at the bank, did I?' she puffed and rested forward on the handlebars.

'No, but you can tell me without stopping for yet another breather.' Paul winked at her. 'I suppose this is because you received another letter from Simon?' He waved at her to keep pedalling. 'Go on, what did he say?'

'I couldn't really put it off any longer. I explained everything to him and he asked to see my credit card statements and gave me an application form to complete. He was lovely,' Bea said thinking back to the sweaty little man she'd met the day before. 'He probably looked much like I do now.'

'What did he say, Bea?'

She shrugged. 'He's going to check out my figures, but doesn't think it'll be good news for the entire amount Simon wants.'

'Why not? You earn a decent wage surely?'

'Not that good, obviously.' Bea stopped pedalling again. 'He's sending out an estate agent to value the house and they'll be able to make a more informed decision after that. I should know later this week, hopefully. At least then I'll have a better idea about what I'm dealing with.'

'Good for you. I'm sure it'll be good news. And if it isn't you'll just have to try at another bank.'

'I have,' admitted Bea. 'This is the third bank I've contacted. I did the other two online and spoke to someone, but they weren't positive either. I tried this one as Mr Peters knew my aunt and I've banked with them since I was a teenager when Aunt Annabel opened an account with them for me. I only looked at the online sites to see what I could expect. I didn't think it was going to be so difficult. It's not as if I owe money all over the place.'

Paul stopped his running machine and went over to sit at a torturous looking contraption in the corner. 'Did he remember you?'

Bea nodded. 'He did. I was going to ask him if he recalled her mentioning anything about A Jersey Kiss, but he started chatting about Aunt Annabel and how they'd known each other since primary school then he went off on a tandem and I stopped listening.'

Paul let the handle he'd been pulling on revert back to its original position and stared at her thoughtfully, before bending over laughing hysterically. He wiped his eyes with the backs of his hands, before laughing again.

'What?' Bea frowned.

'I presume you meant "tangent".'

'Sorry?'

'Never mind,' he said starting his workout again and shaking his head. 'You carry on.'

'I don't think he works full time any more, he's probably near to retirement age if he's known my aunt for so long, and it seems fairly difficult to get an appointment with him, but I think he's my best bet to get the mortgage secured.'

Bea took a few deep breaths to try and slow her panting. She couldn't wait for her session with Paul to finish. It was one thing doing this exercise lark for fun, but another entirely when she had so much decorating work she should be doing during any free time. 'That's it,' she said climbing off the bike. 'I'm off for a shower and then home.'

Bea raced home the following lunchtime with her shopping. She struggled into the house with the three overflowing shopping bags and dumped them down on the worktop in the kitchen.

'You should have asked me to help you carry those,' Luke said, poking his head around the kitchen door. 'You don't usually come home at lunchtime.'

Bea quickly unpacked the frozen vegetables and pushed them into her fridge freezer. 'No, but today I've got to spend the afternoon with a client on his yacht.'

'Sounds fun.' Luke raised his eyebrows and smiled, catching a tin of soup as it rolled off the side.

'Not really. He's a nice bloke, but I've got so much to do back at the office that I really don't need to take time out to sit and chat, but I registered his boat for him the other day and he isn't often over in Jersey and wanted to treat me to lunch.'

'On his boat?'

'Yup,' she said finishing packing away her food and turning to face him. 'You don't have to look so concerned, I'm a big girl and I'm more than capable of taking care of myself.'

Luke laughed. 'I didn't think you couldn't. You seem pretty feisty for a titch.'

Bea placed her hands on her hips and narrowed her eyes. 'Really? Do you want to see how feisty I can be?' He shook his head. 'Anyway, Tom will be coming along.'

'Tom Brakespear?'

Bea nodded, not letting on she was aware they knew each other. 'He's the director I report to at work.'

'Right.' Luke nodded thoughtfully. 'Well, I suppose I'd better get on. I don't want you complaining that you're paying us to stand around gossiping.'

'Haha, very funny,' she said, unable to miss the change in atmosphere between the two of them. 'Coffee?' She wondered if it would be more sensible to terminate his contract with her. Then again, as Tom had said, surely to do such a thing without any obvious reason would make him wonder why she'd changed her mind. She pulled off her black linen jacket, hanging it over the back of a chair. 'I've got time for a quickie before I have to race off and I'm too thirsty not to have one myself.'

'Please,' he answered, leaning back and half-sitting on the edge of the table, his palms resting on either side of him. 'Are you still sure you want us to get on with the plastering in the hallway?'

She passed him his drink, studying his face in an effort to try and spot any hint of criminal behaviour. Idiot, she thought, what would a money launderer look like anyway, you and me that's what.. It's what made them so hard to spot. 'I'd love to say leave it, but if anyone slams the front door, or even closes it with slightly too much force, plaster rains down on them, and it'll only get worse. So, if you can organise to have someone start as soon as possible, I'd be grateful.'

Bea wished she could simply ask him about his business partner and what went wrong, but couldn't risk becoming involved in something that could end up with her losing her home, or even worse, having to move in with her father and stepmother. She shivered.

'You OK?' he asked.

Bea nodded. 'Fine, just a bit stressed that's all.'

'Your ex?'

'Yup, he sends me texts every so often with a countdown of the days until D-Day.'

'D-Day? What the hell is that?'

'Debt Day.' She rolled her eyes. 'He's a moron, what can I say?'

'I wish I could do something to help you, Bea. Really.'

She smiled at him. He obviously meant what he was saying. 'Thank you, but I'll think of something. Losing this house because of him is not something I'm going to let happen that easily.'

'I'll see you two tomorrow,' Bea said to Shani and Paul as she left their flat. She pushed her hands into her bag to find her car keys, catching her nail on an old paperclip at the bottom. 'Damn.' She sucked her finger, groaning when she heard Mel shouting from along the precinct towards her.

'Hey, wait for me.' Bea could hear the click clack of her sister's heels as she ran along the pavement towards her. 'I know you can hear me.'

Knowing when she had no choice, Bea turned slowly, forcing a smile onto her face. 'Melanie, I'm in a rush to get home, can't this wait?'

'No. I gather you've been seeing Tom, what's-his-name from years ago? Why didn't you tell me?' She pushed her huge Dior sunglasses up onto her head.

50

'It didn't occur to me that you'd be interested.' Bea wondered how long it would take Mel to turn the conversation into one about her wedding. She listened as patiently as she could manage.

'But he's gorgeous. I always liked him.' She seemed lost in a memory for a couple of seconds. 'He reminded me of one of those immaculately suited sixties film stars, without the cigarette, though.'

Bea shook her head and laughed. She doubted Mel remembered Tom at all. 'You hardly met him, so I don't know what you ever found to like about him. Apart from maybe the way he dressed.'

'Rubbish.' Mel frowned, or tried to. Bea stared at her sister's forehead; there wasn't a line on it. 'Have you had Botox?'

'Don't be ridiculous.' Mel waved the notion away with her perfectly manicured hand. 'I'm twenty-five, why would I need anything like that?'

Bea smiled. 'Mel, I was born with more lines on my forehead than you have now. There isn't even one.'

Mel attempted to raise her eyebrows, or so Bea suspected. She tried to hide her amusement. 'Now, I was thinking, if you're seeing Tom, then he'd make a perfect best man for Grant.'

What? 'Grant doesn't even know him.'

'Who cares.' Mel tapped Bea's arm and lowered her voice. 'He'd look perfect for the wedding photos.'

'Never mind his wardrobe,' Shani said coming out to join them and shooting Mel an irritated glance. 'Sorry, I couldn't help overhearing your comments.'

'That's because you must have been listening at the door.'

Shani smiled. 'Really, Mel, you should run a shop or a salon. Your interest in grooming and fashion is wasted on a legal assistant.'

'Maybe,' Mel said. 'but I earn far more as a legal assistant, which is why I can afford to buy the clothes I like and pay someone else to do my manicures.'

'Mel is right, though,' Paul sighed, carrying out a tuna melt and taking a bite from it. 'I always found it hard to imagine

51

Tom as a scruffy uni student; he was always so smart whenever I saw him.'

'He wasn't ever scruffy, that's why it's hard to imagine. He was the only immaculate student I remember mixing with, which is probably why I fancied him so much. He always smelt so clean.' Bea laughed at the memory. She couldn't help picturing Luke, not at all smart, scruffy in fact, but always smelling so heavenly.

'I think we can all understand why Bea would find Tom attractive. Can't we, Shani?' Paul said, nudging Bea. 'Stay with us, love.' Bea could see he was trying to make a point, but wasn't sure why he was determined for Shani to grasp it. 'Let her take some risks in her life. You do,' he added.

Shani narrowed her eyes, but ignored him. 'When are you going to ask him all about his situation with his wife, ex, Bea?'

Bea wasn't sure when the conversation had moved on from Mel's wedding to her dating plans. She recalled Shani admitting to her about a crush she'd had on Tom years before when they'd been dating, and Bea wondered if she still could have any feelings for him. Maybe that was what concerned Paul right now? 'I don't know what all the fuss is about,' Bea said ignoring her suspicions. 'He told me they've signed the separation papers. And after Simon it feels, um …'

'Safe?' Shani volunteered.

'Yes, I suppose.' Bea nodded, not too sure she liked to admit this point. 'He's easy to be around. I know him and, to be honest, I don't feel like I'm going to fall for him in any way.'

'At least he's not the sort to mess you around,' Mel said, checking her mobile for messages and quickly texting someone. 'He seems very loyal and must have married that Vanessa soon after leaving uni.'

'Which is probably why he took years to return to Jersey. He must have visited his family over here at some point, but I've never bumped into him in all that time. He does seem loyal though,' Bea said. 'And even though she was the one to have the affair, he doesn't sound bitter in any way.'

'Mmm.' Shani shrugged. 'Then he's a bigger man then most would be. I'm not so sure I'd be happy to forgive something

52

like that. You weren't either, Bea.'

'Bea is going to do whatever she decides, so let's not psychoanalyse why she is seeing Tom,' said Paul before taking another bite of his lunch and staring at Mel. 'Have you had something done to your forehead?'

Mel glared at him. 'No.'

'Anyway,' Shani interrupted, 'if Tom's getting a divorce, then she's nearly an ex-wife. Take note, the emphasis is on the word 'nearly'. Do you want to be loaded down with more baggage, Bea?' Shani continued; obviously not ready to give up just yet. 'You're still sorting things out with Simon. I know you're old friends and all that, but there are loads more blokes out there to choose from. Why pick someone who's going through a divorce too? Move on from him before you get too emotionally involved. I mean, why go for him when you can take your pick?'

'Yeah, right,' laughed Mel. 'There's such a wide choice of available, sane, heterosexual men out there just waiting.'

'Don't be so smug.' Shani glowered at her.

'What the hell is your problem, Shani?' Mel asked, dropping her phone back into her bag and pulling the strap up onto her shoulder. 'Bea's more than capable of watching out for herself.'

'I am, and I'm enjoying being single for a change. Maybe it's a relief being with someone who says something and means it, rather than Simon who always said the right thing and was getting up to all sorts behind my back.' Bea was growing tired of their bickering. 'If you must know, I'm seeing Tom this Friday.' She patted Shani's hand. 'This isn't a great romance. We really are just friends. Relax, what can possibly go wrong?'

Six

September – Digging for the Truth

Bea glanced out of the hall window to see if the taxi had arrived yet and spotted a note on the hallstand that Luke must have left earlier. 'Please leave back door open tomorrow morning. Will be bringing round paint samples for you to look at. L.' She smiled. His untidy handwriting on the torn piece of paper was similar to others he'd left her over the previous few weeks. Like the writer, she mused, straight to the point and abrupt. Could this man really be involved with something underhand and illegal?

She heard the taxi's tyres crunching on the gravel outside the front door and, pushing further thoughts of Luke to the back of her mind, Bea gave Flea a kiss on his tatty head and grabbed her jacket and bag.

Bea paid the cab driver and walked into Sammy's Bar. She glanced around the noisy room, but couldn't see Tom, so bought herself a vodka and tonic and took a seat at a small table with a clear view of the entrance. Tapping the table with her newly painted fingernails, Bea surreptitiously glanced down at her watch for the fifth time. She was contemplating whether to order another drink, or leave, when the door opened and in strode Tom.

His eyes twinkled as he smiled at her. 'Hi, gorgeous,' he said, striding across the room dressed in his trademark bespoke suit, his sandy hair combed to one side. 'You look perfect, as usual.' Unable to help grinning back at him, Bea couldn't help notice the admiring stares he was getting from other women in the bar.

He leant down and kissed her on both cheeks. 'Good to see you tonight,' he said settling down in the seat opposite her. 'I'll get us some drinks.'

'Red wine for me, please.' She watched him go to the bar and when he turned to smile at her, she pointed to the Ladies. Tom nodded.

Inside, she washed her hands and touched up her lip-gloss. Hmm, she didn't look too bad, considering she'd been painting for a couple of hours since getting home from work. Bea rubbed her thumb across her newly applied nail varnish. She'd missed having decent nails.

'I could do with the weather dropping a few degrees,' Tom said, undoing the button on his linen jacket. 'September, and it still feels like mid-summer.'

Bea took a sip of her drink as he looked her up and down. She wanted to ask him about Luke's involvement with the money laundering case, but could see he was about to say something.

Tom leant across to her, and taking her lightly by the wrist, pulled Bea towards him. She could feel his breath against her ear, and wondered if he was going to kiss her. 'The label from your knickers is hanging out of the top of your trousers,' he whispered, trying unsuccessfully to stifle his laughter.

'Oh,' muttered Bea, quickly tucking the offending label back inside her pants, while surreptitiously glancing around the bar to see if anyone else could have possibly noticed her faux pas.

'Hey, don't look so embarrassed,' he said, 'it looked sexy. I didn't want to tell you, but thought you'd like to know.' He winked at her.

'So,' she said, mustering as much dignity as possible. 'How're things going with your separation?'

He looked at his drink, a grimace passing across his previously happy face. 'Well, if you're sure you want to know?' She nodded. He sat back in to the chair and turned his wine glass by the stem for a few seconds. 'As I told you I found out she was seeing someone else, she actually had been for about eighteen months.'

'That's awful. How did you find out?' Bea winced at the unfeeling way her question had come out. 'I meant who told you?'

'I wasn't told exactly. She was meeting up with a guy who I discovered was one of the beneficiaries of one of the bigger trusts I looked after. I've had bi-annual meetings with him over the past five years, and we've always got along well. So, last year, instead of meeting up at the office, he suggested we go out to lunch and discuss everything away from the office.'

Bea was surprised that Tom appeared so happy to tell her everything, and wondered if maybe it was because she'd asked him after he'd had a drink. She waited for him to continue.

'Well, you know how it is,' he said. 'Do business, have lunch, knock back a couple of glasses of wine. Him that is, not me,' he explained, raising an eyebrow. 'He started to relax and began telling me about this woman he was seeing.'

'How horrible,' Bea murmured, wishing she had ignored Shani, and not been quite so nosy after all.

'Not at first,' he continued quietly. 'He didn't know he was describing my wife. We chatted like old friends and he told me how great she was and although she had a husband the marriage was all but over. How it was only a bit of harmless fun for both of them.' He shrugged at the memory. 'I agreed with him on that point, too. It never occurred to me for one second the poor fool we were discussing was me.'

Bea winced, bloody Shani, now she felt truly intrusive. 'When did you realise?'

'It was at the following lunch, six months later. I asked him how everything was going and he happily told me, although this time mentioning her first name, and describing her titian hair. At first I felt a little unsettled, but shrugged off the notion.' He made a loser sign with his thumb and forefinger. 'I thought I was being paranoid. Up until that point, it had never occurred to me Vanessa could ever be unfaithful. Then, when he said how he looked out for her drop-head silver Audi, the penny dropped. I mean, let's face it, Jersey is a small enough place and there aren't that many of the same car, especially ones driven by redheads.'

'What did you do?' Bea remembered exactly how sick she felt when her aunt had sat her down and told her that she'd caught Simon making out with someone in his car.

'Nothing,' he replied, his face expressionless for a moment.

'Nothing? What, nothing at all?' It didn't sound like the Tom she had known all those years ago.

'You married in your early twenties too; didn't your family and friends warn you that you were rushing things?

Bea nodded. 'My stepmother must have told me dozens of times that it would end badly with Simon.'

'Anyway, what's the point? It wasn't as if he knew who I was. I mean think about it, he was a good client of mine, until then we'd had an excellent business relationship.'

'But he was sleeping with your wife,' she said.

'Exactly, my wife. She was the one being unfaithful. And let's be honest, if you have to get divorced, and to me there is no other option when there's no trust left, I was going to need all the money I could get for legal fees. I didn't need to lose a good client. Well, not just then anyway.'

Bea couldn't think what to say to such a revelation. 'That sounds so calculated,' she said, shocked at his callous admission.

'It does when you say it out loud.'

She put her hand over his. 'How horrible. So what's happening now?'

'Everything's in the hands of the solicitors. We've gone for a year's legal separation, like I explained to you the other week. She still doesn't know he's my client.'

'Really?'

'He knows. I told him when I left the company and moved to where I am now.' Tom smiled triumphantly. 'It was one hell of a shock to him, too. I can still picture his face. He didn't know what to do with himself.' He squeezed Bea's hand. 'Can we change the subject now?'

'Of course. Sorry.'

Tom looked at the clock above the bar. 'I've booked a table for us at Giuseppe's, if that's OK?'

'Perfect.'

Bea was relieved to get out into the warm evening air. She couldn't remember being out to dinner with someone other than Simon. 'When we were dating we never went to restaurants

58

together.' She laughed.

'No money, which is why I'm enjoying taking you tonight.'

They entered the dimly lit restaurant. Bea looked forward to seeing Giuseppe. 'I used to come her quite a lot with Simon.'

Tom frowned. 'You should have said, I could have booked for us to go somewhere else.'

'Don't be silly, this is great. You can't beat the food.'

Giuseppe welcomed them with open arms. '*Cara*, I'm so sorry about you and Mr Porter splitting up,' he whispered as he gave her a brief hug. 'He says though that you're very happy now and have both moved on.' Gio looked across to where Tom was waiting for her by their table. 'And I can see he was telling the truth. I am pleased. He is a handsome man, no?'

Bea nodded. 'He is, Gio.' Gio pulled back a chair for her and Bea sat down.

Tom smiled. 'Do you remember we were thrown out of that pub the first summer we were seeing each other when we got drunk with the drummer from that band?'

Bea chewed her lip. 'You mean you got drunk. I had to get you home afterwards and my aunt panicked when I was late back.'

'I remember, you wanted to take over the world,' he teased her. 'You insisted you'd be a millionaire by the time you were twenty-five. What happened?'

Bea sighed. 'Life got in the way. Anyway, what about you? You were supposed to be running your own multi-national business by now.'

He shook his head. 'I know. Disappointing, aren't we?'

'Never mind,' said Bea holding her stomach to ease the pain caused by so much giggling. 'We only didn't succeed because our priorities changed. And we've still got loads of time to achieve stuff.'

'True,' he said quietly. 'What do you want to do most?'

'When Aunt Annabel first died, I thought I wanted to continue with her gardening designs and carry on with the one she was taking to the Chelsea Flower Show this year.' She pictured Annabel with her designs in her shed. 'But although I grew up with her teaching me stuff about gardens, I've got my own garden to keep going and need to find a way to buy out Simon. I don't have a sponsor for the show and to be honest I don't have the expertise to see it through.'

Tom smiled at her. 'You're still grieving over her, Bea. Most of my memories were of your aunt chatting to us while we lay in the sun, or her bullying me to mow her lawn or something. She was a big character and brilliant at her designs. You're doing well enough just trying to keep her home together for her. That's enough for anyone to deal with on their own.'

'Thanks, Tom. It's good to hear you say that.' Bea swallowed the lump in her throat and pushed away a memory of passing bulbs to her aunt as she planted them. 'I sometimes don't know how I'll manage it. I try and remember the fun bits of my aunt, but I miss her too much to be able to do that very often.'

'You're doing very well. Just hang in there and focus on fighting that shit of an ex of yours.' He looked up and Bea blew her nose on a tissue from her bag. 'Ah this looks delicious,' he said as Gio put a plate down in front of each of them.

'Er, Tom,' she said, suddenly noticing Giuseppe was cashing up and the waiter was watching them with a tired expression on his face. She waved her hand in front of Tom to get his attention. 'I think we've outstayed our welcome.' She motioned to the empty room. 'We're the last people here.'

'When did that happen?' Tom asked, before quickly finishing his drink, and nodding at Giuseppe for the bill. That paid, he stood up. 'Come on then, let's make a move.'

Taking her by the hand, they said their goodbyes to Giuseppe and his staff and Tom led her outside where he immediately flagged down a passing taxi.

He shouted Bea's address into the cab's window, and helped her into the back. 'Bea,' he murmured huskily, sitting down heavily next to her. 'I've had a wonderful time with you again tonight. It's been fun catching up about us and not having to concentrate on work issues.'

'Tom, I was wondering, while we're not at work, if you'd be able to tell me more about this Luke business. You know,' she mouthed the words 'money laundering' so that the taxi driver couldn't hear her. 'I just can't quite believe he could be involved, as you seem to think.' There, she thought, she'd voiced her doubts to him.

Tom took her hand, all humour vanishing from his expression. 'I understand how difficult this must be for you, but I can assure you he is involved, or I suspect he is.' He thought for a moment. 'I know I shouldn't, but come to my office on Monday and I'll show you the irrefutable proof that I'm not lying to you about this.'

Bea grimaced. She'd ruined their evening by bringing this matter up. 'I wasn't insinuating that you'd lied, Tom, but it seems so unlikely.'

'You know him that well, to believe him incapable of something like this then?'

Bea shook her head. 'No, but ...'

He put his arm round her and gave her a hug. 'I know, I'm so sorry. It's difficult to be involved in something this distasteful, whichever way you're connected. I do understand your concerns, Bea. You're right to ask me for proof, and on Monday I'll hopefully show you that you can trust me.'

Bea sighed. 'Thank you. You must think me so rude to ask you this after the lovely evening we've had?'

'Not at all. Once you can see for yourself the seriousness of the situation, it'll help you keep Luke in his place in your mind. It doesn't have to be too difficult; he's carrying out work for you, nothing more. I'll give you a ring in the morning, if that's OK?' he asked, as the taxi moved through the noisy St Helier streets. 'Not too early, I promise. Maybe I could take you kayaking?'

'I'd like that,' she agreed, wishing she felt a little less miserable. 'But not before ten, though. I have to make the most of any lie-ins I can get nowadays.' She didn't mention that she wanted to avoid Tom bumping in to Luke, who she hoped would have seen to any work his men needed to do and left her house by that time.

The taxi drew up at the front of her house and Bea opened the cab door. 'Thank you for a lovely evening,' she said, kissing him on the cheek and getting out. She watched as he waved back and the taxi disappeared into the darkness.

She bent to cuddle Flea as soon as she got into the house. It would be good to finally see some proof about Tom's allegations against Luke, Bea decided, not wishing to think about how awkward it would then be to deal with Luke when he came to the house. Bea removed her make-up and was thinking back over her evening, when the phone rang. 'Bloody hell, that was quick, Flea,' she laughed. 'He must live very near here to get home so quickly.'

Bea slumped back onto the bed, picked up the phone, and placed it immediately against her ear. 'When I said after ten, I meant ten in the morning,' she teased.

'Am I talking to Beatrix Potter?' demanded a controlled, clipped, female voice, tinged with what Bea assumed sounded like a definite threat.

Well, it certainly wasn't him. 'This is Beatrice Porter, and if you don't mind me stating the obvious, it's one-thirty in the morning,' she retaliated, irritated by the caller's aggressive tone.

'Never mind the fucking time,' the woman screeched. 'What the hell were you doing with my husband?'

Seven

Bea Stings

'She said what?' Shani gasped when she phoned her as soon as she'd ended the call with Vanessa.

'You needn't sound so excited about it,' Bea said, annoyed that Vanessa's call had given her such a fright.

'Sorry, you must have been spooked being in that house all by yourself.' Shani lowered her voice. 'You can't do anything about it tonight, so why don't you snuggle up to Flea and try to get some sleep? I haven't got any classes first thing tomorrow, so I'll be able to come over to your place after ten. We'll discuss everything then.'

'I want to go round to her place and give her hell.' Bea said. 'Her call was so unexpected I didn't have time to think of anything clever to say.'

'You don't know where she lives,' Shani said, 'and anyway, losing your temper with her probably won't solve anything. Let Tom sort his shitty wife out.'

Bea had to agree. Vanessa was Tom's problem, not hers. She lifted Flea onto her bed, and settled down for the night, relieved to find she was a little dozy despite everything and put it down to the alcohol she and Tom had consumed earlier in the evening. She closed her eyes and let her mind wander until she fell asleep.

Bea heard Shani's battered Astra backfiring down the driveway as she hurriedly finished dressing the following morning. She pulled on a pair of pink cut-off trousers and ran to open the front door to be instantly engulfed in a bear hug by Paul. 'Oof.' Flea barked in protest.

'It's all right, little man.' Paul let go of Bea and stroked

63

Flea's head before standing back up again. 'Poor you,' he said, leaning back and studying her face for a moment. 'Shani told me what that cow said to you last night.'

'You've heard then?' Bea asked, knowing full well Shani would have told him as soon as she had put down the phone. 'Come through.' They followed her down the long passageway, and into the kitchen.

'Blimey, it's lovely and cool in here.' Shani shivered. 'We're dying up in our flat. It's too hot in the summer and freezing in the winter. I'm starting to hate it there.'

Bea leant back against the cool metal of the Aga. 'Never mind the weather; I need to talk about last night.'

'I can't believe you're the other woman this time,' Paul teased, rubbing Flea's back as he stretched against him. 'Not like you at all.'

'Not funny, Paul,' Shani said, joining Bea in front of the Aga. 'Just pour us some water if you haven't got any cans of lemonade or something similar. It's too hot for tea anyway.'

'It's not funny,' agreed Bea, rubbing her arms to warm up, suddenly feeling chilled. 'I don't need to be dealing with this.' She stood from one foot to the next, retying her ponytail. 'I'm the last person who'd want to upset someone's wife. Don't forget I know how she must feel. I certainly felt like saying the same to Simon's Claire.' That felt odd, she thought. Simon's Claire. It used to be Simon's Bea.

'Sit down,' Shani said. 'Now take a deep breath and tell me exactly what else she said to you.'

Bea did as she was told. 'Tom told me they were legally separated, which is pretty much the same as being divorced. I mean, to be separated you have to sign a legal document stating you're no longer living together, don't you?' She waved her hand at Paul, declining the proffered biscuit barrel in his hand. 'I can't believe he lied to me. It's not as if we're dating as a couple, or anything. We're supposed to be friends.'

'You don't know he has lied yet.' Paul sprayed her with crumbs, as he munched on a digestive. 'Maybe she's the one telling porkies, or she could have been dipping one time too many into the Merlot.'

64

Bea took a deep breath in an effort to stop her temper from rising. 'She screamed at me like a complete nutter calling me all sorts of things. I'm not a slag, or what else did she say, oh yes, a bitch. Bloody cheek too, in the circumstances.'

Shani slammed her hand down on the work top. 'Will you just tell me what she said? We'll deal with the unfairness of it all later.'

'You love taking charge, Shani,' mumbled Paul, trying not to giggle, as they pointedly ignored him.

'She had the nerve to threaten to make my life a living hell if I ever saw him again.' She shuddered at the memory. 'I think she meant it, too. Let's face it, this is a big house to be rattling around in at the best of times, but when someone makes threats to you in the middle of the night, it takes on a creepiness that I've never noticed before.'

'I can imagine. She probably even looks like something from *The Texas Chainsaw Massacre*,' Shani said, taking a seat at the table, and motioning for Bea to sit in front of her.

'It's all right for you to sit there and joke, but it's me who'll be smacked in the face.'

The doorbell rang. 'Sit down,' Shani said. 'Paul will deal with whoever that is.'

'Oh, thanks,' he said, grimacing. 'What if it's the mad woman?'

'You're such a hero, Paul.' Shani took the biscuit tin away from him. 'Baby. I'll go then.'

'I will,' Bea said. Shani got up and pushed Bea back into her seat. Bea fell back wondering how someone so tall and skinny could still have so much physical strength. 'Leave this to me.'

Paul leaned towards Bea after Shani had marched out of the kitchen. 'She loves being the one to sort everything out. She's the same whenever someone kicks off at the gym. Always has to barge in and give everyone hell.'

'And you just let her, I suppose.' Bea smiled at him, imagining Paul, almost a foot shorter than Shani, letting her take charge of any dramas. Bea strained to hear who was at the door. At first she couldn't hear anything at all, and wondered what Shani could possibly be doing. She then heard whispers and giggling getting louder as Mel and Shani made their way to join them in the kitchen. 'It's Mel. I've said she can come in because she's brought food with her.'

'Hi, Mel,' Bea said, sensing Shani had given her sister a hurried, abridged version of events. 'Why don't I go and heat these up?' Bea took the chocolate croissants from her sister. She'd forgotten she'd invited them and Mel for breakfast, so couldn't expect them to leave her in peace before they'd eaten. Anyway they were here for her and another drama. When had her orderly, seamless life dissolved into this chaotic mess?

Paul looked up as she returned from locating the percolator from its home in the pantry. 'Never mind, Blondie, we'll get through this one, too.'

Bea shrugged. 'I know I'm a bit useless, but I'm not totally hopeless,' she said, placing cups and plates on the bleached pine table in front of them.

The phone rang. 'Hello?' said Bea, relieved for the distraction.

'Hi, Bea, it's me,' said Tom, his voice cheery. 'Sleep well?'

'As a matter of fact, no,' she admitted, still cross with him for lying to her about being separated from Vanessa.

'Why? What's the matter?' he asked, beginning to sound a little unsure.

'The matter, Tom, is your wife.' She waved the phone at her intent audience for them to be quiet so she could hear what he was trying to say. All three were now paying full attention, their croissants and hot drinks freeze-framed in mid-air.

'Vanessa?' he asked.

'Who else?'

'I'm coming round.' Tom sounded anxious. 'And you're going to tell me everything.'

Bea went to argue, but he'd already slammed down the phone before she'd uttered a single syllable.

She pointed at the phone. 'He's on his way.'

'Great,' cheered Shani. 'Now I get to see what he looks like after all these years.'

'I only remember him vaguely. I suppose it's because I was so much younger when you saw him,' said Mel, tearing off

66

mouthfuls from her croissant before devouring them with relish after dipping them into her coffee.

'That's disgusting, Mel. Anyway, I'm surprised you remember him at all.' Bea shook her head.

Paul rubbed his hands together to remove the crumbs. 'He was always hot, though we were only friendly because of you.' He grinned at Bea. 'I bet he's aged badly.'

'He hasn't.' Bea stood up. 'I'm going to take a shower.'

'What?' they cried in unison.

'You don't mind looking like hell in front of us,' laughed Mel. Shani nudged her and shook her head.

'I'm going upstairs. Can you three tidy up a bit?'

'What for?' frowned Mel, tearing apart a second croissant.

'My kitchen is a tip. Give it a quick tidy up while whilst I'm upstairs, please,' she said, walking out of the room.

'She's always shouted and stamped her feet when she's in a state about something,' mumbled Mel, chewing her breakfast, and completely ignoring Bea's request.

'If I had my way,' Shani said, 'he wouldn't get a chance to see inside the house at all.'

'Bugger it, I'm not tidying up for him,' said Mel. 'It's not as if she'll notice if we don't.'

'I can still hear you, you know,' called Bea from half way up the stairs.

She was almost finished roughly drying her hair when she heard the doorbell ringing followed by Mel's flirtatious giggle. So typical of Mel, thought Bea smiling, she didn't take long to forget whose side she was on.

Bea pulled on her oldest jeans and a faded T-shirt that had seen better days, but was at least clean and was ready for action. After all, she decided, they may only be friends and she didn't want to appear to be trying too hard, but she did have her pride. What little there was left of it.

She took a calming breath just before entering the kitchen, and saw Tom standing in front of her friends. She couldn't help thinking how they resembled the three wise monkeys, as they sat at the table next to each other, studying him in silence. Tom's face was grey, causing his green eyes to appear more intense than they usually did. Bea could tell he was doing his best to appear friendly. As disturbed as she was by the call, she couldn't help feeling sympathy for him, having such an accusatory audience.

'Tom, let's go through to the living room,' she said, sounding less angry than she had on the phone. 'We'll be able to talk in private through there.' She narrowed her eyes at the threesome who had purposefully ignored her telepathic pleas to go, staying exactly where they were at her kitchen table.

As soon as they were alone, he took her gently by the shoulders. 'Bea, I'm so sorry. I know how this must look, but I promise you I haven't lied about anything. I've told you pretty much everything there is to know about Vanessa. We do get along well, but it's purely for the children's sake, even though I don't see them nearly as much as I'd like to. '

Much as she had enjoyed Tom's company, she wasn't desperate in any way for a social life, and had had enough of being on the receiving end of lies and dramas. Bea told him everything that had been said between her and Vanessa the previous night. She stepped back from him. 'Tom, as much as I've enjoyed your company, I really don't need to be dealing with a psycho woman right now or indeed at any time.' He went to interrupt, but she held up her hand to stop him. 'This is too intense for me. I've got more than enough to be coping with right now and I don't want us to fall out if we have to work so closely together. So I think the best thing you can do is concentrate on sorting out whatever issues you two have, once and for all.'

Tom's shoulders stooped. He stared back at her for a moment. 'You're right, of course. It would be selfish to expect you to get involved with me after what's happened.' He leant forward, kissed her lightly on the cheek, then left without saying another word.

Hearing the front door close, the others called Bea back to the kitchen.

'Well?' Mel nudged her on her way to busy herself with the percolator.

'Not for me, thanks,' Bea said, beginning to feel

waterlogged. 'I don't know why you're bothering to ask me, you were all listening, I presume?'

Paul shrugged. 'You know we were. So he's gone, now what?'

'It's a shame,' she said finally. 'He was fun to be with the other night and he makes life at Malory's bearable.' How typical there has to be a hiccup somewhere, especially such a major one.

Mel handed out the drinks.

'Well, you all said I should give dating a go.' Bea smiled at their serious faces. 'I think I've had my fill of it for now.'

'Right,' said Paul. 'Anyway, I've heard tales about him liking a little flutter.'

'He's a gambler?' Shani widened her eyes.

'That's what I heard.' Paul's eyes glistened as he turned to Bea. 'So whether or not the wife is a problem, you don't need to get involved with someone who is addicted to losing money.'

'You know,' Bea said shaking her head wearily, 'sometimes living on an island can get really tiresome. You know you shouldn't listen to rumours about people, they're usually untrue.'

She turned to Mel. 'How are things coming along with Grant and your wedding plans?'

'Oh all right, I suppose,' she muffled, in between taking mouthfuls of another croissant. Bea couldn't understand how Mel remained slim, as she never seemed to stop eating, and certainly didn't ever exercise.

'Only all right?' asked Shani grimacing at Mel eating. 'Aren't you ever full?'

'You must have bought the entire newsagent's wedding magazines, and I know for a fact you've been on the internet scanning wedding planner's websites for ideas,' Paul winked at her.

'I only asked you to check out one woman for me, Paul, and that was supposed to be in confidence.' Mel sighed. 'I've been scanning the glossy magazines too; I need all the help I can get.' She put down her cup and studied her immaculate manicure with satisfaction. 'You know, I only agreed with

Mum to hold the wedding in May because I was certain we would easily manage to plan everything in that time, but it's not as simple as I thought it'd be.'

Shani and Paul glanced at Bea, but she wasn't in the mood to row with her sister, not today. It was exactly four months since Aunt Annabel had died and eight months and one day until she had to find Simon's money. It seemed like forever ago that she had kissed her aunt's forehead that last time, the tenth of May was coming around a little too quickly for her liking.

Shani motioned for Bea to say something first. She shook her head. Shani glared at her with her best schoolmistress look then turned her attentions to Mel. 'You know you only have to ask and we'll help you in whatever way we can, don't you?'

Bea stifled a groan; the thought of having to spend more time with her stepmother with wedding plans was almost more than she could contemplate. 'Yes, of course,' she said, relenting with as much good spirit as she could muster.

A smile slid across Mel's mouth. 'Really? I wasn't sure you'd want to still help me now that you know when we want to have the wedding. Thanks. Obviously I'll need to pass everything by my mum first, but then I'll let you all know what you can do for me.'

Paul widened his eyes at Bea. She tried not to smile at him, aware she'd been cornered into helping too. He hurriedly snatched his napkin from his lap and held it up to his mouth to try and stop his giggling from being heard.

Despite being surrounded by her closest friends, Bea suddenly felt very much alone. She stared out of the French doors and decided it was time to *be* alone.

Mel glared at Paul, nudging him hard.

'Ouch. That hurt,' he whined, still laughing, but now frowning in pain at the same time.

'Good. My wedding is no joke,' she pouted. She looked at Bea. 'I know we have our differences, but you'll only have to deal with this wedding and then you won't have to cope with my mum's desperation to make sure I'm seen as number one daughter in Dad's eyes.'

Bea's eyes widened. 'I didn't realise you were so aware of

what she does.'

'Yeah,' Paul said. 'We all thought you were a bit switched off where your mother's game-playing was concerned.'

Slamming her hands, palm first, onto the pine table, Mel glared at Paul. 'I don't want you to bother if you're only getting involved so you can take the mickey out of me and Mum at every opportunity. It is my wedding, Paul, despite your loyalties to Bea and her obvious annoyance about the date, but this is something that will have to last me for ever. Bea has a right to insult my mum, you don't.'

'Mel,' Shani snapped. 'He didn't mean to be horrible about Joyce, but I don't think you see the full extent of how badly she treats Bea.'

Bea stood up. 'That's enough. I'm a big girl now, Shani, thanks. I don't need anyone looking after me and I'm perfectly capable of standing up to Joyce, if I feel the need to do so.' She turned her attention to Mel. 'We're happy to help you plan the wedding. I don't like the idea that it's going to be on Liberation Day, but you were aware of that when you set the date. I'm more concerned about the crap Dad will be coping with, and if I can make it any easier for him, I will.'

Mel didn't reply for a moment. Bea waited for her to speak. 'Fine. Not exactly the enthusiasm I was hoping for from my own sister, Bea, but it's better than nothing. You're probably a little down now that your relationship with Tom has gone down the pan.'

'It was hardly a relationship,' Bea said, standing up and collecting their cups. 'Listen you lot, I've got a lot to catch up with here, if I ever want a weekend out of this house again.'

Mel picked up her bag, and slung it over her shoulder, 'I've got a wedding to plan,' Mel said pointedly.

'I was hoping to chill out here for a bit,' Paul moaned.

'You can, if you pick up a paintbrush and do something useful.'

Shani grabbed at her car keys. 'I would, but I need to get off. I've got to try and pin Harry down.'

'Everything all right?' Bea touched Shani's tanned arm lightly 'You're looking a little peaky. You're probably

71

'overdoing it at that gym.'

'Hah, I don't think so,' Paul laughed. 'She's been signed off all week.'

Bea raised her eyebrows and stood in front of Shani. 'Why? You never said you'd been unwell. What's the matter?'

'Thanks, Paul,' Shani snapped before looking at Bea. 'I'm fine. It was just a stomach bug, nothing more.'

'You let me know if you need anything,' Bea said. 'I know I'm probably caught up with all my problems at the moment, but that doesn't mean I don't want to know everything that's going on with you. We should catch up sometime, just the two of us.'

'That would be nice,' Shani said, hugging her quickly and following Paul out of the room.

Eight

October – Budding Romance

Bea ran up to her room and changed back into her old tracksuit. 'Come along lazybones,' she called to Flea, who was snoring soundly in his basket. With a slight groan he stretched, and eventually followed her downstairs.

'Smell that?' she said. 'That's the scent of the end of summer.' She picked a reddening leaf from a nearby acer. 'Such beautiful colours.' She gazed at the acre of green expanse before her and sighed. 'I'd better get a move on and mow this, otherwise it's going to be even more of a jungle out there.' She was grateful for Tom's recent help in keeping the lawn mown and remembered teasing Simon about his determination to mow the lawn every week during previous summers, insisting he didn't dare let it get out of control. Now she appreciated what he had meant.

Unable to face the mowing at that particular moment, Bea went into the kitchen and after flicking through several dog-eared recipe books, found Aunt Annabel's hand-written note showing her how to make a batch of lemonade. She told herself she wasn't putting off the work, simply preparing a thirst-quenching drink for when she'd completed the arduous task. That done, she placed the jug of lemonade carefully into her fridge and went back outside.

'It's not going to cut itself,' she groaned, aware she couldn't justify paying someone for a task she was perfectly capable of carrying out herself. 'No time like the present, I suppose,' she told Flea, breaking into a jog towards the old brick stables at the back of the house where she kept the mower, as well as all the decorating paraphernalia, before she could think of a reason to change her mind.

73

Maybe her aunt had hidden her mysterious item out here somewhere? She stood on the concrete floor staring up at the rafters and trying to think of any hiding places there could be in this place that she could have missed. After a brief and unsuccessful search that only uncovered an ancient chest containing moth-eaten books, she decided to give up looking for the day.

The mower was sitting exactly where Tom had left it three weeks before. Bea stood and stared at it for a moment, hands on hips as she contemplated asking him to come around and do it for her once again, but since the incident with Vanessa she'd done her best to be as friendly to him as possible in a professional capacity only. After all, they did still have to work together and there was no point in giving him the wrong impression that she may want something more from him, even if it was to help mow the lawn.

Bea filled the dusty red tank with fuel from the can nearby, hoping she wasn't doing the wrong thing, spilling a few dribbles of petrol onto her hand. 'Sod it.' Bea shook her hand to get the majority off and walked back into the kitchen to wash her hand. As she replaced the towel back on the rail, she spotted a piece of folded paper on the floor and bent to pick it up. It was Luke's latest invoice with a note pointing out extra plastering that he'd noticed needing replacing in the back bedroom. It must have fallen onto the floor when she'd opened the door letting in a draught. She dialled his number.

'Sorry, I only saw your note last night and it was too late to give you a ring.'

'About the plasterwork?'

'Yes,' she said thinking how sexy his deep voice sounded on the phone. 'I know you're coming to the end of the work now and to be honest I can't afford to do much more work, in fact I'm going to have to …' Bea held the phone away from her ear. Was that voices outside in her driveway? 'Simon?' she whispered before realising Luke was calling her name. 'Sorry, I was distracted for a minute.'

'Is everything all right?'

Bea sighed. 'Yes, I …' It was bloody Simon. What the hell

was he doing at her house, again? She ran over to the French doors and pushed them open wider. 'Hey, what do you think you're doing? Get off my property now.'

Simon carried on talking to someone she didn't recognise.

'Bea?' Luke shouted concern obvious in his voice.

'Sorry, Luke, I've got to go.' She ended the call before he was able to answer, furious with Simon.

'And this is my ex-wife,' Simon smiled as if he'd just introduced her as a tiresome teenager.

'Yes, and this is my house,' she said holding her hand out to the man in a bespoke grey suit. 'And you are?'

'I'm the estate agent your, er, ex-husband contacted for a valuation on this property.' He glanced down at his black leather clipboard and then smiled awkwardly at her.

Bea raised her eyebrows and stared at Simon. 'Why?'

Simon sighed. 'Beatrice, we both know the bank will send someone to value this place in your favour. I'm not an idiot, I remember your aunt talking about Mr Peters, the bank manager who she dealt with for the last two hundred years, or whatever. I'm bringing in someone to make sure I don't get cheated out of my share.'

'You shit. If Mr Peters was so easily influenced I would have raised the money to buy you out by now.'

Simon's triumphant expression made Bea grit her teeth in irritation. 'So you have been trying to sort out our little problem then?'

Bea glared at him.

'Good to know. D-Day will soon be upon us. Only seven months now.' He looked around the garden. 'However, I'm perfectly entitled to bring in an independent valuer and that's what I've done. So, if you don't mind finding something else to do, we'll get on.'

'No, you don't.' Bea grabbed Simon's arm. 'You can come inside,' she said to the estate agent who stepped from foot to foot as he pretended to be intrigued by her herb garden. 'You, Simon, can bloody well wait out here.'

'This way.' She led him into her kitchen trying to remember that it wasn't the poor agent's fault Simon had involved him in their problem.

'Don't worry; I'll only be a few minutes.' He forced a smile, making Bea feel slightly guilty at dragging him inside so hurriedly.

'See?' Simon said tapping his watch at her ten minutes later. 'That didn't take too long, now did it?'

Bea turned her back on them and began walking back towards the stables, stopping abruptly when she heard another vehicle coming down her driveway.

'Oh God, here comes the cavalry,' Simon sneered, shaking his head as he pointed at Luke. 'Come on, let's get out of here. Bye, Bea, see you in court.'

She frowned and turned to see Luke striding across the gravel towards her. 'Are you OK?' he asked, ignoring Simon's pained expression as he passed and focusing on her.

Bea's stomach flipped over. He seemed so concerned for her. 'I'm fine, thanks, just another confrontation with my adorable ex-husband.'

'What the hell did you ever see in that man?' Luke said in the direction of Simon's disappearing car.

Bea shrugged. 'He's very handsome, and believe it or not, can be great fun.'

'Hmm, maybe he's changed a lot.' He smiled.

Bea laughed. 'Or maybe I've woken up and can now see the real Simon that was well hidden for so long. Would you like a drink, or something?'

'No.' He shook his head, his untidy curls settling in a way that made Bea want to push her fingers into them. 'You cut our call so abruptly, I didn't know what had happened and wanted to make sure everything was OK.'

'That's kind, thank you, but I'm fine now he's gone.'

Luke looked at her for a few seconds. 'While I'm here, I just want to check on something the men mentioned to me about the hallway,' he said, before walking to the back door and into the house.

Bea smiled to herself as she returned to the mower and pushed the heavy machine around the side of the house, across the gravel driveway and onto the lawn.

Red in the face at the exertion, she thought back to Simon telling her how to start it. Pushing forward the bar and holding up the handle, she leant forward, grabbed the handle, and gave it a strong tug. Nothing. Bea breathed in, took hold of it once more, and bracing herself, pulled as quickly and as hard as she could. Again, nothing happened.

'Balls,' she yelled in frustrated rage. Several attempts, and two broken fingernails later, she couldn't understand how anyone could manage to hold up the brake bar, while at the same time being able to lean forward to yank the end of the rope with enough energy to make the machine burst into life. It was simply impossible. Or, she decided, probably broken.

Bea kicked the mower, achieving nothing more than the satisfaction of inflicting a dent onto its rusting bodywork, and was battling with herself whether or not to find a hammer to smash the useless creation to bits.

'Having problems?' Luke asked as he ambled over towards her, his long, jean-clad legs making short work of the distance.

Bea could feel her face reddening; so much for independence. 'This bloody thing doesn't work,' she stammered, fully aware the exertion had left her unattractively puce in the face.

He grinned at her. 'Let me have a try.' Luke raked a hand through his messy, wayward hair and stepped over to the mower.

Bea pushed her hands into her pockets and waited to see if he had any better luck with the useless machine.

Luke roughly rolled up the sleeves of his denim shirt, revealing tanned, muscular forearms, and started the mower on his first attempt.

'I thought it was broken,' she explained, feeling ridiculous for making such a fuss.

'There's a knack to these things,' he said, shrugging. 'Years of practice as I was growing up certainly helped. Tell you what, why don't I do this for you, and you can make us both one of your excellent coffees?'

'I've got something much more tempting than coffee,' she

77

said thinking about the lemonade cooling in her fridge. When she noticed Luke's surprise at her comment, she hurriedly changed the subject. 'Do you know how much lawn there is?' Bea asked, perplexed by his offer to do such a tedious task. 'It goes up the other side of the driveway too, as well as down past the orchard.'

He raised an eyebrow. 'Tell you what then, I'll do the main lawn areas now, and leave the less obvious areas for another day.'

Bea couldn't believe his offer, but had no intention of turning it down. She loved pottering in gardens, sowing seeds, dead-heading, and even planting, but the prospect of walking up and down pushing a mower, especially the part where it had to be repeatedly emptied, left her cold. 'Well if you're certain you don't mind, it would be a great help. Thanks.'

She almost skipped into the house, and as soon as she was sure he couldn't see her from her vantage point behind the dining room window, took a sneaky look at the handsome bearded man with the untidy hair, and deep blue eyes she couldn't help finding so mesmerising. He was like a big bear. A sexy, big bear. It was wonderful to enjoy the chance of appreciating his powerful physique fully for once. She watched his long legs pacing back and forth in straight lines across her wide, overgrown lawn and felt a warm glow inside.

'For heaven's sake.' She stepped back from the full-length window, nearly stepping on Flea and causing him to yelp in protest. She was relieved Tom's promise to show her the paperwork had been delayed by an unexpected project keeping them apart at work for the last few weeks. She wasn't going to think of Luke as guilty until she saw proof that he was. Bea hugged herself. Luke was so different to Simon and Tom physically; it wasn't like her to be attracted to someone so rugged. She smiled.

Bea calculated it would take him well over an hour to finish his task and long enough time for her to be able to sort through her wooden seed box in the potting shed.

'I saw a door open on one of the stables,' he announced from outside the door, what seemed like moments later. She stopped tidying away the spilt compost from the worktop and looked up at his damp chest. 'I presume the mower is kept in there.' Bea nodded.

'Thanks so much for doing that. I've been dreading tackling the mowing for weeks.' She brushed the peat off her hands as he looked around the walled-in garden, wondering what had taken his eye.

'Are those Jersey Lilies?' he asked, pointing to a clump of pretty pink flowers with tiny red crosses on their petals.

'No, I'm not sure what they are.' Bea pointed to the larger pink lilies nearby. 'Those are Jersey Lilies, *Amaryllis belladonna*. To be honest my godmother always thought the Guernsey Lilies were prettier; they're smaller, daintier.'

'I like those first ones, they're unusual. Would you like me to take a picture of them and ask my uncle if he knows what they are? He's a horticulturalist or something like that.'

'If you like, thanks.' She watched him take a quick photo of the flowers with his mobile. 'I suppose I should know what each of these plants is called if I'm to learn how to look after them all properly. Do you want to come in the house to freshen up a bit?'

Luke followed her to the house and she watched as he bent down to remove his boots. He washed his hands and face at the sink and Bea handed him a towel to dry himself before going to take the jug of lemonade out of the fridge and placing it onto the table. She wasn't sure if she was disappointed or relieved that he chose not to remove his top. He went to sit opposite her, leaning his bare forearms on the bleached pine of the table. Bea had to force herself not to stare at the golden hairs covering his skin.

'I'll come and do the rest of your mowing another day, if that's OK?'

'Only if you're sure you don't mind. I was hoping to employ a gardening firm to come and sort it all out, but I can't afford to.'

'Well, it's one hell of a garden to look after.' He didn't take his eyes off her as he spoke, and Bea was unable to tear her gaze away from him.

'Luke, as well as the garden, I also want you to know how grateful I am for the work your men have done here,' she said. 'Their standard is so high and I've heard horror stories about workmen beginning a job and disappearing half way through, sometimes for months.'

'I know what you mean,' he nodded. 'It's a pet hate of mine, which is why we don't take on work unless we know we can complete it without messing clients about.' He sat back and stared at her for a while.

'Not out with your friends today?' He glanced towards the kitchen door, as if expecting them to suddenly appear through it. He narrowed his eyes and stared at her. 'On the phone you were going to tell me something about the work, but you didn't actually say what it was.'

'I'm not sure how much more I can afford to do here. I'll physically do as much as I can and I owe it to my aunt to keep her garden perfect.' She said, not sure how to continue with the conversation. 'Lemonade?' she asked, indicating the crystal jug in the middle of the table. 'I thought you might appreciate this more than coffee after all your hard work.'

'Looks good.' He took a sip of the cool drink, the bitterness making him blink.

Bea stifled a giggle. 'Mmm, I think this batch is probably a little tart, but it's the coldest drink I have, unless you'd rather have water, or coffee, of course.'

He cleared his throat, shaking his head slowly and wincing. He smiled. 'No, this is fine,' he said, his voice raspy. 'It takes me back to my misspent youth.' He crossed his legs at the ankles, stretching his long legs out under the table and grazing her ankle.

Bea didn't move away from his touch. 'Hardly very misspent, if you were drinking lemonade,' she teased happily pushing the renovations to the back of her mind.

'It was what we added to it that was a naughty.' He raised an eyebrow.

'What was it? Gin? Vodka?' she asked, enjoying the banter between them.

Luke laughed. 'Granny's cherry brandy.'

80

Bea grimaced. 'Gross. I bet you only did that once?'

He nodded, watching her silently for a moment or two. 'Now that the mowing has been partly done and we're both free agents today, why don't we make the most of this great weather and take a trip to the Ecrehous islands?'

'In your boat, you mean?' Bea hadn't expected this, but what was stopping her? He sat opposite her and waited for her to answer.

'We could take our lunch there; make the most of what's left of the day. I think we could both do with some time off, don't you?'

Bea was sorely tempted, despite knowing she should keep her distance from him. Sod the investigation for once, she thought, it was only lunch after all. 'Why not? I've never been to the islands before and who knows when I'll get an offer like this again?' she said. She'd just have to be careful not to say anything that could raise his suspicions and alert him about anything.

Luke stood up. 'Great. The sea should be pretty calm and now that most of the holiday-makers have left, we might even find we're the only ones there.'

'Sounds perfect,' she admitted, liking the prospect even more than she'd expected to. 'I'll just phone Shani and ask if she can pop in later to take Flea out for a walk and keep an eye on him while I'm away,' she said, checking Flea had enough food and water. She quickly phoned Shani and, satisfied that she would be round to the house in an hour or so, followed Luke out to his truck. She tucked a stray strand of hair behind her ear self-consciously. 'I've always meant to go there.'

'Good,' said Luke. 'Then it makes our trip even more fun.'

As they drove through the country lanes across the north of the island to St Catherine's Bay, Luke told Bea all about Alphonse Le Gastelois, a recluse who fled to live for fourteen years on one of the main islands in the sixties when he was accused of molesting children.

'But it wasn't him, was it?' Bea said remembering back to hearing her stepmother tell stories about the Beast of Jersey and how he'd terrorised the islanders, especially those living in the east all those years before.

'No, poor devil.' Luke indicated to turn down towards the bay. 'They caught the Beast. Poor Alphonse was brought back and there was talk of giving him compensation for everything he'd gone through over those years. I should think there were a few red faces over that, too. Look,' he pointed out to the Channel. 'Over there, the Ecrehous.'

Bea peered out of the window and saw the islands, looking like nothing more than a cluster of rocks poking up out of the sea about halfway between Jersey and the coast of France. 'People don't actually live there, do they?' she asked, wondering if she should already know the answer.

Luke shook his head. 'No, but several of the islanders own huts on the main islands, and you can rent one of them, The Old Customs House, from the Parish of St Martin.'

Bea couldn't wait to get out there, and wasn't sure if she was more excited about going on his boat or seeing these intriguing little islands for the first time.

He parked the car. 'Just popping in to the café. I won't be long.'

Bea leant against the railings and breathed in the warm salty air. 'No, I'll come in with you.'

She watched from the doorway as Luke walked over to the owner. 'Good day today, Barrington?' he asked.

The older man, with his untidy hair and mahogany tan, smiled when he heard Luke's voice. 'It certainly has been. It's been packed all day today.' He suddenly noticed Bea standing further back. 'What are you doing here?' he shouted, opening his arms wide to welcome her. 'Come and give me a hug.'

Bea laughed. 'Hello, Barrington. Sorry I haven't been down here for so long.'

He held her by her shoulders and studied her for a moment. 'It's OK, your dad told me you were working on that house of yours. Not having too much trouble from that ex, I hope?'

Bea shook her head. She wasn't going to give the old man any reason to worry about her. 'Nothing I can't handle.'

'Good.' He frowned and looked up at Luke. 'You two come here together, did you?'

Luke nodded. 'We did. I've invited Bea to join me for lunch on the Ecrehous. Got any cooked lobster we could take with us?'

'I've got a couple here, just cooked for someone, but you can have them, I can get more from one of the fishermen on the slipway.'

'If you're sure,' said Bea, not wanting to cause him any extra work.

Barrington slapped Luke on the back. 'For this lad, and you of course, m'darlin', I'm only too happy to give them to you, well, at a little over cost, that is.'

Luke laughed. 'Great and we'll also need something to drink and maybe a baguette if you have one going spare.'

Barrington looked over his shoulder to his chef. 'You got that, love?'

The amused woman nodded. 'Two minutes.'

Luke went over to the till to settle up. Barrington immediately put his arm around Bea's shoulders and led her outside. 'Good chap you've got there, my love,' he said. 'It does me good to see you happy. I always thought that Simon was going to break that heart of yours one day. He talks the talk, he does, but only when he wants something. You're far better off without him.'

'That's what Aunt Annabel said too,' Bea said, her voice choking with emotion.

'She was a good woman. Did I tell you I asked her to marry me once?'

'Yes,' Bea laughed. 'But she married Uncle Antonio instead and you've never got over it.'

Barrington shook his head and gave her a tight hug. 'I loved my Sylvia, but Annabel was my first love, that's no lie.' He motioned to Luke waiting patiently at the counter for their lunch. 'He'll look after you, young Luke. Have fun.'

'I don't need looking after, Barrington, but thanks anyway.' Bea kissed him on his cheek. 'We're only going for a bite to eat; it's nothing to get excited about.'

He pursed his lips. 'If you say so.' He glanced over her shoulder. 'Here he comes. Now you two youngsters have fun.'

'We will,' she said, shaking her head and giving him a quick hug. She caught Luke's eye and he smiled at her. He seemed very fond of Barrington too, and she wondered how they knew each other.

'Come along,' Luke said taking her by the hand. 'We can't listen to this old reprobate all day, or we'll miss the tide, and you don't want to have to only see the Ecrehous from a distance. The rocks are vicious out there, we have to time this well.'

Once Luke had showered and changed and they'd cast off, it took Bea a little while before she got used to the movement of his beautiful wooden boat. She relaxed against the open door to the wheelhouse. Gazing up at the high mast, she wondered how often he hoisted the sails, or if it was easier to use the engine to get anywhere.

'Engine,' he said smiling at her.

Bea narrowed her eyes, wondering if she'd spoken her question out loud. 'What?'

'You were thinking about whether or not I make use of the wind or diesel to get from place to place on this beauty of mine.'

Bea laughed. 'Yes, I was. Why don't you use the sails though?'

'I do, when I'm further out to sea.' He looked across at the breakwater and Bea followed his gaze, watching St Catherine's receding away from them.

'I really should come here more often,' she said, breathing deeply and closing her eyes in the sun.

'St Catherine's, or on my boat?' Luke teased, as he steered the boat.

'St Catherine's,' she said, not opening her eyes, but aware he was watching her.

'Well, I'll just have to make sure you enjoy your trip enough for you to want to come again, shan't I?'

'Yes,' she said. 'This is bliss. Do you ever see dolphins?'

'We do, especially when the sea is warmer. They swim by the boats and Barrington sees them quite a lot from the café.'

Bea leant back, resting on her elbows, and watched Luke, so

comfortable with his boat, as if it were a part of him. She ran her fingers along the varnished handrail. 'It's so classical,' she said. 'You must have to spend a lot of time working on all this wood.'

He shrugged. 'I love beautifully crafted things and this boat is a bit of an obsession of mine.'

'So, you're in no rush to finish the restoration of your cottage then?'

Luke laughed. 'No, which is just as well.'

'Why?'

'I might be selling it sooner than I'd assumed.' Before Bea could question him further, he pointed back to Jersey's shoreline, at the rich green trees and tiny coves, then across to the Normandy coast. 'Perfect, don't you think?'

Bea nodded, aware that he'd opened up to her more than he'd intended doing. 'I really don't make the most of living on this island, you know.'

'Most people don't,' Luke said. 'I think life gets so busy sometimes we forget to enjoy everything we have around us.'

She felt the engines slowing down and saw the little group of islands nearby. 'They're so pretty,' she said. 'Like something in a picture book.'

'Not so inviting in the winter and damn frightening during a storm,' Luke said, dropping the anchor and moving their bags of food and drink from the galley into the dingy at the back of the boat. 'Here, let me help you.'

She took his cool hand and tentatively stepped down into the small boat. 'Thanks,' she said, holding on tightly until she was safely seated.

Luke showed her around the small islands, and Bea couldn't get over the tiny, one-room huts, used mainly by fisherman, then more recently by the lucky local families who owned one of them. She peered into another window. 'Why doesn't anyone live here?' she asked.

'No fresh water supply,' Luke said, leading her over to a small cove and laying out a blanket for them to sit on as he took out their lunch. 'Holidaymakers have been coming to stay here since Victorian times.'

'Can't say I blame them.' She took a plastic plate with the freshly cooked lobster and a dollop of yellowy mayonnaise from his hands. 'This is heavenly,' she said, unable to remember anything more perfect. 'Thank you for bringing me here today.'

Luke smiled at her. 'My pleasure, I'm glad you're enjoying yourself.'

'Tom,' Luke said after a few minutes.

'What?' Why did he want to know about Tom, Bea wondered.

'I think I saw him here a couple of months ago.' Luke didn't look at her, but thoughtfully took a drink from his bottle of water.

Bea shook her head. 'I doubt it; Tom hates the sea, from what I remember.'

Luke stopped eating and looked at her. 'Does he have a couple of children?'

Bea nodded, wishing he'd drop the subject. 'He does, they're quite small.'

'Then I'm sure it was him. I thought I'd seen him somewhere before when I saw you both at your house that evening. I'm sure it was here, although I can't be certain because I was in the boat at the time and he was onshore.'

'I think you must be mistaken. I can't see him coming here. He once told me about nearly drowning at Green Island when he was small, so he's very wary of the sea. I know he doesn't like boats. So it can't have been him.'

Luke didn't look too convinced. 'You're probably right. How's that lobster tasting?'

'Delicious,' said Bea, feeling better now he'd changed the subject.

They finished their lunch in silence and Bea relished being with him in such a tranquil place, with nothing but birds and the sound of the waves breaking against the rocks to disturb them. After tidying up, Luke helped her to her feet. 'Fancy seeing more of the islands?' he asked.

Bea nodded. His dark blue eyes, shining with a carefree enthusiasm she didn't often get to see, made her want to take his face in her hands and kiss him. As if he'd heard her thoughts, he abruptly stopped walking, turned and grabbed hold of her. Then, pulling her tightly against him, he kissed her; his cool lips hard against hers. Bea forgot everything and was lost in the moment.

Then, gently letting go of her, he sighed. 'You're so beautiful,' he said, before taking her hand once more and leading her across the sandy beach.

Bea felt like she'd been hugged on the inside somehow. The touch of his firm hand around hers as he told her all about the old Abbey on the little island of La Maitre, and how the French had invaded twice in the nineties, meant that she couldn't quite concentrate.

'I remember my Dad ranting about that,' she laughed. 'I'm glad they didn't get them back though.'

Luke looked surprised. 'They'd have a fight on their hands if they really tried to.'

'Typical Jersey boys,' she giggled. 'So patriotic about your island.'

Luke helped her back into the dingy and passed over the bags containing the remnants of their lunch. 'And why not? It's worth fighting for, don't you think?'

She wasn't sure if there was more to what he was saying, so decided to simply nod her agreement.

Luke drove her home, entertaining her all the way with anecdotes about Barrington and how he had upset one woman for not letting her pay for three ice creams with a credit card.

'But that's ridiculous,' said Bea. 'Surely she couldn't expect to pay for so little with a card?'

'She did, and was irate when he asked for payment in cash. Caused quite a stir down at the café, that did.'

Bea giggled. She could picture Barrington sending the woman on her way. 'He's the most generous man most of the time, but I've never known him have a problem telling someone exactly what he thought of them.'

Luke laughed. 'Me, neither.'

Not wanting her perfect day to end, Bea asked Luke if he wanted to come in for a drink. She finished her second glass of

87

wine and looked up at his tanned face. 'I've had such a lovely day today,' she said. 'It was like being on holiday somehow.' She felt heady and more alive than she had in years, and couldn't help noting Luke's muscles. 'I don't suppose you ever need to go to the gym, do you?'

Luke laughed. 'Never have the time. I'd rather get my exercise outside in the fresh air than in some sweaty gym.'

Bea pictured Simon and Tom, who worked out at the gym religiously each week. She had been so absorbed in admiring Luke's physique she'd forgotten to listen to what he was saying. She wasn't sure how she should answer. 'Um, yes?' she offered hopefully.

He laughed, 'You haven't been listening to a word I've said, have you?'

'No. I mean, yes,' she stuttered, her face reddening. 'Sorry, I was in a world of my own.'

'Somewhere enjoyable, I hope.'

If only he knew, thought Bea trying not to smile widely. 'It was very enjoyable.'

Luke sat at his side of the table, glass of wine in hand, sipping it slowly, and watching her intently from over the rim. 'You're very beautiful.'

'Shall we move into the drawing room?' suggested Bea, feeling mellow, but unsure how to reply. It was so long since she had felt such an attraction for anyone she couldn't quite remember how to react to it. 'It's getting rather chilly and I can light the fire in there.' She didn't like to add how she'd prepared the fire earlier expecting to be spending a quiet evening alone with a good book and a glass or two of rosé.

'Of course.' Luke carried their drinks and followed her into the vast, cream room, settling down on the sofa, as she lit the fire.

Bea took her place at the opposite end to him. Dragging a cushion onto her lap, she drew her legs up underneath her.

'Why do you do that?' he asked, passing over her glass.

'Do what?'

'Feel awkward, when being given a compliment.'

'Well, how do you think I should reply?' she asked.

He moved towards her, gently taking the cushion from her hands and tossing it over to the opposite chair. Then, moving closer to her, he put one hand behind her head and he kissed her. 'You taste wonderful, too.'

Bea's heart almost stopped. The pressure from his firm lips, and the feel of his tongue gently exploring her mouth, caused her senses, already hazy from alcohol and long-suppressed lust, to go completely haywire.

One minute, there were light delicate kisses on her face, neck, her throat; the next urgent discarding of clothes, as he kissed her lips, his hands moving deliciously over her skin. Bea sighed as Luke laid her down gently onto the Persian rug in front of the fire. He kissed her before lowering his head to her breasts, sending exquisite shards of ecstasy through her entire body.

'You're so perfect,' he whispered hoarsely, a hand caressing her thighs, moving slowly upwards between her legs, the dampness there betraying her feelings for him. Then, just when she thought she couldn't take any more, Luke finally entered her. Bea clasped him to her as they moved, her pleasure increasing until she climaxed seconds before he did. Luke groaned, holding her tightly, as Bea's felt her body exploding into a million, tiny pieces.

Nine

Not a Bed of Roses

The next morning, Bea woke to the sound of heavy rain battering against her bedroom window. Wearily opening one eye, she took a tentative look towards the chink of grey light beaming through her heavy, silk bedroom curtains. Her head felt fuzzy, and her mouth was parched. Reaching over to her bedside table, she patted around aimlessly, until her fingers touched the plastic of the ever-present bottle of water. She took a sip in an effort to wake up.

As Bea leant forward to sit up, her foot skimmed past a warm leg. Someone murmured behind her. Her eyes snapped open, sending a shooting sensation burning through her dehydrated brain. Turning slowly, her gaze fell on Luke, lying asleep on his back, muscular arms bent above his head, his tousled dark hair framing his handsome face, looking peaceful and content. Bea's heart contracted and more than anything she wanted to kiss him again.

Taking the opportunity to survey his hairy chest, she managed to retain enough self-control not to push her fingers through it. It didn't stop her from feeling like a voyeur, though. He was beautiful, even more so when he was sleeping and the intensity in his face disappeared. The rest of the time he appeared to be concentrating, on what she wasn't sure, but hoped it was his partner leaving him with so many financial difficulties and not his own involvement in them. She pushed away the thought.

The sheet only covered him from the waist down, but Bea could tell he was completely naked underneath. She had for so many years only ever shared her bed with Simon, and couldn't help gazing on this perfect specimen of manhood lying right next to her, completely relaxed, as if he was perfectly at home. She felt different with him, somehow, wanted him more desperately than she could recall wanting any other man. Her intense attraction to him unnerved her. So unlike Simon or Tom, the only other men she'd ever slept with; they'd made her feel beautiful and cared for, and had always wanted to please her, but never like Luke had done. She hugged herself at the memory of making love with him.

She pulled the sheet up around her as Tom's words about Luke being investigated seeped, unwelcome, into her mind. Losing Aunt Annabel was hard enough, being betrayed by Simon was a different kind of cruelty, but to let herself fall in love with this man when she'd been warned about his financial problems was nothing more than careless.

'Damn,' she murmured, wishing, yet again, that Tom had thought to keep his information to himself. She needed to distance herself from Luke, however much she felt the urge to be with him. She tried to get more comfortable in the bed, but moving her legs woke him up.

'Morning, beautiful,' he murmured, his voice croaky, as he stretched. He smiled up at her and, noticing her expression, narrowed his eyes. 'What's the matter? Didn't you sleep well? Hangover, I suppose. I must admit, I'm feeling rather heavy-headed too.'

'Luke?' she whispered awkwardly.

'What is it, sweetheart?' He pushed himself up on his elbow, his expression gradually changed to one of concern. 'What's wrong?'

'We had sex.'

He smiled. 'Yes, we did.'

'And?'

'And, it was wonderful,' he replied, placing his hands behind his head.

This felt too perfect, too dreamlike. Why had she not simply refused to go with him on his boat the day before? She wasn't an idiot and knew what she could and couldn't say. Bea couldn't help smiling as she looked down at him.

Luke put his arm up and, placing it around the back of her neck, gently pulled her down on to him, kissing her. Bea melted into him, relishing the feel of his mouth on hers as she lay on top of him.

His hand moved down towards her bottom. The shrill ring of his mobile startled her. 'Ignore it,' he whispered.

The ringing continued.

Eventually, with the mood broken, Bea pushed away from him. 'You'd better answer it. Maybe it's something important.'

'I'm sure it can wait.'

Bea wondered why he was so determined not to answer the call right now. 'I'll go and take a quick shower, leave you to it,' she said, handing him his still ringing mobile.

She got out of bed and with a quick glance back at him could see he was frowning at the screen. He looked up at her and smiled, probably waiting for her to leave the room. Bea went into the bathroom and closed the door behind her. She could hear his voice though the door. He sounded irritated. She stepped into the shower and, turning the tap on, stood under the spray of water and soaped her body. Something was wrong, or was she just being overly sensitive? Maybe Simon's deceit had coloured her perspective of how others lived their lives.

Bea found Luke standing in her kitchen wearing only his faded blue jeans. 'Feeling better?' he asked, passing her a mug of steaming black coffee and kissing her lightly on the neck, making her shiver. 'Mind if I take a quick shower?'

Bea's heart pounded as she watched him walk out of the room. His toned arms, back, and tousled hair making her wish they were once again back in her bed. She smiled. He was delicious and so opposite to everything Simon had been. Such a relief.

The phone rang and Bea answered it after a couple of rings. 'Hi, Shani,' she said, recognising the number. 'I can't really talk now. Can I give you a call later?'

'Yes, of course, but let me quickly tell you about that hunky builder of yours.'

Bea groaned. 'You're such a gossip. Go on, what tittle-tattle have you learned at the gym this time?'

'Did you know he was living with a model; legs up to her armpits, or so I heard. They've been together on and off for years.'

Bea's legs seemed to lose some of their strength. She quickly pulled out a chair and slumped down onto it. 'What?' she whispered. 'Are you sure?'

'Damn right. They were seen together only the day before yesterday. She lives on his boat with him. Lucky cow.'

Bea felt as if Shani had slapped her. Hard.

'Bea? Are you there?'

'Yes,' she murmured. Hearing Luke's footsteps on the landing as he walked towards the stairs, she took a deep breath and tried to clear her mind. 'I have to go, Shan, but I'll call you later.' Bea ended the call without waiting to hear Shani's answer and took a sip of her coffee, ready to confront Luke.

'That's better,' he said, taking her in his arms and kissing her, his damp hair sticking up at all angles. Bea shivered at his touch, hardly able to look at his tanned face. She knew he could never be hers, not in the way she would like him to be. She let him hold her for a second longer, not wishing for the moment to end and lose the weight of his arms around her. The pain of knowing how perfect it felt to be made love to by Luke only compounded her misery that he belonged to someone else and she was probably nothing more than yet another conquest.

She pushed him away. Luke frowned. 'What's the matter?'

'This can't happen again,' she insisted, staring at the steam coming from her cup and ignoring his confused, but gentle, expression.

'Why ever not?' He frowned, ignoring the drop of water falling onto his face from his wet hair.

Bea struggled to find her voice. She had to look away from him. She wanted to be with him, but she could not ignore he had a girlfriend. Wasn't the threat of the investigation against him enough to put her off, she mused? I'm so stupid, she decided, aware that by spending time with him she might be putting into action something that could result in her losing her home. Annabel's house. No, she owed too much to her aunt and her trust in her to let that happen, despite how much she couldn't help feeling attracted to him.

A black look shadowed his face. 'If you don't want it to happen again, then it won't.'

Bea moved away. She'd hurt his feelings and didn't want him to get the wrong idea. 'You have a girlfriend.'

He raised his eyebrows. 'You knew that when we slept together last night?'

'No, Shani phoned a few minutes ago and told me.'

He shook his head slowly. 'It's not like that.'

'OK, then,' Bea said, determined to know for certain the extent of his relationship with this woman, 'just answer me this? Do you live together?

He smiled and folded his arms. 'She stays on my boat sometimes, but that doesn't mean ...' He shook his head. 'Bea, we're just friends.'

Bea swallowed the lump forming in her throat. 'Have you ever slept with her?' She didn't want to know the answer, but wasn't going to be made to look a fool yet again by some man, however gorgeous he might be. 'Well?' she asked when he didn't answer right away.

Luke sighed. 'Yes.'

Bea stepped back and leant against the sideboard. 'So she lives with you and you've slept together, but you're just friends. Sorry, Luke, we're not looking for the same things, obviously,' she said. 'I'm going through a divorce and however it may look to you, I really don't go in for one-night stands.'

He walked up to her and stood so close she could smell the soapy scent of his skin. 'Bea, look at me.' He lifted her chin, but Bea kept her focus on the floor. 'I don't know what you think I'm looking for, and I can see that the situation with Leilani sounds a little odd, but you must believe me when I tell you that there really isn't more to our relationship than friendship now.'

'Now?' Bea couldn't hide her anger towards him. 'I really think it's best if you just leave.'

Luke stared at her for a moment. She could see he was upset, or was it annoyance with her for being so, what was it Simon called her, oh yes, middle-class. Well, middle-class or not, she wasn't going to put up with being anybody's second best again.

'You've obviously made your mind up about me already, so I'll let you get on. Goodbye Bea,' he said, leaning forward and kissing her on her cheek. 'I'm sorry it had to end this way.'

Me too, thought Bea, letting him see his own way out.

'I can't believe he has a live-in girlfriend,' Bea admitted to Shani on the phone the following day after work. With her voice lowered, she gave a vague outline of what she'd said to Luke.

'How could you have known if he didn't tell you? Bastard. If nothing else though, it'll do you good, getting a taste of a new man. Out with the old, and in with the new, I say. So it's not the end of the world, is it?'

That's a matter of opinion, thought Bea miserably trying to push away the memory of her night with Luke. 'I feel so stupid.' She wished she'd never taken his number from Mel and called him about the building work. She'd been doing so well before that. Her house might have been crumbling, but she'd slowly been learning to cope without Annabel and her anger towards Simon had helped her deal with his betrayal. Now, it all seemed so raw once again. 'He wasn't happy when I argued with him about his girlfriend.'

'Are you surprised?'

'No,' Bea said miserably. 'He's probably relieved to have had a lucky escape from the mad divorcee.'

'Relax,' Shani said. 'He had fun that night too, don't forget. You shouldn't be so hard on yourself. You're young, free, and single. You've been firmly crapped on by your louse of an ex-husband, and you deserve a bit of spice in your life. Sleeping with a guy doesn't have to mean you should then have a full-blown relationship with him. This isn't the Dark Ages, you know.'

Shani was right. 'Yes, look at you and Harry. How is he by the way? I still haven't met him, as far as I know,' Bea said.

Shani groaned. 'He's hot and sexy and driving me nuts.'

'Why?' Bea couldn't help smile. Shani was always so in charge of her men; she only wished she was as tough on hers.

'Nothing much, just a little disagreement we're having at the moment.'

Bea could tell something wasn't quite right. 'You're always so in control of your men. You are OK, aren't you?'

Shani sighed. 'When have you known me not to be? Tell you what, I'm booked up for a few extra classes this evening, but I'll give you a call tomorrow. Maybe, if you're not already busy, we can take a walk on the beach with Flea.'

The thought appealed to Bea. If only she could discuss what Tom had told her with Shani, but she'd signed a confidentiality agreement when she joined Malory's and couldn't divulge any information about a client, even if it was about Luke. 'Lovely, and Shani?'

'Yes?'

'Why don't you bring Harry along sometime? It would be good to get to know the man in your life. It feels weird not knowing him at all. A bit too mysterious, if you ask me.'

'Bea?'

'Yes?' Bea replied hopefully.

'Shut the hell up. You and Paul will meet him when I'm good and ready, and not before.'

Bea laughed. She knew when she was beaten, and replaced the receiver feeling sure Shani was behaving a little too secretly; then again, thought Bea, I'm probably being over-anxious about everything. Shani was nothing if not tough and never had a problem admitting if something was wrong in her life and then, mused Bea, sorting it out without needing anyone's approval or assistance.

Shani and Bea drove straight to L'Etacq. As soon as he was allowed off his lead, Flea ran onto the beach and immediately turned his attentions to killing strands of black seaweed.

'So, Shan, how are things going with Harry?'

'You're not going to let this drop, are you?' Bea smiled and shook her head. 'Not so good. In fact I haven't heard from him for about a month.' She kicked a lump of sand with the toe of her worn, white trainer.

'A month? Why, what happened?'

'No idea,' Shani said, looking away from Bea.

Something wasn't right. 'Are you OK? You would tell me if there was something wrong, wouldn't you?'

Shani picked up Flea's ball and threw it towards the edge of the tide for him. 'Of course. Now stop going on. When have you known me to have a problem I couldn't cope with?'

Bea couldn't think of one solitary occasion where Shani was unable to deal with something troubling her. 'True. Maybe it's just me.'

'It is, now shut up.'

Bea picked up a piece of pale green glass, frosted by the sand and tide, and brushed the dried sand from it before dropping it again. 'Did I tell you the bank manager has called me in for another meeting?'

'No, when?'

'Next week. I'm hoping Simon's estate agent did a decent enough valuation so that I'll be able to get the full loan, but I'm not feeling all that confident.'

'What will you do if you don't get enough money to pay Simon off?'

Bea shivered and breathed in the salty air. 'I've had sleepless nights over this, Shan. If I don't come up with the money then I'm going to have to sell the house. He's entitled to half.'

'But that's unfair. Annabel loathed him ever since she found him with Claire that night, and she left the house to you, not him.'

Bea picked up Flea's ball and threw it again for him, watching as his ears bounced up and down behind him as he raced off like a little grey gazelle after it. 'I know, it seems bloody unfair to me too, but I inherited it while we were still together and so it's considered a matrimonial asset, according to Simon.'

'But you've signed separation papers now.'

'Yes, after Aunt Annabel had died, not before. So, if I do sell,' she continued, the frequent nausea flooding through her as it did every time she tried to contemplate the chance of an unsatisfactory outcome, 'I suppose I'll have to move in with Dad and Joyce until I sort something out.'

'You'd go mad having to move in with that old bag.' Shani grimaced. 'You always hated being in the same house with her whenever your dad insisted you go and stay with them, even when you were small.'

'I think she found it harder having me there, it messed up their little family somehow, which is why Dad agreed to let me spend most of my childhood with Aunt Annabel.'

'I don't know why they ever made you go back home again.'

Bea had spent many miserable nights wishing they hadn't. 'Me neither and it never lasted very long, but I suppose it would have looked bad at her charity lunches if her husband's dead first wife's daughter was sent to live somewhere else.'

Shani picked up a piece of driftwood and threw it for Flea. 'Despite his inability to stand up to Joyce, your dad does love you, don't forget that.'

Bea smiled. 'I know he does. He's just too under her thumb to be able to show it very much. Poor man has spent most of his life doing things he doesn't want to so that she'll be kept in a good mood.'

Shani whistled for Flea to bring back the piece of wood. 'What's wrong with that dog, he doesn't understand he's supposed to bring the thing back if he wants me to throw it for him again.' She shook her head. 'It's a shame that Joyce always stirred you and Mel up. You're always so competitive towards each other.' Bea nodded. 'Do you think that's why she chose Liberation Day to hold her wedding?'

Bea didn't doubt it for a second. 'More than likely, but the date's set now, so I have to deal with it.' She didn't add that she also had to try and find a way to get through the day without falling apart. 'I've no idea what she was thinking.'

Shani folded the front of her jacked over her stomach. 'I can't believe we all liked Simon once, little shit.'

Bea smiled. 'I know. It makes me wonder if I can really trust my judgement in people,' she said, thinking again about Luke. 'I'm not sure if he was the one who fooled everyone with his charm, or if we're all, and I mean me in particular, simply gullible. Getting back to Harry though, you do know if you need any help you can come to me.' Bea stroked Shani's arm nearest to her, before calling Flea back from the edge of the sea. 'However, I do think if Harry won't speak to you, then maybe you should go to his surgery. He'll have to talk to you then.'

'Don't worry, I will. Now,' Shani said, 'Although how I ended up sleeping with a dentist, I'll never know. Tell me all about you and that delicious man you slept with the other night.'

Bea cringed. 'What's there to say? I thought we had something special, but obviously I was the only one who felt that way. I want to know more about Harry.'

Shani groaned. 'He's a little older than me and comes to boxercise classes. I think he's hot, but I'm not sure how I really feel about him right now.'

'OK, I know when you've had enough interrogation for one day.' Bea nudged her and whistled for Flea. She bent to put on his lead. 'Anyway, it's getting cold out here and I can tell by the way he's panting that Flea's overdone the running up and down after seagulls. Let's go.'

Ten

November – Dishing the Dirt

Bea hadn't come across Luke at all for the two weeks since they had spent the night together. She tried to push the whole episode further to the back of her mind, as she made a few notes in one of the meeting rooms at work. Although she couldn't help feeling slightly deflated, even though she had been the one to tell him to leave. Surely if he felt anything for her at all, he could have contacted her on some pretext?

Her mobile rang. Bea scrambled to find it in her pocket, aware she should have it on silent in the office. She quickly answered it. 'Hi, where are you?' Tom said. Bea tried not to let her disappointment show. 'I've called your extension and walked by your desk, but couldn't see you anywhere. I need to chat to you about a couple of things, if that's all right?'

Bea tucked the phone between her ear and shoulder, continuing to scribble her notes. 'Talk away; I'm just putting together a few details from here for one of my clients. I've come into Room Three to get a bit of peace so I can concentrate.'

'I'd rather we speak out of work?'

She thought he sounded quite unsure of himself. It wasn't like him at all. 'I can meet you outside here if you like, say, in about half an hour; we could get a coffee and have a chat then.' Bea didn't know why Tom couldn't simply make time to talk to her at the office. Maybe, she mused, he wanted to keep their friendship away from prying eyes. She'd heard enough gossip at Malory's to not want her private life being the next bite being passed around.

'So, Tom,' she said, finding him outside the coffee shop a little later. He handed her a latte and went to kiss her on the

101

cheek. 'I thought we could take a stroll along the promenade overlooking the marina.'

'Sounds good to me,' she said happy to be outside for a while.' How are things?'

'I wanted to let you know Vanessa and I have been speaking about what happened, and you can rest assured it won't happen again. She understands how rude it was for her to phone you like she did.'

'That's a relief, I suppose,' she said, not sure why he was bringing this up so many weeks after Vanessa's phone call.

'I was also wondering if you and your friends would like to join me at the opening of The Dark Side?'

'The what?' Bea frowned, taking a sip of the milky drink.

'The Dark Side,' he explained. 'It's a new nightclub. The opening night is next weekend. So, if you're not doing anything else, I was hoping you might want to come along?'

It sounded like fun, but she wasn't sure. Then again, it wasn't as if she had anything else in her diary for the foreseeable future. Bea knew she could do with letting her hair down for a change and somewhere new and exciting sounded tempting, and fun. She hesitated. 'I'll speak to the others,' she said after a moment, 'and get back to you. I'm sure neither of them will want to turn down an offer of an opening night anywhere.'

'It's great to see you again.'

'Tom, you can see me most days at work.' It was good to see him too, she realised. How did he manage to look so immaculate when the wind was so strong? She suppressed a smile, pushing away the thought of how much hairspray he must use to keep his hair in place.

'I've got something to show you,' he said, opening an attachment on his phone. 'I have to be careful at work and these files are confidential, so I thought I'd take a photo and show it to you that way.'

Bea waited silently, not wanting to have to see the proof of Luke's guilt for herself. Tom handed her the mobile. Bea's mood plummeted when she read the report on headed paper from the financial commission confirming her worst fears about

Luke. He was under investigation and she knew as well as Tom did that there had to be enough evidence against him to at least cause them to investigate his finances. Her hand began to shake so she quickly gave Tom back his phone. 'So, it is true,' she said, wishing more than anything that he hadn't shown it to her.

She took a deep breath and began walking. Walking down here always relaxes me, she thought, but not this time.

'You didn't think I'd lied to you, did you?' Tom came up beside her, concern obvious on his face.

Bea realised what she'd done. It wasn't Tom's fault Luke wasn't the man she'd hoped him to be. Like Simon, she'd read him wrong. When would she learn, she wondered, holding tightly onto her cup. 'Sorry, no. I suppose I was hoping you'd been wrong.'

'I'm not. I'm sorry, I know you're upset.' Without any notice, he grabbed hold of her in a bear hug with such force it almost took the air from her lungs. 'Thanks for agreeing to meet me today,' he said over her shoulder. 'It's been great to clear the air.'

Bea waited a second or two before gently pushing him away. 'Tom, you do realise I'm only agreeing to go out to the club as a friend, don't you? If you're going to get the wrong idea, then I'm going to have to turn down your invitation.'

He shook his head, looking hurt. 'Not at all. You've made your feelings clear and I understand where you're coming from. I want us to be friends, too. We've known each other for so many years it would be a shame not to spend some time together outside that air-conditioned breezeblock we call an office.'

'We'll see. I'm not going to get in the middle of whatever odd situation you and Vanessa have between you. I'll give you a call about going to The Dark Side, but knowing Shani and Paul, they'll be only too happy for an excuse to go out and party.'

Tom went to kiss her on the cheek, but stopped before actually doing so and raised an eyebrow. 'Sorry, force of habit,' he said. 'I'd better get on, I'm meeting a client in ten minutes at the other end of town, in Colomberie.'

She watched him go, wondering if maybe she was doing the wrong thing accepting his invitation at all, then again, he was essentially her boss and she didn't really have any reason to be anti-social towards him. She looked up, coming eye to eye with Luke as he drove past. Her stomach contracted and she pushed away the memory of those lips pressing down hard on her own. Bea pictured the image Tom had shown her, unable to force a smile as Luke nodded to acknowledge her before driving on.

Knowing she was going to be out for several hours, Bea double checked Flea's water and ensured that the heating was on low for him. She then drove into down to meet Tom, Shani, Mel, and Grant at The Dark Side. Paul turned up a few minutes later with Guy, a French chef he had met the previous month.

'He wanted to make sure they had some sort of a future together before introducing us to him, or so he says,' Mel whispered from the corner of her mouth as she eyed Guy up and down. 'I love his olive skin. He's lovely, don't you think?'

'He's hot,' Shani murmured, as they stared at the tall, brooding Frenchman. 'Don't you just love that accent? How he's managed to keep him a secret I'm not sure. Mind you, I've been so involved with my own stuff I probably wouldn't have noticed if he had moved him into the flat.'

'He might have done,' Bea laughed. 'I think they look cute together, the tall, dark Frenchmen and the little, blond Jersey boy. They look happy together.' It was the first time Bea had seen Paul with anyone since his long-term partner had broken his heart by leaving him to return to Canada five years before.

'Now, if he wasn't gay, I'd be in there like a shot,' Shani said not bothering to hide her attraction to Guy. 'Why is it that the lush men are always gay?' she pouted. 'Do you know Paul always smells like a balmy day on a desert island?'

Bea raised her eyebrows. 'He does?' she asked, trying to imagine exactly how that was supposed to smell.

'Sure, and never ever has beer breath.'

'He wouldn't have beer breath,' Mel argued. 'He doesn't drink beer.' She took Grant's hand. 'Come on, let's go and find other people to talk to.'

Bea looked around the darkened room with its purple lighting and mirrored dance floor. 'Love's young dream,' Bea murmured to Shani, wishing she didn't feel just a touch of envy at their happiness.

'Love's young drips, if you ask me.' Shani rolled her eyes, smiling at Paul as he and Guy came up to them.

'Don't take any notice of her.' Paul joined them. 'She's only jealous.'

'Oh bugger off, Paul.' Shani shook her head emphatically. 'You wouldn't get me being all soppy like that in public. Shouldn't you be getting the drinks in? It must be your round by now.'

'No problem, your ladyship.' He patted his pocket. 'Plenty in here to spend tonight, but you can come and help me carry them.' He flounced off towards the chrome bar at the other end of the cavernous room, taking Guy by the hand, a wide smile on his cheeky face.

Tom laughed, as he watched Shani striding after Paul, her long, toned legs on display in the shortest skirt that barely covered her knickers. 'I'm beginning to think you're surrounded by mad people.'

Bea secretly agreed. She held her hands up and nodded. 'I know. And what's more, these are my closest friends, so there's no hope for me. Guy seems fun though, don't you agree?'

Bea watched as Shani, bored with waiting at the crowded bar, swayed her hips as she wandered across to the dance floor and waved her arms in the air as she lost herself to the music. Paul followed and mimicked her, while Guy was left to buy the drinks.

'It's like something from one of those documentaries on 1970s discos in New York,' Tom joked. 'Except these two haven't quite mastered the moves.' As he took a gulp from his Budweiser someone caught Tom's eye, and he nodded at them at the other side of the room.

Bea couldn't see who it was over the mêlée of people crammed into the darkened club. She then noticed Shani gesturing frantically in her direction. She looked round the room, but couldn't find what all the fuss was about.

Tom turned back to face Bea. 'Look at ...' he started, before a hand landed heavily on his back. Tom turned round mid-sentence and, his shoulders tensing, he forced a smile. 'Luke,' he shouted, over the noise. 'How are you?'

Bea frowned. She hadn't expected to see him here.

'You know Bea, of course,' Tom said, sliding his arm around her shoulders. Bea shrugged him off.

Luke's mouth twitched. He nodded at Tom. Was that contempt she spotted in his glance? He looked at Bea and his expression softened slightly. They stood transfixed for several seconds. Luke found the power of speech first. 'Of course,' he answered his deep blue eyes boring into hers. 'You won't have met Leilani yet.'

Bea then noticed movement next to him. Her heart plummeted when she saw that one of his shirt-clad arms was casually slung around a tall, tanned brunette, who she couldn't help noticing was wearing the same diamante Jimmy Choo shoes she had lusted over with Shani the previous week in the latest edition of *Vogue*. Bea didn't think she'd ever met anyone this glamorous and impossibly beautiful before. No wonder Luke was seeing her; Leilani was utterly gorgeous and even taller than Shani.

She looked down at Bea and smiled. 'Hi, I'm pleased to meet you,' she said, before turning her attention to Tom, who, Bea couldn't help noticing, was dumbstruck at the vision in front of him.

'This is Tom and Beatrice,' Luke said, his smile showing of his white teeth to perfection. His beard appeared to be clipped and only a little more than designer stubble. They made an incredibly beautiful couple, and Bea wanted to cry. She forced a smile.

'God, they even have matching teeth,' Shani said from behind her.

'What a typically English name,' Leilani drawled sexily.

Bea's insides hurt, they had contracted so much, and try as she might, she couldn't help sneaking another peek at Luke's face. He wasn't looking as happy as she'd expected him to, although his lips did draw back into a smile when he caught her

106

looking over at him. Tom gazed appreciatively at Leilani's impossibly high bosom. It was almost at his eye level, and he was six feet tall. Bea couldn't imagine where Luke had found this woman. She had certainly never seen her in Jersey before.

'Nice to meet you, Leilani,' Tom said to her chest. As both men turned their attention to her, Bea noticed how Leilani discreetly moved one of her endless legs slightly in front of the other, to show off its perfection, while at the same time, managing to push her already high chest further up. Bea knew in no uncertain terms that she could never hope to compete with anyone as impressive as this Amazonian standing in front of her.

'Lukey has been showing me round the countryside you have here on Jersey. Everything is so quaint, although I have to admit to being a city girl at heart. As far as I can make out, you either turn left or right, when you go for a drive in this little island, and still end up back in the same place one hour later. There's not much space here to escape to, is there?'

'We say in Jersey,' Shani said pointedly. 'Not on Jersey.' She leant towards Bea. 'Lukey?' Shani murmured a little too loudly. He looked at her, but Bea couldn't tell if he was annoyed or amused.

'Manhattan is more my thing,' Leilani continued, oblivious to Shani's sarcasm. Bea suspected Leilani was used to dealing with jealous females. She couldn't help being amused by Shani's instant dislike of Leilani though; it made her feel much better.

'So you're on holiday then?' Tom asked, not appearing at all fazed by her insulting comments about his place of birth.

'How long are you planning on staying in Jersey?' Bea said, feeling happier at this news.

'I haven't decided yet. I suppose I'll be here for as long as Lukey wants me to be.' She stroked his tight, hard bottom that unfortunately Bea remembered only too well. She stiffened at the memory. Bea cleared her throat. Leilani pouted at Luke. He replied by giving her a slow smile that was so sexy even Shani stood still and gawped.

'What is it that you do?' Tom asked, unable to take his eyes off her.

'I'm a model,' she announced, smiling at him as if to prove her point. 'Runway mostly, but I specialise in stockings and lingerie.' She pointed one foot forward, and raised her finely waxed eyebrows.

'Well, it was nice seeing you again,' Luke said. He glanced down at Bea. Then taking Leilani's hand, added, 'We'll catch up with you all later. Have a fun evening.' Before leading her away across the dance floor.

'It was lovely to meet with you,' Leilani added over her shoulder at Bea. She oozed sex, and Bea doubted she had ever felt as thoroughly self-satisfied as Leilani now seemed. Bea wanted to dislike her, but apart from her close proximity to Luke and her perfect looks she couldn't honestly do so. What little confidence she had managed to muster before leaving the house had now vanished. And, as for Lukey, well, Bea decided, she could keep him.

'Wow,' Shani said. 'He is shit hot.' I know, thought Bea. 'But Lukey?' said Shani once again.

'I think all the sex they must be having has turned his brain to mush.' Bea grimaced at the thought.

'He could turn my brain to mush any day.' Shani glanced away from Luke's receding back and noticed Bea watching, hands on her hips. 'Oops, sorry.'

Bea shrugged. 'No, you're right, he's gorgeous, although I thought that performance was a little staged, didn't you?'

'That bloody smile wasn't. It could have set fire to my pants.'

'Ladies,' Tom said, reminding Bea that he was still there. 'Can I get you both a drink?'

Bea winced at Shani and turned to him. 'Yes, please.'

Bea stared after them, as they moved away, horrified when Luke looked back over his shoulder and caught her. She was unable to tear her eyes away. However, Leilani instantly noticed him looking, and pulled him closer to her, winking at Bea. 'Come on big boy, let's have some fun,' she said, kissing his neck. Luke took her hand away from his buttock and led her to the bar, where he whispered to her for a few seconds before turning his attention to the barman.

'Well,' Mel said later, when the girls visited the Ladies. 'It didn't take him long to get over you, did it? How typical of a man.'

Bea could have killed Shani. She had only admitted to her that they'd slept together, but now regretted being so open, and stupid. She must have told Mel and now her sister would never let her forget what she had done.

'Two entirely different things,' Bea assured her through the locked door, grateful for the time to gather her thoughts. 'It was a friendly meal, nothing more.'

'He kissed you.'

'So?' Bea felt instantly bad for suspecting Shani of gossiping about her behind her back.

'Er, you had sex?' Mel said, rather more loudly than Bea would have liked.

'Thanks, Shani,' she called to the next cubicle. So she had told Mel about their phone call that morning.

'Sorree.'

'So what? Now he has a proper girlfriend.' Despite her bravado, Bea felt thoroughly fed up, and she struggled to zip up her tight trousers.

'Melanie,' interrupted Shani pointedly. 'None of us are in a position to criticise Bea's choices. After all, you've had your problems in your relationship with Grant. Hey, look at me with Harry.'

'Harry who?' Mel said sarcastically. 'I don't think any of us have been allowed to meet him yet, but I suppose you're right,' Mel said, reapplying her crimson red lipstick. 'Though Bea, he can't have been that hurt by you being so weird with him, after all he took no time to replace you, and you have to admit, he looked happy with Leilani. So at least you don't have to feel guilty about anything.'

'I wasn't feeling guilty,' Bea said, brushing her hair and wishing it was straight and shiny like her sister's rather than curly and wild.

'I know he's not all tailored and suave like Tom, but you were attracted to him enough to have sex with him.' Bea grimaced. Mel made it all sound so matter-of-fact and somehow sordid.

'I just don't understand, that's all,' Mel added, her expression one of concern. 'You don't jump into bed with guys, so you must fancy him, a lot.'

Bea shrugged, trying to make light of her reactions to Luke. 'What's your point, Mel?' Bea asked, bored with her sister's interest in her non-existent love life.

Mel narrowed her eyes. 'What I don't understand is why you'd sleep with him, even if he's a little rugged and messy looking, and then give him the brush-off?'

Bea groaned. She was too embarrassed to tell Mel about discovering that Luke had a girlfriend only after they'd slept together and couldn't divulge the information Tom had given her about the suspected money laundering, but her sister was a legal assistant and knew how these things worked. She considered her words carefully. She wanted to prove to herself that her instincts weren't completely crap. Maybe if she could find out more about Luke's money laundering activities then at least she could feel a little less vulnerable by her attraction to him.

'Tom told me something about him and as much as I may like him, I stand to lose my professional integrity, not to mention my freedom, if I allow some sort of closeness to develop between us. Sleeping with him was just a one-off. A moment of weakness I mustn't allow to happen again.' She watched Mel trying to make sense of what she'd just told her. 'At least for the time being.'

Her sister wasn't stupid and would be able to put together various scenarios that could link Tom's, Luke's, and her own business connections. At least she hoped she could. She waited for a moment.

'Ahh.' Mel raised her eyebrows at it dawned on her. 'I think I understand your predicament now, and if it's what I think it is then it's definitely better that you don't have anything to do with someone who could be involved in, shall we say, washing.'

Bea nodded miserably. 'I know.' She put her hairbrush back

in her bag and clipped it closed. Life stank sometimes.

Shani shook her head. 'I have no idea what the hell you're both prattling on about, but if that's the case then am I to take it that Tom did a good thing by tipping Bea off about Luke?'

Bea caught Mel's eye and pulled a face at Shani's unintentional use of one of the two words they'd made a point to exclude from their conversation. 'You could say that,' she said as they left the loo and returned to the others.

She was soothed slightly by the sight of Paul grimacing, as he relayed an amusing anecdote to Tom who threw his head back, laughing loudly. Guy watched Paul, happiness lighting up his fine features, his black eyes glistening with adoration. Noticing Bea walk up to him, Tom smiled over at her. 'You all right?'

'Fine thanks. Shani had some gossip for us two. You know how it is.' She was going to relax and enjoy her evening out. She didn't have to worry about Tom causing her emotions to go into meltdown. She studied his sea green eyes, as he bent his head towards Paul to catch the punch line of a joke, noticed Luke out of the corner of her eye as he leant against the bar, his back to Leilani. He didn't seem at all bothered that his girlfriend was flirting with the barman right in front of him. When she looked back at Luke she noticed he was staring directly at her with an intensity that was confusing. She saw Mel had noticed too, so glanced quickly up at Tom who seemed to be listening to Paul and Shani, who were now debating whether or not the club manager was gay.

Mel gently took Bea's hand nearest her and in a rare moment of sisterly affection gave it a light squeeze. 'We'll talk tomorrow. I'll have a think; see if I can maybe find out more about the case against him. Try and switch off until then,' she whispered into her Bea's ear.

Bea sighed. Somehow this was more painful and heart breaking than finding out Simon had been unfaithful to her. It seemed ridiculous, but true. She'd been drawn to Luke and it concerned her that her instincts could be wrong. What an emotional mess, and this time she had no one else to blame.

Eleven

Never Enough Thyme

Luke watched Bea leaving with Tom. He couldn't miss her reaction to Leilani and knew she'd assumed they were sleeping together. There was more to her emotional distance towards him than his relationship with Leilani, surely? Bea was an independent woman, a professional who didn't need validation through whatever man she was seeing, but he should have insisted she listen to him about Leilani; then again, if she'd told him the same story, would he have been willing to accept that there was nothing going on between them? He doubted it. He wasn't going to let her believe that he was moping around after her, especially now she seemed to be spending time with Tom Brakespear again. What the hell was going on between those two?

'Honey, are you sure you don't want to invite me onto your boat for a nightcap?' Leilani raised an eyebrow. 'It's closer to here than my hotel.'

He shook his head. 'No, I think you should go back to your room.'

'You never used to be so reluctant to sleep with me.'

Luke laughed. 'And you never used to be so forward.'

'It's that Beatrix girl, isn't it? Something's happened between you.'

Luke shook his head. 'It's Beatrice, and it's none of your business what, if anything, has gone on between us.'

'Lukey,' she teased, kissing him on the cheek and sliding her hand down to his crotch. 'Go on, you know you want to.'

'Stop it.' He laughed, taking hold of her wrist and pulling her hand away. He tried to sound stern, but it didn't work, she knew him too well. 'We both know that you're only here for a few months, and that whatever was going to happen with us finished years ago.'

'You were my first love.' She smiled, tilting her head to one side and flicking her long hair behind her shoulder. 'We could still make it work if you wanted to.'

Luke couldn't help thinking back to those days when everything in his life seemed so much clearer. He'd thought himself in love with Leilani, and he probably had been, after all she was good fun as well as very beautiful. But he had more pressing matters to consider now. His business was in a mess and despite his better judgement he knew he had strong feelings for Bea.

'What?' Leilani asked, resting a hand on his thigh. 'You're not thinking of changing your mind are you?'

'No, I'm not.' He laughed, taking her hand and placing it back on the seat beside her. 'Right, you can sleep in one of the cabins tonight if you like.'

Leilani pouted. 'I've never had anyone play as hard to get as you are now and I don't like it.'

'Too bad, now where will you be sleeping? I'm shattered and have to get up early in the morning, so I need to get you settled.'

'I'll sleep in the other cabin, then. If you're sure you can't be persuaded. It's just a shame you won't be in there with me.'

'You'll be fine, stop sulking.' Amused at her persistence, he thought back to his younger self. He would never have turned down such an appealing offer.

With enormous relief Bea finally arrived home. She couldn't wait to shower and somehow wash away the memory of seeing Luke with Leilani at the club. She began removing her makeup and did her best to push away the thoughts creeping into her aching brain, but as much as she tried she simply couldn't help thinking about him being in this room with her that night.

Bea had no choice but to admit that while she may have strong feelings for Luke, he meanwhile, was having the time of his life with someone else. And worse still, she was a leggy model.

Bea sat down heavily on the edge of her bed. Her life had

been mapped out in front of her since she was a teenager. She'd always planned on living in her own home with a supportive husband and two children. She tried not to get too miserable as the memory of her miscarriage seeped into her mind. Her baby would have been starting nursery school about now. She pictured her aunt sewing name labels into endless pieces of her own uniform and had always imagined doing the same for her own little boy or girl. It hurt to know she'd missed out on something so life enhancing. The children might not have come along, but she had thought Simon to be 'the one' when they married and they did have this house, even if he'd resented her aunt being here with them. It hadn't occurred to her that her life would ever change from what she'd expected. Any detours from her life plan had never occurred to her.

'No wonder I'm making such a mess of it all,' she groaned miserably. 'I didn't see this coming.'

The following morning, bored by her self-pity, Bea went through to the small room her aunt had used as a study and sat down in front of her untidy desk. She lay her hands palm down on the scarred wooden surface and sighed. If only she'd solved the puzzle of the Jersey Kiss. It must be something important if her aunt had included it in her will. Maybe she would find some reference to it in her aunt's papers. She pulled open the middle drawer and lifted out the mass of papers, sifting through one invoice after another. Nothing giving any reference to a mysterious item in there, she thought, frustrated by her unsuccessful search.

Pushing her hands to the back of the drawer to check she hadn't missed anything, her fingers touched something. Bea took out several small envelopes she vaguely recognised. She read the childish scrawl on the front of each one and breathed in the faint scent of her aunt's perfume. Reading one of the letters she'd sent to her aunt from boarding school, Bea was instantly transported back to the misery she'd experienced being away from everything familiar to her.

She replaced the invoices and her letters back neatly into the desk and checked the other six drawers. Nothing. Wondering if her aunt had maybe filed something away about the legacy, she spent the following two hours carefully working her way through the dusty lever arch files on the bookcase.

Bea had scoured every inch of the study, but apart from her old letters and a few heartfelt ones from Antonio, she'd only really found paperwork relating to the garden. She remembered standing in here with her aunt many times over the years with Annabel proudly showing her plans for designs that she'd won prizes for at flower shows. She'd even discovered several of her school photos and a certificate for coming second in a painting competition, but nothing that could possibly relate to the Jersey Kiss.

Bea went out in to the garden, pushing the orange plastic wheelbarrow half filled with weeds and dead wood, and as she walked to the compost heap behind the walled garden, she came to the conclusion that she was perfectly happy without a man in her life. She just needed not to lose this house.

Paul had a partner and Shani would no doubt work things out with Harry, or find someone to take his place. She needed to persuade Mr Peters at their meeting that she deserved the loan, buy Simon out of his share of The Brae, and take back some sort of control of her life. The thought cheered her up.

A couple of hours later, Bea had worked her way through several flower beds, noticing that she needed to plant more thyme for next year. Never enough thyme, she mused. She'd managed to clear her head a little and work through her dilemma about the men in the life. She showered and changed, tying her damp hair up in a scrunchie, and then padded through to the kitchen in her worn bunny slippers to make a desperately needed mug of coffee and read through the papers. It helped to immerse herself in other people's chaos as she skimmed the gossip columns.

'It's only us,' Mel shouted from the hallway. 'The front door was unlocked, so we've invited ourselves in.' Bea's heart sank several levels; she knew that tone. It was her sister's organising, over-the-top-cheerful one. Not what you needed at any time, but especially not on a rare chill-out day. Had she forgotten about their conversation the previous night?

'Through here,' she answered, willing herself to sound

116

welcoming.

'Hi, hon,' said Shani, pulling a face from behind Mel's back. 'Mel and I were talking about the wedding and I just knew you would hate to be left out.'

Cow, mouthed Bea, unable to help smiling at her disloyal friend. Shani winked back slyly, as Mel busied herself filling a cup with boiling water and dunking a herbal tea bag in it.

'Right, listen to me, ladies,' started Mel. 'I've had an idea.' Bea suppressed an anguished groan. 'I didn't initially want to have any bridesmaids, but I think I'd like to have them now. I don't want to have to choose between my friends, you know how sensitive people can me. So, I thought you two would be perfect. My sister, who everyone will expect to be one, and you, Shani. You're so opposite to look at and both so different to me, we'll look great in the photos. Isn't it perfect?'

Bea shot a rabbit caught in headlights glance at Shani, who gave her a knowing look.

'Well? What do you think,' Mel asked excitedly, arms held out. 'Think of all the fun we can have. Getting dressed together, our hair and make-up, manicures. What could be more fun?'

Struggling for an acceptable answer, Bea racked her brains. 'Um, yes,' she answered lamely. 'Although …'

'What do you mean, although?' Mel's lengthy, French-polished extensions tapped a rapid chorus on the pine table.

The embryo of an idea was rattling around Bea's addled brain and she forced herself to pursue it. She knew she had to make her excuses now, or go along with the horrible bridesmaid idea for the next few months. If she didn't come up with a suitable alternative, photos of themselves in peach crinoline dresses or some other hideous creation would forever haunt her and Shani. 'What about Grant's nieces?'

'Who?' Mel asked, eyes lighting up.

'His sister's twins,' agreed Shani, immediately making the most of Bea's brilliant idea, relief flowing across her exotic face. 'Yes, your soon-to-be nieces, you have to think of them at a time like this. They'll be devastated not to be included in your special day.'

Bea nodded, chewing her lip, knowing the little girls would

117

more than likely be delighted to be asked, and even if they weren't, thought Bea, there are times when adults have to pull rank and this was one of them.

'What about them? I presumed you would be having them, to be honest,' enthused Bea, running with the idea now that Mel hadn't immediately rejected it. 'They can walk ahead of you down the church aisle scattering rose petals from a tiny wicker basket, or something.'

Mel looked suspiciously from one to the other and thought through the suggestion. 'What, as well as you two, or instead of?'

'I think two are probably enough, so you should have the little ones only.'

Mel thought about it briefly and Bea had to hold back a sigh of relief when her sister's face slowly broke into a broad grin. 'Of course, why didn't I think of it? It's a great idea and a good way to score points with his mum.' She clapped her hands together gleefully. 'Clever girl.'

'That's what Shani and I are here for, to help you plan your day as perfectly as possible.' She smiled, relieved beyond belief that her idea had been so eagerly accepted.

'But what about you two,' Mel added, her face filled with concern. 'What will you do on the day if you're not going to be my bridesmaids?'

Shani folded her arms across her chest. 'I can help with organising the setting up of the marquee or whatever else you may need me to do.'

'Yes, are you still going to have it at your mum's and Dad's? You're more than welcome to have it here if you want, you know?' offered Bea, crossing her fingers behind her back.

'Thanks, but this is your house, where you and your aunt have memories, they're not mine, Bea. My childhood was spent at home with Dad and my mum and anyway Dad's already drawn up a plan of the layout and matting leading from the driveway to the inside.'

Bea pushed away the hurt that Simon's insistence that they hold their wedding reception at a hotel instead of in this garden had caused her aunt. She'd never forgiven herself for giving in to him on that. 'Whatever you want, it's your day after all.'

'Great idea,' Shani said, oblivious to the tension. 'I've always envied you being able to walk down steps out at the end of your parent's garden straight onto the beach.'

Mel smiled. 'It's going to make the most of the view with one of those marquees that have windows all along the side of the sea view. Then, he said that if the weather is good they'll roll up that side so we're almost holding the reception outside.'

Bea said thoughtfully, 'I can arrange flowers and the table settings can be put together from the plants here. Or, if you prefer, I can do something different.'

'You can both start by helping compile a list of who to invite. I'm scared of missing someone, and must make sure I don't forget anyone who might buy one of the expensive items I intend to have on my wedding lists.' Noticing Shani's frown, she added pointedly. 'There will be cheaper bits on it too, for the tighter guests.'

'How rude,' Shani teased. 'Just don't forget any great-aunt Ethel, or you'll never be forgiven.'

'I do have one problem,' frowned the excitable bride-to-be.

'What?' Shani asked, as Bea glanced back at an article she liked the look of.

'Not what, but whom?'

'Well, whom then?'

'I need to invite Luke and Leilani,' she said tentatively, looking from one to the other.

'What? Why do you have to?' Shani argued, ignoring Bea's frantic mouthing to shut up as she didn't need Mel to interrogate her yet again.

'I have to, he's an old friend of Grant's.'

'Take no notice,' Bea interrupted, 'of course you must invite him.'

'And I'll invite Tom for you, although I've no idea who can accompany you.' She pointed a long finger at Shani. 'After all Paul's now with Guy and Harry never seems to be around, so you'll be by yourself once again. I could try and find another of Grant's friends to act as escort for you, if you'd like?'

'Don't you dare.' Shani glared down at Mel from her lofty

119

height.

'Surely Harry will be coming with you?' Bea asked. 'And I'm sure Tom will want to come, so he can be my plus one.' Tom being her partner rather than some stranger Mel might link her with suited her far better.

'I didn't think you two were dating again?'

'We're not,' Bea said. 'We do work together though and if you want me to have a partner I'm sure he'll step in. I'm not bothered either way.'

Shani crossed her eyes and pulled a face, making Bea giggle. Bea knew the arrangements could only get more complicated and that there would be further rows between now and the big day. She needed to keep these chats with Mel as light as possible to be able to face them.

'Well if you two aren't going to be my bridesmaids, and I'm to only have the twins, then I think I'll ask Leilani to be my chief bridesmaid,' Mel suggested. 'I think I need to add a little extra touch of glamour to the occasion, don't you?'

There was a sharp intake of breath from Shani. 'Are you completely insane? You can't ask her.'

'Why not? She'd look fantastic and could watch over the twins.'

'Don't be so bloody ridiculous, she probably hates kids.'

Bea rolled her eyes. 'Mel, she's a model, not a nanny.'

'I know that.'

'Well as pretty as you may be, Mel,' Bea tried again, 'Leilani is a professional model, and I wouldn't have thought you'd want to give her the chance to upstage you on your big day.'

'Which she bloody well will,' Shani insisted glaring across the table in disbelief.

Mel grimaced. 'Honestly, you two are so easy to wind up sometimes.'

Bea and Shani shook their heads at each other. 'Is this going to take much longer?' Bea asked, forgetting her plan to keep things light and be nice.

Mel shrugged. 'Whatever,' she looked at her watch. 'I'm going to go home and change. I'm meeting Grant later. I'll leave you two in peace. Oh, and Bea, I haven't forgotten what we discussed last night. I'll get back to you as soon as I find out any info.'

Bea thanked her and saw her out, relieved to have peace restored once again. 'She can be so exhausting at times,' she said to Shani later as they sat quietly together chatting in the snug watching an episode of her favourite soap opera.

'I've been thinking,' Shani said. 'If you need help paying off that mortgage.'

'The one I haven't got yet?'

Shani rolled her eyes. 'Yes, that's the one. Well, I thought I could always move in here with you and pay you rent?'

Bea thought for a moment. 'I'd love that, but what about Paul? Wouldn't he miss you?'

'I doubt it; he seems to be spending most of his time at Guy's flat at the moment, so he'd probably be relieved.'

'Good, I'm glad,' Bea admitted. She loved the idea. 'It'll be just like when we were younger and at boarding school.' But even though the extra money from Shani was better than nothing, it still wasn't nearly enough to help her sort out her finances.

'I can't believe how miserly Simon is being with you, though.'

'I think it's probably because I'm insisting on keeping this house and going against his wishes,' Bea said, staring into the dancing flames in the nearby fire. 'But I've had enough of doing what he dictates, and this time, I'm going to do whatever I can to keep my house, whether Simon likes the idea or not.'

Twelve

December – Twisted Vines

Simon arrived at the house a few days later. Bea had just ended a call with the bank arranging a meeting with Mr Peters in the New Year to discuss her mortgage application and her relief to have a definite appointment was short-lived. She stood on her doorstep glowering at Simon as he took out an envelope from his briefcase and handed it to her. 'I'm running out of patience with this crap. I know you've tried at a couple of banks, but you'll just have to rethink things or agree to sell this dump. Why you even care about this garden now Annabel is dead, I don't know. You don't even know that much about gardening.'

'I wouldn't expect you to understand.'

He went to place a hand on her shoulder, but she stepped back and his hand fell away. 'I didn't mean for all this to happen, you know?'

Bea folded her arms creasing the envelope in her hand. 'No?'

'Of course not. If your aunt hadn't said anything about seeing me kissing Claire that night, then we'd probably still be together.'

'That's crap, Simon, and you know it.'

He marched down the front steps to his car and turned to face her. 'Fine, but we don't have to be so angry with each other all the time.'

She took a deep breath. 'We wouldn't be if you weren't so dead set on me having to sell this house.' Without waiting for his reply, she turned and stepped back into the house, slamming the front door.

She tore open the envelope and unfolded his letter with shaking hands. '*Claire's due date is only a month away now*

123

and I need money to buy the furniture we need to complete the apartment before then. I think I've been more than fair with you, Beatrice. The sooner this matter is finalised the sooner we can both move on with our lives.'

'Moron,' she shouted, as a thin layer of plaster dust fell onto the sheet of paper in her hand. It was time to contact Mel and ask her to sort out the injunction against Simon. She was not going to put up with his unwanted visits anymore. She phoned Mel and told her to go ahead and draft something up for her. Enough was enough.

'It's about bloody time,' Mel said. 'Don't hold back from sending it to him either. He needs to be put in his place.'

Bea agreed.

That evening Bea sat in the drawing room carefully turning tatty pages of her aunt's notebooks trying to take in some of her tips and work out if the sketches inside related to any of the plants she recognised. It was only five months until D-Day; what was she going to go? The phone rang. Bea thought about not answering, but when the shrill ringing continued she got up and picked up the phone. 'Hello?' Bea said, trying not to show her irritation at being disturbed.

'Hi,' said Tom. 'Sorry to bother you, but I was wondering if I could pop round for a chat this evening.' She didn't answer. 'If that's not a problem, I mean?'

She wasn't really in the mood to see anyone after Simon's appearance.

'Look, Tom, I'm not in the best frame of mind and if it's all right with you I was looking forward to an early night.'

'Why, what's the matter?'

'Nothing new, I'm afraid.' She couldn't be bothered repeating what had happened with Simon.

'Bea, I know you well enough to know you're hiding something. Is there anything I can do?'

'Thanks, Tom, but it isn't anything you can help with,' she said miserably, sitting back down again and taking up her cup of coffee before giving in and relating the entire conversation with Simon earlier in the day. 'So you see I just have to shut up and deal with it. It's tough, but life stinks sometimes. I can do

124

without further legal fees and will have to delay some of the work on the house, yet again, to pay for it, but I can't have him coming here whenever the mood takes him.'

Tom sighed. 'Sorry, Bea I can imagine how you must feel. I'll leave you to your early night, but if there's anything I can do, promise you'll ring me.'

'All right then,' she said. 'I'll speak to you soon.' After he had ended the call, Bea wondered what he'd wanted to come and talk with her about that couldn't be discussed at the office. It couldn't have been that important, surely, or he would have come round and told her about it. She looked over to the corner of the room where her aunt had always placed the Christmas tree. 'Maybe I should put one up,' she said to Flea, who continued to snore in reply. It just didn't feel like Christmas this year. 'Maybe not.'

She picked up the books again and pulled her legs up onto the settee to get comfortable. If only she could close the shutters and the rest of the world out and be left to her memories. She shut her eyes and rested her head against one of the worn velvet cushions. Shutting out everything was so tempting. She snuggled up and let her mind wander back to happier days when she and Simon had had so many plans. Aunt Annabel singing tunelessly in the potting shed pushed the image of her and Simon away and Bea couldn't help smiling. Her aunt looked up at her standing at the doorway. 'There you are, darling,' she said. 'Be a good girl and stop wallowing. Go and fight for what you want.'

Bea opened her eyes and sat up, waking Flea with her sudden movement. Glancing around the room to check her aunt wasn't actually somewhere near, she rubbed her eyes. 'She's right, I need to get a grip and stop feeling so miserable.'

Over supper at Shani and Paul's top floor flat the following evening Bea pondered how her two best friends managed to work together and live in such a small space without wanting to wring each other's necks.

The attic flat, originally Paul and his previous boyfriend David's, was bright and always inviting. The small lounge somehow appeared bigger with only a two-seater cream settee and a matching armchair taking up the floor space, with a plain oak sideboard along one wall, displaying nothing but a wooden bowl fashioned from the wood of a cherry tree that had been blown down in Paul's aunt's garden near Ludlow in the great storm of 1987. She couldn't imagine how he managed to cook in the tiny kitchenette. It didn't seem much larger than most wardrobes, with only a two-ringed hob, kettle, toaster, and a tiny sink. Paul pushed back the veil of tiny coloured glass beads hanging from the doorframe and handed her a glass of wine.

'I feel bad living in such a big empty house when you two have to share everything here.' Bea could understand why Luke had been so surprised that she lived in The Brae alone with all those empty rooms.

'You can always take her ladyship here to live with you,' he said.

Shani looked at her thoughtfully. Bea could tell Shani was desperate to tell him about her suggestion that she move in with Bea. Neither of them wanted to upset him though. Shani pulled a face at Paul. 'Thanks,' she said. 'I thought you loved sharing with me.

'I do, but your untidiness drives me mental. I've never met such a messy female. Did you know, Bea, this one sleeps in an old 1930s bed her grandmother passed down to her and every time she brings some poor unfortunate bloke home with her I have to wear ear plugs, the bloody thing squeaks so much. The whole house must know when she's having a shag.'

Bea spluttered and nearly spat out her drink. 'Charming.'

'Cheers, Paul.' Shani glared at him. 'We can't all be neurotic about keeping everything in the right place.'

'A little bit of discretion wouldn't go amiss,' he teased. 'Supper's ready and waiting.' Paul handed Shani a glass of sparkling water and Bea a glass of Shiraz. 'Grab a plate and help yourself.' He indicated various tubs of different Thai food.

'You're not drinking, Shan?' Bea frowned. She'd never known Shani to turn down alcohol before. 'Are you sure everything's all right? You're not pregnant are you?'

Paul and Bea laughed at Shani's horror-struck expression.

'No, I'm bloody well not.'

'Well, it's not like you.'

'My stomach is a little delicate at the moment,' she said, glaring at them both. 'Not that it's any of your business.'

'All right, calm down.' Paul handed Bea a plate of food. 'Get this down your neck.'

'It smells gorgeous,' Bea murmured, forcing herself not to rush the delicious-tasting food. 'Where did you pick this up from?'

'Rosa.'

'Who?'

'Rosa, she's a Thai lady and married to one of the managers at the Studio. She'll cook you whatever you like and is so reasonable. She'll even come to your house and cook the meal for you if you're having a dinner party, but we don't exactly have much room in ours, so I asked her to do it at her home instead.'

'This is so tasty. What a great idea.' Shani said, her mouth half full. 'I haven't had anything this good in ages.'

Bea made the most of every mouthful. For someone with a dodgy tummy Shani was certainly bolting down her food. 'You don't seem to be off your food then,' Bea said. 'Only alcohol.'

Shani tilted her head to one side and pursed her lips. 'My stomach has been a little sensitive.'

Bea frowned. "What do you mean?"

'Yeah, there's nothing delicate about you,' Paul laughed.

'If you must know, I've got a UTI and I'm taking a course of antibiotics.' She scooped a forkful of food into her mouth and chewed. Swallowing, she added. 'Anything else you'd like to interrogate me about?'

'Gross. I wish we hadn't asked now.' Paul grimaced.

Bea laughed, noticing Shani's amusement at his horrified expression. 'Me too.'

'So,' Paul asked, filling his plate with more food. 'What's happened recently, apart from you both mooning over Luke Thornton with a horse between his muscular thighs?'

Shani waved her fork in the air. 'Sorry Bea, I can't forget how amazing that polo match was in the summer. Don't you

127

think it was pretty intense?'

Bea laughed, enjoying the image of Luke galloping across the beach. 'It was. I'm definitely going to go again next year, if they hold the beach polo again.'

'Yes,' Paul scowled. 'I still haven't forgiven you two for not including me. You're both so selfish sometimes.'

'It hasn't all been fun this year,' Bea said, telling them about her visit from Simon and then Tom.

'Well, you both know he's not really my cup of tea,' Paul said, sipping from his glass.

'Which one?' Shani asked.

'Either, both, neither,' Paul said.

'Why?' Bea looked at him, fork midway from plate to her mouth with her last bit of rice. 'I know Simon is a waste of space, but what's wrong with Tom?'

'Nothing I can put my finger on, but I can't help having the feeling he isn't all he seems.'

Bea laughed. 'That's ridiculous, there's nothing suspicious about Tom.' She didn't mention that she'd not been so quick to believe his tales about Luke and the investigation until she saw his proof. 'He was actually quite sweet when I last saw him. So, what's wrong with him?'

'Nothing is,' Shani said, mopping up some spilt food from the floor with a piece of damp kitchen towel. 'Just ignore him, I think Tom was lovely to apologise to you and be so sympathetic about shitty Simon. Paul?'

'OK, it was the right thing to do, I suppose,' he relented grudgingly. 'What the hell is that?' he asked hearing the 1812 Overture warble from Bea's handbag.

'I changed my ring-tone when I was bored the other night. It's Tom,' she said, noticing the name on the tiny lit up screen and turned away from her inquisitive friends. After several minutes she ended the call and dropped her mobile back into her bag. 'That was Tom.'

'We've gathered that much.' Paul raised his eyebrows. 'What did he want?'

'You're never going to believe this, but his assistant has been signed off work for three weeks after an appendix operation and he's booked for me to go with him to New York for five days.'

They looked at her. Paul opened his eyes wide. 'You're going on holiday with him? That's a little unexpected, isn't it?'

Bea shook her head. 'Not really. He's always travelling to meet clients. I've gone to London once or twice in the last few years, but never further than that. Wow, I can't believe I'm going to New York in a couple of weeks.'

'Lucky cow. I wish I was going away,' said Shani. 'The break will do you good though and if you get to spend some time with him you might find you hit it off. If not, at least you'll be away from Simon and his crap for a bit.'

'Sounds good, I suppose,' Paul said, refilling their glasses. 'He must be earning decent money if they send him to the States to visit clients. I hope you get to do some sightseeing while you're there.'

'Me too.' Bea laughed, picturing visiting the Empire State building and walking through Central Park. 'I'm so excited, I can't wait.'

'In fact you both must be on decent salaries if you work in trust?' Paul added, interrupting her thoughts. 'Surely you can afford to take out a smallish mortgage for The Brae, and you must earn enough to pay for the work that needs doing to the place?'

Bea shook her head. 'I wish. My job sounds more important than it actually is. Only directors and maybe senior managers earn good salaries in trust and company work. They're the ones that sign things off. I'm one of many in Jersey doing the same job. I'd have to pass my professional exams to reach a higher salary.'

'But you did do exams, loads of them,' Paul argued.

'I've done my ICSA certificate and diploma, which were eight exams in total, but there are loads more to do, unfortunately.'

'Blimey,' Shani grimaced. 'I always thought you were way up there with the big money.'

Bea laughed. 'No. Simon is, which is why, despite what he said in his letter, I know he doesn't need to be chasing me to

129

pay him back. Tom will be on a higher salary than me, but I'm not earning anything spectacular, I can assure you of that. Anyway, Tom's trip is being funded by his client. There'll be a reason we have to hold the meetings in New York and the client will be paying, but he's giving me a great opportunity by taking him with me.'

She thought of Flea. 'Look, I know you're spending a lot of time at Guy's flat, Paul, but I was thinking that if you wanted to, you could both move into the house and look after Flea for me.'

Paul and Shani looked at each other and then back at Bea, and without exchanging thoughts on the matter both immediately nodded in agreement. 'I'd be happy to. Guy works long hours so I don't see him nearly as much as I want to and when he's working I can be here enjoying all this with her.'

'Yes, it suits me,' Shani agreed.

'You go and have a great trip and leave the house to us,' Paul said. 'Although by the time you return we may have become so used to your way of living that we'll make the most of our squatter's rights.'

'I don't think you have them here in Jersey, but as long as you take care of Flea for me, you can stay as long as you like,' she said, liking the thought.

'It's going to be strange though, surely,' Shani added. 'Going away with him to New York?'

'I know, that occurred to me too,' Bea admitted. 'I'm sure it'll be fine, we're there for business, nothing more.'

'New York?' Luke knew he sounded idiotic repeating Grant's words, but he couldn't help himself. 'With that jerk?'

Grant shrugged and nodded. 'That's what Mel said. Only for a few days, though. I'm sure it means nothing. I think it's got something to do with work.'

Luke tried to remain calm. He clenched and unclenched his hand.

'I wouldn't have told you if I'd thought you'd be this pissed. Since when have you been interested in what Bea gets up to anyhow?' Grant checked to see Mel was nowhere near to overhear them, 'Let's face it, I would have thought you had more than enough on your hands with Leilani. She looks a bit of a handful, a gorgeous one, of course, but definitely stroppy.'

Luke could see how ridiculous he must seem to his friend and knew he'd made an idiot of himself. Time to backtrack, he decided. 'I'm not interested in what she does, or who with. I just need to speak to her about a few jobs that she couldn't afford to do at her house and put off. I can't very well do that if she's on the other side of the Atlantic, now can I?'

Grant raised an eyebrow. 'Really?'

He could tell he hadn't convinced his friend. 'The work's nearly done, and I need to get my men onto another site. Time is money, and all that,' he added.

Grant seemed to accept this explanation, or at least, Luke thought, he was pretending to. 'Right, of course it is. How's the court case going with that ex-partner of yours, any news?'

'Nothing.' Luke felt the usual knotting in his stomach as the anger towards Chris kicked in. 'It's been three years now and I think I've pretty much explored every avenue trying to recoup my money, but it doesn't look like I'm going to get anywhere. Serves me right for putting so much trust in him, I guess. I was a bloody idiot.'

'Hey, don't beat yourself up about it. We knew him since we were teenagers, why would you have any reason to suspect he'd be capable of embezzlement? Anyway, you can make it again. You've certainly got the brains and sheer bloody-minded determination to do it,' said Grant, patting him on the back. 'You're a clever bugger, Luke. Making money comes easily to you.'

Luke shook his head. Somehow his bad experience had dampened down much of his enthusiasm and ambition. Knowing everything could simply vanish overnight took away some of the excitement building up his business had once held for him. 'It's the principle that drives me nuts. How could I be such a lousy judge of character?' He signed. 'What the hell was I thinking to have trusted him with everything like I did?'

'I know, mate. I know, but you're just going to have to move on from this and the sooner you do it, the better for you it'll be.'

Luke knew his friend was talking sense, but couldn't help

thinking there was something about Tom Brakespear that reminded him very much of his ex-partner. An underlying slyness he couldn't ignore. And whether Bea could see through him or not, Luke was not going to let some slimeball hurt her. She was far too special for that, even if her lack of feelings for him continued to sting. He thanked Grant for telling him about Bea's trip, he also wished he'd told him earlier, when he would have had a chance to think of a way to put a stop to it.

'Is this Leilani's?' Grant held up a tiny pair of cut off denim shorts he'd spotted on the seat in the galley. Luke nodded. 'You're a lucky sod. I mean, I love Mel, of course I do, but she's so bossy I'm a bit nervous she's going to merge into her mother as soon as we're married.'

Luke laughed and snatched back the shorts, throwing them into the small cabin Leilani had sometimes slept in. 'She's always leaving her gear around the place, and before you get any ideas, we're not sleeping together.'

'Bollocks.' Grant laughed. 'Pull the other one.'

Luke stopped marking out his route to St Malo. 'We're not.' Why was it so difficult for people to believe? 'She's fun and loves winding people up, but she's really only here for a couple of months for a break before she decides which offer she accepts.'

Grant shook his head. 'And you believe that, do you?'

'Yes. Now, let me check this bloody map or I won't be taking you across to St Malo tomorrow and you'll have to get the ferry like everyone else.'

Thirteen

Crossing the Pond

'Helloooo?' Paul announced his arrival at The Brae on the day Bea was to leave for America. He dragged a massive holdall behind him as he climbed the wide oak staircase.

'We're up here,' Shani called.

'Why do you never think to lock that front door of yours?' Paul asked. 'Anyone could walk in to the house.'

'Anyone just did,' Shani giggled.

'I'll pretend I didn't hear that comment,' Paul said, amusement obvious in his tone. 'I've brought everything I should need for my stay here. Is it safe to come in or will I be traumatised by all your big pants?' he asked outside Bea's bedroom door.

'Shut up and get your bum in here,' Shani shouted from inside Bea's clothes-strewn bedroom. 'She doesn't have any big pants, not that I've ever seen anyway.' Shani laughed. 'She's doing well, though it was touch and go for a bit.'

'You can't change your mind about going.' He squeezed Bea's shoulder as he passed behind her to check his reflection in her dressing-table mirror.

Bea shrugged. 'I know, but I'm a little nervous about going.'

'You're OK with Tom, don't worry about it.'

'It's not Tom that bothers me, it's how I'm going to manage at the meetings.'

'Shut up. You'll be brilliant.'

'Yes, I'm being a wimp,' she said feeling a little better. 'You do know Guy is more than welcome to stay here, too?'

Paul nodded. 'Thanks, I'll tell him.

'How's it going with him, still blissfully happy?'

'*Parfait.*' He clapped his hands together. 'He's so perfect.

Not all men are selfish sods, apparently.'

Shani pouted. 'Not the gay ones anyway, the rest bloody well are.' She turned to Bea. 'Paul came with me the other night when I went to see Harry at his surgery.'

Paul grimaced dramatically. 'I take it by the expression on his face,' Bea said. 'that it didn't go down too well.'

'Nope.' She shuddered as if reliving the experience.

'I think it's over between them.' Paul stroked Shani's arm. 'Poor love. You do really have the hots for him, too.'

'I'm so sorry. Maybe he's just had something on his mind. He'll probably be fine in a few days.' Bea hoped she was right. Shani looked so sad. She must like him a lot, Bea decided.

'He'll have something on his mind if he doesn't already,' Shani said, before closing the lid of Bea's case and zipping it up. 'There, I told you it'd all fit in.'

'What do you mean?' Bea asked. 'Has something happened between you both that's bothering you?'

Shani shook her head. 'No, it was just a throwaway comment, that's all.'

Bea wasn't convinced. Shani would tell her if there was anything worrying her, but only when she was ready. She hoped she didn't take too long about it though. She glanced at Paul.

He shrugged. 'I've already asked her all about him and she's strangely reluctant to confide in me too.' He turned his attention to Shani. 'Aren't you?'

Shani scowled from one to the other. 'No. I haven't told you anything because there's nothing interesting to tell. Now, can we please stop talking about me?'

Bea was relieved Paul and Shani had agreed to house sit for her time away. They knew where everything was kept, so there hadn't been too much to go through with them. They both adored Flea, which was a relief because Bea was sure he'd pine for her while she was away. At least, Bea thought, Shani would be able to have a trial run living in the house and could make sure she liked it. Then, if she changed her mind, she wouldn't have to go through the difficulty of breaking the news about moving to Paul.

'I'm going to be making us healthy meals each day,' Paul

134

announced to Bea as she ticked off items from her packing list after they had finished their baguette, Camembert, and red wine bought from the market earlier in the day. 'I won't know myself having an entire kitchen to play in, even if it is a horror from the seventies.'

'Cheeky sod,' Bea replied. 'When and if I ever get the money to be able to update my kitchen, I will, but until then you'll have to be grateful for my orange Formica one.'

'Shame. I know your kitchen is ancient, but compared to our two-ringed hovel, it's almost state-of-the-art. I can't wait to cook in it. By the way, which rooms do you want us to sleep in?'

'I've made up a bed in the other room overlooking the walled garden and put clean linen on my bed. So I'll leave it up to you two to decide which you prefer. Make yourselves at home and have a great time, just don't forget to feed, water, and walk Flea.' They pretty much knew Flea's routine, but she went over it with them anyway and made sure they knew what food to feed him and that he was used to half a treat every night when he went upstairs to bed.

'I'm sleeping in your room,' Paul said. 'Flea can be my roommate for our stay, although he can share with Shani when Guy's here for the night. We're going to have a brilliant time with all this space.'

Paul and Shani grinned at each other with barely suppressed excitement. They looked to Bea like a couple of teenagers being allowed to stay at home for the first time whilst their parents went away on holiday. 'You're welcome to use my car, don't forget,' she said. 'Thankfully it's old and fairly battered, so I won't notice a few extra dings.' Her blue Mazda had seen better days and had been her pride and joy when Simon had bought it for her years before. Since then it had seen a lot of action, mainly due to her lack of concentration, and had already been treated to a few re-sprays.

'Shani, please speak to Harry, but maybe wait to see if he contacts you in the next day or so first.'

She nodded. 'I'll try. I've left him a couple of messages at work, but he hasn't called me back yet.'

'Well, don't worry about it.' Bea patted her arm gently. 'You can only do your best. If he doesn't call you back, then we'll think of some other plan after my holiday.'

Tom rang the doorbell. Bea hugged her two friends as he grabbed her small suitcase. She slung her bag over her shoulder and hesitated for a moment, looking at her friends. 'Well, here goes,' she said walking towards the door.

'Go on.' Shani pushed her out. 'Make the most of the peace.'

Tom leant over to Bea as she settled herself in the front seat of his BMW. 'I can't wait to show you New York.'

Bea grinned like an idiot. 'I'm so excited. Bye you two,' she said out of the window, waving frantically, 'And be careful.'

'Yes, now bugger off,' Paul shouted.

Bea was determined not to worry about Shani during her trip. She knew there was nothing else she could do and Paul had assured her he would contact her should there be any problems with Harry. She leant her forehead against the plastic of the aircraft window, gazing down in awe as the plane descended over the water and New York's JFK Airport several hours later. She was relieved she'd been able to sleep for much of the night flight and couldn't wait to go and see all the places she'd dreamt about for so long.

After a brief panic by Tom that they had lost his suitcase, they were met by a driver and taken through the busy Manhattan streets, like corridors through the shiny skyscrapers above them.

Bea had to hold back from squealing in excitement as an enormous, red fire truck hurtled past them. Fire fighters kitted up, serious expressions on their faces, was even more exciting than she'd imagined. She watched in awe as they barely slowed down to manoeuvre through the throng of yellow cabs and cars. They gave a loud blast on the horn to announce their presence to any driver foolish enough not to have already noticed them. Bea thought back to all the movies she'd seen growing up featuring these romantic heroes. 'Oh, yes.'

Their driver pulled over by the curb. Bea looked up at the

golden canopy nearby. 'Wow, you never said we were staying at the Waldorf Astoria,' she squealed, stepping out of the car and craning her neck upwards, unable to come to terms with the height of the buildings all around her. 'This is so beyond anything I'd expected,' Bea gasped, already in holiday mode and after her initial concerns about being with Tom, determined to make the most of her trip and enjoy every second of it.

'Thank heavens for that.' He glanced over at her, taking hold of the handle of his suitcase, before picking up hers with his free hand. 'I wanted to book somewhere you'd enjoy, so you'd forget about everything at home. We're going to have a great time and although we have four meetings, I've scheduled them to run as closely together as I dared to give us some time to see as many of the sights of this amazing city as possible.'

Bea nodded and couldn't help feeling how thoughtful he'd been. The vitality of the energetic city was infectious and her nerves subsided a little. 'This is amazing,' she said. 'It's even better than I'd ever hoped it would be,' she said honestly.

Tom laughed. 'We haven't been anywhere yet. You wait until you see inside the hotel,' he said, waving up towards the canopy of the Waldorf Astoria. 'I wanted to book us in here because I know how you love old movies and Art Deco, but we don't have the best rooms, I'm afraid. There's only so far I can push the budget.'

Bea followed him inside and pictured the different films that had been shot in this very place. Relishing the abundance of deco features all around her, she smiled. It was as if time had stood still and they were back in the thirties. 'Incredible,' she breathed, feeling like a child experiencing their first trip to Disneyworld.

'Our rooms are this way,' he said as soon as they'd checked in, leading her to the lifts.

'Give me half an hour to unpack, then I'll meet you down in the lobby,' she said, checking her laptop was fully charged. 'I'll just have a quick look at my emails and meet you downstairs.'

He looked a little disappointed, but didn't say anything, just showed her to her bedroom and held the door open for her.

She didn't want him getting the wrong idea and thought it

137

best she make it clear from their arrival that she still intended keeping things between them platonic, reminding herself that she was here for business reasons only and had no reason to feel at all guilty. Tom knew how she felt, or at least should do by now. She wasn't about to rush into bed with anyone in the near future, unlike her mistake with Luke. Damn, why did she keep thinking about him? She opened her case and hurriedly hung up her clothes, before freshening up, quickly logging onto the Internet to deal with any outstanding messages she might have received, and going to meet Tom.

She saw him straight away, sitting under the huge ornate clock, his mobile against his ear as he carried out what looked like an intense conversation. He seemed to sense her approaching and ended the call, slipping the phone into the chest pocket of his thick tweed jacket.

'Looking as gorgeous as ever,' he said, taking her hand and kissing her cheek. 'Come along, lovely lady, I have such a short time to show you so much of this magnificent city, and I don't want to waste a moment of it.' He led her out onto the noisy streets. 'We can grab something to eat at a deli on the way.'

Bea gasped as they stepped outside onto the sidewalk. She still couldn't believe she was in New York, and it really was even bigger and more impressive than she could ever have imagined.

'So,' said Tom interrupting her thoughts. 'Where to first?'

Bea shook her head and laughed. 'I've no idea.'

'I was thinking we could start close and move on from there. Grand Central Station, then on to the Chrysler Building, and maybe make our way down towards Battery Park. They've got the damaged Sphere that used to stand in between the Twin Towers. I think it gives people hope to think those massive constructions crashed down on top of it, and although it's pretty dented, it's still obvious what it was originally and it survived.'

'I'd like that,' Bea said, feeling the need to see something that would give her hope things would turn out right in the end.

'And then I thought that maybe we could take a boat over to Ellis Island. What do you think?'

Bea nodded. 'Sounds perfect,' she giggled. Tom's

excitement almost matched her own and she was more than happy to be led wherever he thought best. She had looked up New York on the Internet, but found it impossible to choose what she wanted to see most. There was far too much choice.

Even the diners they ate their meals in were like something out of a Hollywood movie. 'Did you notice the rear car lights in each booth?' she asked him as they walked back to their hotel later that evening, exhausted, but relaxed and happy.

'I know.' He nodded. 'Everything, right down to the light switches in the Gents seemed to be from the fifties.'

'Good food, too,' Bea said. She'd been thrown by the magnificence of it all, and the only downside had been the several calls and texts Tom had received to his mobile. 'Tom,' she said, unable to help from asking. 'Why are you getting so many calls? I would have thought they'd be monitoring your workload back at the office. I know they're covering mine. Is something the matter back in Jersey?'

He shook his head. 'No, nothing at all,' he assured her, although Bea couldn't help noticing her question had somehow unnerved him, deflating his previously buoyant mood rather more than a simple question should do.

'It's not a problem,' she said, wishing to alleviate his defensiveness. 'I was a little worried something might be wrong.'

Tom immediately stopped walking, taking her by surprise. 'Leave it, Bea,' he snapped. 'It's a few calls; nothing for you to be concerned about.'

She didn't like his tone, but thought better of arguing with him. After all, it was thanks to him that she was on this trip and having a good time. Then again, she mused, it wasn't the calls that bothered her, but his reaction to them. 'Whatever,' she said. 'I didn't mean to pry.'

The following day after a morning filled with back-to-back client meetings, she persuaded Tom to leave the paperwork until later and go with her to the Top of the Rock at the Rockefeller Centre. 'Look at the view,' she said pointing out across Manhattan, past the magnificent Empire State Building that had featured in so many films from her childhood, and over to the East and Hudson Rivers, the sunlight glistening like a gold and yellow liquid ball above them. She took a couple of photos to show Paul and Shani.

'I can't believe you've persuaded me to come up to the seventy-sixth floor, never mind that I'm actually outside. I'm terrified of heights usually.'

'You're doing very well. Try not to think about it,' she said, taking his hand and leading him over to the other side before he could start to panic. 'Look over there, isn't that stunning?' she asked, as they gazed out over the rectangle of green in the middle of the city. 'Isn't Central Park incredible? All that green in the middle of this amazing city!'

'Shit,' Tom said, pushing his hand into his pocket and withdrawing his mobile. 'Fucking phone never stops.'

'So, don't answer it then.' Bea's initial relief at the sound of his phone receiving a text was instantly replaced by irritation. She knew he would have to read it and see what it said. She was building herself up to say something, when her own phone bleeped. She raised her eyebrows and immediately locked eyes with Tom. Bea didn't know who looked more astonished, her or Tom. She turned away from his amused expression to see who had sent the message to her.

'Luke?' she said, instantly wishing she'd thought not to speak his name out loud.

'What does he want?' Tom glared at her.

'He's asked me to call him as soon as possible,' she said, staring at the text again. 'It must be something important.'

'Of course,' Tom said, the sarcasm obvious in his voice. 'Funny that.'

'Tom, this is the first time Luke has contacted me, and I don't think I'm wrong to think it must be something important.'

'Fine, ignore me. I just worry about you getting involved with him, especially since you know what he's connected with, Bea. You really should distance yourself from him as much as you can,' Tom said, texting a reply on his own phone.

'I haven't forgotten,' she said, wishing she could. It wasn't Tom's fault Luke was being investigated, she thought, feeling a little mean for being so annoyed with him.

'Luke,' she said, walking to the other side of the open space to gain some room between her and Tom. She checked her watch and quickly made a calculation. 'I've just realised it's ten thirty at night in Jersey.' She knew something must be really wrong for him to call her at that time.

'Now, don't panic, Bea,' he said, his calm, deep voice causing her stomach to flip over. 'It's nothing we can't deal with.'

'What isn't?'

'You have a burst pipe in the main bathroom.'

'What?' she said, trying not to panic at an extra cost she would have to find money to cover. 'How?'

'I've checked it out, and your pipes are pretty worn in places. After all,' he added, 'the house is nearly a hundred years old, these things happen.'

'Not on my budget they don't,' she said, trying her best to sound light-hearted.

'Don't worry about the cost.'

'That's easy for you to say,' she said, swallowing the lump forming in her throat. She knew she shouldn't have gone away, not when she still had to try and somehow finalise things with Simon.

'Bea?' he said, quietly, making her stop and take a breath.

'Yes?' Her heart pounded at the thought of having to find the money for another large invoice.

'You mustn't worry about anything. I can sort this out. I'm just calling you to ask if it's OK to do some exploratory work on your plumbing while you're away? We don't want this happening again. It's a good thing Shani and Paul are staying here and noticed the water quite quickly. If it had happened while they were away, or even at work for the day, it could have ended up being very costly, and you don't want water damage after you've finished your renovations.'

'I don't want them at all,' she said. She tried to work out how she could possibly pay for this. She hadn't even considered any plumbing work and was at the limit of her budget already.

'You're worrying,' he said, his tone gentle and quiet. 'Don't. It's fine, really.'

Bea glanced over at Tom. He'd finished his call and was making his way over to her, a set expression on his face.

'Bea?' Luke's voice interrupted her thoughts. She did trust him when he said not to worry, which made knowing about his business activities even more upsetting. She wished she was back in Jersey and could see for herself what had happened. Was he telling her the truth about the lack of damage, or was he trying to keep her from panicking? 'Bea, speak to me.'

Tom had almost reached her. She could tell he was in a bad mood and now was no time to have Luke on the other end of a call. 'Sorry, yes. Do whatever you feel you have to. And, Luke?' she added. 'Thanks for sorting this out for me.'

Luke switched off his phone. She couldn't wait to get off the phone from him, no doubt to carry on enjoying her holiday with that creep. He picked up his can of lager and took a mouthful, leaning back against the pillow on his bunk, the rocking of the boat unusually doing nothing to soothe his frustration.

'Tom Brakespear,' he said, almost spitting out the words. He couldn't help distrusting that man. How had that jerk ended up in New York with Bea, while he was back here, waiting for her to finish enjoying herself with some other bloke across the other side of the Atlantic?

He picked up his phone and scrolled down to The Brae's phone number and pressed.

Shani answered after only two rings. 'Did you speak to her?' she said. 'I hope you didn't give her too much of a fright. I don't want her trying to race back here, thinking we can't sort this out without her here. If anyone deserves a holiday right now, it's Bea.'

Luke smiled. He loved Shani's devotion to her friend, and felt good that she was so doggedly determined to look out for Bea. 'I assured her it was fine. She's told me I could do whatever I needed to. So, tomorrow I'll come back there, turn the water back on again and start checking the other pipes. I don't want this happening again.'

Shani sighed loudly. 'Brilliant, thanks. I hope you didn't mind me phoning you, but I didn't know who else to call, and I know Bea would have done the same.'

Her words cheered him up a little. It was good to think of Bea turning to him in a crisis. 'No problem. Now don't worry and I'll come to the house first thing in the morning.'

'Luke?'

'Shani?' he replied.

Shani smiled. 'Tom's not the problem between you two, you know? She probably feels a little guilty.'

Luke pushed himself up onto his elbow. 'What do you mean?' His good mood instantly evaporating.

Shani groaned. 'Forget I said anything. Night,' she said, abruptly ending the call.

'Shani?' What had she meant by guilty?

Almost immediately his phone rang. 'Shani, what could Bea have done to feel guilty about?'

'Shani?' Leilani asked, making him curse himself for not bothering to check the number calling him before opening his mouth. 'Isn't she Bea's podgy friend?'

'Don't be nasty. Anyway she's not fat, far from it.'

Leilani groaned. 'You men are all so blind. Anyway, why do you need to know about Beatrice being guilty of something?' she asked, obviously not intending to be fobbed off.

'Never mind her,' he said. 'Why are you phoning this late?'

'Don't try and change the subject. I was wondering if you needed a little company tonight?' she suggested, her voice softening. 'It's so boring here.'

Luke laughed. As spiteful as Leilani might be sometimes, he thought, her spoilt diva-like behaviour amused him. It never mattered to her if people disliked her. Then again, he thought, he much preferred her when she was being generous and funny. 'You're staying in a five star hotel, and they're treating you like royalty.'

'So, can I come over?' she asked, ignoring him.

'No. I'm tired and have to be up early for work. I'll come over and see you after I've finished. Maybe we could go for dinner somewhere. You choose, if you like?'

'I don't like,' she said. He could picture her perfect mouth pouting in irritation.

143

''Night, Leilani,' he said. 'Sweet dreams.'

Bea drafted the minutes from their meetings and completed as much of the report for the directors about their time in New York as she could. She wanted to check everything was in order and that she had not forgotten to include details of any of the funds the client had discussed with them. Before sending an email back to the Jersey office, she went to ask Simon a query about one of the action points and noticed him ending yet another phone call. She knew their client was on a flight to Boston and was fairly certain they had covered everything in the meetings, so was unable to contain her annoyance with Tom. She confronted him on their last evening away during a walk towards Central Park. 'Why so many phone calls?' she asked, keeping her voice as level as possible.

'I explained to you already.' He squeezed her hand lightly before letting it go, as they crossed the road towards the wall of the park.

'Tom.' She stopped walking as soon as they reached the entrance across from the Dakota Building where John Lennon had been murdered. 'What's going on? If there's a problem, I'd like to know. Maybe I can help in some way.'

He backtracked to be next to her. 'I promise you it's just the odd hiccup at work. Vanessa's phoned once or twice to speak to me about stuff, you know, like the children. So stop worrying unnecessarily. Let's just enjoy our last night together and make the most of this incredible city.'

They moved on again, but Bea couldn't help feel a niggling doubt in her mind. She wanted to know what he was hiding from her, and assumed it must be something to do with Vanessa, though why he should hide anything about her, she couldn't imagine.

'You were great in the meetings. I knew you would be,' he said as they returned to the hotel. 'Well done, it's not easy dealing with some of these clients.'

'As long as you put in a good word for me back at Malory's and make sure my annual review is brilliant, I'll be happy.'

'I'll only ever write the truth,' he said. 'Though thankfully in your case, it will be very positive.'

Bea looked at him for a moment and decided to keep her thoughts to herself. Pacified, she smiled up at his concerned face. 'That's good to know.'

Their week at an end, Bea struggled to get comfortable on the plane, not managing to sleep throughout the night flight to Heathrow. 'It's a pain that none of the airlines fly directly to Jersey anymore,' Bea said, covering herself with a blanket and resting her feet on her bag.

'I know, the most tiring part of any trans-Atlantic journey, for me at least, is having to get from Heathrow to Gatwick and wait for the next flight home. It always adds so many extra hours to any trip.' He frowned. 'I don't want to go back to the real world,' Tom moaned miserably.

'Nor me,' Bea fibbed. She'd loved every second they'd spent visiting the sights in New York, and was determined to return, hopefully with Shani or Paul to show them everything she'd experienced, but she was ready to get back to her house. 'I'm dreading finding out about the burst pipe damage.'

She could feel him tense up and could have kicked herself for mentioning anything to do with Luke. She didn't need another lecture about being careful around him, as if she was a kid and didn't know how to behave. They checked in for their flight back to Jersey, going through their own emails and messages to pass the time and Bea was relieved when their flight touched down at Jersey Airport and she was nearly home. They shared a taxi from the airport, but sat in silence most of the way, both lost in their own private thoughts. Tom helped Bea with her bags when they arrived at the house.

'You can tell we're home, the weather's miserable and damp, unlike the cold crispiness we enjoyed in New York,' he said, placing her bags down onto the doorstep. 'I'll give you a call later,' he promised, getting back into the cab and waving as it drove off. Bea couldn't help noticing his mobile was already against his ear before the car even reached the turn of her driveway.

Fourteen

Bare Branches

Flea barked frantically at the front door and Paul, no doubt having been waiting for her return, pulled open the heavy door with a flourish. 'Cupcake, how the devil are you?' he bellowed, dramatically holding her at arm's length and scrutinising her up and down as Flea jumped up at her legs, crying and whimpering for her attention. 'Mmmm,' he mused. 'I don't know if it's all that sightseeing, or maybe a little sex was on the agenda?'

'Stop it.' She punched him in the shoulder and shook her head. 'Why do you always have to bring everything down to sex?'

'Whatever it is, it's given you that healthy glow. And you, sweetie, are glowing.'

'I don't know how,' she groaned. 'I'm knackered and the jet lag hasn't even hit me yet.'

'Bea,' said Luke from the top of the stairs.

'Hi.' Bea, cringed, narrowing her eyes at Paul for mentioning sex in front of Luke. 'I'm just coming up to see the damage,' she said, bending down and making a fuss of Flea, hugging and kissing his soft grey head.

Paul grimaced. 'We've kept our eyes open around here, but neither of us has come across anything that could be the Jersey Kiss your aunt left to you.'

'Never mind,' Bea said, trying to imagine for the hundredth time what it could possibly be. 'It's so frustrating not knowing. I wish she'd left me some sort of clue.'

'Me too,' Paul said frowning. 'I hate not knowing things. Right, you'd better go and see to your gorgeous builder, and I'll make us all a cup of tea,' he whispered, giving her a quick hug. 'Just leave the case; I'll sort it out later.'

Bea ran up the stairs, hoping her flushed face had calmed down a little by the time she entered the bathroom. 'So? How's it going here then?'

Luke put down the wrench he'd been using to sort out a pipe and turned to her. 'I hope you didn't panic when I called you?' he said.

Bea felt him studying her and could tell he'd not only heard what Paul had said about her and Tom having sex, but also that he believed it. Damn Paul and his big mouth. 'Not too much,' she said, forcing a smile.

'Fibber,' he smiled. Bea couldn't help staring back at him, her stomach doing somersaults as his gaze penetrated somewhere deep inside her.

Bea tried not to laugh. 'Yes, but don't tell anyone,' she said.

'Do you take sugar?' shouted Paul from the bottom of the stairs. 'I can never remember.'

Bea shook her head. 'He's talking to you, by the way. He knows I'm sweet enough.'

Luke raised his eyebrows. 'Yes, well, that's probably a matter of opinion,' he said. 'Two, please,' he called to Paul, without taking his eyes off Bea. 'As you can tell, I'm not very sweet.'

Bea giggled. 'That's a matter of opinion, too.'

'Teas are on the table,' shouted Paul from the kitchen, causing the moment to pass.

Luke glanced up, but then went back to work on the pipes. 'So, how was your holiday then?' he asked without looking at her.

Bea didn't like the sudden distance between them. 'It wasn't a holiday. We were there to meet with a couple of clients, but it went well, thanks,' she said. Luke didn't need to believe she was sleeping with Tom and it wasn't as if it was any of his business, or if he was even interested, she thought. Probably didn't actually give a damn whether she slept with Tom, or not.

'Coming down?' she asked, moving closer to the door.

Luke followed her through to the kitchen. Bea motioned for him to take a seat and went to lean against the familiar heat of the Aga, watching as Flea, content to have her back where she belonged, returned to his warm bed and watched her out of one open eye.

'So, can I ask what this Jersey Kiss is that I keep hearing you lot chatting about?'

Bea explained. 'So you see, Aunt Annabel left me the house and something else. It's important enough for her to mention in her will, but no one seems to have a clue what it is exactly, even her lawyer. It could be in this room for all I know.' Bea shrugged, wishing again Aunt Annabel had left a clue of some sort.

Luke thought for a moment. 'I can't think what it could be, a painting maybe, or some jewellery?'

Paul sighed. 'So you're as useless as we are at guessing then?'

Bea laughed. 'Don't be mean, Paul, you're just irritated because you hate not knowing things.' She rubbed her face, careful not to smudge what was left of her makeup. 'Talking of mysteries, where's Shani?' she asked Paul, having noticed her friend's absence for the first time. 'I'm surprised she's not here to hear all my gossip. She's all right, isn't she?'

'She's very all right, actually.' He rubbed his hands together gleefully. 'In fact, at this very moment she's with Harry at the hospital having a scan.'

'What?' Bea gasped, unable to believe what he'd just said.

'Hey, don't jump to conclusions. Harry's the one having the scan, not her; bad back or something, an old rugby injury.' He handed her a drink, and making himself comfortable, taking a seat opposite Luke at the table. 'When she didn't hear from him, she went to the surgery to talk to him again.'

'And did he speak to her properly this time?' Bea asked. Paul nodded. 'Good, I'm so relieved. I knew she'd been putting on a brave face about him not contacting her.'

'Maybe he had his reasons; he could have been caught up with other things. You don't seem to have much confidence in men,' Luke said, his face serious.

'It depends on the man.' Bea raised an eyebrow, trying to make light of her comment. It didn't seem to work.

'I have to agree with her,' Paul said. 'Harry phoned as soon

149

as he received a note she sent to him saying she wanted to discuss something and after a brief chat, agreed she could go with him to the hospital. Although that sounds an odd place to talk about things if you ask me, most people would go for a drink. I think she's being cagey about him because she's probably discovered he's married, or something.'

'I hope not, she'll be devastated if he has been lying to her.' Bea said, feeling Luke's gaze on her and wishing he wasn't in the room for this conversation. It wasn't as if he knew her friends, and she didn't want him making assumptions about them.

Paul leant his chin on his palm. 'Damn right. She's been so much happier since taking control of the situation, so maybe she's beginning to see a way forward. I have to say, she's loved it here with all the space. I think it makes her feel more secure, somehow.'

Bea was tempted to tell Paul about her offer to Shani, but stopped. It was Shani who would want to do that. 'I can't wait to see her. When do you expect her back?'

'Soon,' he grinned. 'I just hope everything went well at the hospital. I don't want her fretting about something else.'

'Me too.' Bea rubbed her hands together. 'It's even colder here than in New York,' she said. 'I'm going to take a day or two to get used to it again.'

Shani walked in before Bea could say anything else. She noticed Luke first and smiled at him. Bea felt a frisson of envy course through her, as he responded in the same way. Why didn't she feel like she could relax so completely with him? Why did she have to fall in love with him? There was far too much going on in her life to allow that to happen.

'How did it go?' Paul asked Shani as she dropped her heavy handbag onto the floor next to her.

'I think this is my cue to leave,' said Luke, finishing his drink and getting up. 'Loads to be getting on with.' Bea watched his retreating back.

Paul pretended to follow him out of the room.

'Stop it,' Bea whispered, glaring at him before smiling and pointing for him to sit back down.

'Well he's so sexy.' Paul raised his eyes heavenward. He turned his attention to Shani once again. 'You were saying, Shan?'

Shani folded her arms and shrugged. 'Nothing to tell.'

Bea didn't believe her for a second. She studied her friend and could see Shani avoiding catching her eye. Then it dawned on her. How could she have been so blind? 'Shan, that's not entirely true, is it?'

'What do you mean?' Paul nudged Shani, but she ignored him.

'Shani, I know you denied this before, but I can't help wondering if you are pregnant?' whispered Bea, aware she had to be careful of her next words. 'Please don't feel you can't speak to me about it if you are. I know I've had problems having a baby, but that doesn't mean I wouldn't be excited for you.'

Shani looked across at her but didn't react.

'Shit, Shani. You're not, are you?'

Shani took a deep breath and shook her head. 'I don't know where you two get these ideas from, but I'm not pregnant, so shut the hell up and stop going on at me.'

Bea wasn't sure if she believed her or not, but it was hard to tell just by looking at her. Her boobs didn't seem much bigger, if at all, and there was no sign of any baby bump that she could see. She glanced at Paul who shrugged. Shani was wearing baggier clothes, but then she often wore loose-fitting outfits. 'As long as you're sure you're OK,' Bea said eventually. 'I'd hate to think you couldn't confide in me about something like this, or anything at all for that matter.'

Shani shook her head. 'Bea, I'm fine, now stop agonising over me. You've got enough on your plate without imagining problems.'

'She's right,' Paul agreed. 'You do have enough going on, and,' he looked Shani up and down, 'she looks the same as ever to me.' He thought for a moment. 'Something is wrong, though. Is he married? Is that it?'

Shani raised her hands in the air. 'Yes,' she shouted. 'He is married; happy now?'

'Of course we're not happy.' Bea scowled at Shani for being so nasty. 'We're only trying to find out what the hell you're hiding, because it was obvious that something was wrong.'

'Well, now you know everything.' Shani looked up at Bea and shrugged. 'I know, it's disgusting, but I promise you I honestly believed him when he told me he was divorced.'

Paul scowled. 'The bastard. Will you tell his wife?'

'Of course not. What do you take me for?'

Paul shook his head. 'I can't believe you never said anything, to me at least. I mean, we live together and you still never said anything.'

'I know. I'm sorry. I wasn't sure how to tell you,' she said. Then turning to face Bea, she asked. 'Not after what Simon did. Do you hate me, Bea?'

'Don't be ridiculous, of course I don't,' she replied. 'At least you're not pregnant, now that would be lousy. For you, I mean.'

Shani sighed. 'I'm not, so there's no need to worry about that.'

'When did you find out he was married?' Paul asked, sitting down next to Shani.

'I only found out from his business partner yesterday, when I phoned Harry to arrange a time to meet for his scan. His partner and he had rowed and he told me Harry and his wife had only briefly been separated. To make matters even worse, he then told me Harry has done this sort of thing before and one of them *had* been careless enough to fall pregnant.'

'What a creep.' Paul scowled as well as he could with his Botoxed forehead. 'Thank God that hasn't happened to you. I'd have to track him down and kill him.'

'Stop being so dramatic,' Bea said. 'You know exactly where to find him if you wanted to do that.' She turned to Shani. 'Don't beat yourself up about it; we'll be here for you.'

Paul hugged her. Shani began to cry. 'I'm such an idiot.'

'Rubbish,' Bea said, stunned to see her usually bolshie friend so upset. Shani never cried. 'He's a worthless piece of scum; how were you to know?'

'You're gorgeous, and don't you ever forget it.' Bea leant across the worn pine table and handed Shani a tissue before taking her friend's hands in hers, giving them a reassuring squeeze.

Shani pulled her hands away and straightened her top. Bea could tell she was embarrassed and that it was time to change the subject. Shani obviously wasn't in the mood to say anything more about the subject.

'Now, why has no one told me how Guy happens to be, or in fact where he is?'

'He's still hot.' Paul kissed his fingers. 'In fact, I believe I've met the only other truly perfect man in the entire universe.'

'Who's the other one?' Shani teased, a little colour seeping back into her face.

'Me, of course. Guy's perfect though. He's kind and generous, and happy to take our relationship as slowly or as quickly as I like.'

'You told him about your ex, David, then?' Bea asked. Paul nodded. 'Good, I'm pleased. At least he knows you're wary of being hurt again.'

'He says he's happy to be with me and get to know me properly.' He winked at them. 'We're having so much fun together.'

'I think I'm going to cry again,' Shani sniffed, pulling the used tissue out of her sleeve and blowing her nose.

'For heaven's sake, what the hell is wrong with you?' Paul asked. 'Are you sure you're not having a baby? My mum always goes on about how emotional she was when she was expecting me.'

'What?' Shani frowned. 'I told you I'm not pregnant, so stop going on about it, will you?'

'I only meant … never mind.' Paul shrugged.

Bea had had enough of the bickering. 'I've got tons of washing to catch up on,' she said, thinking about Luke and wondering what he was doing up in her bathroom. 'And knowing you, as I do,' she pointed to Paul, 'you'll need an in-depth chat with Shani about her revelations on the Harry front.'

'Yes and I think you should speak to Luke. We've been asking him about Leilani and he insists she's nothing more than a friend. Maybe you were wrong about her,' Shani said, standing up and grabbing her bag. 'You're obviously attracted to the bloke.'

Bea nodded. 'I am, but I've got to sort out this business with the house before I can concentrate on anything, or anyone, else,' she said. The last thing she wanted was to end up getting into the same situation as Shani and having to deal with a man who was already in a relationship. 'I'm just not going there.'

'I haven't told you about Luke interrogating me the other day, have I?' Shani said, raising her thin, dark eyebrows and taking a roll of mints out of her bag. 'It was when I phoned him in a panic about the water seeping out of the bathroom,' she said. Bea listened silently, wondering what she was going to say next. 'He asked how you were, and when I said you were on holiday in New York he seemed rather surprised. Although, to be honest, I did have a sneaking suspicion he already knew you were away.'

'Did he ask who I was with?' Bea couldn't help asking, a familiar knot forming in her stomach.

''Fraid so.'

'And by the disappointment in his tone, he wasn't impressed.' Shani popped a piece of chocolate into her mouth. Bea felt better by his annoyance at her trip with Tom. It was short-lived. 'Then the next day, I passed that new coffee shop, you know the one on the corner of New Street and King Street, and he was having a coffee with that Amazon woman.'

'Leilani,' Bea murmured, her mood flattened. Serves me right, she thought, for thinking he might actually be interested in me. 'Never mind that, it's Christmas soon and I want to know what we're doing.'

'I have to spend the day with my parents, as usual,' Shani groaned. 'I've no idea why, they don't seem to enjoy themselves and always end up having a row.'

'Ah, yes.' Paul pursed his lips together. 'I know we were planning on sharing a turkey *a deux* here, but Guy has asked if I'll meet him at his flat after he's catered for the hundreds at the restaurant. He insisted you must come too, so no arguments.'

Bea shook her head. 'No, I'm not going to interrupt your first Christmas together. I'll be fine here.'

Paul scowled and shook his head. 'No chance. It'll be your first Christmas alone and without Annabel, I'm not having you feeling sorry for yourself here.'

'I'll be fine. Anyway Dad's asked me to join them this year.'

Shani swung round from the doorway and nearly tripped over, grabbing the door handle at the last minute before she completely lost her footing. 'And you said yes?'

'I did,' Bea lied, laughing at the disbelief on both her friend's faces. 'The wedding's coming up and I thought I should try my best to build whatever bridges I could before then.'

'Rather you than me having to put up with Joyce for a whole day.' Shani laughed. 'She hates you.'

Bea shook her head. 'I know which makes it all the more fun that Dad invited me, don't you think?' Seeing she'd convinced them, Bea watched them leave, heads together as they whispered no doubt about her plans for the twenty-fifth. By the time they discovered the truth, she'd have spent a quiet, but peaceful day alone with Flea, a bottle of champagne left over from her birthday, and no one to interrupt her watching the stack of DVDs she'd been keeping especially for that day.

After they'd gone, Bea walked up the stairs to speak to Luke. He didn't seem to notice her arrival and Bea made the most of being able to watch him work. He bent down over the pipes and she could see the top of his bottom where his jeans had slipped a little. Now that really was the sort of builder's bum she could get used to looking at, she thought. Such a shame he was with someone else.

Luke turned and caught her appreciative glance at him. 'What's so amusing?' he asked. 'And why are you smiling at me like that?' He put his hands back and pulled his jeans up a bit. 'Were you laughing at my backside?'

'Hardly laughing,' she said, aching to cross the room and kiss him. 'I was wondering how long you were going to be, or if you wanted a drink?'

'I'm fine thanks,' he said, sitting back on the heels of his plaster-splattered boots. 'Nearly done here for today.' Bea was unable to stop staring at his tanned face as he contemplated some thought. 'I was wondering if you'd like to come for dinner on my boat some time?'

Taken aback by the unexpected question, Bea raised her eyebrows in surprise. 'Yes,' she said, before giving it any thought. 'I'd like that.' Then remembering what Shani had said about him seeing Leilani, shook her head. 'No, better not.'

'Why?' He stood up and watched her, his intense gaze and closeness making her not sure whether she wanted to kiss him or cry.

'Because you have a girlfriend and I'm not going to be anyone's second choice.'

'You really can't find it in you to trust me, can you?' he said, turning his back on her and bending down to continue with his work. 'I hope it's not too late when you do finally realise that I'm not the guy you seem so desperate to think I am.'

Fifteen

January – Icy Breezes

Bea was walking Flea down on Greve De Lecq beach with Paul and Shani, who wanted to stay occupied and keep her mind from dwelling on her situation with Harry, when her phone rang.

'I'm useless with this thing,' Bea said struggling to retrieve it from her jeans pocket, which was bulging with change, old carrier bags, and kitchen paper. 'Hi, Mel, how are you?' she asked, noticing the number on the screen.

'Fine, but I can hardly hear you; it's a really crappy line.' She sounded put out that Bea wasn't going to be having the usual lengthy chat with her.

'It must be the wind. I'm on the beach.'

'Huh, rather you than me. Anyway, I phoned to ask if you remembered to buy the tickets for us to have a table at the Christmas charity ball this weekend?'

'Charity ball?' Bea turned her back to the wind in a vain attempt at muffling the noise.

'Yes, for Burns Night, the one with the black-and-white only dress code.'

'Oh yes,' Bea remembered, thinking she had better get on and buy something to wear for it. 'The tickets arrived in the post while I was away.'

'Great, I don't suppose you've managed to find the time to shop for your outfit yet?'

'You presume right.' She pulled the collar on her jacket up higher to shield the phone from some of the wind. 'Flea, get away from the sea.'

'OK, then we must arrange to go shopping to get ourselves sorted,' continued Mel. 'And Shani, she needs to find something a little less, um, obvious.'

'Mel, don't be rude,' Bea said, wondering why her sister felt the need to put people down like she did.

'What was that all about?' Paul asked, pacing along beside her, his pedometer firmly attached to the waistband of his jeans.

'Only Mel,' she puffed, doing her best to keep up with him. 'About Burns Night, we bought tickets, remember?'

Shani and Paul looked at each other vacantly for a moment. 'Never mind the ball, we still can't forgive you for lying to us about spending Christmas with your parents,' she said. 'Mel told us you hadn't gone, so you must have spent the day on your own. I was horrified to think of you with only Flea for company.'

Bea wasn't surprised to discover that Mel had told them; she never could keep out of other people's business. She wrinkled her nose. 'I know, I'm sorry about keeping it from you, but I quite enjoyed not having to bother sitting around a dining table, and anyway Flea is great company; he doesn't argue back or give me a hard time about anything,' she said smiling at them both in an effort to soften her words.

Shani shook her head. 'You're impossible, but we love you anyway.'

'I forgive you, sort of. Right, about the ball.' Paul waved Bea on, encouraging her to keep up the pace. She stuck her tongue out at him. 'You could look a little more excited.'

Shani groaned. 'I don't have anything to wear.'

'Which is why I gave in to Mel when she insisted we go shopping tomorrow afternoon. We'll find you something incredible,' Bea said, stopping and bending over to catch her breath, her hands resting on her knees.

'Sounds OK, but I'll decide what I wear, not your sister.' Shani drew to a halt with her and crossed her arms over her stomach.

'Stop chatting, you two, we're supposed to be jogging and getting you fit.'

'Stop nagging, Paul.' Bea pulled a face at him. 'The only thing you get from jogging is a saggy face.' She turned to Shani. 'I can't really afford to buy something for this ball, but I haven't much choice. I wish I hadn't agreed to go now. I hate buying something new, especially as I'll probably only wear it once or maybe even twice.'

'Me too,' nodded Shani, stretching her calf muscles.

Paul shook his head slowly and smiled at his miserable friends. 'For pity's sake, what's the harm in going a little wild? Anyone would think you were your aunt's age the way you act sometimes. I know you have a lot of responsibility resting on your bony shoulders, little Bea, but you have to lighten up and think "bollocks to the rest of the world" and have some fun.'

'I think I've had my quota of wild for the foreseeable future,' Shani grimaced.

'Well, I haven't,' he shouted, making Flea look up and run towards Bea. She took the opportunity of the dog's bewilderment to attach his lead to his red collar.

'I agree with Paul. I think we should treat ourselves. We haven't done so for ages and it's for a worthy cause.'

'Weren't we lucky finding this closing down sale?' she whispered, nodding at Shani's reflection in the mirror when she came out of the changing room wearing an empire-styled dress, in white, with a tiny black satin ribbon running under her breasts. 'Your boobs seem bigger than they did before.'

'Rubbish,' laughed Shani. 'I think it's just the style of the dress.'

'I adore my dress.' Mel twisted and turned, looking at her reflection from every angle in the one-shouldered creation she'd tried on. 'I'll have to make sure Grant hires a tuxedo soon, otherwise he won't get round to doing it.'

Bea picked out a sleeveless, chiffon-covered, beaded dress from the few she'd narrowed down her choice to and carried it into the changing room. The weight of the dress helped the feel of luxury. Pulling back the velvet curtain from her changing room, she crossed over to the mirror. 'I feel really glamorous in this one,' Bea said, wishing Luke was to be her partner for the night rather than Tom. She held her hair up at the back of her head. 'I think perhaps I'll make a booking to have something a little Hollywood done to my hair for the evening, too.'

'I know we've all got to watch our cash flow at the moment but I think it'll be fun to treat ourselves for once. We may as well make the most of this.'

'It's perfect practice for my wedding day.'

Shani groaned. 'Why does everything always have to come back to your wedding, Mel?'

Mel ignored her. 'I'm especially looking forward to the auction; I can't wait to see exactly what's in the lots.'

'This is going to be fun,' Bea said, determined to ignore the pain she was already experiencing thanks to her exquisite, black, four-inch stilettos, which pinched the front of her feet tortuously, but they'd been the only ones in the charity shop that would go with her dress. She hoped they'd loosen up a bit as the evening wore on.

'Tom, you look *trés* James Bond,' Paul said, looking him up and down in his dinner jacket. 'Grant, you've scrubbed up well, too. I'm so impressed. I can see Mel's influence here, so don't even try to deny it.'

Bea laughed as Paul, immaculately groomed, his blue eyes sparkling, bowed theatrically. 'As you may notice, I've splashed out on a new black silk cummerbund and bow tie as well as a spray tan.'

They stared in silence when Guy strode into the room. 'Wow,' said Mel, eyes as wide as a bush baby's.

'Thank you,' Paul said, smiling with self-satisfaction.

'Not you. Him,' she said, pointing at Guy. 'I'm sorry, but you're wasted as a chef, Guy.' Mel shook her head as she stared at the six-foot, dark-haired vision in front of her. 'You should be gracing billboards across America, not be encased in a stuffy kitchen somewhere.'

'Very Ralph Lauren, don't you think?' Paul linked his arms with one of Guy's and smiled up at him.

'Time to get into the taxi,' Tom shouted, taking Bea's hand in his. 'You look very beautiful tonight.'

Bea sat down in the seven-seater taxi and smiled at him. She tried not to think about Luke, wondering if he'd be at the ball too, and had to force herself to laugh at the jokes as the car took them to the nearby manor at St Ouen. As soon as the car stopped, Tom helped each of the women out and Bea looked across at Shani's cousin Paige and her fiancé Jeremy outside the huge white marquee especially erected in the grounds of the walled garden for the evening.

'This is amazing,' Bea gasped, trying to take in every detail, as light dripped from the grand, crystal chandeliers overhead and circular tables, covered with their crisp white linen tablecloths, showed off rose and lily of the valley displays in the middle of each one.

'Stunning,' Shani said, taking a glass of apple juice from the waitress. Bea caught her eye and when Shani smiled, she pushed away the nagging doubt in her mind and picked up a glass of chilled champagne.

'Not drinking tonight?' Mel asked, raising an eyebrow as a pipe band welcomed the guests in to the event. Shani ignored her. 'It is pretty incredible,' Mel said, barely able to contain her excitement. She pulled her chiffon wrap over her shoulders and took a glass of Buck's Fizz.

'I've never been to a ball before,' Paige admitted breathlessly, taking a glass of champagne from the nearest tray. 'I'm relieved they've got heaters in here, it's freezing outside.'

Paul threaded one arm through Shani's and the other through Guy's and led them further into the room.

Tom took Bea's hand and squeezed it gently, leaning down towards her. 'Did I tell you how beautiful you look this evening?' he whispered.

She kissed him on the cheek. 'Only about twenty times. But hey, carry on if you feel you must.'

He studied the table plan and pointed over to one in the middle of the room, near the dance floor, where the auction was to take place later. 'This is perfect,' he said. 'We won't miss anything sitting here.'

The Master of Ceremonies welcomed the guests, announced the arrival of the Seigneur. Bea wondered what it must be like to own this beautiful place and know that Charles II had hidden here when he escaped centuries before. Once the Seigneur and his wife were seated, the rest of them took their places.

161

'Did you know that Charles II gave this Seigneur's ancestor the land where New Jersey now stands as a thank you for letting him come and stay here?'

Bea did recall her father telling her the story. 'Yes, it's why they named it New Jersey. I told some Japanese clients that a couple of years ago and I'm sure they didn't believe me.'

'It does sound a little far-fetched,' Paul said. 'I can see why they'd find it a bit unlikely.'

Bea couldn't help noticing Shani's quiet mood, but didn't want to draw attention to it, especially with Mel there.

'These savoury tartlets are orgasmic,' Mel declared, rather louder than Bea suspected Grant would have liked. She lifted her napkin so he couldn't see her giggling. 'How can anyone make stinky goats cheese and red onions taste so heavenly?'

A grey-haired couple on a nearby table turned to glare at Mel reproachfully. Grant pulled a face, but Mel simply winked at them. 'Try it,' she said to the woman. 'You won't regret it.'

'Mel, that's enough.' Bea gave her sister her fiercest glare, which was difficult when she couldn't get her mouth to stop smiling.

'I hope Paul's happy,' Shani whispered to Bea as they watched Guy and Paul walk across the dance floor to study the lots. 'He deserves to be.'

'I agree and he's been a good friend to both of us,' Bea said, picking up her glass of wine, her words tailing off as she spotted Luke talking to two older men at the far end of the room.

'Fuck me,' Shani sighed. 'He scrubs up well.'

'His beard's gone,' Bea said, barely able to think straight at the transformation in front of her. She was just about managing to force her attention away from him when he seemed to sense her and gazed directly back at her. She smiled before looking away, but couldn't help glancing back at him, only to find him still watching her. He raised his glass to her and smiled before turning back to continue his conversation.

'He could make a fortune on the telly,' Shani said, having another look at Luke. 'And I'd love to know why you keep finding reasons not to go after him, Bea, because I can't think of one.'

Bea wished she couldn't, either. She took a gulp of her drink to steady her pounding heart. Who knew that face had been hidden under all that facial foliage?

'Everything all right?' Tom asked, returning to the table from the Gents and looking round the room to see what had diverted her attention. 'Everyone seems very quiet at this table. It's time to get the party started, you lot.'

She struggled to retain her composure and cleared her throat. 'Yes, sure,' Bea replied, her voice high and shrill. 'I can't get over what an incredible place this is.'

'I'm taking this as a practice for my wedding,' Mel said, glancing around the room. 'It's given me a few ideas about décor and I've been picturing where I'd seat my guests. Which tables to put everyone and all that.'

Bea desperately wanted to sneak another look at Luke, but forced herself not to. What was wrong with her, she wondered, annoyed at her own stupidity. Luke might be the most stunning guy she'd ever seen, but she couldn't ignore the money laundering business.

The small band that Bea had hardly noticed upped the beat of their quiet background music and began to play a little louder as the Master of Ceremonies announced the first dance. Tom took Bea by the hand. 'Come on, let's show them how it's done.'

She laughed. 'As long as you're not expecting me to be any good at this waltzy sort of dancing,' she said, as he led her to the dance floor.

'Rubbish,' he argued, placing one hand lightly on her waist. 'It's nothing to worry about. Anyhow, as the man it's up to me to lead you, and if you are unable dance to this, then I'm not doing it correctly. Relax and enjoy the dance.'

She did as she was told. 'Hello,' said a baritone voice that haunted Bea's dreams. Tom tensed and looked over her shoulder at Luke.

'Good evening, Luke, Leilani.' Tom smiled stiffly, continuing to dance and not faltering a single step, unlike Bea. As they passed by, Leilani narrowed her heavily made-up eyes at Bea, but Bea smiled at them both, still counting the steps in her head.

'I didn't know they were here,' Tom said quietly.

'Me neither,' she fibbed, wondering if she'd misread Tom's accusatory tone, and why she was lying to him? They danced to several more songs, but didn't pass Luke and Leilani again. Bea supposed they must have returned to their table.

As soon as Tom and she were seated again, and he was busily replying to a text on his mobile, she subtly motioned to Shani that she was going to the Ladies. Shani followed. 'Shit, he looks hot,' Shani gasped. 'You could burn your fingers on that man.'

'I know,' Bea agreed quietly, trying to get used to Luke's new, improved appearance.

'I thought he was probably just friends with Leilani, but she looks very possessive of him, don't you think? Like a lioness protecting her ... well, not her young exactly, but you know what I mean.'

Bea laughed. 'I do, although I wish he hadn't asked me to dinner when he was at my house the other day. I don't want to think of him as being two-faced, like Simon.'

'Now that is depressing.' Shani reapplied her matt-red lipstick. 'Then again, after what happened between you both that night, maybe you could be right. Don't worry about it now. You're here to enjoy yourself. Make the most of this brilliant party.'

Bea nodded, wiping below her eyes with her fingers where her eyeliner had smudged slightly in the heat of the marquee. 'I'd better actually go to the loo, I suppose.' He had a girlfriend, she reasoned silently for the umpteenth time as she washed her hands. She needed to get a grip.

She sat back in her seat and watched Paul, who was looking happier than she had seen him in years. Someone coughed quietly next to her ear. Bea turned and came face to face with Luke, crouching down next to her in between her and Tom's chair.

'Hi, I was wondering if you'd like to dance with me,' he said, his arm resting on the back of Bea's chair. He looked across at Tom. 'You wouldn't mind your beautiful partner having just one dance with an old friend, would you?' he asked.

'Of course he wouldn't,' Bea said without waiting for Tom's reply. Luke grabbed hold of Bea's hand and led her onto the dance floor.

She could sense Tom's eyes boring into the back of her and at the same time noticed Luke's gaze on her. 'Thank you,' he said. 'You're looking incredibly beautiful tonight, although I have to admit I miss seeing those bunny slippers.'

'Stop it,' she said, trying not to laugh. 'What are you playing at?' Bea asked, aware he was holding her so firmly in the arch of her back that the entire length of his body was pressing alarmingly next to her own, sending disobedient, delicious feelings coursing through her.

'Can't a friend ask his pal to dance?' he whispered in her ear, holding her tighter to him.

Bea swallowed. She could feel the hardness of his chest against her breasts. Her mouth was almost completely dry. 'Of course you can,' she replied breathlessly.

'I didn't think you and Tom were seeing each other any more,' he said, the heat of his hand firm against her back.

'We work together and neither of us had a partner for the evening.'

'I could have been your partner if I'd known you were free.'

Bea pushed away the idea. 'But you're here with Leilani, aren't you?' she said, feeling him tense slightly at her answer.

'We're friends, that's all, Bea.'

'So you say.'

He watched her silently for a few moments, his expression dark, and Bea had to concentrate on not looking away from the intensity of his gaze.

'If I can believe you when you tell me that there was nothing between you in New York, why don't you listen when I tell you that whatever happened between Leilani and me is all in the past?'

Bea breathed in his citrusy aftershave and glanced up at his perfect lips so near to her own. It was wonderful to see them properly for once. Damn Tom for telling her about the investigation. An icy breeze seemed to grip her insides.

'Bea?'

She couldn't allow herself to be with him. She couldn't lose her house, but at least she had her appointment with Mr Peters in the next few days. She took a deep breath. 'There's too much going on in my life right now for me to get involved with someone, Luke.'

'I could help you sort whatever it is you're dealing with, you only have to ask.'

She wished it was that easy. She pulled him closer and relished being in his arms. This was the most she could allow herself for now. It would have to be enough. 'Thank you.'

'I wish you'd tell me what's holding you back,' he said, lowering his head to whisper in her ear. I wish I could, too, she thought, her entire body tingling when he kissed her lightly on the neck just below her jawline. The music ended and Bea went to move away, but he held on to her tightly. 'One more dance?'

She let him take her back in his arms. 'Luke, we talked about this.'

'No. We didn't. You decided for both of us that I wasn't right for you, but I've got no idea why, and I don't believe it's because of Leilani.' His breath was hot against her neck. She wanted to kiss him, feeling almost light-headed. 'I can't begin to imagine why you believe Tom to be more suited to you than me.'

'I told you, we really are just friends.' Bea took a deep breath in an effort to control her emotions. She daren't give him false hope. She gazed up at the desolate expression in his deep blue eyes and wanted him more than she had ever wanted anyone in her entire life. She swallowed, aware that she had to come up with some excuse for her behaviour. 'Anyway, Luke, you're not ready for the kind of relationship that I want.'

'You don't know that.'

'I do. And about that night ...'

'What happened that night was wonderful.' He stopped dancing for a moment and stared at her.

She made a step to force him to dance again, not wishing to draw any more attention to them than was necessary. 'Please keep dancing,' she pleaded. Luke moved once again. 'Whatever you may say, you can't ignore the fact you have a girlfriend. So it's not as if you're even free to be making a play for me in the first place. Tom's a good man, and he is just a friend; he's also my manager at work and we do have to get along.'

'And he makes you feel safe, is that it? Is that what you truly want, to feel safe?'

Sixteen

Fenced Off

'Right now, yes, it is actually.' She turned her head away from him but not quick enough to avoid his lips grazing hers so lightly she wasn't certain whether or not she had imagined it. She had never wanted to kiss anyone so desperately, but she had no choice. She owed it to herself to be sensible.

He sighed and let her go. 'I'm sorry you don't trust me, Bea. I wish you did.'

'It's time you went back to your friends.'

He fell silent. 'If that's your final word on the matter, then I'd better escort you back to your table.'

'You don't have to.' Bea forced a smile on to her face since she didn't want anyone else to see how upset she was. 'Really, there's no need,' she added turning her back on him and returning to her table. She sat back down and noticed Tom watching in silence as Luke held out her chair for her. He gazed down at her briefly before returning to his own group of friends.

Tom's phone bleeped. 'I'd better deal with this,' he said, making towards the direction of the Gents.

'Bloody hell, Bea, what are you playing at?' Mel whispered, watching Luke return to his seat.

'That's the second time tonight someone's asked me that question,' she answered.

'Quick, shush, Tom's on his way back,' Paul whispered through clenched teeth, no doubt loving every second of the unexpected drama. 'Look, everybody, the auction's about to start.'

'This is a relief.' Guy shook his head. 'You English, I thought it was the French who were the passionate ones. Where are your stiff upper lips and coldness? This is not at all what I expected. It is, though, far more interesting.'

The moustachoid auctioneer stepped up to the podium and banged his gavel. Bea breathed a sigh of relief. Now everyone would stop focusing on her and concentrate on the main event. Tom immediately put in a bid for the first lot: a crate of six bottles of Cristal. Bea watched the short bidding war Tom was having with a couple of other like-minded men. She clapped when Tom won, even though he ended up paying far more than she thought was necessary. Tom cheered and gave a little bow as everyone clapped.

'Well done,' Paige congratulated him, clapping. 'That's my favourite champagne. Not that I've been lucky enough to try it more than once.'

'Then you must take a bottle home with you.'

'Lot number two,' announced the auctioneer. 'Is a gourmet meal for two at The Grenadier's Boot, which I'm sure most of you know is a top-class local restaurant set neatly on St Aubin's Bay overlooking the small harbour.'

Bea had only been there once before with Simon for their first anniversary. She remembered back to when they had sat outside on the patio, overlooking the water and with the waves gently lapping against the harbour walls, making long forgotten promises to each other and felt sad for the innocent woman she had once been. She hoped she'd never be foolish enough to fall in to that trap again.

Jeremy was bidding against a puce-faced man, who looked about to explode out of his dress shirt as it pulled dangerously at the jet buttons down its front. 'I know him and he's a right sod,' he confided rather too loudly across the table. 'His ex-wife used to work with me, horrible man.'

'Yuck, he's revolting.' Mel pulled a face. 'What on earth does the redhead hanging off him see in him?'

'His excessive bank balance, Lamborghini, and a penthouse flat in St Jean Cap Ferrat, maybe?' Tom suggested with a smile on his face. 'It seems amazing how some women find these things so attractive.'

'Eugh.' Mel winced. 'So that's what a gold digger looks like.' She shuddered. 'I couldn't sleep with him no matter how many flashy baubles he may have stashed away.'

'I don't think it's his baubles she has to sleep with.' Grant laughed loudly at his own joke. Mel glared at him, as Paul and Shani tried to stifle their laughter. 'Keep going, mate,' he said to Jeremy as he concentrated on the auctioneer.

'Yay,' Mel cheered. 'Our table has outbid the competition again.'

Jeremy kissed Paige hard on the cheek. 'There you go, my sweet, I'll take you there for a treat on your birthday.'

Bea couldn't help smiling at Paige's proud expression. It made a pleasant change to see her friend look so excited. She'd often wondered why someone as meek as Paige had ended up with Jeremy, but couldn't help thinking that despite his occasional bossiness when he reduced Paige to tears, he probably needed an adoring, compliant wife to make him feel important. It made her even more relieved to think she didn't have to put up with Simon's arrogance on a daily basis.

Bea tried not to fidget as the following twenty lots were fought for. 'And now the main lot of the evening,' said the auctioneer. They stopped talking and Bea noticed how everyone paid attention; everyone, of course, except Luke, who humiliatingly caught her peaking over at him when she thought he wouldn't notice. She quickly looked away, pretending to be as entranced as the rest of the partygoers in what was happening at the podium end of the marquee.

'Can you imagine how romantic it must be to take a long weekend ballooning in the South of France?' Mel asked no one in particular.

Bea spotted Tom lifting his hand to start the bidding. 'Tom, you're spending a fortune tonight,' she said quietly not wishing to make a scene, but worried that he seemed to be spending so much when he'd confided in her recently about the difficulty he had paying for Vanessa's home as well as his own on his salary.

'It's for a children's hospice, you can't get much more worthwhile than that,' he snapped.

Bea looked at Tom's main opponent as the bids quickly rose. She could see that the immaculate older woman with her impressive helmet-like hair-do was more than capable of paying whatever the lot went for. She wasn't so certain Tom could compete. When even she pulled out of the running, Bea gave a sigh of relief.

The auctioneer held up his gavel. 'Any more bids? Do I hear two thousand, six hundred anywhere?'

The guests peered silently around the filled marquee, expectant faces looking at each other, waiting with to see if anyone would have the nerve to bid against Tom. 'Going once, going twice.'

'Three thousand.' Luke winked at Tom, his dark eyes twinkling mischievously.

Bea's held back a groan. The last thing she needed was for Luke to show Tom up. He probably wouldn't intentionally do it, she mused, but Tom would definitely take it that way.

Tom squared his shoulders and glared at Luke. 'Three thousand and fifty.'

Luke stood up and nodded at Tom. 'Three thousand, one hundred.'

Bea cringed. What the hell was wrong with them both? Neither had money to throw around and here they both were trying to outbid each other. 'Three thousand, two.'

'Three thousand and three.'

Bea glanced around to see who was cheering. Someone started clapping and soon most of the audience were joining in. 'This is ridiculous.'

'Chill,' Paul laughed. 'It's for charity. So what if they're showing off in front of you.'

'And five hundred.'

'Don't talk rubbish,' Bea said, trying to think of a way to stop them. 'Neither of them can afford this.' What the hell were they both doing?

Mel squealed in excitement, clapping her hands together rapidly. 'This is so exciting.'

'Four thousand,' bid Tom, unwilling to back down, his face set like stone.

'Four and a half.' Luke's smile slipped for a second, but Bea doubted many people noticed.

'Five,' Tom shouted slamming his palm on their table and

sending several glasses crashing over. Bea and Shani leapt up to grab hold of the drinks and stand them upright again. Paige covered the spilt liquid with their napkins.

The auctioneer held his mallet in Luke's direction. 'Do I have any increase on the bid?'

Luke shook his head. 'No, I've reached my limit.'

'All done then. Going for five thousand pounds. Going once, going twice,' the auctioneer pointed his mallet in Tom's direction, 'sold to the gentleman on table twelve, for the generous amount of five thousand pounds, thank you, sir.' He turned to Luke. 'A grand effort on your behalf too, sir.'

Bea stared at Tom. He did look a little stunned. She took hold of the cuff of his jacket and gently pulled him down to his seat. 'Don't you think you got a little carried away?'

Tom ran his finger around the neck of his dress shirt and cleared his throat. 'Of course not,' he smiled. 'It's for a children's charity, after all.'

'Well done, Tom,' Mel cheered, holding up her glass to toast him. The others picked up their glasses and Shani and Bea took hold of their empty ones and smiled at each other. 'To Tom.'

Tom bowed. 'Thank you. Mind you, that man's a bloody lunatic,' he muttered as he sat down.

Bea glanced over at Luke. She didn't like to point out that the man shaking hands across the room with the other members of his party had been the one with the sense to pull out of the bidding. They slapped his back and seemed to be commiserating with him for his loss. Bea noticed he didn't appear to be at all upset about it. Leilani put a lean, tanned hand on his shoulder and nodded over to Bea. Bea smiled and looked away.

'She resembles a rather elongated Great Dane, don't you think?' Paul whispered in her ear.

Bea giggled. 'That's a little mean, Paul. I wouldn't mind having legs as long as hers.'

'Nah, you're little and cute, like me,' he said, winking at her. 'Who wants to be a beanpole like her?'

'Thank you.' Shani glared at him. 'There's nothing wrong with being tall and skinny.'

'Yeah, whatever.' Paul pulled a face and Bea laughed.

Luke stood up and marched directly to their table. A broad smile on his face, he held his hand out to Tom. 'No hard feelings, Tom?' Bea wondered if he was aware just how furious Tom probably was with him.

Tom rose, shook Luke's hand. 'Hell, that's what these evenings are all about,' he said, pumping Luke's hand up and down enthusiastically. 'Spending far over the odds for something we don't even need, for charity.'

Luke took Bea's hand and bent his head to kiss it. 'I hope the lady enjoys her trip.'

'I haven't been invited to go yet,' she replied, irritated by his presumption.

'I'll see you guys later then.' Luke nodded to the rest of the party before returning to his group and Leilani who, Bea noticed, managed to pout without looking ridiculous.

'How could Tom manage to pay all that money for something?' Shani leant over to Bea, whispering. 'I thought his ex-wife and kids were costing him a fortune.'

'I would have thought that with his financial problems the last thing Luke Thornton should be doing is bidding for anything at all,' Mel said. 'Don't you agree, Grant?'

'There's more to his finances than you would think,' Tom said.

Bea grimaced. 'Tom? Should you really be saying things like that?'

'No, of course not, sorry,' he said guiltily. 'That was uncalled for.'

Paul nudged Bea gently. 'I think you did very well, Tom,' he said. 'I'm glad someone on our table will be leaving with a few lots. It makes the evening more fun, especially when the rest of us couldn't afford to bid for anything after paying for the tickets and these clothes.'

Cheered by this observation, Tom visibly relaxed. 'Don't be silly, Paul, they rely on selling the tickets. The auction is just the icing on the cake, and if someone is mad enough to go completely overboard at least the charity benefits in the end.'

Bea was grateful for Paul lightening the atmosphere of their group. She heard the band strike up the first notes of a tune and went with Tom on to the dance floor when he took her hand. 'I wonder what we would have been like if we'd married?' he said.

Startled by his observation, Bea hesitated. 'I hate to think,' she said, making a joke of it.

'We never argued much and we got along pretty well.'

Bea agreed, hoping he wasn't going to try and ask her out on a date again. 'True.'

'I don't suppose you'll want to come with me on my holiday?'

She shook her head, but smiled at him. 'No, Tom. Maybe you could take the children away with you? I'm sure they'd enjoy a trip away.'

She glancing at her watch, pleased to note it was nearly the end of the evening.

'You and Tom were getting a little cosy tonight.' Shani said, as she pulled up the duvet in Bea's spare room. 'Is there something you want to tell me?'

Bea looked out of the window through the darkness to the coast of France and the lights of the distant houses. 'Er, no. So don't expect any gossip from me. He's off to Manchester to meet with a client tomorrow, so won't be at the office for a few days, either. Sorry to disappoint you.'

'A relief?'

'Yup.' Bea sat on the end of Shani's bed and rubbed her blistered feet. 'I don't know why I let you persuade me to wear those shoes. They nearly killed me tonight.'

Shani puffed up her pillow and leant back. 'They didn't seem to bother you when you were dancing with Luke, I noticed.' She held up her hand to stop Bea from interrupting. 'I know you insist there isn't anything going on between you and Luke, but I definitely caught the two of you exchanging looks tonight, several times in fact.'

Bea sighed. 'Let's not talk about him, Shan,' she said, wriggling her toes and groaning. 'I'm glad you're staying here tonight, it's lovely knowing there's someone else here for a change.'

175

'Why not? I don't care what you say, I know you well enough to see that you fancy him like mad. Which means that there's some other reason why you're keeping your distance from him, and I've no idea what it can be.'

Bea stared at her tired reflection in the dressing-table mirror. God, she looked awful. 'It doesn't matter what I think or feel about him though, does it?'

'Why would you say that?'

'Because he's with someone else,' she said, hating her voice for cracking like it did and giving away the depths of her feelings to Shani. 'I know he keeps insisting he isn't, but they go everywhere together and she stays with him most of the time.'

'Maybe she's the one who's after him and he doesn't realise it?' Shani tilted her head, her face sad. 'Or have you thought that maybe he believes you and Tom have more going on between you than you actually do?'

'Why would he even think about me when he's with someone as beautiful as her?' Bea walked out to the hall. 'Who knows? Anyway I'm shattered. I'll see you in the morning.' She went to her bedroom and closed the door behind her and sitting down heavily on the end of the bed. Shani opened the door and stood in her doorway. 'You're gorgeous too,' she said. When Bea laughed, Shani added, 'And you're far more fun than she could ever be. I'm sure Luke isn't really interested in anyone as shallow as her, model or not.' She turned to leave the room, then turned and tapped the side of her nose. 'There's something going on between the two of you that I don't understand, but one of these days I'm going to work it out or force you to tell me what it is.'

Bea woke early and getting up quietly, so as not to disturb Shani, she dialled Luke's number as soon as it was a respectable enough time to do so. 'Yes,' croaked a deep female voice.

Bea panicked, and slammed down the phone in horror. Leilani. Furious with herself for daring to believe him when that they weren't together and for not having the foresight to consider Luke would probably be with Leilani, Bea pushed her jealously to the back of her mind. She paced her bedroom floor, trying to work out the best way to contact him without raising Leilani's suspicions, finally coming to the annoying conclusion that she would simply have to wait.

Bea was frustrated that she couldn't arrange to see him. She knew she should keep her distance from him, especially as when his girlfriend was right beside him in his bed. The picture forming in her head of his toned body wrapped around Leilani's perfect perma-tanned limbs gave her a sick feeling deep in her stomach. However hard she tried to remember what Tom had told her about Luke, she still couldn't help her feelings. It didn't help when he acted the way he had at the ball. She needed him to know that he couldn't play with her emotions. He had a girlfriend and it wasn't fair on either of them to play games.

She didn't want to wake Shani, so decided that maybe today was the perfect day to start jogging, after all despite her best intentions, she hadn't been jogging since going out with Paul and Shani recently. It would do her good to run on the beach, she decided. So, dragging on her tracksuit and tatty trainers, Bea kissed Flea goodbye and promised to take him out for a walk later. He was getting too old to want to do anything more energetic than walking. She pushed a few pounds into her pocket so that she could buy the newspapers on the way home, grabbed her phone, and drove to Grouville Bay.

Bea remembered to stretch her legs gently to warm up and took a few deep breaths of fresh air. 'Ahh,' this was more like it. She walked down the cobbled slipway and gazed appreciatively at the sea and the tough surfers as they rode the rolling waves on their colourful boards.

After taking several more deep breaths, she became a little dizzy. Too much, too soon, she decided before setting off at a slow jog. 'Phew,' she grumbled, 'this is far harder than it looks when Paul and Shani do it.' After only about fifty yards she was panting and if it hadn't been for the other fit runners pacing away along the beach, she would have allowed herself to collapse in a heap face down onto the damp sand.

Bea forced herself on, one step after the other for as long as she could bear to. She could hardly breathe, her chest was tight, and her calf muscles were burning. There was nothing for it but to casually slow to a walk and then stop. Bea stood feet slightly apart, hands firmly on thighs, bent over, puce in the face and gasping for air.

Having finally managed to slow her heart rate to somewhere near normal, she turned to walk back up the slipway to the catering van, to compensate her efforts with a Galaxy and a large coffee when her phone shrieked the 'Dance of the Knights' by Prokofiev. 'Bloody Paul,' she moaned, 'I wish he'd stop messing about with the ringtones on my mobile,' she said, wishing he didn't love watching *The Apprentice* so much. With shaking fingers she pressed the green button as she paced along, eager to reach the liquid refreshment she had promised herself. 'Hello?' she panted.

'Is everything all right?' Luke whispered. 'Leilani said she answered my mobile, but the person on the other end rang off. I checked my phone and saw it was you.'

'Argh,' she screeched, as her trainer caught a stone, tripping her up so she landed in an ungainly heap, cracking her knee on the concrete path, grazing her hand, and sending her phone flying out in front of her with a loud clatter. 'Shit, shit, bollocks,' she grimaced, rubbing her knee hard and brushing away the tears of pain that seemed to come from nowhere. She grabbed her phone. 'Luke, I …'

'Stay where you are. I'm coming to get you,' she heard Luke shout just as she held it back against her ear. 'Where did you say you were?'

'Just off the first slipway, Grouville beach,' she breathed. 'But I'm …' the phone went dead. 'Fine,' she added. Bea held the phone in front of her and stared blankly at the screen. 'Sod it.'

She pulled her trouser leg up and winced when she spotted the blackening bruise and beads of blood already on her knee, then remembered Luke said he was coming. 'Oh hell.' She covered her leg again and tucked loose blonde strands behind her ears to try and look reasonably human. He was going to see her unwashed and sweaty, and after only having run fifty yards.

It then occurred to Bea that Luke didn't have to know that she had only run approximately twenty paces before nearly suffering a coronary. And anyway, what did that have to do with anything?

Yes, let him come, she decided. Let him think she did this thing every Sunday, like Bea was damn sure Leilani did. An annoying image sprang uninvited into Bea's mind of Leilani, her endless toned legs, tanned to perfection in the tiniest micro shorts, pacing comfortably along the beach as her long hair flowed elegantly behind her. Cow.

Bea hobbled towards the van, something that she did most Sundays, but usually with Flea ambling along at the end of his lead, sniffing for other dogs who dared walk the same route as he, before lifting his leg to pee and regain some invisible ownership of his imagined territory. 'Morning, Des,' she said, trying to sound more cheery than she felt now that she'd finally managed to regain some composure.

'Bleedin' 'ell, Bea, you bin runnin'?' he teased, taking in her dishevelled appearance. 'That's not like you, my love.'

'Yes, but keep it to yourself, won't you?'

'Want your usual?'

Bea nodded. 'Yes, please.' She tidied up her hair and smiled at him when he handed her a coffee, bar of chocolate and her newspaper, and passed over several notes. 'It won't do any harm people thinking I take regular exercise, will it?'

'What people's that then?' he asked, scratching his head.

She spotted Luke running towards her. 'Bea, what happened?' he demanded urgently.

She turned to Des, her eyes wide with embarrassment. 'People like him.' She motioned discreetly, doing her best to ignore her stinging knee.

He stifled a guffaw with little success, as he handed her a cappuccino and a Galaxy. 'See ya next week then, love.' He winked.

Bea turned to Luke. 'Morning.'

'Morning? What happened?' he panted, looking her up and down. He pushed a hand through his messy fringe. Bea was painfully aware his hair was still tousled from racing straight to her from his bed.

She stared at him silently, intent on remaining as composed as possible. 'Nothing, why?'

Luke's concerned expression morphed into one of fury. He grabbed her by the elbow.

'Hey,' she glared at him, 'my coffee.'

'Sod your bloody coffee, you said something had happened,' he accused angrily.

Bea shook him off. 'No, I didn't. You presumed something was the matter. You cut me off before I could finish what I was saying, if you remember.' She turned and walked off, her chocolate bar pushed into her pocket.

He soon caught up with her. 'Do you realise how infuriating you can be sometimes?'

'Now you listen here –' Bea glared at him.

'No, you listen. When I phoned you back, you sounded like something was wrong. I thought you were hurt.' He noticed her torn tracksuit. 'There's blood seeping from your knee.'

She glanced down at her leg. 'I slipped when I answered your call. I was slightly out of breath, that's all,' she sniffed. 'I'd been for a run.'

He thought for a moment, confusion spreading across his angry face. 'Christ, you sounded like you could hardly breathe,' he argued, confused. 'That must have been some run. Anyway why didn't you phone me back if there was nothing wrong? You knew I was coming to find you.'

She stopped, causing him to stride ahead for a couple of paces, and having to double back to continue his onslaught. 'Bea, you phoned me at some un-Godly hour this morning, if you remember?'

'Surely Leilani can't be very impressed that you've come here to meet me?'

Luke shook his head. 'I didn't feel the need to tell her, if you must know. So, now that I'm here, you may as well tell me what was so damn important it couldn't wait?'

Bea shrugged. 'I did phone you, but only because I wanted to arrange to see you, so when you cut me off so abruptly, the best thing seemed to just let you come here.'

180

His hands fell by his sides 'You wanted to see me? Why?'

'To discuss this thing.' Bea was beginning to feel a little awkward. This wasn't going to plan. He was supposed to have, what? She wasn't quite sure.

'Thing?' he mocked. 'Are you still drunk from last night?' Bea stared at him in silence, trying to figure out what to say next. 'Well go on then. I'm waiting,' he shouted.

'Last night, Luke, your behaviour was ridiculous.'

He raised his eyebrows. 'Because I bid against Tom?'

'No, that isn't what I meant.' She took a sip from her cappuccino, immediately wishing she hadn't when she scalded her lip.

'Well?'

'Coming over to our table, being sarcastic and insinuating things by staring at me, and then again when we were dancing. *Then* there was that ridiculous business with the auction.'

He looked down at her. 'You're lecturing me?'

'I'm just saying!'

He ignored her protests. 'Do you realise how badly you're behaving?' He stared at her, his eyes searching hers for answers. 'I thought there could be something between us, but it seems I was wrong. Fair enough. But I've caught you looking at me as if you're searching my face for an answer to something, and I've no idea what it is.'

Bea couldn't look him in the eye. He was right, only she couldn't tell him the truth.

'Fine, I'll leave you to carry on with your jogging then.' He marched off towards his car 'Bloody woman,' she heard him curse.

Bea watched him leave, wishing more than anything that she could afford not to care about his past. If only Simon didn't want half of her house, if only she didn't need to keep her job to be in with a chance to get that sodding mortgage. She walked towards her car, pulling her keys from her pocket as she balanced the coffee and papers in both hands. If only bloody Tom hadn't told her about the investigation.

She dropped her bar of chocolate, hearing it break in its wrapper.

Seventeen

February – Pruning the Deadwood

Bea didn't have to look at the calendar to know it would have been Annabel's birthday today. She stood outside her kitchen door holding the neck of her coat closed as she drank her coffee and stared out across the walled-in garden. 'I miss you,' she whispered; glad to be alone with her memories. Bea wished she could go back one year to the birthday treat she'd surprised Annabel with. 'It isn't every day you're seventy,' Bea recalled telling her aunt when Annabel had expressed horror at how much her gift must have cost. 'Anyway it's from me and Simon. He's done all the arranging and booked the tickets for the mystery walk with the Kew guide and for us to see *Les Misérables*. We have him to thank for this really.'

Was it only me who was shocked at Simon's double life, she wondered. She shook her head and held tightly on to her mug. No, Aunt Annabel had always been fond of him, too. Bea tried not to think how devastated her aunt had been when she'd discovered him with Claire. She hated to think that her aunt's heart attack could have been brought on by that devastating night when their three lives had changed forever. She breathed in the crisp, frosty air and swallowed the lump restricting her throat. She'd shared enough tears for Simon and her aunt would hate for her to spend today crying. No, she'd begin her day by visiting Aunt Annabel's grave and take her some of her favourite orange roses.

'I know they're shop bought,' Bea murmured her warm breath frosty, aware that there were one or two other people close to the immaculate grave, its wooden cross looking out of place among the other engraved stone creations, 'so I've brought you the hyacinths too. I didn't kill them off this year.

There's one in blue and one in pink.' Bea smiled. 'You never could decide which colour you preferred.' She breathed in the familiar scent which took her back to so many winters watching the ritual of her aunt first planting the bulbs and then watching them flower on the kitchen windowsill. It was a tradition she was determined to continue.

She picked up the vase and, noticing there wasn't any water, sat back on her heels to get up and fetch some. 'Here, let me.'

Startled by Luke's voice, she stood up quickly, nearly dropping the vase in her hand. 'What are you doing here?'

'I hope you don't mind me intruding, but I saw your car as I was driving past and realised it must be a special anniversary of some sort. Your mum, or your aunt maybe?'

Bea cleared her throat. 'It would have been Aunt Annabel's seventy-first birthday today.'

'I presume you planted the hyacinths especially for today, then?'

Bea nodded. She could feel herself welling up and turned away from him. 'I was just …'

'Let me.' He took the empty vase from her hand and walked away.

Bea watched him and struggled to retain her composure. She didn't want anyone to be too kind to her today. It would be too much to bear. She crouched back down and placed the hyacinths either side of the cross, pushing their enamel containers slightly into the ground so the wind couldn't disturb them.

'Here you go,' he said, handing her back the vase three-quarters filled with water, their hands grazing lightly as she took it from him.

'Thank you,' she said, taking the vase and placing the roses into the water. She rested a hand on the cross. 'I can't wait for this ground to settle and be able to order Annabel a proper gravestone. I gather you have to wait about a year, though.'

'Yes, something like that.' He placed a hand lightly on Bea's shoulder. 'I hope you didn't mind me coming here. I'll leave you in peace now.'

Bea put her hand up until she could hold his fingers. The

warmth of his touch on her shoulder was strangely comforting. 'I don't mind you coming here. Thank you for looking out for me, it was kind.'

As his footsteps receded along the narrow path, she could almost hear her aunt's approval. Aunt Annabel liked strong men. Her Antonio had been a well-built man, always needing a strong team of polo ponies to take his bulk. She'd definitely like the idea of Luke working with his hands. She never did understand people's preference for working in offices. Bea's breath caught in her throat as emotion got the better of her. She sat back on her heels and cried for a few minutes. 'I'm so lost right now,' she whispered, placing her hand on the cold wood of the cross. 'Surely things would have to get better soon.'

Bea arrived at her father and stepmother's home a short while later. As usual it hadn't occurred to either of them that maybe this might be a day when Bea wouldn't want to have to talk about her sister's wedding plans. It was easier for her to go and get it over with than to row about it endlessly though, so she forced a smile on her face and went in.

'I've invited Tom,' Bea heard Mel say as she let herself into the house. 'He doesn't have a partner either, so I thought Bea, oh there you are.' She said looking confused at Bea's unhappy expression. 'I was saying you're pairing up with Tom for the wedding.'

'I'd really rather not, though, Mel.' She had no intention of staying a moment longer than was necessary.

'Now, now, girls,' her dad said, standing up to give her a bear hug and looking equally as fed up at the discussion. 'No fighting. Mel's right, though.'

'I don't have a problem with it, but why should it matter if I take a partner or not?'

'Because then I can deduct your 'plus ones' from the invitees.' Mel took her crystal-covered biro and scrawled out the writing next to Bea's name and then Tom's on her spread sheet.

Bea scowled at her sister. What was she on about? She looked at her dad for a clue.

'Mel and Joyce have got a little enthusiastic with their

invitations and Grant has finally put his foot down.'

'Not Grant,' Mel groaned. 'Dad's the one being selfish.' She pulled a face at him. Bea could remember when that princess-look of hers used to work, but she must have been all of five years old at the time. She tried not to be irritated with her sister.

'Thank you, Melanie,' Joyce snapped, coming through to the living room carrying a tray of biscuits. 'I think your father is being perfectly reasonable about this.' She looked Bea up and down. 'You've got here then? I thought we said ten-thirty, not eleven o'clock,' she said pointedly looking at her watch. 'I do have a list of items to work through today, Beatrice. We can't all be spending time wallowing.'

Bea ignored her and sat down, soothed by her father's glare in Joyce's direction as he left the room. She knew he'd have a go at her stepmother when she'd left, but a part of her wished he'd do it in front of her. Just for once.

'Melanie tells us she's inviting that handsome chap, Luke, is it, and his model girlfriend. So you and Tom will have to team up. I won't have any argument on the matter.' She hesitated for a moment. 'Although I do think that refusing to allow any more than one hundred people in the marquee is probably a little too conservative, Eric. Your precious lawn will grow back if we do decide to hire a larger marquee,' she shouted over her shoulder in the general direction of his study, where Bea presumed her father must now be working.

'I think a hundred guests are more than enough,' Bea said. 'You can't have that many friends, and neither side have large families, do they?'

'Beatrice, I'll thank you to keep your opinions to yourself,' Joyce snapped, pursing her lips together and raising her chin in her usual aggressive manner when anyone dared to disagree with her. Bea remembered when she was little being terrified of this woman, until she saw Annabel stand up to her and give her hell. Bea smiled to herself. That was the night when Annabel told Joyce and her father that Bea would be moving in with her for good. It had been the happiest day of her life, until her wedding day.

'Are you listening to me?'

186

Bea blinked and tried to recall what Joyce had been saying. 'Of course.'

'You've had your big day and I won't allow you to try and ruin your sister's, whatever misguided loyalties you might have about that date.'

Bea shook her head and glared at Mel. 'I just think out of all the days Mel could have chosen for her wedding, Aunt Annabel's first anniversary is a bit insensitive.'

'You're so selfish.' Joyce pursed her thin lips together. 'You've always thought more about that old woman than you did anyone else.'

'You wonder why?' Bea murmured under her breath.

Her father returned to the room. 'What's all this shouting about?' He looked over at Joyce, who for once closed her mouth and didn't answer. 'I told you that I wanted this to be a calm chat and let's keep it that way. I want Mel's day to be a perfect at yours was, Bea,' he said, ignoring Joyce's badly concealed moan. 'I agree the date is a little unfortunate, but it's booked now and maybe it's not such a bad thing to have something happy for us all to focus on for the ninth of May.'

'Maybe,' Bea said, unconvinced, especially because she was the only one who'd actually had any affection for Aunt Annabel. She suspected her father had a soft spot for her aunt, but never showed it as Joyce seemed so sensitive about Annabel being Bea's mother's sister and a reminder that Joyce wasn't the first woman he'd loved in his lifetime. But not wishing to give her father more grief than he suffered most days, she nodded. 'Mel tells me she's come up with a suggestion for you to keep Simon away from the house?' he added.

'Yes, an injunction, but he's retaliated by getting his lawyers to send me a letter threatening a court date on the tenth of May.'

'Probate ends on the tenth of May,' her father said quietly. 'He doesn't waste any time, does he?'

'No, but I suppose whatever happens it'll be a relief to get it all finalised at last.'

'Have you been to the bank yet?' Bea nodded. 'No luck then?' Bea chewed her lower lip and shook her head. 'Never mind, you'll have to keep trying. You know I would help if I could.'

Joyce stood up. 'Don't you dare say if it wasn't for this wedding, Eric.'

'I wasn't going to, Joyce. This wedding might be expensive, but even this couldn't pay for half the worth of that house.'

'Yes, well some people don't know when they're well off, do they?' Joyce snapped, giving Bea a pointed glare. 'You sister doesn't have a house of her own yet.'

'Mum, stop it,' Mel said, slamming down her biro. 'Annabel was nothing to me. She was Bea's mum's sister, so why would she include me in her will? Honestly, you do irritate me sometimes.'

Bea didn't know who must looked more stunned at her sister's uncharacteristic outburst at her mother; her, her father, or Joyce. When no one spoke, Mel took hold of one of Bea's wrists. 'Look at your hands, Bea,' she said, turning over her hand and inspecting Bea's ruined nails. 'A farmer would have better manicured fingernails than you.'

'I doubt that somehow,' Bea said. 'But I promise I'll get a manicure before your wedding.' She thought it was the least she could do. 'Do you want to come with Shani, Paul, and me to a winter fayre this afternoon after we've finished here?'

'She's not going anywhere until we finalise these arrangements,' Joyce snapped.

Mel thought for a moment then smiled. 'Oh God, go on then. Where is it?' she added, without looking up.

'It's such a gorgeous day and the fayre is in Gorey Village near Shani's parents' house. Her mum is the chairwoman of the Women's Voluntary Guild, or something like that, as I'm sure you'll remember. Shani phoned me last night and asked if I could muster up some helpers.'

Mel glanced up at her. 'What would we have to do? And why does she need us to help? I thought her mum is the most organised person in the entire cosmos.' She smiled at her mum. 'Apart from you, of course.'

'Apparently, there was a monthly lunch party that most of them attended at one of their homes and it seems like they've been poisoned.'

'Poisoned?' Mel laughed in disbelief.

'Well, you know food poisoning.'

'Sounds strange to me,' Joyce said.

'There's nothing sinister about the request, her mum just needs helpers for two of the stalls. She's managed to persuade her cousin Paige and her fiancé Jeremy to help, so I can't really say no, now can I?'

Bea would really rather have not bothered to go either, but she liked Paige and knew that if she had been roped in then Shani would be in her mother's bad books if she didn't go. Even so, she thought, she wished her friend would stop feeling she had to take charge of her all the time, especially when she had so much DIY to get on with, however she didn't mention her thoughts to Mel and waited to see if she would agree to go.

'It sounds like a good idea to me,' Bea's dad said, giving her a kiss on the cheek. 'You two should get going. We've agreed that we won't be hiring a larger marquee, we know your plus one and Tom's are being removed from the list, and by the time we've pruned the deadwood,' he raised his voice a little, 'and Joyce realises our neighbours from twenty years ago do not need an invitation, then I think the numbers should tally pretty well. We can discuss this again later in the week.'

'Put like that,' Mel shrugged, 'How can I refuse? Grant's busy anyhow and these damn wedding preparations are stressing me out. I need to get away from them for a bit.'

'It'll probably do me good to have time away from the smell of paint and white spirit.' Bea smiled, relieved to have a reason not to spend any more time in Joyce's company.

'Look at all the cars already parked here,' Bea said as she tried to figure out where she should park her dusty car. The only space she could see was between two shining Mercedes and, with her lousy parking she thought it preferable to draw up on the roadside instead.

'What is it about bangers that people never bother to wash them?' Mel looked back at Bea's ancient Mazda.

'I daren't,' Bea joked. 'The thing would fall apart if you wet all the rust.'

189

Having been given their orders for the day, Bea led the way to their pitches. It never ceased to amaze her how Shani, with her toned features, had such a matronly mother. Mrs Calder's robust frame was supported by such short legs that Paul couldn't help commenting on how different her build was to Shani's. Her steel grey hair, pulled back into a tight chignon, framed the powdered face with beady, black eyes that never missed a trick and pursed, cherry matt-red lips Bea was sure had never uttered a gentle word to anyone.

'Step to it,' she bellowed. 'I want these stalls ready for visitors as soon as you can. No point in wasting time.'

'Blimey,' said Mel, indicating the elderly women scuttling around the room answering Mrs Calder's orders. 'This lot are terrified of her.'

'Aren't you?' Paul laughed. 'I wouldn't cross the old bag.'

'Hey, that old bag is my mother.' Shani punched him on his shoulder. 'Only I'm allowed to criticise her and don't you forget it.'

'I can see who the next generation of old bags will be led by,' he laughed, before running off with a tray of cakes he'd been supposed to take to an old lady's stall.

'Steady on, young man,' Mrs Calder's voice bellowed across the room. Voices hushed and Bea giggled as Paul stopped messing about and mouthed an apology.

'So, you all understand. Melanie and Paul, you are to man the second-hand bookstall and Beatrice and Shani, you can have the preserves.' Mrs Calder pointed to the rickety trellis tables laden with jam-filled jars of all shapes and sizes.

'Come along then, jump to it. Lady Dulbury will be arriving in half an hour to open the fayre. I need you all to make sure your stalls are immaculate and presentable and don't forget, one of you needs to be in charge of tying the moneybag round your waist. You'll find more than enough change in them, so do be careful not to lose them. At some point today a photographer from the *Gazette* will be here to cover the event and I don't want any of you letting the side down.'

'Whose bright idea was it to help out today?' whispered Paul behind his hand to Bea. 'I'd rather be moping by myself than being bossed around here.'

'I'm not deaf,' Shani said, her voice quiet. 'Now stop messing about and come with me.'

'If you're not careful you're going to morph into your mother,' Paul giggled ignoring her. Mel grabbed his wrist and dragged him to their stall.

'No. No. No, Mrs Baxter, not like that.' Mrs Calder pounded over to the cake stall, her sensible brogues slapping the hard earth lawn where the poor white-haired old lady fumbled with a disintegrating Victoria sponge.

'Quick, let's look busy,' Shani said, frantically tidying up their stall.

Bea didn't argue. She nudged her gently. 'You must take after your dad.' She raised a playful eyebrow.

'Thankfully, I think I do. Do you know, when I was small I was sure I was adopted and even had the guts to ask her once.'

'Phew, that's brave,' laughed Bea at the thought of it. 'What did she say?'

'She told me not to be so rude and sent me to my room without any supper.'

They were mid-titter when Shani's mother noticed and made her way back over to their stalls. 'I presume by the chit chat that you two are satisfied with your presentation?'

'Yes.' They nodded, almost standing to attention and trying not to laugh.

She surveyed the trestle table and all that it held for a few seconds before sighing loudly, her whole body quivering as if to emphasize her concerns. 'It'll have to do, I suppose. You are amateurs after all, and I must be grateful for whatever help I can find today.' She clapped her hands together and marched off once more to check on the others.

The jostling and elbowing in front of their stall slowly began to subside. 'We've all done extremely well, don't you think?' Shani shouted from the middle of the hall three hours later.

'Most of our jars have been sold,' Bea said to Shani proudly. 'Even the boxes hidden under the table to restock are almost gone.' Bea looked down at her own bag containing two jars of damson and raspberry jam she'd bought for herself and her parents. 'I'll just pop these last few jars on the stall, see if we can sell them too,' she said. Sensing someone there, she stood up, arms full of jars, and placing them on the table, asked, 'Can I help you?'

Luke held a carrier bag full of books. 'Yes, please,' he said.

Eighteen

Mole Hills

Startled by his voice, Bea looked up, knocking over two of the jars. 'Hell,' she said, as he instinctively reached to catch them before they hit the ground.

Luke smiled at her, his eyes sending signals through her entire body as she hurriedly tried to think of a reply. 'Well done,' she said, impressed by his instinctive reactions.

'Well?' he asked, waiting for a reply.

Bea frowned. 'Sorry?' Why did she find it so hard to stay focused when he was around?

Luke shook his head. 'Can I buy a couple of pots?'

'Of course you can, as much as you like,' she said, unable to stop her lips drawing back into a wide smile. 'Anyway, what are you doing here? I wouldn't have thought this was your sort of thing.'

He looked around at the other stalls. 'I could say the same to you. However, my excuse is that this is my parents' home and my mother is on the committee with that old battle-axe over there.' He inclined his head in Mrs Calder's direction.

Bea leant towards him, 'Lower your voice,' she whispered. 'She's Shani's mother.'

Bea laughed when Luke's eyebrows nearly disappeared into his fringe. 'Poor girl. Doesn't take after her though, does she?'

'No, thankfully not,' Bea giggled. 'So, do you always help out at these things then?'

He shook his head and shuddered. 'No, only when they're held here, which thankfully is only once a year. My mother always asks me to hang around to help with any heavy carting about, and I don't really mind. It's a bit of fun, and I'm usually paid with a couple of ciders from that stall, and Jersey Wonders from over there,' he said, indicating a converted ice-cream van behind him.

'What a surprise,' Leilani said, suspicion souring her voice. 'When Luke suggested I come here today, he didn't mention you might be working here, Beatrix Potter. Isn't it delightful how we keep on bumping into each other? I suppose we have to expect it on this tiny island of yours.'

Bea forced a smile, determined to be pleasant. 'Leilani, have you been enjoying the fayre?'

'It seems a little more interesting now I've seen you're here. I thought there would only be old ladies fighting over tea cosies, or whatever you call those horrible knitted coats for teapots,' she said, approaching Luke and snaking her arms through his like a particularly clingy feline. 'Lukey,' she said, raising an immaculately sculptured eyebrow in what Bea presumed was supposed to be a sexy look. 'Your mother asked me to find you. She needs you in the other room to help re-arrange some tables.' She turned back to Bea. 'I gather the afternoon teas are more popular than they had anticipated.' She took one of his hands in both of hers and began pulling him towards the house. 'Ta, ta, Beatrice,' she said over her shoulder in a mock English accent.

Bea ignored her and caught Luke's eye. He mouthed an apology and smiled at her before following Leilani.

'God, I hate that rotten cow,' Shani said from behind her. 'Hey, I'm thirsty, do you mind holding down the fort for a bit?' she asked, crossing her legs as only someone expert in yoga could manage. 'I can get us some lemonade after I've visited the Ladies room.'

'Not at all, off you go.' Bea watched as Shani walked off, wondering what was different about her.

'Young lady,' said a tiny old woman in front of her. 'Please can you help us?' Bea nodded, hoping Shani wouldn't be long with that drink. Her throat was parched, and she wished she'd thought to bring a bottle of water along with her for the afternoon. 'We've just enjoyed the most delicious afternoon tea and were told that the jam they served with the scones is being sold on this stall. But we can't decide between the strawberry and the damson.'

'How about buying one of each?' Bea asked, giving them her brightest salesman smile.

'We only want one jar each though,' the shorter of the two women replied.

'Well, why not buy a different one and if you have a spare container at your home you can take half each out of the jars and swap,' she said, holding up two jars.

After a few more minutes of debate they did as she had suggested and she gratefully handed each one a jar and took their coppers. 'This bag is heavy,' she said to Paul and Mel when they came over to join her and see how she'd done. 'Why can't people use pound notes instead of all these coins, and most of them are coppers. You'd think they'd be pleased to still have pound notes over here. I don't know why they stopped them in the UK.' Bea stepped from one foot to the other to try and alleviate her aching feet. Raking her hands through her hair, she pushed it back off her flushed face. Where was Shani with those drinks?

'You look a bit flustered,' said Paul, coming over to join her.

Bea heard a distant boom. 'What was that?' she asked, looking around to try and see what had caused it. It didn't appear to have come from very far away.

'No idea, but I'd like to know what's going on over there,' he said, motioning through the double doors over the thinning crowds to the parking area where people began congregating around a car. 'I wonder if Leilani has been upsetting the locals again?'

Bea looked over to a group of about fifteen people. There did seem to be an awful lot of arm waving going on, as well as raised voices. Bea craned her neck in an attempt to find out what was so interesting, but couldn't see past them to find out.

'Anyway where's Shani got to?' Paul asked, taking her attention away from the on-going drama.

Just at that moment, she noticed Shani hurrying over, holding a cup of tea out in front of her in each hand trying to concentrate on not spilling them as she made her way through the bustling people. 'Here you go,' she said as soon as she reached Bea. 'Sorry I was so long. There's some sort of problem near the entrance, but I've no idea what and it's too sodding cold to go and find out.'

Bea blew on her tea and peered through the people in front of her. Absorbed by what was happening, she took a sip of the hot drink, the shock of it scalding her mouth, causing her to swallow it the wrong way, which nearly choked her.

'Arrgh,' she spluttered, coughing and frantically fighting for breath. Shani took her cup from her and slapped her heavily on the back several times.

'Oh dear, do be careful,' Leilani mocked. 'We wouldn't want you to choke now, would we?'

Bea turned and gasped for air in the face of her nemesis. 'Leilani,' she rasped, her throat raw from all the coughing. 'I'm sure Luke could do with your help somewhere?'

'Actually it's your help I need right now,' he shouted, striding up to her stall and pointing at Bea. Leilani glared at him.

'Mine? What for?' Bea asked, still attempting to clear her throat. Luke didn't look very happy, she noted. In fact, he looked furious. She wasn't so sure she wanted to know the answer.

'Is that your Mazda on the road?'

'The blue one?' she asked.

'Yes, the dusty one, parked in front of the sign saying 'No Parking'.'

Bea grimaced and nodded. 'Ah, yes?'

'Good. Keys handy?'

'Yes.' She didn't try to fathom what exactly was going on.

'Right. Come with me,' he said, his tone not allowing for argument. He took hold of Bea's hand and pulled her through the crowd of nosy women trying to see what was going on.

'You're going now?' Leilani shouted. Bea turned to see her head about all the others, the fury on her face obvious and knew that if looks could kill a person, she wouldn't even have time to say good-bye.

'Yes, right now.' He pulled Bea out of the hall and across the lawn, pushing his way through the throng of people and over to her car.

'Where are we going?' she asked, fumbling with the ignition, relieved to finally manage to start the car at her second attempt.

'St Catherine's Lifeboat Station. Hurry, I should be there by now.'

'Really?' Bea glanced at him, and then putting her foot down, narrowly missed a hire car.

'Indicating might be a good idea next time,' he said, his voice softening. 'And thanks, by the way.'

Bea shrugged, breathless from the unexpected excitement of what was happening. 'No problem,' she said, finally getting onto the road and putting her foot down on the accelerator. 'What's the urgency?'

'Didn't you hear that loud bang a few moments ago?'

'Yes,' she said, feeling a little foolish that maybe she should know what was going on.

'That's the boom letting the crew know there's a shout, or a call out. Someone's in trouble, and if people parked where they should do,' he pointedly cleared his throat, then smiled at her, 'I wouldn't have been blocked in at the fayre.'

'Ahh,' said Bea, realising he meant her. 'Sorry about that.'

'Turn here,' he said. 'I didn't mean you, either. If you'd have parked where you should have done, I would never have got to the station in time to join the crew.'

'You're a member of the crew? Aren't you nervous?' she asked, wondering how many other things she didn't know about this man.

'No. Once the adrenaline kicks in, which is pretty much as soon as the alarm is sounded, I don't feel anything, but the need to get out there, and get to the job.'

'I suppose whenever that bang is sounded whoever is on duty must have to get to the station as quickly as possible?'

'Yes. The first ones to arrive that make up the crew for the lifeboat, launch her, and then any others who get there later wait to see if they're going to be needed.'

'How brave,' she said, turning to glance at him.

He shook his head. 'There are far braver men than me. I'm

197

just doing something that matters to me.'

Within minutes they reached the lifeboat station. Bea could see men running inside from hastily parked cars. She stopped and Luke immediately leapt out. 'Thanks for the lift,' he said, before racing towards the building and disappearing inside. Bea decided to wait and see them launch. Within moments huge wooden doors were pulled back and a converted tractor pushed the boat down a huge concrete slipway and onto the beach, smashing straight into the waves, engines already roaring and the crew kitted up inside. Bea gasped, impressed with their actions. She had never experienced anything quite so dramatic before.

She thought she spotted Luke, but couldn't be too sure, then stepping out of her car to get a better view, she watched them disappearing into the distance. The vessel turned left and Bea wondered if they were going towards the Ecrehous.

'Blimey,' said Shani when Bea arrived back at the stall to find them packing up the last few jars. 'You never told us he was in the RNLI.'

'I didn't know,' Bea said, hoping Luke wouldn't get into any difficulties wherever he was.

'Who'd have thought he would be a secret hero?' Shani nudged Bea with her elbow.

'I can't say it surprises me,' Paul said. 'Let's get out of here before the Amazon reappears and gives you a slap for running off with her man.'

'I was hardly running away with him,' Bea said, helping them pack up and thinking that chance would be a fine thing.

Shani's mother thanked them for all their 'admirable effort'. 'Quick, let's make our getaway before she finds anything else for us to do,' Paul laughed as they hurried over to Bea's car. Bea rested two jars of jam on the roof as she unlocked her car door.

'I still can't get over Luke being a real-life hero,' Paul said. 'Here, give those to me.'

Shani quickly snatched them off the roof. 'No chance. These are mine and Bea's; you said you didn't want one. Too late now.'

Bea watched as Shani held the two jars high above Paul's head so he couldn't reach them. She took a breath to speak, but was distracted by the way Shani's sweatshirt pulled against her stomach.

Bea's mind was in turmoil. How had she not noticed? Why hadn't Shani said anything to her? For once she was relieved that the others chatted continuously all the way to their homes. Bea dropped Mel off and then Paul at the shopping precinct, eventually arriving back at The Brae.

'Come on, let's get inside,' she said to Shani, barely able to contain herself.

As soon as they were in the kitchen, Bea turned to her friend. 'I can't believe you're pregnant and you never said anything.'

Shani's mouth dropped open, then her face slowly reddened. 'How do you know?'

'Seriously?' Bea stared at her friend's rounded stomach. How had she not noticed it before now, it was hardly a molehill? 'Harry?' Shani nodded. 'How far along are you?' Shani didn't answer, but sat down with her head in her hands. 'Shani, when's the baby due?'

The doorbell rang as they stared at each other in silence. 'Bloody hell, what's going on in here?' Paul laughed. 'You two look like crap.'

'I thought you were going straight to meet Guy?' Bea said, wishing she'd been left alone with Shani at least until she'd found out about the baby.

'I was, but I wanted to bring you these,' he said holding out a brown paper bag. 'And tell you that I'd just bumped into one of trainers from the gym.' He looked from Bea to Shani, eyes shining with excitement. 'You'll never guess what's happened.' He shrugged when neither of them spoke. 'The vice squad came to the studio this early this morning.' He waved his hands in the air. 'I must have had my phone switched off, which won't go down well with the owners, but it was my day off. Anyway, they got the receptionist to let them in so they could search the lockers and everything. I wonder what they were looking for?'

'Did they find anything?' Shani asked quietly.

'No, thankfully, but it's a little odd, don't you think?' He sighed deeply, his arms outstretched. 'Hey,' he said, his immaculate eyebrows knitting together in curiosity. 'Have I missed something?'

Bea looked at Shani and then back at him. 'She's pregnant.'

Paul dropped the bag onto the table before pulling out a chair and sitting down in silence. 'And she didn't tell us?'

Bea squeezed Paul's shoulder. If she was upset at Shani for not confiding in them, how bad must he feel? 'How did I not notice this?' He shook his head slowly. 'Shan?'

'So, was that business about Harry needing a scan all crap?'

Shani nodded and pulled something from the depths of her bag. 'Here, I can see you're both practically holding your breaths,' she said, holding out a piece of paper towards them. 'It's a copy of the scan of the baby.' She pointed to the black and white image.

'I can't believe it.' Paul murmured, snatching the picture from her fingers and studying it for a moment.

'Do you hate me, Bea?' Shani looked at Bea for the first time.

The pleading in her eyes made Bea well up. She walked round the table and gave her a hug from behind. 'Don't be stupid, of course I don't hate you.' She hesitated, then couldn't stop herself from adding. 'I am disappointed, though.'

'I was dreading that,' Shani said, wiping her eyes with a tissue. 'I'm pregnant with a baby I didn't plan, or originally want, and you lost the one you wanted so badly.'

Bea shook her head angrily. 'That's not why I'm disappointed. I can't believe you kept this from me.' She noticed Paul's confused expression. 'Us,' she said, correcting herself. 'Why did you keep something this important to yourself and why didn't you tell us what was going on when be asked you about this before?'

Shani shrugged. 'You have all the crap going on with the man who left you soon after your miscarriage and he,' she said pointing at Paul, 'is in love with someone for the first time since being heartbroken. I thought you both had enough happening.'

'And?' Paul didn't sound convinced. Neither am I, decided Bea.

'I discovered Harry was married and then I really didn't know how to tell you.'

'Idiot,' said Paul, squeezing her hand for a moment before squinting at the picture of the scan. 'I'm sorry, but I can't make this out. Will one of you please explain what exactly I'm looking at?'

Bea sat down and took Shani's hands in hers. She couldn't stand seeing her friend in such turmoil. Shani was always so open with them both, or so Bea had always believed. She must have been very worried about upsetting them if she managed to keep something this monumental to herself. 'It was devastating when I lost my baby,' she said quietly. 'And I admit that I do find it difficult to come to terms with my miscarriage and dealing with the date when my baby was due, but that doesn't stop me being thrilled for you.' She touched Shani's arm. 'You're going to be a lovely mum; you know that, don't you?' Bea smiled at her, attempting to reassure her. 'I'll be fine, whatever you choose to do. You having a baby will be something we can all look forward to. Something good we can enjoy. I can't believe you've gone through this by yourself.' She took a deep breath. What must Shani have been going through these past few months?

'What about Harry?' Paul asked. 'What did he have to say about the baby?'

'When I told him I was pregnant, when we went for that scan, it was after the appointment that Harry told me he was back with his wife.'

Paul groaned. 'Bastard.'

'I still hadn't quite believed his partner about him being married until that point, so to hear Harry calmly tell me about her was a bit much to take in.'

'I'm not surprised,' Bea said, wishing she could confront Harry and give him hell for what he'd done to her friend. 'We're here for you, whatever happens, Shani.'

Paul glanced at the kitchen clock. 'Damn, I only popped in on my way to see Guy. You don't mind if I race off, do you? He starts work soon and I need to see him about something before then.' He bent down and kissed Shani on the cheek. 'Don't fret about this. Sod Harry, you've got us two and we'll be all the support you need.'

'We'll catch up with you later,' Bea said. 'Shani and I can carry on chatting.' She waited for him to give Shani a quick hug and reassure her once again. Bea had an idea, but waited for Paul to close the door behind him before speaking. 'Can you stay at the flat with a baby, do you know?'

'I don't think so. That was another thing I knew I'd have to discuss with Paul.'

'You have already offered to do this and the baby doesn't make any difference.

'Really?' Shani narrowed her eyes. 'Are you sure it wouldn't be too much? I did love it when I stayed here. Too much, probably.'

'I can't have you going to some tiny bedsit when I'm rattling around by myself here. Let's face it, Shan, I have six bedrooms and only use one for me, and another as an office, which I only use to keep track of the work on the house. It's the perfect solution, surely?'

'But I wouldn't be able to pay you much as I won't be working for a few months.' Shani moved a cushion behind her in an effort to try and get more comfortable.

'I've thought about that and to be honest every little will help. It'll also be company. I didn't realise how lonely I would get living in this place all by myself with just Flea to talk to. The only problem I can see us having is with Paul. He's going to be upset to be losing you as a flatmate. It's going to be bad enough for him not having you every day at work, without you moving out, too.'

'I know,' Shani said, thoughtfully stroking her round bump. 'How on earth am I going to tell him?'

'I'm not sure. Maybe I could ask him to move in here, too?' she said. They all got along well together and another person helping towards the mortgage would be a great help. 'I do think moving in here will be the best way forward for you and the baby, though.'

202

'Yes, but what if it's one of those ones that cries all night long?' Shani asked.

'Then you'll just have to have one of the rooms at the back of the house,' Bea teased. 'I'm joking,' she said, patting Shani's bony knee when she looked concerned.

'I'd love to live here. I can't think of anywhere else I would rather be. I'm not sure if Paul will move here too, but there's no harm in asking him. What about finances? How are we going to sort out paying for things?' She held a hand up to stop Bea interrupting. 'I'm not moving in here without paying my way. You can't afford it, and it's against my principles.'

'Fine, at least we've agreed you should move in here. That's a start.'

It mattered to her that Paul didn't feel excluded, so to ask him too would be perfect. She could tell Shani didn't want to pass up her offer, and Shani had already raved about living here in the countryside with the lawns, orchard and areas of the garden, so pretty and private. Bea suspected her friend would love the idea of parking her baby's pram in the fresh air in her garden, especially knowing it would be safe there.

'Do you know,' Shani said eventually, 'even Harry's lack of interest in our baby can't dampen my mood now I know I don't have to start traipsing the streets finding somewhere suitable to live.'

'I think we both need a cup of tea,' laughed Bea. She picked up the brown paper bag Paul had left behind. 'Here, we'll need plates, too.'

Shani opened the bag to reveal the spongy cakes. 'Jersey Wonders, perfect.'

'Yes, I thought you'd say that,' Bea said, concentrating on keeping the tone of her voice cheerful. 'Full of fat and sugar, and perfect for celebrating baby news, not that he knew that when he bought them. Mmm, these are still warm.'

Nineteen

March – Darkest Days

Bea struggled to decipher her aunt's handwriting in the notebook. Why had she ever thought she could stand a chance of keeping up with her aunt's good work? She was already finding it impossible to manage it.

She picked up a brown bag of snapdragon seeds and carefully opened the twisted top, trying not to lose the precious seeds her aunt had collected from her garden the previous year. Taking a small container, Bea dipped it into the tub of peat she'd collected from the bins outside and went to pour it into the little pots, accidentally knocking over the brown bag and scattering the seeds all over the shed floor. She threw down the pot and burst into tears of frustration.

Why was she bothering with all this? Simon was right, Aunt Annabel wouldn't be here to see any of it and no one else was interested in the damn garden. She sat down on the old wooden stool and sobbed.

'This bloody house,' she groaned. Maybe Simon was right and she should simply sell it and move on. She didn't have any fight left in her. But, even though she was currently overwhelmed by everything she'd lost – her aunt, her marriage, and her baby – she knew she couldn't lose this house, too. And anyway, where would Shani and her baby go if she actually did sell up? How could she have got things so wrong?

When had her happy marriage become a sham? She'd always thought Simon so perfect, now she was hard pushed to even try and recall why she'd fallen for him in the first place. Had she ever been in love with the real Simon, or had she imagined he'd possessed those qualities she thought she saw in him? Mel had once accused her of marrying Simon so quickly because she was too desperate to create the happy family she'd been excluded from when her mum had died. She'd laughed at Mel then, but maybe, Bea mused, her half-sister had actually been right.

She blew her nose on a crumpled tissue and went back into the house. Though it was early, she opened a bottle of rosé and lit a fire, then sat back into the huge overstuffed sofa in the darkness of the drawing room with only Flea and a box of tissues for comfort. The soothing golden glow of the fire for once did nothing to improve her mood. She started on her way to get hideously drunk. She was in love with a completely unsuitable man who could end up causing her to lose her job and if she wasn't extremely careful, her freedom, too. What the hell was she playing at, and why was everything so complicated?

Bea went to pour herself another glass and finding the bottle empty, decided to get another from the fridge. The lights in the house flicked once and then went off completely. Bea carefully made her way in the darkness to the window. She looked out, but couldn't see any other lights nearby. 'Bloody power cuts,' she said, hoping she didn't need to find money to pay for the house to be rewired as well as everything else..

Turning too quickly, she caught her temple on a corner of an open cupboard door she must have forgotten to close properly earlier. Bea winced in pain. Tentatively, she put her fingers up to her head to rub it better, but instead felt the warm stickiness of blood. 'Hell, that hurts,' she moaned. Stunned and a little wobbly, she quickly padded in her slippers over to the sink to soak a wedge of kitchen roll in cool water.

Bea held the wet mass up to her head. She returned to the drawing room, thankful for the screw cap on the bottle of wine, and poured some into a glass. Her head was pounding. Maybe it was time to go to bed. No more melancholy for her. Enough now. She got up slowly, surprised at how dizzy she felt.

The phone rang on the table next to her. 'Hello?'

'Bea? Is that you?'

'Who is this?' she asked, cupping the phone in between her ear and chin. Hearing Luke's voice, she settled back down onto the couch.

'It's Luke. I wanted to phone and thank you for getting me to the boat in time for the launch the other day. I think I could have been a little snappy with you and I wanted to apologise in case I had been.' He was silent for a moment. 'Bea, are you all right?'

Why had she answered the phone, she wondered. She knew she was in no state to talk to anyone about anything, especially him. She'd had too much to drink to allow herself to talk to him without saying the wrong thing.

'I'm fine, thanks.' Bea wiped away a random tear from her puffy eyes with a handful of damp, disintegrating tissues. ''Night,' she put the phone down. She would sleep in here tonight. It was cosy and the fire should keep going for the next few hours.

Sometime later she became vaguely aware of a banging noise. Bea dragged a fresh tissue from the near empty box and blew her nose. Flea barked and ran to the front door. The banging was repeated. She pushed the blanket off and ambled blearily over to follow the dog, opening the door tentatively and peering around it to see who was making all the noise. Her eyes focused on Luke staring back at her, his face unsmiling. She pulled back the heavy door. 'What's the matter?' she asked blearily, her voice sounding odd even in her drunken state.

Luke couldn't believe his eyes. The moon shone into the doorway lighting up someone standing with one hand on the door and dried blood down the side of her face. The person vaguely resembled Bea. Only this person had a pale face, eyes so puffy they were almost closed, and hair that had once been held back in a band that was now sticking up at angles and mussed up all around her blotchy face.

'Luke, can this wait until tomorrow?' Bea asked, pushing her hands through her untidy hair and beginning to push the door closed. She stepped back from the door and turned away from him.

Luke couldn't imagine what could have happened to her. Dread filtered through the pit of his stomach. He put his hand

207

out and caught the door before it slammed shut and followed her silently inside. There were no lights on in the house and the only light seemed to come from the full moon outside. Without saying a word he followed her, sitting down opposite as she settled back down and made herself comfortable again. She seemed unaware that he was still in the room.

'Bea,' he said, keeping his voice as gently as he could and glad of the light from the flames in the fireplace. 'How did you hurt your head?'

He watched as she slowly raised her hand and lightly touched the cut. 'Ouch,' she said, flinching, her gaze troubled. 'I think it was on a cupboard door. Stupid really.'

Luke forced what he hoped was a reassuring smile. 'Is there anything I can do?' he asked.

Bea looked up at him. He felt a pang of sadness at the pain in her eyes. Something had happened between her dropping him off at the Lifeboat Station and now. He couldn't imagine what it was. 'Is it Simon?' he asked, his intuition kicking in.

She thought for a moment and then nodded slowly. 'I'm such an idiot,' she murmured sleepily, touching her head once more.

'Of course you're not,' he soothed, not sure if she was telling him the truth. 'We can talk about this in the morning.' Gently pulling her hand away from her head, he leant forward and checked her cut. It was difficult to see it clearly, but he didn't think it was still bleeding.

'I don't think it's that deep, but we should get it looked at.'

Bea shook her head and immediately winced.

'Come on, I'm not going to argue with you over this' he said, determined to make sure she was OK. 'It shouldn't take long.' He stood up and putting his arms around her, helped her to stand.

She didn't speak on the way to the hospital, but closed her eyes and seemed to be in a world of her own. Luke talked constantly, partly to keep her awake but also because he was nervous. She seemed so withdrawn and sad, and he hated seeing her like this.

The A & E Department was very quiet and Luke was

relieved when Bea was seen by a doctor within thirty minutes. 'She's fine,' the doctor said after taking Bea away to examine her. 'You can take her home now, but she'll need someone to stay with her for the night.'

'That's no problem,' Luke assured her, putting his arm around Bea's shoulders and leading her outside.

He was relieved to get Bea home again. 'Right, let me help you up those stairs and get you settled in bed. Hopefully you'll feel much better in the morning.'

'No," Bea said. 'I'll be fine sleeping in here.' She gave him a hug. 'Thanks for being so thoughtful and looking after me. You don't have to worry about me though. Why don't you go now, I'll be fine.' Without waiting for him to answer, she walked through to her living room and settled down on her settee.

He followed her. 'I'm not going anywhere.'

'Fine.' She lay back and closed her eyes.

He pulled a chenille blanket from the back of the settee to cover her and sat back down, watching her silently, the flickering shadows from the fire taking him back to that memorable evening they'd slept together.

Luke added several logs to boost the fire and tried to make sense of his feelings for her. He knew he was attracted to her, wanted to take care of her somehow, but she seemed to have more than enough to deal with at the moment. How attached was she to Tom? Damn him. It was one thing knowing Tom was good at his job, but another having to watch him spend time with Bea. Luke shook his head. How did Tom manage to get so close to her, when all she seemed to do with him was find reasons to push him away? Why was she holding back from him? He was sure there was something, but what? He didn't get it. She couldn't really believe there was something between him and Leilani, surely? He was sure that must be some sort of excuse.

While preparing coffees in the kitchen the next morning, Luke answered the phone hanging on the wall by the fridge on its first ring. 'Hello?' he said absent-mindedly, stirring sugar into the steaming black liquid.

'Who's that?'

'Who's this?'

'I asked first, oh sod it, it's Shani.'

'Luke,' he volunteered, trying not to sound too amused at her obvious surprise.

Silence. 'Er, morning, Luke. Um, is the lady of the house there please?' Shani asked, excitement emanating from her voice. He suspected she was thinking he and Bea must have slept together to find him here so early in the morning.

Luke placed the coffees and two plates of buttered toast on a tray. 'She is, but she's a little caught up at the moment. Can I ask her to give you a call when she comes round?'

'Comes round? Is she OK?'

Damn, thought Luke. Why had he chosen those particular words? He thought for a moment and remembering what close friends the two women were, knew he had to fill her in on the previous evening. 'Shani, she's not all right as it happens.'

'What do you mean?' Luke could hear the concern in her voice.

'I phoned her last night to thank her for the lift to the call out, but she didn't seem to be her usual self. So, I came round here and although she wasn't particularly happy to see me, I couldn't in all conscience leave her.'

'You've been there all night?'

'Yes, but it's not what you're probably thinking I'm about to wake her now.'

'Do you know what's wrong?'

He would love to, he thought, but didn't say so. ''Fraid not. She does have a nasty cut to her temple though, and will no doubt have one hell of a headache this morning. I don't envy her.' He hoped he hadn't said too much, but felt pretty sure Shani needed to know exactly what happened in case Bea tried to make light of everything. She needed help sorting whatever it was out, and her best friend was the perfect person to do so.

'She's got rather a lot on her plate at the moment, and to be honest I haven't helped.' Shani groaned. 'Unfortunately none of her problems are things anyone else can help with, only she can deal with them. Simon is so controlling, and she's going to have to find a way to sort him out once and for all. Although I've got a niggling feeling there's something else wrong, but she hasn't confided in me about it. Look, I'm going to ring off now, so I can come right over.'

'Thanks,' he said, relieved Shani was on her way. He knew Bea wouldn't be happy to see him here when she woke up. Hell, he thought, he'd be horrified to come round after a heavy night to find her sitting watching him. He couldn't help having feelings for Bea and had suspected from the first time he met her she could be different to any other woman he'd ever known before now. Up until now, though she'd always seemed so strong and in charge of everything, but seeing her in such a state last night had concerned him. Seeing Bea so fragile, he wondered what could be worrying her so badly. He knew she loved the house and was worried about losing it, but he had to agree with Shani, there must be more to it than anything they were aware of, but what?

Shani arrived and thanked Luke for sitting with Bea for the night. 'Let me know how she is, will you?' he asked, making a quick note of his mobile number for her on the notepad by the door.

'Will do,' said Shani, concern for her friend written all over her face.

As he opened the front door, she called to him. 'Luke?'

'Yes?'

'How will you explain to your girlfriend where you've been all night?'

'She's not my girlfriend.' Then again, he thought, aware that Leilani had a habit of pitching up at his boat on odd occasions and usually when he least wanted to see her. She was going to be impossible and surely throw a tantrum over him staying out all night, especially when she discovered that he was at Bea's, which she no doubt would.

Bea heard the front door close and stretched. She recognised Shani's voice and watched through blurry eyes as her friend entered the room. 'Ooh, my head,' Bea groaned, pushing herself up slowly, holding the side of her head with one hand. 'Hey, how did you get in?'

Shani stared at her thoughtfully. 'Luke let me in.'

Bea frowned and tried to process Shani's words. 'Luke? Here? I don't understand. Ouch.'

'He told me he'd found you in a really bad way and didn't like to leave you alone.'

Realisation dawned on Bea like a slowly dripping tap. 'Oh no, I think I vaguely remember.' She looked up at Shani, another movement that hurt like hell. 'Even my eyes hurt.'

'I know, and you look a mess,' said Shani, holding out a mug for her to take. 'Drink your coffee, then you can freshen up. You'll feel much better then.'

Bea, not having the emotional or physical strength to argue, let Shani take charge. Catching sight of her puffy pale face, swollen eyes, and cut temple, with the angry purple and black bruising glaring back at her in the ornate mirror on the wall, she groaned in anguish that anyone, let alone Luke, had seen her in such an awful state.

After luxuriating in a hot lavender bath, Bea took a couple of painkillers. She was feeling a little better. Shani wanted her to make an appointment with a doctor to ensure her head didn't need a couple of stitches, but Bea insisted it wasn't necessary. Instead, she suggested they make the most of the colder weather and go out for some fresh air. They walked along the paths in between the World War Two gun placements and bunkers at Noirmont Point and watched Flea sniffing intently for rabbits.

'Is it because of the baby?' Shani asked eventually. Bea shook her head. 'What's really the matter, then? I'm sure you're keeping something from me and it's making me nervous.'

Bea once again wondered how much easier it would have been if Tom hadn't confided in her about Luke's problems with the police and his money laundering suspicions.

'You can tell me anything, you know that, don't you?' Shani said.

Bea felt guilty and nodded. She needed to somehow explain things to Shani without breaking the confidentiality code she had to live by as a trust officer. She spent her working life looking after others' trusts and companies and it went against her principles to discuss business when she shouldn't.

'Bea?'

Bea chewed her lower lip. 'Shani, it's not that I don't want to tell you, but I'm not allowed.'

'So, it's not about the baby? I know that must be hard for you to take in.' Bea shook her head again. 'Who's it to do with?'

'I can't tell you that either, sorry. It's nothing for you to worry about, though. It's more to do with work.'

'Tom.' Shani pulled a face. 'I might have guessed.'

'Sorry?' Bea pulled on Flea's lead when he walked too close to the deep steps of a bunker. Why was Shani always so intuitive? 'Why do you mention Tom?'

Shani stopped walking and stared at her, hands on her hips. 'I knew he would have something to do with it.'

Bea stood and shrugged. 'It's difficult and Tom hasn't actually done anything wrong.'

'So, tell me. You work for the same company and he is your manager, after all. '

'He knows something that he felt I should be told, that's all,' Bea eventually confided, reining in Flea's lead to get him back to the pathway once more and out of the bracken.

Shani stared at her, a confused expression on her face. 'This has something to do with Luke, I presume?'

Bea gasped. 'You don't know anything of the sort. I've told you I can't discuss this and I really am not supposed to.'

'OK, so how come he can tell you then? I don't get it.'

'He told me to make sure I didn't inadvertently get myself into a difficult situation.'

'With Luke.'

Bea rolled her eyes. 'Will you forget about Luke, for pity's sake? I can't tell you anything else.'

Shani shrugged and began walking again. 'All I know is that something is playing on your mind and I don't like it.'

Bea hugged Shani. 'Neither do I, but there's nothing I can do about it.'

Shani stroked her rounded stomach. She stopped and took Bea by the arm. 'It'll all work out, just hang in there.'

'I hope you're right.' If it doesn't, she was just going to have to deal with it.

Shani pushed her chin deeper into her red woollen scarf. 'I wonder if Luke's boat is one of those out there?' She pointed, changing the subject. 'Mind you, it does look a little rough today.'

'I doubt it. He's moored at St Catherine's over the other side of the island. I suppose living on his boat while he does up his cottage is an obvious place for someone who loves the sea like he seems to.' She inwardly cringed at the thought of him spending all night watching her sleep. What had she said to him? God, her head was still pounding. 'Anyway, I have more pressing matters to worry about. I need to sort out this money for Simon.'

Shani groaned. 'If only you could discover what this Jersey Kiss thing is and maybe you could sell it. If she your aunt left it to you in her will then it must be worth something.'

'I know,' Bea said, shivering and doing up her ancient Burberry mac. 'But I've looked everywhere for it. There isn't any paperwork that I can find no paintings that look valuable and certainly no jewellery. If I don't find a way out of this financial mess, I'm going to have to seriously consider selling The Brae, and I can't bear the thought of losing everything Aunt Annabel worked so hard to achieve. I'd feel as if I'd let her down badly, not to mention you and the baby.'

'I know you would, but you shouldn't. We need to discuss my rent.'

Bea shivered.

'Bea,' Shani said. 'I know it's sometimes awkward to talk about these things, so I've contacted a rental agency and explained my situation. They suggested I pay you about one hundred pounds per week. Do you think that's enough?'

That sounded fine. She needed to find approximately one thousand, four hundred pounds each month. Shani wasn't an owner of the gym, simply one of the supervisors, and Bea didn't want her to worry about finances. 'Are you sure it isn't too much for you?'

'No. I'm happy, as long as you are with that amount.'

Flea barked.

Bea smiled. 'That's great. I can let Mr Peters know when I meet with him tomorrow.' Bea picked up Flea's ball and threw it for him, smiling as he bounded off like a fluffy breezeblock after it. It had been much quicker working this out with Shani than she'd expected. Then again, Shani never liked to waste time messing about, so she shouldn't be too surprised by the short and decisive conversation.

I wish I could afford to help you out more,' Shani said, wrapping her scarf another time round her neck. 'Why is it so bloody cold, it's March for heaven's sake! 'I'm sick of this weather too.'

'What time is your appointment with the bank manager?'

Bea groaned. 'Nine o'clock. It's the third time he's seen me and the poor man keeps trying to find ways to help because of my aunt, but we're not getting very far. He can only do what he's allowed to do and I suppose I'll be able to find out exactly what that will be when I see him tomorrow."

'Mr Peters will see you now,' his secretary said, showing Bea through to his wood-panelled office.

'Ahh, Miss Philips,' he said indicating a chair and opening a file on his desk. 'I've studied your income and expenditure and how much money you're hoping to borrow.'

Before he could continue, Bea told him about Shani and how much she'd be contributing by way of rent.

He listened in silence and made a few calculations. 'Have to admit I can't quite see how you'll be able to make the monthly payments.' Bea sat up straight, determined not to let him see how much his negativity was upsetting her. 'Ms Philips, much as I would like to help you here, especially as I am such an old friend of your aunt, I'm afraid that at this moment in time, I simply will not be able to sanction a loan for the full amount.' Bea opened her mouth to speak, but he continued, 'Even with your friend moving in to lodge with you, I'm afraid you'll be rather short on funds.'

Bea chewed anxiously on her lower lip. 'I have to find a way to keep the house if I possibly can.'

'I'm sure you do, but I'm governed by procedures and have to make a decision based on those. I suggest you go home and maybe discuss this with family members, see if there is something they can maybe do to help solve this matter.'

'Thank you, I will,' Bea assured him, knowing full well that she wouldn't get anywhere with any of her family. 'My ex-husband needs his money now and I'm not quite sure how my family can afford to help me.' She stood up and shook the bank manager's hand. 'I'll do what I can and get back to you, if that's all right?'

'Yes, of course it is. I will be able to arrange for you to have a partial amount, but it would be less than a third of the value of the house and not the fifty per cent you were hoping for.'

Bea forced a smile. 'It isn't enough, but I'd be grateful if you could put the offer in writing for me, so that if my circumstances change in any way, at least I know what I can borrow.'

'Yes, of course,' he nodded. 'My secretary will forward the paperwork to you in the next few days and should you find an alternative source of funds, then we can arrange to finalise the paperwork at that time. Best of luck, Ms Philips.'

Bea walked across the office to the door, and then turned to him thoughtfully. 'Mr Peters, I've been wondering if perhaps you might recall my aunt mentioning something called, A Jersey Kiss?'

His eyes widened slightly and he thought for a moment. 'I can't say that I do. What exactly is it, may I ask?'

Bea shrugged. 'I don't know. My aunt left it to me, but no one seems to have any idea what it could be and we can't find any records giving more information.'

He tapped his ink blotter with his pen and stared out of the window, looking as intrigued as she'd been when the lawyer had told her about this mysterious legacy. 'I do remember her mentioning some sort of gift to you. I know she was very proud of it, but I can't say for certain that she was referring to this Jersey Kiss. Could it possibly be a piece of jewellery? Her late husband enjoyed commissioning intricate pieces for her.' He shook his head slowly. 'I'm sorry, I wish I did know. Maybe it's a painting, or a sculpture that you've not noticed before?'

Bea hadn't thought to check the house or garden for sculptures. She smiled gratefully. 'Thank you, you've been very helpful.'

'Right,' said Shani, when Bea visited her in a flustered state at the yoga studio after her appointment. 'We'll have to speak to Paul, and let him know I'll be moving in with you sooner than we expected. He'll understand our motives, I should think. You could always consider renting out a couple of the other rooms, too.'

Bea hoped she was right about Paul, and feeling only slightly less panicky, hurried off to work to make up the time she'd taken for her appointment.

Bea sighed heavily as she walked into her house at the end of the long, arduous day. The only sound to greet her was from Flea, snoring noisily in his bed in the kitchen. Bea took off her best navy coat and hung it over the back of her chair. Great guard dog he is, she thought, comforted by his complete lack of concern with the world, and wishing she could be as laid back about everything.

Later that evening, as Bea was microwaving a lasagne dinner for one, Paul phoned. 'Poor babe, the soon-to-be mother has informed me that my loss is to be your gain.'

Bea's heart pounded hearing Paul's voice and tried to make out if he was happy or not about Shani's news. 'Yes,' she acknowledged cautiously. 'We thought if you didn't mind, Shani would have much more space living here with the baby, and of course there's the garden for all the fresh air she needs.'

'Hold it right there,' he interrupted. 'You don't need to give me the prepared speech, I do understand. After all, our lease doesn't allow children, so we'd only have to move soon anyway. Stop worrying.'

'Tell her everything, you little cheat,' Shani shouted in the background.

'Shut up you, I was about to.' Bea could imagine Paul's large blue eyes glaring at Shani in mock rage. 'If you must know, Guy has asked me to move in with him and we've been trying to figure out a way to break the news to the mother-to-be here. We were even contemplating finding a two-bedroom cottage, so she could move in with us.'

Bea realised Shani had snatched the phone from Paul. 'I'm Billy-No-Mates, of course,' he snapped. Obviously, he had taken it back from her. 'Bloody hell, can't a fellow have a simple conversation without being manhandled by some bossy woman? Go away and let me speak to my friend,' he said. 'Now Bea, where was I? Oh yes, you mustn't worry, as now her ladyship is to abandon this unexceptional abode, Guy and I can get on with searching for our love nest sooner than we had hoped.'

Bea gave a sigh of relief. 'Well that's one less problem to worry about. I'm glad to have been so helpful to you both,' she laughed. 'Tell Shani to let me know how and when I can help with moving her things here, though I'm not sure about the rent.'

'No, you don't. This isn't solely a room I'm renting, it'll be two soon, and you're letting me have use of all the house and gardens. I'm not arguing, Bea. If this isn't arranged in a fair way then I can't accept your offer to move in.'

'Shani,' argued Bea. 'You can't afford that much.'

'And you can't afford not to accept it. It is the going rate, after all. I'm not a charity case, and my parents have offered to help me with the rent while I'm not working. Well, my father has. For once he's over-ruled my mother and I had the feeling she'd been given a stern telling-off, because she was far nicer to me when I popped in to see them and discuss this yesterday.'

Bea could tell by Shani's voice that she was calmer about the situation now that her parents seemed to be coming round a little.

'I'll also make sure Harry agrees to assist in some way,' Shani added.

'All right, I give in.' Bea thought through what Shani has told her for a moment. 'We can each put in a certain amount per week for food, and I'll cover the household bills myself. Yes, that's what I'll do. I'll feel much happier then.'

Bea could hear Shani murmuring to Paul and knew by her

muffled voice that she had her hand clamped over the receiver as she discussed the finer points of their arrangements. 'Paul's nodding at me, so he thinks we're on the right track. Great, we'll do it like that then. This is going to be exciting, don't you think?'

Bea giggled. It would be fun, and the thought of having someone to chat to late into the night cheered her up no end. 'It'll take us back to our boarding school days.'

'You only boarded for two terms before your aunt insisted you came back to Jersey,' Shani teased. 'I was left there for an entire year after you'd gone.'

Bea still felt guilty for her aunt's intervention about the boarding school. She'd loved her all the more for bringing her home and it had been after that, when she went to live with her almost full time.

Bea went back to her notes and added in Shani's new agreed rental payments. It made her income appear far healthier than before. However, as generous at it seemed, she still couldn't make the figures succeed in covering the payments she would need to keep a roof over their heads.

She heard a noise outside and realised she hadn't checked if she'd received any post that day. Bea went to the hall to see what delights the postman had delivered earlier. 'Great,' Bea groaned, opening a Court Order Simon had threatened her with. 'This is a nightmare,' she said to Flea, chewing on the end of her biro. 'Damn Simon for wanting so much.'

Twenty

April – Home to Roost

The phone rang, interrupting her thoughts. 'Bea, it's Tom, I've been thinking.'

'You have?' she said half-heartedly staring down at the sheet of paper and covering letter from the lawyer's office in front of her.

'I think I should host a dinner party. Maybe invite several friends, what do you think?'

A dinner party? Bea was stumped and not exactly sure why he was asking her opinion. 'I don't see why not, you haven't really entertained in your flat yet, have you?'

'No, and I want to show my new friends that I've moved on from Vanessa.'

Bea rubbed her neck; it was painful. She must have been looking down for too long, she decided. Bea leant her chin in her hand. 'Fine.'

'Will you help me with the food?'

Aww, so that was it. Bea thought for a second or two. He sounded so unsure of himself, she didn't like to refuse. 'OK.'

'Brilliant, thanks, Bea.' He hesitated for a moment before adding. 'Is everything all right?'

'I'm having a bad day, that's all,' she explained, making an effort to be friendlier. It wasn't as if he was the one demanding money with menace. 'Being broke isn't improving my mood, Tom. Now, who were you thinking of inviting?'

'Us, of course' he replied, his voice softer. 'Your two friends, Mel, Grant, Luke and Leilani, and I thought that other couple from the Burns Supper evening. What are their names? Oh yes, Paige and Jeremy. I thought ten would make a decent number.'

Bea's mood took another nosedive. So he'd meant her friends then? And what about Guy? 'Actually, it'll be eleven with Guy don't forget.'

'Oh yes, sorry, I'd forgotten about him.'

She ignored his reaction. 'Anyway why would you want to invite Luke and Leilani?' she dared to ask, her stomach doing somersaults. She hadn't seen Luke since he had sat up with her all night when she was in that dreadful state. She shuddered to think of how humiliating it was going to be to see him again.

'They appear at the same parties we go to and anyway I have to deal with him in business, so why not? I don't think he and I will ever hit it off, but she seems very pleasant. In fact, she was the one who phoned me the other day and suggested we should all meet up.'

'She did?' Bea wondered what Leilani's motive could be for trying to set this thing up. She wondered if Luke knew anything about it, but doubted it. Maybe he'd turn down the invitation anyway.

'Yes, so it seems a little odd if I don't. I thought if I held the meal, then at least it would be over and done with.'

'I suppose so,' she replied. 'As long as you don't talk business, I'd hate to let anything slip about this damn investigation. Any idea how much longer it should going on for?'

'I don't know exactly, but it won't be too long now.'

Bea sighed. 'Do they still think he's guilty?' She didn't dare hope he'd give her the answer she wanted.

Tom didn't speak for a few seconds. 'I'm not sure. His partner's the main culprit, that's something I'm sure about. Luke is probably guilty by association more than anything, but we still have to make sure we don't let anything slip about it, OK?'

'Yes, of course.' She couldn't help smiling. Guilty by association wasn't the same as consciously committing a criminal act. That had to be better, surely?

'Fine, then it's settled. I'll give everyone a call and plan it for a week on Saturday, and let you know how you can help closer to the time. Speak soon.'

She put down the phone and took a deep breath. Flea opened one eye to glance at her before immediately falling back into a deep sleep. 'You lucky bugger, I wish I was a dog sometimes.'

'Blimey, how on earth did you manage to hide all this stuff in your room in the flat?' Bea said over her shoulder as she carried yet another box of books from her car into the house. 'Couldn't you have weeded out the ones that you've read and do something with them?'

'I love my books.' Shani pulled a bag over her shoulder and took a bin bag of clothes in each hand and followed her friend up the stairs and into her designated bedroom at the back of the house. She dropped the bags on to the bed and leant against the window sill, staring out over the orchard beyond. 'This is a perfect view,' she panted, turning to Bea. 'I can't think why you don't have this room.'

Bea emptied the bags. 'I prefer the view of the veggie garden, although I admit nothing can beat this one when the apple blossoms are in full bloom.'

Shani leant out of the window and breathed in deeply. Bea couldn't help smiling. This was going to be so lovely, having someone to share all the wonderful things about this place. 'I don't know how to thank you, Bea. You've been a life saver offering this room to me.'

'Rubbish.' Bea shook her head. 'I need your money and you and the baby need a roof over your heads. I think we're evens. Don't you?' Bea shrugged. 'Anyway, I've been looking forward to having you both here so much. We're going to have so much fun.'

Shani turned to face her and leant against the wall, resting both hands on her rounded stomach. 'Thank you, for not making me feel like a parasite.'

'Stop it,' Bea said, upset to hear her friend talking about herself in such a way. 'You're only feeling like that because of Harry treating you so badly.'

'I suppose so, but at least when he phoned me at work yesterday he did promise he'd help me out financially, not that he has much choice legally. Although he still insists he doesn't want anything to do with us once the baby is born.'

'Now why don't you start unpacking and putting some of these clothes away before they crease too badly? I'll go down and get another couple of bags. If we keep at this, we should be finished in an hour or so.'

'Hey there,' shouted Paul up the stairs. 'We've brought another car load.'

'Well, grab what you can and start to bring it up here if you want,' Bea bellowed back at him. 'Bloody hell.' Bea laughed seeing Shani's face reddening as she attempted to fold the mountains of coloured fabrics into neat piles on the crumpled bed. 'We're going to have to start putting boxes in the attic soon; there simply won't be enough room down here for all this stuff.'

Paul walked into the room and laughing and held up a pair of Shani's size eight jeans. 'I doubt you'll be wearing these for a while.'

Bea snatched them out of his hand and shook her head. 'For that mean comment you can take these few boxes up to the attic.'

'What, now?' He widened his eyes and grimaced. 'I hate attics; they're filthy places, full of smelly old things.'

She laughed but, forcing a stern look on her face, stood with her hands on her hips and held up the jeans. 'And while you're there you can have a rummage to see if you can find any paintings that could be the Jersey Kiss. I still haven't discovered what it was, but I'm sure it's probably a painting. I don't remember Aunt Annabel wearing any unusual jewellery, so I doubt it's that.'

'All right, I'm going.' He picked up one of the boxes and left the room. He waved Guy to follow him. 'You can come with me; I'll need you to hold the torch.'

'You do know he's secretly going to have a ball up there,' Shani laughed. 'He's so nosy; it'll be his idea of heaven, especially if he does find this painting.'

Bea doubted he'd find anything worthwhile. All she remembered being stored in the attic was old furniture and a few trunks of clothes, some of them dating back to when her aunt was at boarding school decades ago. 'I've been meaning to go through everything, but the thought of all the spiders hiding up there in the eaves is enough to put me right off.' She shuddered.

'This is so embarrassing. I didn't realise I had so much. And these things.' She held up the jeans. 'Paul's right, they may as well be thrown away; I can't imagine ever fitting into them again.'

'Of course you will.' Bea held them up. 'You'll lose all your baby weight in no time; you've always been so skinny. Anyway, when you go back to work all that yoga will pull everything back together before you know it.' She threw the jeans back on the bed.

They separated Shani's boxes into items she wanted to keep in either her room or the baby's and boxes to go into the attic out of the way. 'Phew, I'm exhausted. All this lifting and moving things around is harder than you think.' Bea fanned her hot face with a gym brochure. 'It'll be good to store that lot out of the way for a bit, at least until we know exactly what's happening with this place,' Bea suggested. 'If I do stay here there's more than enough room to give you your own living room, if you like.'

'Are you two actually going to help us, or are you expecting me to cart this lot up those rickety steps?' Paul complained shouldering the half-open door back against the wall and struggling in to the room laden with a box stuffed full of ornaments. 'I found this on the landing. You don't half have a mountain of tat here, Shan.'

'You didn't find anything interesting up there then?' Bea asked hopefully.

Paul shook his head, brushing a determined cobweb from his hair. 'I've had a quick peek, but nothing that could be your painting. It's very dusty and full of trunks, a scary coat stand covered with strange-looking furs, and old bits of furniture. I think you'll need to sort it out at some point.' He shrugged. 'Even if you don't find what you're looking for, maybe your aunt kept some stuff of your mum's up there.'

His suggestion gave her a jolt. She'd approached her aunt so many times when she was small about her mother's belongings, but Aunt Annabel had always rebuffed her, saying that it was too upsetting for her to go through them. She'd promised to show Bea at some point, but they'd never got round to it. 'I suppose I can look at her bits now without worrying about upsetting Aunt Annabel. I don't think there's anything mysterious up there, though. I just think she missed Mum so much she hated thinking about losing her.'

'Strange, when you think what a tough old bird your aunt was,' Shani said, smiling at Bea.

She nodded. 'I'll leave you to it and put the kettle on,' Bea said, leaving the room mainly to have a think. She'd got so used to not being allowed into the attic, apart from the time she'd snuck up there when her aunt was out, that it hadn't occurred to her to do so. What would she find?

Two hours later, having boiled the kettle on the Aga, Bea called them to sit down at the kitchen table. 'At least we've found homes for most of your bits,' Bea said enthusiastically.

'Yeah,' Paul agreed, finishing off a custard cream with relish. 'Thank heavens you had the baby's room for us to fill, too.'

'I don't understand where I hid all this stuff at the flat.' Shani pushed her hands through her short unwashed hair looking confused.

'I do, your room was always a tip,' Paul groaned. 'I'm not going to know what to do with all the space now you've moved out.' He laughed when Shani pulled a face. 'I'm only joking. I'll miss you really.'

'Anyway,' Bea said passing them their drinks, 'we can take the next few weeks to go through the rest of your boxes and bags and whittle down what you don't need and do a car boot sale or something. We're going to need to decorate the baby's room soon anyhow and can do it all then.'

'At least we have Tom's dinner party to look forward to,' Guy added.

'That's another problem,' moaned Shani miserably. 'I have to find something I can still fit into.'

Bea smiled at her reassuringly. 'It's one thing you don't have to worry about. I have more than enough clothes to lend you and I don't have the excuse of pregnancy for wearing them.'

'Great. What will you wear?'

'No idea. I would like to buy something new but we know my financial status, so it's out of the question.'

'Why don't you ask Mel if she has anything you could borrow? You look as if you've lost quite a bit of weight recently,' said Paul. 'I have a sneaky suspicion you haven't been eating properly. You don't want shitty Simon to think you're losing weight because you're missing him.'

'I can always make you some meals for your freezer if you wish,' Guy offered. 'From what I hear of your ex-husband, he sounds like the type of man who would only see your thinness as proof you pine for him.'

Bea shuddered at the thought. 'What a revolting idea.'

Paul leant back in his chair and sighed contentedly. 'I think that's a great plan, Guy. Thanks.'

Bea shrugged. 'Normally I'd say not to worry, but the idea that we can eat your food is too good an offer to turn down.'

'Yeah, thanks,' Shani agreed.

Bea noticed how pale and exhausted she suddenly seemed. 'Right, I think it's time we let Shani go and have an early night. Don't you agree, boys?'

'I'm fine.' She stroked her stomach gently.

Paul shook his head. 'No, Bea's right. You look worn out.' He motioned to Guy for them to leave. 'I think it's time we left you in peace and made our way home, too.' Paul stood up and took the empty mugs to the sink. 'I wonder what Tom will expect you to make for Saturday, Bea?'

'I don't know yet,' answered Bea, following them to the front door. She was dreading Saturday but didn't want to admit that to her friends. She would just have to put a determined smile on her face. After all, she mused as she waved goodbye to them, how awful could it possibly be?

Twenty-one

Heat and Shade

'Chateaubriand?' shrieked Shani a few days later as they pottered in the garden dead-heading the numerous rose bushes lining the driveway. 'How the hell do you cook that?'

'I've no idea.' Bea waved her secateurs in the air. 'And before you explode, I've already told him that if he wanted Chateaubriand, then he'd have to make it, but that he should rather serve something else for his guests instead.'

Shani stood with one hand on her stomach and the other on her back. 'What, like tuna melt or spag bol, you mean?'

'I'm holding a weapon, Shani.' Bea pursed her lips and narrowed her eyes.

'Scary. Ouch, damn roses. And what did he reply to that?'

'Guess.' Bea cut several roses and put them to one side, when Shani didn't answer she added, 'He said he was only joking, and you know how useless I am at knowing when people are joking.'

Shani stopped sucking the blood from her pricked finger and, eyebrows raised in disbelief, shook her head slowly.

Bea laughed. 'Why are you glaring at me?'

Shani smiled and sighed. 'Did we miss something in our teen magazines? Didn't they write hints about ways to avoid men who are full of their own self-importance?'

Bea shrugged. 'I've no idea; now stop moaning and get on with what you're doing. At least we've both decided what to wear for this meal of his. That at least is some sort of achievement for both of us right now.'

'True,' Shani said. 'You look lovely in Mel's red shift dress and nude shoes. I said it would suit you, but you wouldn't believe me.'

229

'Yes, I know, I'll listen to you next time you make such a fuss.' Bea pushed down the cuttings in the bucket with her polka-dotted gloved hand. 'I still can't believe she agreed to let me borrow it.'

Shani nodded in agreement. 'She wants us to get together for the final wedding arrangements next week; I can't think of any other reason she's lending you clothes right now.' Shani winced and rubbed her bump rapidly. 'Ooh, I'd place bets this baby is going to be a professional rugby player. He kicks like a horse.'

'Sit down for a bit and take a break.' Bea indicated the low wall by the driveway.

'You never did say what he's going to cook for Saturday.' Shani bent down carefully, panting lightly to take the edge off the pain.

'No idea. It's a shame Guy hasn't been asked to do the cooking.'

'I'd be looking forward to it far more if he was. I'm surprised he was able to get a night off on a Saturday, too. I've got a feeling poor Guy has been forced into taking it.'

'Perfect timing,' said Tom, opening the heavy bleached oak door and pecking her lightly on the cheek. He turned to lead her towards the kitchen. 'Come and check if this is OK, will you?'

Bea lifted the foil and breathed in the smell of the perfectly cooked joint. 'Looks and smells great.' So he had been joking when he'd asked her to make the Chateaubriand.

'Mel will kill you if you get fat on her dress,' Shani whispered from behind her.

Tom covered the meat, careful not to splash his immaculate chinos and Hugo Boss pink shirt, and then walked with her into the neutrally decorated lounge. He poured Bea a glass of wine from a crystal decanter.

'Thanks, just what I need.' She took a sip and carefully placed the glass down on the dining-room table, noting that it looked as if a ruler had been used to place each piece of cutlery at precise distances from each other. 'Apple juice?' he asked Shani.

Paul and Guy arrived. 'Shan, you're looking voluptuous, for

once,' Paul said, pointing at her boobs. 'You look so different with those, or are you wearing a clever bra?'

'Stop it,' Guy said, hugging Shani. 'You're looking very beautiful tonight.'

Shani smiled. 'It's me and a clever bra. I thought I'd make the most of having something to show off for a change.'

Tom marched over to them, holding a glass of wine in each hand. 'Great to see you both here,' he said, fawning over Guy in such an obvious way Bea knew Paul would be teasing him the following day. 'I've done my best, but the food won't be to your standard.'

'I'm certain it will be delicious,' Guy said. 'It is a treat not to be the one catering for others.'

Tom smiled as if not quite sure whether he was being teased not. 'Well we'll soon find out.'

The doorbell rang and Tom hurried to welcome Mel and Grant in to the apartment. Luke and Leilani followed closely behind. She was wearing a short, olive-green shift dress that Bea suspected no one else she knew could carry off so well. Tom and Grant stared at her, both forgetting to close their mouths for a few moments.

'Shani, you look blooming,' Luke said, seemingly oblivious to the intense focus on his partner. 'Hello, Bea, it's good to see you again.' He pushed back his hair. 'Red suits you.'

The soft tone of his baritone voice sent Bea's stomach into rapturous somersaults. 'It's good to see you too,' she replied, her voice a little higher than she would have liked. Grateful to hear the doorbell ring once more, she took the opportunity to leave Luke talking to Shani and opened the door to Paige and Jeremy.

After a few drinks, Tom showed everyone to their seats. Bea noticed Luke's designated chair was diagonally across from her own and couldn't help sensing his gaze. By the time they got round to eating the delicious New York cheesecake Tom had bought from the French patisserie in town, she managed to find a break in Leilani's constant chatter. 'How's it been living on the boat?' she asked, thinking of the storms they'd experienced the previous week.

231

'Exciting is probably the best way to describe it,' he said, his blue eyes twinkling. 'Summer's definitely the best time to live on-board though, especially if you don't like rough weather.'

'Have you always had boats?' Shani asked. 'I hate them, and once got sick before the ferry had even left the harbour.'

'It's true,' Bea laughed, recalling the day they'd decided to visit St Malo for lunch. 'The water was like a mirror, nothing moved at all.'

Shani nodded. 'I really am crap on the sea. It ruined our day because all I did the whole time we were in France was moan about having to come back again that evening.'

Luke shrugged. 'Sailing doesn't suit everyone. I've always had boats, from very small ones when I was a teenager and saved up to buy this one. I wanted a boat like *Trojan*, for years and when the opportunity arose to buy her, I was determined not to miss it.'

'Sounds very like *Swallows and Amazons*,' Paul laughed, sounding as if he had already had one too many to drink. 'Can we come and have a look on board?'

Tom frowned at him and turned to Luke. 'What type of boat is it?'

Luke sighed dreamily, 'She's a magnificent Rampart, forty-two-footer.'

Tom didn't seem any the wiser and Bea decided he probably had no more idea about boats than she did. 'When was she built, then? I mean, if you've lusted after one since your childhood, she must be something special.'

'She's much older than me. She was built in 1955, and made of wood. She takes more looking after than a fibreglass boat, but I love the character these older boats have.'

Bea couldn't help noticing how his eyes sparkled as he spoke lovingly about his home.

'Where is she?' Paige asked, dabbing her mouth with her napkin.

'She's moored in the marina most of the time, and I've been sleeping on her while I'm carrying out the renovations at my cottage in St Catherine's.'

'But surely that's not allowed?' Paige asked. 'Aren't there

regulations about living on boats?'

'Not really.' He gave Bea a meaningful glance and half smiled. She flushed at the memory of their trip to the Ecrehous together.

'Luke doesn't stay there by himself all that much,' Leilani interrupted, nudging Luke as she raised a perfectly waxed eyebrow, her innuendo blatant. 'Personally I can't see what all the fuss is about. It's an old boat and not very high spec as far as I can tell and, let's face it, this is hardly the climate to be living on-board, is it?'

Luke shook his head and sighed. 'It probably depends on what you're used to.'

By the time Tom served coffee in the comfort of the cream living room, Leilani was holding court with Paige, Jeremy, Tom, Mel, and Grant, telling them stories about her experiences on the runway. 'Catwalk to you guys.'

Shani and Guy whispered and giggled in the corner of the room and Bea watched silently. Luke walked over to her and sat down. Leaning back into the cream leather settee, he turned his body to face her. 'Shani tells me she's moved into The Brae with you?'

Bea nodded.

'I could have helped with her stuff. I gather she had more than she expected hidden away at her flat.' He smiled at the thought.

'I've no idea where she's been hiding it all.' Bea raised her eyebrows. 'It's all stored away now though and it's made me realise I should also tidy up my attic; the Jersey Kiss could be stored up there somewhere.' She took a sip of her drink and relaxed further into the seat. 'It's lovely having her in the house,' Bea admitted, staring into her half empty glass.

'I've missed you,' he murmured, so quietly she wasn't sure if she had imagined the words.

Bea blinked in surprise and looked up at his serious expression. 'Sorry?' She glanced around the room, relieved no one appeared interested in their conversation.

'You heard me,' he said gently, not taking his eyes away from her. 'I've enjoyed being with you tonight. Can't we put everything behind us and start again?'

Bea didn't have to consider his invitation. 'Yes, of course,' she said, wishing it was that simple.

He smiled at her and Bea felt her heart pounding as her breath shortened. She studied his rugged face.

'Is everything all right?' he asked. 'You're looking a little tense this evening.'

Bea sighed. 'It's nothing.'

'Bea,' Luke said, placing his hand on hers. 'Tell me, maybe I can help.'

Why not, she thought. If he was crafty enough to find a way to launder money then maybe he could come up with some idea how she could sting Simon. She told him about the court order and her desperation to sort things out.

Luke thought for a moment.

'I've thought of something you can do,' Mel said, sitting down next to Bea. 'You want to apply for a Martin Order.'

'What's that?' Bea had heard of a Mesher Order, where the wife is given enjoyment of the home until an agreed time, usually when the youngest child had finished their education, but they didn't have children. 'I've never heard of it.'

'I've heard of one of those,' Luke said thoughtfully. 'They're pretty rare though, aren't they?'

Mel nodded. 'I don't know why I didn't think of it before. Too much time listening to my mum fretting about this wedding, I suppose.'

Bea wished she'd hurry up. 'What is it though? Tell me.'

Mel leaned closer to Bea. 'It's where one party signs over the property to the other's name.'

Bea narrowed her eyes in disbelief at his suggestion. 'You seriously believe Simon would agree to sign over The Brae to me. Just like that,' she clicked her fingers.

'You never know,' Luke said. 'It's worth a try.'

'I'll definitely ask him, but I'm pretty sure he'll tell me to bugger off.' She sighed, wishing Mel's suggestion had been remotely achievable.

'Think about it,' he said, 'maybe there's a way to persuade him.'

'I'm sure we'll find some way round this,' Mel said. 'We just need to have a damn good think.'

'Listen up everyone,' Leilani said, standing in the middle of the room. Bea tried not to show her annoyance at Leilani interrupting their conversation. Leilani held up an almost empty wine glass and beamed pointedly at every one in the room. 'Lukey didn't want me to say anything tonight.' She pouted prettily, her immaculate lipstick unmarred by the three-course meal. 'But I'm too excited to keep it to myself any longer.'

Bea looked quizzically from Leilani's exotic features back to Luke. He shrugged. 'I've no idea what she's talking about.' He shook his head. 'Never could cope with much alcohol,' he joked raising his eyebrows. Bea giggled, enjoying his disparaging remarks against the perfection of womanhood showing off in front of them.

'Lukey and I are to be married,' she squealed, theatrically throwing her arms out to encase her audience.

'What?' Luke's eyes widened. Bea's heart pounded, but she couldn't move and watched as Paige immediately congratulated Leilani with kisses and hugs. 'I know, I know. Isn't he darling?' Leilani blew a kiss at Luke who sat motionless, staring back at her in silence. 'We haven't had a chance to choose a ring yet, but it needs to be exactly what we want.'

Bea, a stabbing jolt in her solar plexus, tried her best to make sense of what she'd just heard. She looked away from Leilani and focused on the cream carpet. She heard Luke swear under his breath and felt him push himself up from next to her, watching as he crossed the room in one stride to his bride-to-be.

'I think it's time we were leaving,' he announced, his voice a monotone and his expression like granite as he took Leilani firmly by the elbow. 'Thank you for a wonderful evening, Tom.' He shook Tom's proffered hand before turning to Bea. 'It was good catching up with you.'

Bea, unable to form any words, looked straight into his eyes, making a valiant attempt at hiding her confusion and hurt. She decided she must have taken what he had said to her, during their intimate conversation, the wrong way. I'm a fool, she thought, forcing her mouth into a smile which she suspected more resembled a grimace.

'Good for Luke,' Tom cheered closing the front door behind them. 'I never saw that coming, did you?' he asked Paul.

'Nope.' Paul stole a glance at Bea who did her best to reassure him by trying to look as happy as the rest of the group. Paul stood thoughtfully for a moment. 'I suppose when you feel the time is right to do these things, you just get on and do it.'

'Well,' Mel interrupted defensively, 'at least they won't be able to book anything before my wedding day. I don't want Leilani overshadowing me.'

'She couldn't do that,' Grant said, for once saying the right thing. 'You're far prettier than she could ever be.'

Paul squealed. Bea wasn't sure if it was because of Grant's comments to Mel, or that Guy had probably kicked him under the table to shut him up.

'Don't forget we're meeting on Monday at lunchtime to visit the florists with Mum,' Mel said, oblivious to any undercurrents. 'I think I've now made a definite decision about the flowers.'

The party seemed to have reached a natural end. Paige and Jeremy said their goodbyes and as Tom showed them out, Bea and Shani went to the kitchen to make a start of filling the dishwasher and washing up glasses. 'What the hell was that all about?' Shani whispered over her shoulder.

'I'm meeting Mel at the florists.' Bea emptied the dregs of the wine glasses in the half sink and began washing the fine crystal glasses.

'You know what I mean. What the hell was that business with Leilani and her wedding?' She flicked Bea lightly with a tea towel. 'I saw you all cosied up on the settee with Luke, and the stunned expression on your face when she made her announcement.'

Bea stared at the bubbles on the glass she was washing. 'I'd rather not talk about it right now if you don't mind.'

'I'm sorry, Bea. I don't know what he was saying to you, but I'd bet a pound to a penny he didn't see that coming either.'

Bea turned to face Shani. 'He certainly didn't argue with her,' she snapped. 'I'm confused, that's all. I think he means one thing and then something happens to make me realise I've totally misread the situation. I've made a bit of a twit of myself. It doesn't matter, don't worry about it.'

'Hey, girls.' Tom strode into the room. 'Please don't worry about clearing up. My cleaning lady has agreed to come in for an extra couple of hours tomorrow morning to do it all.'

'On a Sunday?' asked Shani, staggered that anyone would need to pay someone to clear up so little mess.

'Yes, she said she's happy to have an excuse to get away from her husband for a bit, and its extra money, so who am I to argue?'

Shani shrugged. 'Fine, you don't have to tell me twice. We may as well head for home and leave you in peace.'

'Thanks for a lovely evening.' Bea gave Tom a kiss on the cheek. 'Everyone had a great time.'

'Yes, I thought it went well. I'll let you all get on your way then and see you at the office on Monday. Thanks for coming.' Tom patted her on the back, returning to Mel and Grant in the lounge.

Shani looked sideways at Bea. 'Er, I would ask what that was all about, but you won't answer me truthfully, so I shan't bother. Ouch, this baby can't half kick.'

'Poor you, maybe he'll end up being a premier league footballer and keeping his mother in the manner she wishes to get accustomed to.'

Shani dried her hands. 'Don't think I've missed you changing the subject just now.'

Bea held the door open for her friend. 'Come on, let's go,' she said. It was time for her to stop wasting emotion on someone who was already spoken for. Enough was enough. Bea knew it was time to move on from Luke and focus on her future. She had a lot to sort out, and now was the time to get on and do it.

Twenty-two

First of May – The Scent of Lilies

Bea sniffed the intoxicating perfume of the lilies of the valley she'd picked from the garden earlier that morning and scrolled down her phone directory to find the number for her lawyer. It was nine days to crunch time, or D-Day as Simon had teased her, and she was relieved she had taken the day off work. Bea was also glad she'd thought to use the same man her aunt always went to.

'I'm sorry Annabel's house is considered part of your marriage settlement,' he said, shuffling papers in the background. Bea didn't know how he ever found anything on his permanently untidy desk. 'I know it seems very unfair to you, and I know she would be unhappy to think Mr Porter benefiting in any way from her death. I think the best thing we can do is include in my court papers confirmation that your aunt had booked an appointment to see me, but died before she was able to do so.'

'Do you think it'll help?'

'I can't be certain. The judge has to base his judgment concentrating on the legalities of each case, not the emotions behind them.'

Bea chewed her lower lip; this was so frustrating. 'What about the Martin Order my sister told me about?' Bea needed some good news, and wasn't sure how much longer she could afford to keep up this fight against Simon.

'It's a good idea, but in all reality, unless you have something with which to bargain or a way of persuading your ex-husband, then I think you'll be hard pushed to get him to accept this suggestion. By agreeing to the order he will, in effect, be giving up any rights to the property or any monetary gain from its sale.'

'Mmm, I can't see him doing that.' Bea chewed her lower lip for a moment. 'But you think it's worth a try?'

'Definitely. You won't lose anything by speaking to him. I could write to him formally with the suggestion, but I think sometimes these things are better dealt with on a more, shall we say, personal level.'

Bea also knew how much a letter from him would cost her. She checked her watch, concerned that she was being charged for every six minutes he spoke to her. 'I thought I'd speak to his girlfriend,' Bea said, picturing going to Claire's apartment and knocking on her door.

'Worth a go, and Beatrice? Your aunt was a close friend of mine for many years; I want you to know how proud of you she would have been.'

Bea swallowed the lump in her throat. 'Thank you.' The last thing she wanted to do was sell The Brae, but if all else failed then she wouldn't have much choice. She didn't relish the thought of having to move Shani out either. Not when she'd been so relieved at the thought of moving in with her baby, but whether she liked it or not, Bea knew she was running out of options, as well as time. She glanced up at her wall calendar. 'First of May, only nine days until court.' She ruffled Flea's head.

She thought through her plan and decided that the best chance she'd having of getting anywhere with Claire would ideally be when Simon was away on one of his business trips, but she had no idea if he had any booked in the next few days, but as long as she went to the apartment when he was out, that was all that mattered.

Bea's alarm on her mobile pinged. 'Hell,' she groaned, already running late for lunch with her stepmother and Mel at Chica's Restaurant. She couldn't wait for the wedding to be over and not have to spend so much time with them, but it meant a lot to her dad, so she grabbed her keys and went to collect them, wishing she'd thought to meet them there, rather than give them a lift.

They waited for Mel to pay for a pink crystal she had fallen in love with in the adjoining shop. 'It'll be perfect to hang in my bathroom window,' she said dreamily. 'Oh look, Bea, there's ...' Mel started, leading the way out of the shop and into the small courtyard.

'Who've you seen, dear?' Joyce asked, looking through the window to where diners were seated around numerous metal tables and chairs eating their lunch alfresco under the overhead gas heaters.

'Er no one, it wasn't anyone,' she insisted, grabbing Bea by the arm and pulling her away through an archway towards the car park. 'I think it's full here, let's try somewhere else.'

Intrigued by her sister's reaction, Bea turned to peer over Mel's bony shoulder and was astonished to see Tom, head bent towards Vanessa, as he listened to something she was saying.

'Please don't cause a scene,' Mel begged, pulling her intrigued mother with her free hand. 'Let's go and have lunch somewhere else.'

Joyce took her lead from Mel and, hating a drama more than most things, nodded her agreement. 'Yes, darling, let's go.'

Bea frowned and followed. Why would she want to make a fuss? Surely they didn't still believe that she had any feelings for Tom, she thought, irritated by their persistence, but not minding leaving before sitting through lunch. Aware Tom had spotted her, she gave a discreet wave. His serious expression contradicted Vanessa's triumphant one. Bea walked to her dusty car. 'Everybody in,' she said.

Bea had barely closed the front door on her arrival home when the phone rang. Noticing it was Tom's number, she decided to ignore it. The answer-phone clicked in.

'Bea, this is Tom. Pick up the phone. I want to explain about meeting Vanessa for lunch.'

Bea picked up the phone and sat down on the Bishop's seat in the hallway. 'Tom,' she sighed. 'I don't know why you feel the need to do this. There's nothing going on between us and if you and Vanessa want to get back together then I think it's great.'

There was a momentary pause. 'Bea, I only met Vanessa at Chica's because we needed to discuss the children and I thought

241

she wouldn't get all dramatic on me if we met somewhere public.'

'Whatever, it's not my business. I don't really know why you care what I think.'

'What do you mean?' He sounded hurt.

'Tom, we're not seeing each other. I'm happy by myself. We work together and yes, we do sometimes go out in a crowd together, but I really don't have a problem if you go out with anyone else.'

'We get along well though?'

She could hear the neediness in his voice and had to concentrate on not snapping at him. 'We do, and we can still go out for the occasional meal together, but as friends. I hope your ex-wife doesn't think there's more going on between us than there is, because I'm not up for being used as some sort of pawn between you both.'

'Everything's fine. There's nothing going on, really.'

Bea wasn't sure what she was missing, but something didn't feel right about this, she decided.

Later that evening, Bea was pleased to find Shani still up watching television in the living room. 'What's the matter?' she asked, noticing the grim look on Shani's face. Then it dawned on her. 'Mel's phoned, hasn't she?'

Shani sighed dramatically and threw her head back against the sofa. 'She ranted on for over an hour tonight.'

'Oh no, poor you,' Bea laughed sympathetically.

'Poor me, indeed, I had to keep moving the phone from one ear to the other, they were so hot. I thought she'd never go, and she doesn't get hints, even big ones, like 'sod off Mel, I'm knackered'. Thankfully, Grant started complaining about their dinner getting cold.' She pushed herself up and followed Bea through to the kitchen.

'So what's the latest, dare I ask?' Bea sniffed and tried not to smile at the realisation that Shani must have burnt her toast again. She made them both a mug of tea.

'You mean, apart from you catching Tom being seen with Vanessa?' Shani teased.

'I know. Mel and Joyce really can be painful sometimes,

especially when they get together. Those two love any hint of a drama.'

'I suppose he had a good excuse for being out with his ex?'

Bea rolled her eyes. 'Who cares? I think they're trying to make each other jealous, or something childish like that. I'm not going to get caught up in his problems.' She pulled her hair back into a ponytail and twisted a band around it. 'I suppose Mel wants us to meet with her wedding planner again then?'

''Fraid so, and she wants us to help her put the seating plan together next weekend and I couldn't think of an excuse quick enough to get out of it.'

'Balls.'

'Balls indeed.' Shani pushed her swollen fingers through her short black hair. 'The fatter I get the less my brain seems to connect, and as if it couldn't get any worse, guess who's coming to help?'

'Please don't tell me my stepmother will be there, too?' Shani nodded slowly, an agonised expression on her tanned face. 'She is.'

'Thank God we've only got another few days of this wedding stuff,' Bea said.

'You'll never guess what?' Mel asked them as they sat at a stark white table at the wedding planner's studio surrounded by fake flower arrangements, white, pink, and grey chiffon and several heavy black folders. 'Paige bumped into Leilani the other day and she insists they're having an enormous wedding in early September.'

A tingling sensation shot through Bea's chest. She concentrated on not changing her expression.

'So soon?' Shani asked. 'How the hell are they going to book everything at such short notice?'

'No idea.' Mel waved the feather from her pink flamingo pen across her cheek. 'Especially when you think she'll have to arrange hotels and flights and such for her family and friends from the States. I don't fancy her chances of being able to get anywhere decent at this late stage.'

'You have to book at least a year in advance for the better

hotels,' Joyce sniffed. 'I don't know who this young woman thinks she is, but this is Jersey, not Texas, and there aren't many places catering for larger weddings over here. It'll be like an episode of *Dallas* I shouldn't wonder.'

'True,' Mel said looking a little happier. 'I do like Leilani.' Shani snorted loudly. Mel ignored her. 'But she acts like she's something special and she's very spoilt. If she thinks she can pick and choose, she's in for a shock.' She lowered her voice. 'I don't fancy Luke's chances when she puts her mind to having something and not getting it.'

Shani laughed. 'Hey, that's a point. They'll either have to put the date back to next year or at a quieter time this season or maybe just have a smaller wedding.'

'Can't see that happening, can you, Bea?' Mel asked. 'Bea, what's the matter?'

'Nothing.' Bea shrugged. 'I was just thinking.'

'What about?' her stepmother asked. 'Are you feeling all right? You do look rather peaky. I hope you're not going to come down with anything ghastly.'

'I'm fine,' she assured her. 'If Mel has a hundred guests, we can have ten on the top table, with the rest of the guests seated around a further ten tables.'

Shani and Mel stared at each other. 'Weren't you listening?' Mel asked. 'We were saying ...'

'Melanie, I know what you were saying,' Bea interrupted. 'But I'd rather get on with these wedding plans than waste time wondering what Leilani and Luke are doing. Now can we please get on?'

'Quite right.' Joyce raised her eyebrows pointedly at Mel.

The wedding planner re-joined them. 'I think we're nearly in agreement about the main points. The colour scheme ties in beautifully with your dress, and the groom's cravat and waistcoat. Now we want to make sure you're completely happy with the floral arrangements. There'll be no changing your mind after today.'

'But we still have eight days left,' Joyce said, pushing forward her folder. 'I have a few suggestions here.'

'The flowers will need to be flown in, Mrs Philips, and

244

sourced by my contacts in England. There won't be any time for changing minds.'

Bea noticed Shani steal a peek at her, and then thinking better of saying anything, took one of the folders and flicked through it.

'There are some surreal ideas in here. Hey, look at this one.' Shani pointed at an ostrich feather standing in a small iron base in the shape of a bride's shoe with tiny brides and grooms hanging from it at odd angles.

'There'll be none of that tat on Melanie's tables, Shani, thank you very much,' Joyce insisted. 'No, we decided on a shallow vase with one or two orchids floating inside for each table. Simple, yet classy.'

'That sounds lovely.' Bea winked at Shani. 'I think Shani's hormones are giving her strange ideas.'

'Well at least we know my wedding photos are going to be incredible.'

'What do you mean?' Shani looked at Bea and raised an eyebrow.

'Now that Luke is to be Grant's best man, of course.' Bea opened her mouth to speak, but couldn't think of anything to say. What was Mel up to now?

Mel lowered her voice so her mother couldn't hear. 'It did take a bit of persuasion from Grant.' Bea had thought an old school friend was going to be his best man, but wanted to hear what else Mel had to say, so didn't interrupt. 'Since our engagement party, they've spent quite a lot of time together,' Mel said. 'Don't forget they knew each other from school, they go way back. Grant says he still feels guilty for breaking Luke's nose during a rugby match years ago.'

So that's what happened to it, thought Bea, liking the extra character the bump gave his otherwise perfect face.

'I just wish Leilani didn't have to come. No doubt she'll look amazing,' Mel added.

'I bet she will,' Bea and Shani said in unison.

'And you,' Mel nodded at Bea, 'as my maid of honour will be partnered with Luke now. Won't that be fun?'

'Yes.' Bea forced a smile, Mel must have missed the point

when she said she thought the small children should be bridesmaids, obviously Mel assumed being a maid of honour was something else entirely. The sooner this wedding was over and done with the better as far as she was concerned.

'Don't interfere now, Melanie,' Joyce snapped. 'Concentrate on these exquisite place cards.'

'Before your sister rams one up your nose,' Shani whispered, leaning close to Bea.

Twenty-three

Second of May – Blooming Fabulous

Bea couldn't believe how large Shani's stomach had grown and had to concentrate on not staring at it. She was relieved that the wedding would soon be over and she could concentrate solely on her legal problems. Mel was driving her nuts and the atmosphere between Paul and Shani was exhausting. It was only seven days until the first anniversary of Annabel's death and Bea was dreading every second of it. She couldn't believe her aunt had been gone for almost an entire year.

She turned her thoughts to Paul and how terrified he seemed to be about being there when Shani gave birth, and if she was honest, Bea felt the same way. She shivered and patted her mobile. The contact details of the maternity ward were there, the taxi firm number was there, too. There was no need to panic. It never ceased to amaze Bea that someone could live on an island only five miles by nine and not bump into people for years, especially, she brooded, if they didn't want you to. And she was pretty sure Luke was avoiding her. She had kept a low profile socially and, as much as she missed seeing him, she felt it was the only way to deal with being in love with someone she couldn't have. She wasn't sure why he was keeping away, though. It was going to be difficult enough seeing him at the wedding, she thought, hoping she remembered to watch every word she said to him.

'Have you thought more about where we can book to go for Mel's hen night?' she asked Shani. 'We've already left it a bit late to arrange something.' The sun had just forced its way out through a layer of thick clouds after a particularly forceful shower. Everything in her garden shone as Bea pulled on her Wellington boots in anticipation of a couple of hours of therapeutic weeding.

'Really? I thought she didn't want to do anything. Anyway, you think this bulk will want to party right now?' Shani panted, rubbing her back and sitting down on the large pine carver.

Bea laughed. 'You're not that big,' she fibbed, waving away Shani's hand when she went to playfully slap her. 'We have to arrange something for her.'

'I know. How about arranging a night at Effervescence, that's probably the easiest option.'

'Effervescence, that's a brilliant idea.' She thought for a moment. 'What about my stepmother, though? It's not the sort of place I'd imagine her agreeing to go.'

'Tough. We need to book somewhere I can sit for most of the evening. We can eat and then enjoy the show.'

'It's the show that worries me.' Bea grimaced. She'd been to see the brilliant sketch show with the hilarious overly made-up transvestites. It was perfect for a hen party, but not one that included Joyce.

'Why?' Shani pulled a cushion behind the arch of her back and leant against it.

'Because its men dressed as women and some of the jokes can be a bit rude.'

Shani straightened the loose knitted jumper over her stomach. 'Yeah, I forgot about that. Well, it's either that or a quiet meal somewhere else. Not very hen-like though. Mel's hardly the condoms-tied-on-a-hat sort of girl and I can't see Joyce supping her martini from a willy-shaped straw, can you?'

'No.' Bea laughed, an image of her horrified stepmother filling her mind. 'Why don't we ask Mel, just to make sure? We don't want to upset her and have to deal with Joyce's ranting, too.'

'True,' Shani laughed. 'She's tense enough about the whole thing as it is, especially now there's the threat of Leilani competing with her in the bride stakes. Oops,' Shani winced. 'Sorry, I didn't think before speaking then.'

Bea took a weary breath and glared at her friend. 'You've nothing to be sorry for. I've got no interest in what Luke and Leilani get up to,' she lied. 'I'll give Mel a ring now, and then we can book something.'

Bea came back from the phone. 'Surprisingly enough, it's to be Effervescence and Mel told me Joyce will be fine, especially if we open a bottle or two of Laurent Perrier Rosé here before we set off. So that's what we'll do. Mel will bring the booze and I've already phoned and arranged it for Saturday.'

'If I'm still around to join in.' Shani cupped her enormous bosoms as best she could. 'I swear these are growing by the day. I'd give my eye teeth for these to stay this big. Why is it the only time I have enormous boobs, I have a matching belly, too?'

Bea studied her friend. 'You do look different with those, but I think the novelty would probably wear off after a while.'

'Are you kidding?' Shani jiggled them gently up and down. 'I think they are amazing. I'm going to have to get implants once these go down.'

Bea shook her head doubtfully. 'Mel said Guy and Paul are also welcome on the hen night. Apparently they're honorary girls. Joyce won't be too happy, because they aren't girls, but hopefully she'll be too pie-eyed by then to care.'

'You hope.'

'Ladies,' Paul said, stepping in through the French doors. 'I've just got a text from Mel about her hen night. Good choice.'

Bea stood hands on hips. 'I may as well take these damn things off; I can see I'm not going to get any peace this morning.' Resigned, she kicked off her beloved boots and pushed her feet into her bunny slippers.

Bea moved away her legal folder a couple of hours later. 'I can't wait until it's over.'

'What, the wedding, the court date, or my giving birth?' Shani stroked her stomach with both hands. 'It's like some sort of countdown.'

Paul thought for a moment. 'Have you heard from Harry at all?'

Shani's shoulders drooped at the mention of his name. 'I don't expect to now. I'll just contact him when the baby's born, like I agreed to do and we can take it from there.'

Paul stroked her shoulder. 'Sorry, chick, that was a bit insensitive of me.' He turned his attention to Bea. 'I heard Tom's put his new apartment back on the market. Now why would he do that? He's only just bought the place and probably hasn't even finished paying for that expensive furniture. It doesn't make sense.'

'How do you know all this?' Bea wasn't naive enough to think there was no truth at all in what Paul was saying.

Shani sighed. 'You can't do a thing in Jersey without everyone knowing your business.'

'Are you insane?' Mel pushed away the silver sash bearing the title 'Bride-to-be' on it in neon pink. 'I'm not wearing that hideous thing.'

'It's your hen night.' Bea tried in vain to place it over Mel's carefully straightened mane of chestnut hair. 'At least we haven't bought you "L" plates.'

Shani grabbed the other end of the sash and pulled it over Mel's head. 'Come on, let your hair down just this once. You did far worse to Bea when it was her turn.'

'I don't care; I'm not wearing any stupid sashes or badges. I thought I was letting my hair down by agreeing to come here.'

'Forget it, Shan, she's not going to give in.' Bea folded the sash and pushed it back into the paper bag. 'You have no sense of fun sometimes, Mel.'

'I don't spend hours getting ready to go out to look completely stupid. Besides, Mum would be horrified.' She pulled on her grey silk jacket over her matching shift dress and shoes. 'We'd better hurry up and get in the taxi. She's had a couple of glasses of bubbles, so we don't want her to sober up too much before we get there and realise what she's in for. God, I hate hen dos.'

Paul was waiting with Mel's other friends at the bar. 'Wine this way,' he shouted pointing at several bottles. Most of them, Bea noticed, were half empty already. 'I've checked our table and thankfully it isn't right in front of the stage, so we'll have a great view, but there's less chance they'll pick on Mel.'

'Good, I'll leave if they do,' Mel moaned, taking a glass of wine from him and handing it to Joyce.

Joyce sat between Mel and Bea and seemed to enjoy her meal, although Bea assumed the wine was going a long way to keep her so relaxed. She couldn't remember seeing her stepmother so chilled. It made a pleasant change.

'Don't those barmaids have the most enviable figures?' Joyce tilted her head; Bea noticed her helmet hairstyle didn't move a millimetre. 'They should be models, not working in a restaurant.'

Mel grimaced at Bea. Bea knew the moment was coming when it would dawn on her stepmother that those barmaids were in fact barmen. She winced as a vice-like grip attached itself to her wrist and her stepmother turned slightly in her direction. 'Beatrice? Those are men,' she half whispered, half mouthed.

'Um, yes, that's right.' Bea unclenched the nails from their imbedded position in her stinging arm.

'But they're wearing full make up and frocks.'

'I know.' Bea widened her eyes at Mel's horrified expression, knowing that however she reacted to this discovery would be the deciding factor as to whether Joyce panicked or not. 'Isn't it fun?'

'Fun, dear?' She looked aghast at the suggestion. 'Fun?' she repeated, panic rising in her voice.

'Yes, Mum,' Mel agreed, supporting Bea for once. 'You know all the best people come here and it's almost impossible to get a table unless you book months in advance?'

'Are you certain, darling?' Joyce didn't look as convinced as Bea would have liked and didn't take her eyes away from them.

'Mel's right,' Bea assured her. 'In fact the last time I was here, I spent a good few minutes chatting with the Lakeland-Joneses, who were here for their anniversary celebration.'

'Good grief.' Joyce looked astounded by this information. She turned to Mel and then Bea, her bony hand resting on her chest. 'Well, if you're quite sure, darling. I must admit they do look rather spectacular and the food has been sublime.'

Bea watched Paul and Shani at their end of the table, as they tried not to laugh at Joyce's reaction. She rolled her eyes

251

heavenward, pleased they had chosen to come here. The lights dimmed, and Joyce gasped as a six-foot drag queen wearing a two-foot high, candy pink wig sashayed past their table, pursing his lips at Joyce, who watched awestruck as he stepped up onto a podium and announced the start of the show.

'How on earth does he walk in those heels?' she asked as the cast began singing an adapted risqué version of *The Sound of Music*.

By the end of the evening, Bea had given her stomach muscles a far better workout by laughing at the show than she could have managed by going to the gym.

'Thanks so much for tonight,' Mel said. 'I was a little concerned about the venue, to be honest, but I have to admit it's the best party I've been to in years.'

They waved Guy and Paul off in their taxi and Bea laughed when Joyce tried to explain their evening to Dad. He looked a little stunned by her enjoyment of it, too and Bea could see his eyes twinkling as he tried not to laugh.

'It sounds as if your mother has had an educational evening, girls.' Bea and Mel kissed him on his cheek. 'I'll bet she boasts about this to her lady friends for months to come.'

Their taxi dropped Mel off first. 'Thanks again for organising this evening, you two,' she said, ignoring their pleas and paying the driver for her part of the fare. 'It was far better than I expected,' she added, a big grin on her face, before waving and disappearing into her front door.

'Cheeky bag.' Shani sat back into the plastic-back seat. 'She should have trusted us to arrange an amazing evening. Mind you, despite having to go to the loo about a seventeen thousand times and not drinking anything stronger than sparkling water, I had a brilliant time, too.'

'And me,' Bea said thinking back over the evening. 'I was a bit worried when you became hysterical a few times; I had a horrible feeling you might go into labour.'

'I did get a good kicking for most of the evening, but it was worth it. The show is brilliant.' Shani slipped her feet out of her ballet flats. 'Only a week to go until the wedding of the year and this little stranger makes his or her entrance. I can't begin to imagine how it's all going to change my life.'

Twenty-four

Eighth of May

Bea knocked at the door. She'd checked her watch and, aware that Simon was a stickler for routine and would probably be at the seventh hole of the La Rue Golf Club by now.

'I'm coming. Hang on a sec.' The door opened and Claire stared, open-mouthed, at Bea.

Bea couldn't believe how untidy this usually impeccable woman looked. 'I'm sorry to bother you without phoning first, but I thought you might not agree to see me,' she said, staring at Claire's unbrushed hair and smudged make up.

'And you would have been right,' Claire snapped, tightening her dressing gown around her stomach. 'What do you want?'

'I'm sure you're sick of Simon ranting about our finances and me?' she asked, knowing how Simon went on about matters he couldn't control.

'You're not kidding.' She looked Bea up and down. 'I know you weren't expecting him to leave you and I'm sure you're probably resentful of me for having the baby you lost.'

Bea winced. 'Not quite, but carry on.'

'Well, Simon seems to think, and I have to say I believe him, that you're only dragging this on because you can't bear to let him go completely.'

Bea did her best not to show her irritation. Did this woman seriously believe such nonsense? She stared at her and realised that she did. 'Claire, the only person who's causing unnecessary anguish for us all is Simon. I inherited that house; I love it, and don't want to part with it.'

'Yes, but he's entitled to half. He told me.'

'I was left that house by my god-mother, I shouldn't have to pay him any part of it,' she said, not quite sure even she

255

believed what she was saying. 'It's not as if he even needs the money, is it?'

Claire frowned and shook her head. 'No, I don't suppose so.' She stepped back and motioned for Bea to enter the apartment. 'Why don't we sit down? I've got a feeling this is going to be interesting.'

Bea walked in and sat down on one of the sumptuous cappuccino suede sofas. 'It's beautiful in here,' she said, aware how this place and her house were at opposite ends of the spectrum when it came to interior design.

'Thank you.' Claire sat opposite her. 'You were saying.'

'Yes, well, Simon doesn't need the money and if you want our finances to be settled once and for all so that he can be granted his *decree absolute* and be free to marry you, then all he has to do is sign a Martin Order.'

'A what?' Bea explained that it would mean that Simon would transfer the property outright to her. 'And you think he'll agree to that, do you?'

Bea shrugged. 'It's down to you to persuade him.'

'Me?'

'Think about it. I want to move on, whether Simon believes that or not. If we sort out the problem with the house, then the divorce can be finalised. You can marry Simon and your baby will be born into the sort of family unit I know he'd rather be part of.'

'I suppose so,' Claire said thoughtfully, chewing a broken fingernail.

'If you can't get him to agree to this, then you'll need to ask yourself how much influence you do have over him, despite carrying his baby. Also, I'd think you must worry that he left me and moved on to you without any conscience at all. What's stopping him from doing the same to you?' she said, aware she was being a little spiteful, but not caring for once. 'Don't you want to prove to yourself how important you are to him?'

Claire chewed her lower lip. 'Much as I want to argue with you, I admit you're voicing some of my concerns.' She looked at Bea, her puffy eyes showing some uncharacteristic softness. 'I feel bad about having an affair with Simon behind your back.'

Bea shrugged. 'Yes, well that's all in the past now,' Bea said, relieved that she'd at least made Claire think further than her latest wallpaper for once. 'We need to think ahead and I'm sure you want me out of your life as much as I want to be away from it.'

Claire nodded. 'Absolutely.'

'So you'll talk to him?' Bea could barely contain her excitement.

'I will.' Claire stood up. 'He's not going to like it though, you do know that?'

'I do, but I think it's time Simon was forced to put someone else's emotions before his own, and if you're going to have his baby then you need to know that your feelings matter.'

Bea left the apartment. She couldn't help smiling at the thought of Simon's reaction to the suggestion of a Martin Order. 'Let him try and talk himself out of this,' she said as she unlocked her car door, grateful to Mel for coming up with the suggestion.

The night before the wedding Bea tried on her cerise bridesmaid dress and matching bolero jacket with its three-quarter length sleeves. She hadn't been sure about the style when Mel had first told her about it, but they'd shortened the skirt a little and now it felt a bit more like something she'd choose to wear. She picked up one of the satin shoes that had been dyed to match. Mel had also insisted her dressmaker make a handbag in the same shade. The only thing Bea hadn't agreed to was having her shoulder-length hair cut into a neat bob. It would never be sleek like Mel's; she had far too many curls. 'Anyway, I like it wild and loose,' she murmured stubbornly, accepting a fascinator being clipped into her hair was going to be as far as she'd go.

Bea had let Mel book her in for a manicure after her sister had shrieked in horror at the state of her nails. She wasn't sure how she'd be able to type at work with the acrylic tips attached to her own shorter nails, but they did look pretty smart. Bea was surprised to realise she was looking forward to dressing up the following day.

She stepped into her bubble-filled bath to enjoy an hour's reading before trying to get a decent night's sleep and had only managed to read a few pages when her mobile rang. At first she ignored it, grateful when it stopped, but then it rang again and she knew that the caller was someone who was determined to speak to her. 'Bugger,' she grumbled, stepping tentatively out of the bath and dragging a towel around her. 'Shan, why are you calling me on my mobile? I thought you were staying in tonight.'

'I am.' Her voice was strained. 'I'm in my bedroom.' There was a brief pause and some panting. 'I'm in labour.'

'Don't panic,' Bea said, throwing her phone down on her bed. Dragging on her dressing gown, she ran down the landing to Shani's room. 'Shani, are you all right?'

Shani was bent over, leaning with one hand on the bed and the other on her back. 'I need to get to the hospital. Soon.'

'But the doctor said you'd have hours before you'll need to go to the hospital.'

'I've been having contractions for hours. You don't think I'd have called you at the first twinge, do you?'

'Why the hell not?' Bea snapped, immediately feeling mean for panicking. 'Sorry, I'll calm down in a minute.' Bea's heart hammered rapidly in her chest as she tried to remember what they should do next. 'Quick, let's get you down to the car.'

'If you're driving me to the hospital, I think you had better get dressed, don't you?' Shani groaned and held onto her back. 'Shit, this hurts!' She panted a couple of times until the contraction passed. 'I think I've got a bit of time still.'

Bea panicked. 'What do you need me to do?' Her brain had gone into meltdown and for some reason wouldn't cooperate with her.

'Take a deep breath. That's it. Now another one.' Shani rubbed her back and smiled at Bea. 'This is scary but I can't help feeling excited now that it's time.'

'Me too,' Bea said, concentrating on trying to look calmer than she felt.

'I'll get myself down the stairs and you dress and give Paul a quick ring; he should be here in no time.'

Bea left Shani panting and phoned Paul. 'Oh my God,' he shrieked. 'Give me ten minutes max.'

She ran to her room and grabbed the first thing she could find, noticing as she ran into Shani's bedroom that she was wearing her grass-stained jeans and tatty off-white sweatshirt she'd been wearing earlier 'Right, I'll take this,' she said, picking up Shani's overnight case and ran down the stairs to the car.

'Let me help you with that,' she said, taking the seatbelt from Shani in her trembling hands and carefully fastening it around her huge stomach. 'Now where's Paul?' She paced back and forth on the gravel waiting for him to arrive. 'We should have arranged to meet him at the bloody hospital.'

'Calm down, I can hear him now,' Shani shouted, wincing in pain.

'Why don't we just take his taxi?' Shani suggested waving Paul over as he paid the taxi driver.

'No reason to, I'll drive,' Paul said.

'No, you won't.' Bea snatched the keys back from him. 'I'm fine, I'll get us there.'

'Bea, please will you do me a favour and give Paul the car keys.'

'What for?' asked Bea, hysteria rising in her voice with each word.

Shani patted her lightly on the hand. 'Because I want to get there in one piece and you're making me nervous. Why don't you have a stiff drink and go back to bed and try and get some sleep before the wedding tomorrow?'

Paul took the keys from Bea's hand and gave her a kiss on the cheek. 'Stop stressing. We'll be fine and I promise I'll call you as soon as baby puts in an appearance.'

'But I want to be with you.' Bea pushed her head into the window and pleaded.

'I know you do, and I love you for it. But to be perfectly honest, Bea, for once in his life, Paul appears to be strangely calm and I need that right now.' She winced and sucked in her breath. 'I think we ought to be going. Paul will call you as soon as anything happens.'

Paul turned on the ignition and the car flew backwards, only stopping when it collided with Bea's low granite wall. There was a sickening crunch, and he immediately stopped, and took a few breaths.

Bea didn't bother checking her car, but wasn't so sure he was as calm as he was making out.

Shani puffed. 'Take it easy. I only asked for you because I thought you'd be a safer bet than her.' She waved Bea away.

'What?' Paul screeched, becoming more panic-stricken.

'Why am I the calmest one here? Everything's fine; this is all perfectly normal. Now get a grip and let's go. We'll get there in plenty of time. It's not too far, thankfully. I wish I'd kept your taxi and gone in that and left you two here to be hysterical together.'

'That's enough,' Bea shouted, opening the driver's door. 'Get in the back, Paul, I'm driving.' She grabbed hold of his jacket and pulled him out of the car.

A couple of minutes later Shani frightened them both by bending forward, one hand on the dashboard and the other on the mound of her stomach and started to puff and pant again. 'Phew, that was a bad one.' She winced, her face flushed with the exertion. 'At least it's the middle of the night and we don't have to worry about the traffic.'

With almost pathetic relief Paul pointed to the lights ahead. 'Hospital, there's the hospital.'

'Thank heavens for that,' Bea whispered.

'You've both done very well. Now, stop here and let me out of the car.' Shani pushed herself up out of the seat. 'I'll make my way in and start the registration procedure and you park the car and follow with my case.'

Bea nodded and watched her amble off for a second or two, marvelling at her bravery before wheel-spinning towards the car park. She and Paul found the back door Shani had indicated and rang the bell. 'This is terrifying,' Bea said, wondering how she thought she could give birth at any point in her life.

Eventually a tired-looking midwife unlocked the door. 'How do you know we're really here with one of the women in labour?' Paul asked.

Bea glared at him. 'The security is not your problem, Paul, shut up.'

'Because there's a certain look that partners of expectant women have,' said the woman. 'And both of you have it right now. So, do you want to come in, or not?'

They followed her up to the labour ward and waited in the hallway for fifteen minutes. 'What checks do they have to do anyway?' Bea wondered.

'I would have thought getting her bulk onto a bed would be top of their list.' Paul paced along the tiled corridor. 'Why is it so quiet in there?'

Bea shrugged. 'I suppose they're getting her changed and checking the baby is actually on its way.' She hoped it wouldn't be too long until they could rejoin Shani; Bea couldn't bear to think of her being frightened.

'I'd be shitting it, if I were her right now,' Paul said, reading Bea's thoughts. 'There's no going back now, poor girl.'

Bea sat down on one of the chairs and tapped her foot on the floor. 'Why won't they call us in?'

The door finally opened and the midwife waved them over. 'Shani's ready for you both to come in now.' She smiled at Paul. 'You don't need to look so terrified, everything's fine.'

Bea walked in first, her eyes widening at the sight of Shani lying with her long, slim legs up in stirrups.

'And there's another contraction,' the midwife said cheerily. 'Come in quickly, you two, and please try to stay out of the way.'

'Glad you could, argh, both make it,' Shani groaned.

Bea felt lightheaded and doubted it was due to the intense heat in the room; the look of pain across her best friend's usually unlined forehead was shocking. Paul shielded his eyes from the bottom end of the bed. 'They could face the top of your head towards the door,' he grumbled. 'Or have a warning note outside somewhere.'

Bea glared at him. 'Don't be such a baby, you're not having to do anything,' she said through clenched teeth, not quite certain she had heard him murmur something about being traumatised for life. She took Shani's hand in hers, wincing when Shani almost crushed her bones with a grip most men would be proud of as she panted frantically through her contraction. 'Ouch, Shan, can you let go a little?' she complained as Shani sucked on a tube she was holding in her free hand. 'Gas and air?' she asked. Shani nodded.

'I could do with some of that,' Paul said, concentrating his wide-eyed gaze on Shani's face.

'What's the matter?' The young nurse, smiled. 'If either of you think you're going to faint, then go outside. You'll find a water cooler in the hallway.'

Paul shook his head and grimaced.

'Phew, that was a bad one,' Shani said, turning to smile at Paul. 'You look worse than I probably do.' The midwife put on her gloves and examined Shani once again. 'Surely I'll be ready to push soon.' The woman nodded and smiled.

This was going to be a long night, Bea thought. Maybe the thrill of watching new life entering into this world was a little over-rated. She decided should she ever feel broody again, she would have to visit this place; it would soon put her off wanting babies.

'She's had a baby,' Paul shouted down the phone to Guy two hours later, his voice trembling.

'Well, that's a relief,' he teased over the loudspeaker. 'What sort of baby?'

'What do you mean, what sort? A baby.'

'Is it a boy, or a girl?'

'Oh, a girl. She looks so cute and tiny, though she's a bit crumpled still, but I think she'll plump out a bit. I think they said she was three kilos or something, though I've no idea what that is in real terms.'

Bea pulled a tissue from her sweatshirt sleeve and blew her nose.

'Congratulations,' Guy said. 'I can't wait to give her a cuddle.' Paul told him he'd see him later and ended the call. 'You need to take it easy for a while after what you must have been through,' he told Shani, and then frowning looked over at Bea. 'Never mind her, you're looking a bit knackered.'

'You don't look so hot yourself.' Bea peered down into the clear bassinette and felt a tug at her heart as the baby took her little finger in her hand.

'Gorgeous, isn't she?' Shani yawned and although her face was puffy from the effort of pushing, Bea thought her friend had never looked more beautiful. It felt strange to see someone as tomboyish as Shani looking so maternal and serene. She could tell by the adoring way Shani was gazing at her baby that she'd be an incredible mother, with or without Harry's involvement.

'You're so clever and you were so brave.' She hugged Shani, careful not to disrupt the drip in her arm. 'She's lovely. I'm sorry I was so panicky getting you to the hospital.'

'Don't be silly, you were both brilliant in the end. You'd better get a move on; didn't you have to be at your stepmother's an hour ago?'

Bea frowned. 'An hour ago?' She rubbed her eyes and yawned.

'The wedding, it's today.' Bea stared at her trying to take in what she was saying. 'You go and have a fantastic day. Give Mel my love.'

Bea retied her ponytail and checked her watch. 'Shit.' She blanched. 'I'm so late.' Bea pulled an agonised expression, making Shani smile. 'Nooo, I don't want to go.'

Shani giggled. 'Behave yourself, you'll look gorgeous, and you're going to have fun. Take some pictures with your mobile if you get the chance and send them to me.' Bea nodded. 'Oh and Bea, thanks for everything. You've been a star.' Bea sniffed aware her chin was starting to wobble again. She blew her nose. 'No, don't you dare start crying,' Shani said, welling up. 'I'm allowed to. No one's going to see me for hours yet. Mel and your stepmum will never forgive you if you ruin the photos with bloodshot eyes and a big red nose.' She pushed her friends away gently. 'Go on, I'll see you both when it's all over.'

'This is one hell of a lot of trouble to go to, to get out of Mel's wedding,' Paul teased.

'Perfect timing though, don't you agree?' Shani arched an eyebrow. 'I know. I couldn't have really planned it any better, could I?'

Bea shook her head and took one last look at the baby. 'Right, here goes,' she said, trying to raise a little enthusiasm for spending the next few hours with her hysterical stepmother and bossy sister. 'Finally, the wedding day.'

'I need a coffee so strong you could stand a ruler in it,' Paul said, rubbing his face with his hands.

'Bugger coffee,' Bea laughed, hurrying down the corridor towards the car park. 'I think I'll need a couple of vodkas before I'm in the mood to face this lot.'

Twenty-five

Ninth of May – Archway of Roses

Bea drove home in a haze of emotional exhaustion. She didn't care what the time was; she had no intention of leaving the house until she'd had a quick nap, freshened up, and had a hot shower. She phoned her dad to let him know she'd be about a couple of hours late and to ask him to break the news to Joyce and Mel as best he could. Bea washed her hair, unable to stop thinking about the emotional night she'd shared with Paul and Shani. Now the baby was safely here, all Shani's cries of pain didn't seem so disturbing. She couldn't imagine anything more worthwhile than giving birth. She felt the tears welling up and scrubbed her face. 'No time for regrets,' she murmured, grabbing her electric toothbrush and cleaning her teeth.

'Hello, darling,' her father said smiling at her, relief obvious on his lined face. He glanced at the plastic-covered outfit she was holding. 'Give me a kiss and hang your clothes inside, then come and let me show you inside this monstrosity.'

She looked past him to the enormous white marquee covering most of the back lawn of his beloved garden. 'Red carpet?' she said, wondering how long the whole construction had taken to put up, down to the carpet meandering from the driveway into an entrance decorated with an elaborate archway made up of hundreds of deep red roses, lilies and a mass of greenery. 'Wow, you don't do things by halves, do you, Dad?'

'This display wasn't my idea.' He puffed on his pipe. 'When your stepmother refused to lower the amount of invitees, I had no choice but to hire this damn thing. The temporary lavatories cost as much as a smaller marquee. They're out the back. Smart wood panelled ones with porcelain basins and proper towels, no less. None of the usual tat, or so I'm told.' He shook his head.

Bea hoped he'd manage to relax at some point and enjoy today. 'Don't let Joyce catch you smoking again,' she whispered, following him through inside the massive space.

'Let her,' he said, straightening one of the white-covered chairs. 'Look at the top table. We're going to die of heat sitting in front of the windows.'

Bea agreed. 'That is incredible though,' she said, indicating the elaborately iced wedding cake displayed on a small round table.

'Don't even try to estimate the cost of that thing,' he said, puffing on his pipe.

Bea looked at the tiny clouds of smoke coming out of the side of his mouth and gave him a hug. 'Mel's very lucky to have you,' she said, kissing his cheek. 'We both are.' She touched one of the large chiffon bows tied round the middle of each chair to match the bridesmaid's outfits and squinted up at the silky lining of the marquee moving gently in the light breeze, lit by cascades of tiny prisms from the crystal chandeliers, later to be muted to give off a softer glow, that she was certain must have been Joyce's idea.

'She has a thing about lighting,' her dad said, shaking his head once again. 'I'm sure she needn't have spent quite so much on this wedding, so much of it seems like extravagant nonsense.'

Bea believed him. 'The price of the pink feathers in each table arrangement were enough to make my eyes water.'

'The bloody table arrangements for each table cost more than your stepmother's and my entire wedding. Look at the damn things, ridiculously over the top.' Bea murmured her agreement as she took in the elaborate creations, each displaying a large, cream cathedral candle bound in thin rope and ivy, with even more arum lilies woven into the rope and finished off with the large pink feathers. Very odd. 'Flipping heck, she must have commanded an entire nursery's stock of the things. I'd have been more than happy to help, you know. There are so many flowers in my garden right now.'

Her father shrugged. 'It's almost obscene really, when you

think you're paying for all this for only one afternoon. Things have certainly gone up since you and Simon were married.' He turned to face Bea and took her hands in his own. 'Talking of which, I know I can't help you pay him off, especially since this production has expanded into something out of one of those glossy magazines.'

Bea kissed him on the cheek. 'Dad, it's fine, honestly,' she assured him, although she couldn't help feeling a little choked, although she wasn't too sure why, because it certainly didn't have anything to do with Simon. Tiredness probably, she decided.

'No, it isn't, but I can help towards your legal fees. And before you argue, I insist. I want you to beat that sod in court. Annabel and I fell out over you many times over the years, but she loved you, very much, and she wouldn't have wanted him to have half her house, especially not after what he did to you.'

Bea gave him a hug. 'Thanks, Dad that would be wonderful. Now all I need to do is find a way to prove that Aunt Annabel was intending putting in a clause in her will to make sure he didn't benefit from her death in any way.'

'Damn law. Whether you inherited the house when you were still together or not, I don't see how that house can be considered a matrimonial asset; he was messing around with someone else. It's not right.'

'Please don't worry about me, Dad. We've got a brilliant day ahead of us.' She laughed. 'Even if it's all a little over the top and I'll just have to find a way to sort Simon out.'

'Good girl, you remind me so much of your mother when she was your age.' He put his arm around her as they walked towards the house. 'I still miss her, you know,' he said, lowering his voice. Bea swallowed the lump in her throat. 'Right, you'd better get in there, they'll be panicking if they don't see you soon.' Bea nodded, unable to speak for a moment. 'How come you were delayed, anyway?'

She cleared her throat and took a deep breath. 'Shani went into labour during the night. She had a baby girl a few hours ago. By the time I got home, unexpectedly dosed off for longer than I'd intended, and then showered, I ended up being late.'

she explained, relieved to have something else to talk about. Bea nodded her head in the direction of the upstairs windows. 'I'd better go and make my presence felt, before I'm missed.' She hugged him and raced up to the spare room. 'Ooh, your hair looks gorgeous, Mel,' she said spotting her sister having her hair primped and curled. Before Mel could answer she held a hand up. 'I've got exciting news. Shani had a little girl last night.'

Mel squealed, knocking the hairdresser's hand away. She turned to Bea. 'Is she OK? Is the baby gorgeous?'

Bea tried not to laugh at the hairdresser's irritated expression. 'Yes, they're both doing great, although Shani's a bit tired after everything she's been through.'

'Melanie, sit still. You don't have all day to get your hair done,' Joyce said, taking Mel by the shoulders and facing her towards the dressing-table mirror once again. 'That's wonderful news, Bea; now please can you get changed? You're already late and we still have to do something with your hair.'

She held Bea's fascinator up for the hairdresser to see. 'We need this in Bea's hair as soon as she's changed into her bridesmaid outfit.' She smiled at Bea. 'What a relief Shani didn't spend the night here after all. It would have upset Melanie's entire routine and imagine how ghastly it would have been if her waters had broken over my new spare linen.'

'Mum,' Mel shouted, indignant on her friend's behalf. 'What a thing to say.' Before they could descend into a row, Bea left them and went downstairs to the kitchen to make some tea and toast. She was starving and hoped that breakfast would keep her going for the next few hours.

'Coping?' asked her father, listening out for Joyce's high-pitched voice. 'I'm keeping my distance from those two.' He pointed upstairs. 'They're getting more anxious as the hours pass.'

'I know, they're driving each other nuts already.' Bea buttered her toast and ate it hungrily.

'Thankfully the caterers are here and organised, the florist has left, and, although I don't wish to tempt fate, it appears that we're keeping to schedule.' He shook his head and smiled at

Bea. 'Apart from you, that is.'

'Beatrice, get up these stairs immediately.' Bea grimaced at the sound of her stepmother's command.

'I suppose I'd better do as she asks,' she giggled.

After too long being made up and her hair being fussed with, Bea was relieved to be able to change in to her outfit and then help Mel with her elaborate puffball of a dress and veil. 'You look sensational, Mel,' she said, happy to see her sister looking so excited. For some reason they looked even less alike today. Mel, with her shiny, almost black hair all glossy and up in a French pleat and her with her wild blonde hair and blue eyes never managing to look very sleek. Mel looked more like Shani than she did Bea. No wonder people found it surprising to discover they were half-sisters.

'I do, don't I?' Mel said, lifting out her skirt and smoothing down the bodice of her dress. 'Listen, I can hear the cars. Bea, quick, your shoes, hurry up and put them on.'

Bea slipped her feet in to the towering heels and went to rescue the small bridesmaids from Joyce. The smallest one's jaw was set and Bea could tell she was on the brink of rebellion. She took them by the hands and followed Mel and her mother out to the cars. The phone rang, but Eric grabbed it. 'Get them in the car, I'll see who this is,' he said, waving them outside.

'That was Tom,' he said, a few minutes later joining them outside. 'He sends his apologies but has been unavoidably detained somewhere. He said he'll text you.' He motioned to the back of Joyce's head as she rearranged her wide-brimmed hat in the back of the second car. 'Joyce won't be impressed that her table plan is going to be even more out of kilter,' he said, unimpressed with the late cancellation. 'At least Shani has a decent excuse for not turning up.'

Bea couldn't imagine what Tom could be doing. It was a Saturday and surely even he didn't have to work over the weekend.

'He said he would give you a call later and explain,' her father added, shaking his head.

Bea sighed. It didn't bother her whether he turned up or not, but she wasn't looking forward to Joyce finding out.

'What? Oh, Eric,' Joyce snapped, when he told her the latest news, as if it was his fault Tom wasn't going to pitch up. 'This ruins my entire seating plan, Beatrice. This really isn't acceptable.'

'But it can't be helped,' Bea said, slyly passing a sweet to each of the little bridesmaids. 'Let's not worry about it now. This is Mel's big day and we need to make sure she doesn't have any reason to get in a state about something we can't do anything about.'

Bea settled into the back of the limousine, soothed by the smell of the vintage leather seats. Her phone bleeped. She read the text from Tom asking her to go to his apartment later. '*I have something urgent to talk to you about and need your help. Please come round whenever you can, it doesn't matter what time. We can have a quick chat. T x*' He'd never asked her for help before. Bea considered his request and replied, saying she'd go to see him as soon as she could.

She put her phone into the small matching bag and closed her eyes, making the most of sitting still. Not sure how long she'd dozed off for, she was jarred awake by Joyce hissing directions in her ear.

'Get out of the car, this instant.' Bea checked her mascara was still reasonably in place and tripped out of the car. 'Oof,' she said, her breath being forced out of her lungs as someone caught her at the last minute before she managed to plant her face onto the tarmac.

'You OK?' Luke asked, looking as shocked as she probably did. 'That was close.'

'Stupid girl,' Joyce said through gritted teeth, grabbing the other bridesmaids and positioning them behind Mel as she stepped out of her car. 'Always day-dreaming.'

Bea pushed the fascinator from in front of her eyes and back where it was supposed to be. 'Thanks for catching me,' she giggled, more out of shock than amusement. 'That could have been pretty embarrassing.'

'You think that wasn't?' Mel laughed.

'Right time, right place,' Luke said, still holding on to her waist. Their eyes locked and Bea straightened her dress. Luke glanced down at his hands. 'Sorry.' He let go and raised an eyebrow. 'Well, I'd better get back in the church and find the groom. He only sent me out to check if you lot were on your way.'

'See you inside in a minute,' Bea said, watching him entering the church.

'I told you he'd look great in my photos,' Mel said, winking at Bea.

Eric linked arms with Mel. 'When you get inside, we'll follow on,' he said to Joyce pointedly. 'OK, girls, I think this is your moment.'

Bea watched him whisper something in Mel's ear before giving her a kiss on the cheek. She could remember him doing the same thing to her. She gave the little bridesmaids a big smile. 'Ready?' They nodded. 'Come on then, let's help Mel get married.' She motioned for them to start walking down the aisle and stepped into the cool church behind them to where Grant and Luke were standing facing the altar. Unable to wait any longer, Grant turned to look past them to the back of the church, where Mel and her father were standing. His eyes lit up in such a way Bea felt sure they'd always be happy together.

She looked to his left, coming eye to eye with Luke. Her breath caught in her throat; he looked so gorgeous. Her stomach did a lustful flip as they stared at each other. He gave her a little nod and smiled. 'OK?' he mouthed. Bea nodded, uncaring that she'd almost made a complete prat of herself outside moments before.

Joyce waved at her, breaking the spell. Bea passed Paul, already dabbing at his eyes with a hankie. Guy rolled his eyes heavenward and Bea tried not to giggle. Poor Paul, the emotion of the last twenty-four hours was beginning to take its toll on him, too.

'Bea,' whispered her stepmother as she reached the end of the aisle. 'We're sitting over here. Girls, come along.' She noticed Luke talking to Grant and showing him the two wedding rings. Bea was certain Luke would be too well organised to ever forget something as vital as the rings. Grant patted his best man on the back; she was glad that Luke had been asked to take part after all.

The music changed and everyone turned to see Mel begin walking down the aisle, one arm linked through their father's. Bea couldn't help smiling. She looked so beautiful and he so proud. He winked at Bea and she felt her throat constrict. Someone cleared their throat and Grant took a deep breath as he waited for his bride to reach him. Even by Joyce's high standards, Bea could see Grant had scrubbed up well. She couldn't help thinking how lucky her younger sister was to be marrying the man of her dreams in such beautiful surroundings.

Bea looked over at her sister and dad slowing down towards them. He looked so handsome in his suit and cravat, she wished he'd kept some pictures of his wedding to her mum around for her to see; they must have made a beautiful couple. She pushed the thought away. Mel smiled from one side of the church to the other, then over at Grant, her affection for him unmistakeable. Mel held out her heavy bouquet and Bea stepped forward to take it, as arranged.

Bea couldn't believe it was a year already since she'd last laughed with her aunt. She would have given anything to spend the day by herself at home thinking about her. She caught Luke's eye just as a stray tear escaped down her carefully made-up cheek. His smile vanished. He stared at her briefly, before concentrating ahead of him.

The wedding ceremony was soon over, and after seemingly endless photos, Bea was relieved when they were ushered into the waiting cars to be driven back to the house for the reception. She was beginning to feel as if her body was working automatically. Bea wondered how Shani was getting on and, stifling a yawn, she took her place in the queue with the other guests waiting to walk down the red carpet past the assembled line-up. She listened vaguely to the conversations going on all around her, knowing she had never met most of these people before, and would probably never see them again.

She was grateful to finally reach Mel. Bea swallowed a lump in her throat. She felt sure her sister had never looked more beautiful or serene. She congratulated Grant and was getting into the flow of taking a hand, thanking the person who proffered it when it dawned on her that the large tanned hand she had in fact taken hold of was Luke's.

'Why have you stopped?' he teased, his eyes glinting mischievously. 'Don't think I didn't notice you'd kissed practically everyone else before me in the line-up.' Bea laughed, feeling strangely winded and lost for words. 'Anyway, why aren't you standing here greeting people, too?'

She lowered her voice so Joyce couldn't hear her. 'Because I was determined not to be.' She went to give him a kiss on the cheek, amused at his annoyance, only for him to turn his face at the last minute and ended up catching him on the mouth.

'That's more like it,' he whispered.

Bea, embarrassed to have been caught out by such a simple prank, took a breath to say something to him, just as she was unceremoniously pushed forward by a tank of a woman with a harsh blue rinse. 'Move along, young lady, you're not the only person in this line-up.'

Grateful not to be seated at the top table, but next to Guy, Bea couldn't help glancing every so often at Luke who, she admitted, looked more attractive than any man deserved to.

'He really is a perfect specimen, and don't think I didn't notice that kiss he gave you. Not what you would expect from a soon-to-be-married man.' Paul sat down beside her and Guy kissed her on both cheeks. 'Where's what's-her-face, I would have thought she'd be here taking notes and making sure her efforts over-shone Mel's?'

Bea had forgotten about Leilani, though she couldn't understand how she'd managed to do so. 'I've no idea. I'm sure she must be here somewhere. I've been so busy refereeing the bridesmaids I haven't had a chance to notice who was here and who wasn't.'

'Your stepmother is ranting over there about Shani and "he-who-shall-not-be-mentioned" nearly ruining her table plan.' Paul poured them each a glass of wine from bottles sitting on the table. 'She wasn't impressed with Shani's timing, and as for Tom, well, put it this way, I hope he's got leprosy or something nearly as horrible, because I can't imagine an excuse good enough to allow him to cry off at the last minute like he did.'

273

Bea took a sip, relieved to be able to quench her thirst, the coolness of the liquid helping her to feel more awake. 'Poor Shani, as if she could go in to labour on purpose.' Bea raised an eyebrow. 'This hasn't been as tiresome as I'd expected, though.'

'Yes, well you would say that wouldn't you? Kissing the best man like you did. Slut.' Paul pursed his lips.

'Shut up, Paul,' she giggled, narrowing her eyes. 'You're sitting far too close to me to be that brave.'

As they were served their meal, Bea was glad she couldn't see Leilani anywhere in the marquee. 'I wonder where she is?'

Paul shrugged. 'No idea.'

Bea just about managed to stay awake through the meal and then the speeches began. Her father's was as beautiful as the one she recalled him giving at her and Simon's wedding. Then Luke stood up, looking more nervous than she'd ever seen him. He looked over at her and then back down to his notes. She watched him speak and the guests laugh at his jokes and all she could think about was how much she wished he wasn't involved in something that meant she had to keep her distance from him.

Paul nudged her. 'They're calling you, sweets.' Bea couldn't figure out what he meant, then Mel waved her over. 'Bea, come here and get your maid of honour present.'

Bea blushed. Had they all noticed her staring at Luke, oblivious to everyone else? She walked up and took the gift, thanking Mel and Grant, before returning to her table. 'Look,' she said, touched by the thoughtfulness of the present. 'It's the pink Lalique cross that I spotted in the jeweller's the other week.'

The music started up and Paul groaned as the band began to play the intro to 'I Will Always Love You'. 'Oh, please no.' He put his fingers down his throat in a puking gesture. Bea pretended not to find him funny as Grant led Mel onto the dance floor for their first dance. Other couples quickly followed, eager to get up, she supposed, after so long sitting down. Bea sat feeling vaguely conspicuous when Guy and Paul's good mood descended into a whispered row over something.

She spotted Luke coming in her direction and looked around for Leilani. 'Dance with me,' he said, as soon as he reached her. Unable to think of a reason not to, she took his proffered hand. 'Where's Tom?' he asked.

'Tom couldn't make it.' She didn't elaborate further.

Luke stared at her for a moment, his expression softening. 'I see, well I can't honestly say I'm sorry.'

Bea thought it would be rude to agree with him. 'So, where's Leilani?' Despite herself, she was enjoying his closeness and didn't really want to know but felt she should ask.

'California.'

'California?' She stopped moving and frowned up at him.

'Keep dancing or everyone else is going to bump into us.' He lowered his head to hers. 'She's modelling, or something. She had an offer she couldn't refuse.'

'Just like that?' Bea concentrated on not slipping on the temporary parquet flooring; she didn't need an encore of her clumsiness from earlier. Why would someone as clingy as Leilani leave him to fly across the Atlantic just when they should be preparing for their own wedding?

'Yes, so it seems both of us have been left in the lurch. We'll have to look after each other for today, won't we?' He pulled her towards him, as the band played another slow song began.

As much as Bea felt she should sensibly keep her distance from Luke, she was too tired from the excitement of the night before to fight her conscience and it felt pretty good being held by him again.

'I'm enjoying this far too much,' he murmured in her ear, his breath sending shivers up her spine. 'I wish I knew why you keep your distance from me, Bea.'

Bea didn't reply and resisted him for a moment, then gave in to her instincts, relishing the moment of closeness whilst it lasted. The record finished and was replaced by a faster-paced song. 'Let's escape outside for a bit. You can show me round your dad's impressive garden, and maybe we'll get a chance to chat in peace for a bit. I need to speak to you about something.'

Intrigued, Bea let him lead her out to her father's treasured koi carp pond. It felt a little clandestine having her hand in his, but at the same time, the pressure of his hand around hers was sublime. How can something so wrong feel so perfectly natural, she wondered, staring at his broad suit-encased back as she walked slightly behind him.

'Shall we sit over here?' he asked, pointing to the wooden bench away from the marquee, where her father came to relax every morning with his coffee, watching over his precious fish before anyone else in the house woke up and disturbed him. She sat down, relieved to kick off the tight shoes.

'You look very sexy, by the way,' he said softly, sitting down next to her and taking both her hands in his. 'Bea, I have to tell you …' he began, just as his mobile rang, interrupting whatever it was he was about to confide. 'Damn.'

'Ignore it,' Bea insisted, her voice barely above a whisper and not bothering to hide her frustration with the caller.

'I can't, unfortunately.' He kissed her lightly on the lips and frowned as he answered the call. 'This won't take a moment, I promise.' He stood up and walked a short distance away with the phone to his ear. 'Yes? Hi. No, it's fine, don't worry.'

Bea waited for a few moments, feeling a little foolish sitting there, then seeing the serious expression on his face as Luke paced across the lawn and sensing the conversation wasn't going to be a short one, she stood up to return to the reception. Luke motioned for her to wait. When she shook her head slowly, he raised his spare hand apologetically and continued with his call, his face grim. Maybe, she mused as she went back to join the others, it was business. Then again, it was probably his fiancée. The thought gave her a pang of disappointment.

She returned to the marquee, feeling a little foolish for getting caught up in the romance of the day and her suppressed feelings for Luke. Walking through the guests, she was relieved to spot Paul, chatting happily to Paige and Jeremy. She tapped him on the shoulder. 'Hi.' He leapt up and hugged her. 'Where have you been?' Bea hurriedly explained. 'Oh, charming, so he takes you away from the throng and then abandons you to some phone call. So, where's his fiancée? I would have thought she'd be here taking notes for her big day.'

Bea looked over to where Paige and Jeremy were now in deep conversation, before explaining Leilani was supposedly modelling in California. 'Anyway, enough of that, have you spoken to Shani?' Bea asked, knowing that Paul would have phoned her at some point. She had wanted to give her a call a few times during the day, but didn't like to bombard her with calls, supposing she must be exhausted after all her hard work having the baby.

'Happy as a little pig in poo,' he said. 'She's even breast feeding. So revolting.' He winced. 'I told her that her boobs would be dragging along the floor, doing something like that, but would she listen?'

Stunned, Bea said, 'Paul, that's a disgusting thing to say and I'm sure it's rubbish. Honestly, you must let her get on with it. It's not as if we've got any experience with babies, so you're not really in a position to boss her around.'

'She's decided to call the baby Poppy, I gather.' He nudged her sharply in the ribs. 'Look out, here comes gorgeous.'

Bea saw Luke scanning the room, and then noticing her he changed direction and walked over. 'I'm going to have to go,' he said, looking troubled. 'Something's cropped up that I have to deal with.' He kissed her lightly on the lips.

'You're leaving already?' She couldn't help showing her disappointment.

Barrington placed a cool hand on her shoulder. She was very fond of her father's oldest friend and noticed him give Luke a knowing look before turning to her. 'Let the boy go,' he said, nodding at him. 'Thanks, lad,' he said.

Bea watched as the two men shook hands. There was something going on, but she had no idea what it could be. Luke smiled briefly at her. She watched him thank her parents and say his farewells to the newlyweds. Then he was gone.

Bea felt strangely bereft and gave herself a mental telling off for being so ridiculous. 'Now I'm never going to know what that was all about,' she said, attempting to make light of the situation.

'You have to trust him, Bea,' Barrington said, his voice more serious than she was used to hearing it.

'But I don't understand.'

'You will, my love, you will.' He leant forward and kissed her on the cheek. 'Right, I'd better go and speak to that father of yours about a couple of lobsters your stepmother ordered for their lunch tomorrow. Have fun.'

'Damn shame, if you ask me,' Paul said, as Barrington walked away. She tried to figure out what he had meant. 'Now you won't know when Leilani will be back, if ever.'

'Of course she'll be back,' she said, miserable to know she was right. 'They're engaged, aren't they?'

'More's the pity.' Paul frowned at Bea. 'If he's still engaged to that Amazon then he shouldn't have been dancing with you like that, let alone snog you.'

'Paul, you know perfectly well it wasn't a snog.'

'Yeah, whatever you say, sweets.'

Bea was saved from having to argue with him when Melanie called her over. They went up to Joyce and their dad's' spare room to help Mel change into her going-away outfit. 'Hasn't it been perfect?' she enthused, unzipping her enormous dress.

Bea nodded, delighted her sister had enjoyed the wedding she'd always dreamed of. 'It has; now hurry up and change, or you won't give yourself enough time to get to the airport.'

'Can you believe I'm going to Mauritius?'

Bea smiled. 'No, you're very lucky. Now get a move on.'

Mel changed into her new navy silk trouser suit with its little red silk top. Bea brushed out her hair, taking out numerous grips, and then helped her downstairs with her suitcase. 'What the hell have you got in here, gold bullion?'

'Only a few things I might need. I like to have a choice.'

'But you're going somewhere hot; all you need are a few sarongs and bikinis. You could have packed two hundred of the things and they wouldn't weigh this much.'

'I couldn't decide what to take, so I've taken a few extra things, shoes especially. I don't want to look out of place, do I?'

'I don't think that's a possibility. Now let's go and find Grant.'

Bea offered to stay behind and help her parents with the remaining guests, but happily agreed when her dad told her not to worry about it. All she wanted now was to get home and try to catch up on some sleep. 'And you can telephone Tom back, too and find out what exactly was so important he couldn't attend your sister's big day,' Joyce shouted over her shoulder as a parting shot, before rushing back into the marquee.

'Take no notice of your stepmother, and don't worry. We've got everything under control and by tomorrow afternoon, it'll look as if nothing has taken place here,' her father assured her, hugging Bea firmly. 'Surreal really when you think about it.'

After racing home to change and letting Flea out into the garden for a few minutes, Bea ran upstairs, checked Shani's bed and Poppy's cot were perfectly made up for them, and drove Paul and Guy to the hospital.

'Eugh, this stuff is revolting,' Paul said, forcing down a curly edged ham sandwich in the hospital cafeteria an hour later. He took a sip of his coffee and grimaced. 'I can't believe they're letting her come home so soon.' Me neither, thought Bea, dreamily picturing her own comfortable bed. He pushed his plate away from him. 'I wish we could leave straight away, I'm knackered.'

'Me, too.' Bea stifled a yawn. 'But she's insisting she's discharged earlier than they'd really like, so has to wait for the doctor to check her and Poppy over first before they can go.' She hadn't really thought much when Shani had asked her if she could come straight to The Brae. Bea had assumed Shani and the baby would be in hospital for a couple of days, giving her time to make sure everything was in place for them when they did come home with her. She wondered how they'd cope with everything Poppy was going to need.

'I wonder what Harry is saying to her?' Guy said, shuddering as he took his first mouthful of sandwich and dropping it onto the paper plate. 'You don't mind him visiting Shani at your home?'

Bea shook her head. 'No, I'd rather he did see the baby than not bother. He's probably not that bad once you get to know him. I suppose he'll need time to get used to having a baby around, too.' She was about to carry on talking, then spotted Luke paying for a coffee at the nearby till. 'Luke?' He turned to see who'd called him, a frown on his tanned face. 'Is everything all right?' He looked exhausted and was still in his best man suit.

'Not really.' He walked over to her. 'Mind if I sit down with you?' Bea nodded and watched him pull back an empty chair next to her. 'Has Shani had her baby?'

'Yes, last night. Paul, Guy, and I are giving her and the father a bit of personal space before we take her home to stay with me. You?'

He seemed to consider what he was going to say next. Bea didn't think she'd ever seen him so sad and couldn't help feeling anxious about what he was going to tell them. 'I don't think you ever knew my business partner, Chris.' Bea shook her head, wondering where this was leading. 'The phone call I received at your sister's wedding; he was rushed in here with a suspected fractured skull.'

'Oh my God, what happened to him?' she asked, feeling guilty for being so irritated with his earlier caller. No wonder he'd left in such a hurry, she mused, noticing the bruised smudges under his eyes. He didn't look as if he'd slept, his usually close-shaven jaw now sporting five o'clock shadow. 'Is he going to be all right?'

He nodded. 'It turns out it was just a bad case of concussion.' He looked as if he was going to say something further then looked down again.

Bea wished she could hold him close to her, try to take away some of the pain he was so obviously struggling with. There was more to the story, she was certain. 'What is it? Tell me.'

'It's nothing to do with you,' he said quietly, taking a sip from his coffee, then seemingly unsure of his decision, stared across the table at her. 'He was caught at the harbour, trying to abscond from the island.'

'But I thought he went missing ages ago?'

'He did, three years, but he'd sneaked back onto the island at some point and probably never thought anyone would be looking for him after so long.'

'Is there anything I can do?' She knew he was keeping something from her and couldn't help feeling it somehow involved her in some way.

He pushed a hand through his dark messy hair, taking her hands in his. He lowered his voice to a whisper. 'Fine, but if I tell you, promise you won't hold what I'm about to say against me.'

Her stomach filled with nerves, wondering what he could be about to tell her. Was she finally going to have to discuss his part in the money laundering, was that it? She wasn't sure she wanted to hear this. 'Why would I do that?'

'Because it's to do with Tom. At least I'm fairly sure it is. The authorities will just need the proof.'

Bea pulled her hands back and clasped them under the table on her lap. 'Tom?'

Luke nodded. 'I know you and he go way back, but how well do you really know him?'

'Luke, I know Tom very well.' She thought back to Luke's insistence that Tom wasn't all he seemed. She studied her hands for a moment. 'Well,' she hesitated, 'I thought I did. What he's supposed to have done?'

Luke took a deep breath. 'I think he's probably involved in some way in Chris's activities, but I'm not sure how yet.'

Bea felt as if she'd been slapped. 'Seriously?' She shook her head in disbelief. 'I don't think you understand how seriously an allegation like that would be taken,' Bea snapped.

'Look, you've obviously had a shock. I didn't mean to sound so harsh.'

She couldn't take in what she'd just been told, but something niggled at her. 'You can't be serious about Tom. I know you don't like each other, but this is ridiculous. What grounds do you have for making such an accusation? Why would Tom have anything to do with this sort of thing?' She closed her mouth to stop herself from saying anything further. He still hadn't actually mentioned money laundering and to tip him off now would be stupid. She wasn't going to lose her house and chance going to prison.

'Money problems, that's why.' Luke looked around to check

he wasn't being overheard and leant closer to her.

Bea shook her head. 'I can't believe this.' She felt sick at the thought of being oblivious of something so serious. She took a deep shuddering breath.

'Chris had Tom's contact details on him when they took him into hospital, so he's obviously contacted him recently. Chris knew he'd be arrested if he showed his face back here again, so he must have thought his visit here worth it to risk a prison sentence. I assume Tom got sucked into Chris's scheme in a moment of weakness, and once you're involved with these things, I can imagine it's almost impossible to back out.'

Bea heard Luke's mobile bleep. He glanced at the screen and groaned.

'What's wrong now?' she asked.

'It's an RNLI callout. I have to go.' Luke put his hand on Bea's shoulder and looked down at her. 'Don't worry. This isn't your mess.'

'I feel awful,' she said, wishing she'd not believed Tom so easily.

'Don't be silly, it's not as if you could have done anything.' He studied her face for a moment. Was he looking for assurance, she wondered.

'No, but I can do something about it now.'

Luke grabbed her wrist. 'What do you mean? Listen, Bea, I don't have time to argue with you now, but you need to promise me that you'll let the authorities deal with Tom. I was hoping to get to the bottom of this myself, but I've had to hand all the information I've managed to collate to them.'

She didn't answer.

'You don't know who else could be behind this and I don't want you getting involved. It could be dangerous.' He turned to walk away, pulling his car keys from his pocket.

'Well I happen to think I am involved,' she called after his retreating figure. 'He's my manager.' Damn, she'd said it. She chewed her lower lip.

Luke turned and scowled at her. 'I don't care what's going on between you; you need to stay well away from him. Let the authorities sort this out. Understand?' He sighed wearily. 'I'm aware that money laundering is about the worst thing you, as a Trust Officer, could be involved with in business. If you do speak to him about this in any way, you'd become involved and you don't need that.' He shook his head wearily. 'My guess is that Tom won't think twice of implicating you, if he hasn't already.' He stared at her questioningly for a moment. 'Now, I really have to run. He'll probably suspect that the authorities have been informed by now as well as the police. Even the nicest people can turn when cornered, and despite what you may have thought, Tom isn't a nice bloke.'

'You leave Bea to us,' Paul said. 'She can be hot-headed sometimes, but she's not a fool.'

'Hello? I am sitting here you know.' She chewed her lower lip, biting a little harder than she'd intended. 'Ouch,' she grimaced, tasting blood.

Luke sighed. 'I have to go. I can't miss this callout. Bea, I've no idea how long I'm going to be, but you need to do as I say and not do anything rash.'

'You go; we'll make sure she doesn't do anything stupid.' Paul glanced at Bea,

Guy stroked her rigid back. 'He's right. If Tom is capable of doing this, then you never really knew him at all.'

'What do you expect me to do then?' she asked, feeling frustrated by the injustice of it all. 'I agreed to go and see him at his flat later on. He texted me on the way to the church; there's something he needs to discuss with me.'

'What did you just say?' Luke hurried back to her and she repeated everything she'd just told him. He took her face gently in his hands. 'Then make an excuse. You mustn't try and deal with this yourself. Please leave it to the enforcers who are trained to cope with this.'

Bea could see he was desperate to get away, so nodded. 'Fine, I will.'

'Thank you,' Luke took his hands away and smiled at her, his voice betraying his exhaustion. 'Now, I really need to go.'

They re-joined Shani as soon as they'd finished mulling over what Luke had told them. 'I thought you were only going to be twenty minutes,' she grumbled, pulling on her jacket and smiling down at her sleeping baby. 'Now she's sleeping, typical.'

'How was Harry?' asked Paul nosily, settling himself at the end of the bed.

'He was OK, if I'm being honest.' She shrugged and couldn't quite hide a satisfied smile. 'He's promised to set up a standing order for Poppy. It's not what I would have wished for in respect of fatherly love for my daughter, but it serves me right for getting into this mess in the first place. He said he wants to see her occasionally and believes she should know her father, but that I can only contact him via the surgery.' Shani sighed and straightened her baggy top. 'It's better than nothing and maybe one day he'll choose to tell his wife about his other daughter, but for now I have to be satisfied with that. At least he's acknowledged her and I could tell he regretted being such a shit to me over all this.'

'It's a start,' Bea said, giving Shani a hug. 'It's going to be lovely having you both at The Brae. The house needs a bit of life put back into it.'

'Thanks, Bea.' Shani stood up and winced. 'I think I'm going to need a rubber ring to sit on for a few days.'

Paul groaned. 'Too much information, thank you,' he said, picking up Shani's overnight bag. 'You can take those,' he said to Guy, indicating the two flower arrangements she'd been sent. 'Let's get a move on. I need my bed even if the rest of you don't.' He narrowed his eyes and glared at Bea. 'We all need to get to our beds, don't we?'

Bea rolled her eyes heavenward. She still felt the need to see Tom and find out what he wanted to discuss, whatever the others thought.

'What?' Shani stopped them before they left the room. 'I'm sure something has happened. Tell me what's going on, or I'm going to keep you all from getting home.' She picked up the baby and gave her a cuddle.

Bea listened while Paul explained about their meeting downstairs with Luke. 'So you see, Miss I'm-gonna-take-charge has decided to ignore Luke.'

'I never said that at all.'

Paul tilted his head to one side. 'No, you didn't, but none of us are bloody stupid. We all know what you're like when you make your mind up about something.'

Shani put the baby back in her crib and sat down carefully on the edge of the bed. 'What are you up to?'

Bea groaned, closing her eyes with tiredness. 'Come on, Shan, I'm exhausted.'

'We all are, but no one's leaving this room until I hear you speak to Tom and tell him you won't be going to visit him tonight.'

Knowing when she was beaten and too tired to argue any further, Bea dialled Tom's number and spoke to him. 'He wasn't very happy,' she said not surprised when her friends didn't seem to care about that comment. 'I've agreed to meet him in the office early tomorrow morning. I can chat with him there instead, before I have to go to court. Right, happy now?'

Bea settled Shani and the baby into her largest bedroom and saw Paul and Guy off. As she watched their taxi going down her driveway, she couldn't help thinking that maybe the reason Tom had been so easy going about not pushing a relationship with her was so he could use her as his alibi to Vanessa, which would have allowed him the space and time to arrange meetings with his criminal connections. She still couldn't quite believe Tom could be involved in something illegal.

She wasn't sure what emotion she felt more strongly, fury with Tom and his involvement in something so underhand, or irritation at herself. She couldn't believe she had remained friendly with Tom all this time and not suspect his occasionally erratic behaviour. Surely she should have noticed something at work? She'd find out more in the morning, whether he liked it or not. 'Come on, Flea, outside,' she said, picking him up out of his bed and placing him down in the herb garden. 'You must be desperate for a wee by now.' She kicked off her heels and wriggled her feet, waiting for him to sniff around the borders for a bit before coming back inside.

Twenty-six

Tenth of May – Final Harvest

Bea woke to a balmy, sunny Tuesday. The stillness of the warm May day did nothing to help still the nerves causing havoc with her stomach. D-Day. If only Simon had agreed to the Martin Order she wouldn't have to sit across from him in court today. She stood in the shower certain Claire would have put the idea to him, but not surprised he hadn't agreed to it. 'There's still time,' she whispered to Flea as she rubbed her legs dry with the large fluffy white towel. Maybe not, she thought. Simon had never taken the decent way out.

'You'd only have been suspicious if he had agreed to your suggestion,' Shani said, patting Poppy's back lightly, trying to wind the snoring baby a little later in the garden. Shani checked her watch. 'There's still time. You're not due in court until ten thirty and who knows, maybe Simon will have agreed to your idea. He was probably too busy doing something fanciful like taking part in one of the posh parties being held all over the island for Lib Day yesterday to be bothered phoning you.'

'You think?' Bea raised her eyebrows but not her hopes at the thought. 'I suppose I was caught up with the wedding and little miss here having just been born.' She held back from mentioning how hard it had been trying to appear to enjoy the wedding when she'd been grieving for Aunt Annabel during the day.

Shani shook her head. 'Nope, I don't. You're just going to have to face the little shit in court. And hope for the best.'

Bea made a few more notes to her already lengthy list of points she hoped to bring up at the hearing and, unable to eat the bacon baguette Shani had cooked for her, tore off a small bit from the meat and fed it to Flea. 'At least by this afternoon I should know whether or not I'll be keeping my home.'

Shani placed her free hand on Bea's shoulder. 'Whatever happens today you mustn't worry about what Annabel wanted for you. She loved this place and her garden, but above all she loved you and you would have been the most important thing that would worry her. So, whatever happens, we'll deal with it and I'll be there every step of the way.'

Bea sniffed back the tears. 'Thanks, Shan. I know she would only want the best for me, but I'm also aware how much this place meant to her, and to me, if I'm honest. My whole life the only constant thing has been coming here. I don't know how I'd bear to sell it.'

Bea swatted away a fly with her folder. 'I suppose I'd better get moving if I'm to meet Tom. He wants to chat to me before the others get to the office and I don't want to be late for my own hearing.'

'Best of luck with court.' Shani gave her a one-armed hug, waking Poppy, who immediately began to cry. 'Are you sure you don't want me there? I could always ask Mum to look after Popps for a couple of hours.'

Bea shook her head. This was something she needed to do without any worries about concerned interference from her friends. 'No, I'll be fine. One way or another I'm going to be OK. I promise I'll phone you as soon as I know anything.'

Bea parked the car in the closest space she could find to the office and stepped out, pressing it to lock as she hurried through the car park. She could have done without having to come here, she thought as she waited at the side of the road for the lights to change, but if it was confirmed that Tom was involved with Luke's partner in something illegal, she would feel implicated too. She worked closely with Tom. Chris and Luke weren't clients' of hers, she thought with relief, but she couldn't reconcile the Tom she knew with the devious man who had tried to implicate Luke in something illegal. The lights finally changed and Bea stepped out into the road.

'Bea, wait.'

She stopped instantly at the urgency in Luke's tone and

moved back onto the pavement, uncaring that the driver in the stopped car looked at her as if she was a little nuts. 'What are you doing here?' she shouted, as Luke ran up to her.

'Sorry, I didn't mean to nearly get you run over, but when Shani told me you were going to meet Tom, I had to stop you.' He stood in front of her, bent over, his hands on his thighs as he recovered from the exertion of running to her. 'I called your house, but you'd already left,' he panted. 'You can't go in there.'

Bea frowned. 'Of course I can.'

'No, Tom is going to be arrested.' He shook his head. 'I'm sorry, but he's involved in whatever Chris has been doing and they've now got enough evidence to arrest him.'

Bea felt sick. 'Seriously?' She suddenly suspected that Tom wouldn't care if she'd been caught helping him. What the hell had he been going to ask of her? 'I can't believe Tom would want to implicate me in all of this,' she said, aware even she didn't believe what she was now saying. 'Do you think that's what he wanted to do?'

Luke shrugged. 'Who knows? I should think he was desperate for someone to help him.' He stared at her silently for a minute. 'And you're probably the obvious one to ask, working so closely to him and sharing a history together. I'm so sorry, Bea. I know this must be hard for you.'

They both looked up as two police cars came around the corner and parked outside the office. Bea gasped. If Luke hadn't stopped her when he did, she'd be in there now. 'Come here,' he murmured, taking her into his arms and holding her tightly. 'I'm so sorry, Bea,' he repeated.

She put her arms around him, enjoying the comforting hug. 'I can't believe he'd expect me to go along with something like that. The very first thing we're trained to do is look out for cases where people might be laundering, although I've never experienced anyone actually doing it, until now.' She looked up at Luke. 'He knew he'd get caught eventually, surely? This island is so hot on this sort of thing; they have to be.'

'True, but who knows what happened to make him do this.'

Bea stepped away from him. 'But what about you? Chris

was your business partner.' If Tom was involved in all this, what about Luke? She'd seen the papers with her own eyes telling her of the investigation into his business dealings. Was this just some con to make her believe he was innocent, when in fact it was Tom? Bea stared at him, trying to figure out who she could trust.

'You think I'm involved in all this, too?' He narrowed his eyes, then widened them as a thought came to him. 'You actually suspect that I'm the one who's involved in all this, don't you?'

Even now she couldn't tell him about the paperwork Tom had shown her. 'I'm trying to be logical. Both you and Tom suspect your business partner of being involved in money laundering activities. Tom has, um ...' Damn, she wasn't allowed to say what she desperately needed to.

'Tom has shown you proof, is that it?' He glared at her. 'So, you now think that I'm here to twist your mind into helping me cover up for my involvement?'

Bea didn't know what to think. She rubbed her forehead with her fingers, trying to ease the headache that was seeping through her brain. Tom. Luke. Both could be involved in one way or another, purely by their association with Chris. Both were clever enough. Tom had shown her proof, but she looked across at Luke, trying to gauge if she could trust him or not, and the hurt in his expression told her that he hadn't expected her to react in this way.

'I'm sorry, Luke, but I can't talk to you about this.' He looked aghast at her and she hated herself for what she was saying to him, but she had no choice. 'I really want to, believe me, but legally I can't.'

He looked stunned and raised his hands before dropping them back down to his sides again. 'OK, I understand, I think, but please do one thing for me, whatever you think me capable of.'

'What's that?' Bea waited for him to speak, wishing more than anything that she worked in some other profession and that she'd never heard of money laundering before.

'Do not go into that office. If you trust nothing else I've said to you, please do as I ask just this once. You can call Tom later. If I've lied to you about him being arrested this morning, then he'll still be around for you to chat to later on; if he's not, then you know I was telling the truth.'

'You're quite clear what's going to happen?' her lawyer asked her for at least the third time since they'd arrived at the Royal Court.

'Yes, I'm going to leave all the talking to you, unless they allow me to ask one or two questions.'

'That's correct.' He glanced down at the buff folder in his hand and pushed his round, tortoiseshell glasses up the bridge of his nose. 'I put in a request for you to speak when we filed the papers a couple of days ago, but if the judge does ask you to speak, you must ensure you keep to the point. Be clear and do not bring emotions into it at all. Your emotions are not a factor in a court of law. The legal points are all that matter and also whether or not the judge believes your ex-husband should be awarded half the value of the house or not.'

Bea sighed. 'Yes, I understand. No emotions.'

'Easier said than done, don't you think?' Luke walked up behind her and Bea turned to find him looking down at her.

Her stomach did a flip and for a second or two she forgot her nerves. 'What are you doing here?' she asked, guiltily recalling their conversation earlier that morning.

'It's my hearing today.'

Bea nodded, not sure how to react. 'Ahh.'

Luke raised an eyebrow. 'I've been thinking since we spoke earlier. Tom told you they were investigating me, didn't they?' Bea shrugged. He looked relieved. 'I suspected there was something holding you back whenever we –' he hesitated and looked to see whether or not the lawyer was in hearing distance, '– saw each other and I know it took a while for me to twig, but when my lawyer showed me some of the paperwork with Tom's signature on it, I realised he was involved in the reporting of the case and the reason why I'm here today.'

'Tom reported it? He never said.' Bea clenched her teeth together to stop from saying something she shouldn't in the hallowed corridors of the Victorian Royal Court building. 'Why would he do that if he was implicated?'

'Who knows?' Luke shrugged. 'Hey, don't be too angry, he was proved to be right about my partner. However, Tom hoped that by implicating me to the authorities he was providing himself with a smoke screen. What he didn't realise was that I've been waiting for Chris to attempt to return to the island, or trip up in some way, so that he can be prosecuted and I can maybe get back some of the money he embezzled from me.'

A door closed loudly behind Bea and she recognised Simon's clipped tone. She closed her eyes for a couple of seconds to steady her temper. Luke glanced over her shoulder, his expression not altering and took hold of her hand. 'It's going to be one hell of a morning for both of us, don't you think?'

Bea forced a smile. 'You're not kidding,' she said, determined to ignore Simon until absolutely necessary inside the court room. Bea couldn't believe he appeared so relaxed. Here she was almost sick with fear that she'd be forced to sell her home, when Luke was up against a probable jail sentence. 'I don't think I'd be as calm as you in your position.'

'They're only going to decide whether there's a case to be held, nothing more today, thankfully.' He sighed and bent his head down a little, lowering his voice, 'And I'm not as calm as I probably seem.'

Simon walked over and stood next to them. 'Beatrice,' he said ignoring Luke, who Bea noticed seemed amused by the arrogant behaviour, but didn't leave them alone which she was sure was Simon's intention.

'So, you decided not to accept my offer then?' Bea said.

Simon's eyebrows knitted together. 'I hardly call expecting me to hand over what's legally mine without recompense a reasonable offer, and I certainly have no intention of being forced by you, or by Claire, into doing something that stupid.' He shook his head and looked at Luke. 'Watch yourself with this one, she's got more of a sting than you'd think. She might look all sweet and angelic, but she can stand up for herself with the best of them.'

'I've worked that out for myself,' Luke said, giving Bea a cheeky wink to show there were no hard feelings between them. She relaxed a little. 'I'm glad Bea won't allow anyone to bully her.'

'Oh, it's like that, is it?' Simon sniggered. 'Good luck to you, mate, she'll turn on you one day, too.'

'If she does, I suspect it'll be my own fault.' Luke shook his head as Simon walked away. 'What a jerk.'

Bea shrugged. 'He is a bit of an arse, isn't he?' She giggled. 'I listen to him now and sometimes can't believe I ever thought I was in love with him.' She couldn't even imagine being married to him now, even so short a time after their split. It was like remembering a film she'd watched, rather than her own life.

'Mr Thornton, we need to go through now.' Luke nodded towards his lawyer. 'I'd better be off.' He gave Bea a quick hug. 'Good luck, Bea. I hope the judge comes up with the right verdict for you.'

'You, too,' she said, holding him tightly for a moment, trying to take a little resolve from his bravery. 'And I'm sorry I was so awkward with you. I had to watch what I said when I saw you in case I somehow tipped you off that you were under investigation.'

Luke smiled. 'Don't worry. My advocate explained that you could have got up to fifteen years in prison for something like that, and in your position, I'd also keep my mouth shut.'

'Tom obviously showed me the paperwork about you being reported to keep me off the scent of what was going on with him and Chris.'

'I suppose so. He must have known that if you suspected me, then you'd keep away from me and therefore anything I might accidentally say to you that could make you suspicious of his and Chris's activities.'

'I still find it hard to believe he could be so sly.'

'He certainly is that, but at least you now believe me.'

Bea nodded. 'I'm being summonsed,' she said spotting her advocate waving her over. 'Bye then and good luck in there.'

Luke nodded. 'You too,' he said before walking calmly

towards the main courtroom where the magistrate would hear his case. She took a deep breath and entered the wood-panelled smaller courtroom ready to face Simon and her own future.

Bea sat impatiently, waiting for the procedures to be read through and the French swearing in to be announced by the greffier, and couldn't help thinking how smart and dignified the tall, blond officer of the court seemed as he carried out his duty. Resolving to follow his example, she folded her hands in her lap and listened as each different case was heard. Eventually, it was her turn. Her advocate stood up and, referring to the papers he'd filed with the court, began his reasoning why Simon should not be awarded half the value of The Brae.

When Simon's advocate had finished, the judge addressed Bea. 'You have expressed a wish to speak, Ms Philips.'

'Thank you, yes.' Bea took a deep breath to steady her nerves and in an effort to stop her voice from wavering, more from anger with Simon than nerves. 'I understand that because I was still married to my ex-husband when my aunt died and left me The Brae that it was considered a matrimonial asset, but I'm making a request for the court to take into account my aunt's wishes for her home when the decision is made.'

He looked down at his notes for a moment. 'I believe that your aunt, Mrs Annabel Juarez, had booked an appointment with her lawyer and you assume that this was to change her will.'

Bea nodded. She could almost feel Simon's irritation at her daring to speak, but didn't care. She owed it to Aunt Annabel to fight her case as strongly as she could. 'I'm certain of it. The day after my aunt discovered Simon's, I mean Advocate Porter's, association with Claire Browning, she told me that she was going to put a clause in her will to ensure he didn't benefit in any way from her will at her death.' Bea's voice cracked at the memory of her aunt's anger and lack of suspicion that she would die within three days of the conversation.

The judge looked across at Simon and studied him for a moment. Bea wondered if he knew Simon. After all, Simon was an advocate and no doubt represented his own clients in front of this same judge. Bea willed herself to remain positive.

'Yes, the whole situation is very unfortunate.' He turned to whisper something to his greffier, who nodded and handed him a sheet of paper. He spoke to Bea once again after reading it. 'I'm advised by your aunt's lawyer that she did indeed arrange the meeting, that they did have a conversation on the telephone prior to that meeting where she advised him of her intentions towards Advocate Porter and according to your papers, despite your best attempts to raise the value of half your property, known as The Brae, you've been unable to do so.'

Bea didn't dare move. She concentrated on breathing, aware that she was gripping a little too tightly on the wooden partition in front of her.

'You have, however, been able to raise a figure amounting to a little under one third of the value of the property through a mortgage. Taking into account all that I've heard today, I'm going to award Advocate Porter the value of one third of the property. I realise you will still have to fund a further ten thousand pounds to meet the required amount I am awarding to him, but feel that one third is the fair amount in this case.'

Bea wasn't sure if she'd heard correctly. She'd managed to keep her house. She didn't have to sell. Simon's angry whispers to his legal counsel echoed across to her, but she took a deep breath, relieved, but still not quite able to believe that she'd won her case. It wasn't an outright win, but she still had her house and could find the means to buy Simon out. 'Thank you very much.'

She turned to her advocate and shook his hand. She'd done it. The greffier announced the following case. Bea sat down on the leather seat and lowered her head in her hands, just about managing to stifle her laughter. She could stay at The Brae. She hadn't let Aunt Annabel down after all.

Her excitement died down slightly and she sat up straight, composing herself once again. She wondered how Luke was getting on in the next-door courtroom.

Twenty-seven

Eleventh of May – Secret Garden

Since Tom's arrest, Bea had been to the police station to give her statement and now had nothing else to do. She still couldn't get over Tom's involvement, and cringed at the memory of her not trusting Luke enough to believe him the previous morning. Bloody Tom had a lot to answer for. Then again, as much as she felt for Luke she knew she must remember he was seeing someone else and that was something she couldn't do anything about.

Mr Peters had assured her when she'd phoned him after the court hearing to give him the good news that he hadn't changed his mind and that she could have the money to pay off most of her debt to Simon. Bea didn't mind about still needing to locate another ten thousand pounds to completely cover what she owed him; she'd worry about that tomorrow. She didn't care that she'd probably be broke for years. The main thing was that she'd managed to keep her house and Annabel's pride and joy. She swallowed the lump in her throat. 'I did it,' she whispered. 'You knew I could, didn't you?'

She realised the house phone was ringing and ran inside to answer it.' Hello?'

'Bea, please don't put down the phone, I need to explain everything to you.'

Bea shuddered hearing Tom's self-pitying tone. 'No, Tom, I don't think there's anything you have to say that I wish to hear.'

'You have to let me explain,' he whined.

'No, I don't.' She ended the call without giving him the chance to reply. 'Selfish shit,' she shouted at the phone. Bea went to leave the room, but the phone rang again. She left it for a few seconds, then realising the caller had no intention of

297

giving up, answered the phone. 'I told you I had nothing to say to you, and I meant it.'

'Ooh, who's rattled your cage?' Mel said giggling.

'Mel? What are you phoning for, you're on honeymoon.'

'I know, and it's gorgeous here in Mauritius, isn't it honey?' she shouted to Grant.

'This must be costing you a fortune, Mel. Is everything OK?'

'Yes, of course it is. Better than OK in fact.' Bea took a breath to speak. 'Shut up and listen, Grant said I can only talk for two minutes because the roaming charges are astronomical. Guess who we bumped into at the airport?'

'Who?' Bea asked politely, wishing she'd thought to buy a phone that she could walk around the house with. It was warm enough to sunbathe and she couldn't wait to get outside and make the most of the heat.

'Leilani.'

'Leilani?' Bea stopped dreaming about the sun and paid immediate attention. 'But I thought Luke said at the wedding she had taken a modelling assignment in California. Are you sure it was her?'

'I knew that would get your attention, of course I am sure. Come on, how many six-foot models do you know?' she teased. 'She was the one who got my attention, actually. She was furious with Luke, and I suppose not knowing many people in Jersey she needed someone to let off steam to.'

'What did she say?' Bea tried to hurry Mel up with the story.

'It turns out she didn't actually choose to leave him, whatever he may have told you, but she sat him down one day over lunch with the intention of fixing their wedding date and getting all the plans underway,' she could hear Mel taking a long sip from her drink. 'That was delicious. I'll have another daiquiri please, hon.'

'Well, go on,' Bea urged impatiently. 'What happened?'

'I knew you'd want to know. Grant said I should mind my own, but I told him you'd be interested.'

Bea took a deep breath to stop from shouting at her sister to hurry up. 'And you were right, so tell me.'

'Typical bloke, apparently Luke told her in no uncertain terms he had no intention of making that sort of commitment to her.' Bea could barely breathe, desperately aware of what she hoped her sister would say. 'When she argued that everyone had assumed they were engaged, he told her it was she who had been drunk and announced it to everyone without any encouragement from him and she shouldn't expect him to marry her simply because she thought she'd backed him into a corner by telling everyone he would.'

'Wow!' Bea could feel her heart pounding with the unexpected news. 'What happened next?'

'Melanie, your two minutes is up,' Grant shouted from somewhere in the background.

'I'm on the bloody phone to my sister. You get me that second daiquiri and then I'll get off the phone.'

Blimey, thought Bea, nothing much changes with Mel. 'Poor Grant, you don't have to be so rude to him.'

'Shush and listen. What was I saying? Oh yes, well, apparently, Luke pointed out to her that if she were to settle down now, right at the peak of her career, then she'd be doing herself a disservice, and she should return to the States and be the best model she could and not waste her God-given talent.' Mel giggled. 'Or something like that. Personally, I think she exaggerated a bit, but I do believe he told her to go and get on with her career as a kind way of getting rid of her.'

Bea thought for a moment. 'Wow, and she's so beautiful. You'd think he'd jump at the chance to be with her.'

'Hang on a sec, you haven't heard the best bit yet,' Mel whispered. 'Grant's on his way back, so I have to hurry. Leilani believed Luke would fight for her, so she called his bluff by telling him about this modelling assignment she was offered in America, and said that if he didn't commit to her in some way, then she'd accept it and they'd be finished once and for all.'

'No.' Bea was impressed with the girl's gall.

'Yes.' Mel laughed. 'He called her bluff back, or whatever you say, and told her she should take the assignment. That was the day before the wedding. The morning of the wedding he dropped her off at the airport on the way to the church and we met her when we checked in later on. Can you believe it?'

Bea was stunned. 'But I don't understand,' she whispered, trying to take all this news into her head. 'Why would he let me believe she had left him and gone off like that, when really it was him who forced her hand?'

'Don't know, but that's what she insists happened, and surely it would have been better for her to say his version rather than hers. A bit embarrassing to admit the truth like that, maybe it's because she's American. Maybe they're more open than we would be? I don't know.'

Bea laughed, suddenly feeling better than she had in weeks, months even. Leilani had gone and wasn't coming back, not for the foreseeable future anyway.

'Hey, I only told you because I thought you would be interested, you shouldn't sound so thrilled. Poor Leilani was devastated.'

Bea couldn't help feeling amused at her sister's change in tone. She bit her lower lip and took a deep breath to calm down. 'You're right, that was mean.'

Fuelled with this news, Bea ran upstairs to find Shani and tell her.

'You've got to phone him,' Shani said, holding out a soiled nappy.

Bea grimaced and took it between her forefinger and thumb and placed it into a nappy bag.

'Don't be so dramatic, it won't bite. Maybe it's time you let him know how you feel?'

Bea wasn't so sure. 'I don't think so, Shani. Mel did say how he said he wasn't ready to commit to Leilani. If I'm going to be with someone, then I want it to last. I've tried going out clubbing with you and Paul and it just isn't my idea of fun.' Bea picked up the newly changed baby and cuddled her.

'But you're already in love with him,' Shani added unhelpfully.

'I'm not going to argue with you about that.' Bea held the warm baby in her arms and sniffed her fresh, baby scent. Even if she couldn't be with him, it would have been comforting to hear from him, maybe know that he might have some feelings for her, especially after everything that had happened over Tom the day before. She wondered how his court hearing had gone. 'I think I've probably ruined any chances I had with Luke by not believing him,' she said miserably. 'I know he seemed fine in the Royal Court building, but that was just him being friendly. Anyway, I've no idea what that verdict was yet.'

'You mean he could still be guilty and involved with all that laundering business?'

'Possibly.' Her instincts told her that he wasn't involved, but they'd also told her Simon was the love of her life and Tom a good friend.

Shani carried Poppy downstairs and placed her carefully into her pram. 'I'm going to take her for a walk to the shops,' she said, looking happier than Bea had seen her look, possibly ever. 'Do you need anything?'

Bea shook her head, unable to speak for a minute. 'No, thanks. Enjoy your walk.'

They couldn't have been gone more than five minutes when Bea walked back into the house to check her mail. Flicking through the white and brown envelopes in her hand, she spotted the usual credit cards, fuel bill, and one other. She stopped in the hallway and dropping the bills onto the Bishop's seat, tore open the cream envelope. Unfolding the letter inside, Bea read it stopping to try and take in exactly what she'd been sent. 'Woohoo,' she screamed, dancing crazily around the empty room. 'Yes.' She kissed the letter in her hand and punched the air. 'Thank you, Aunt Annabel.'

'Shani,' she shouted up the stairs, before remembering that she'd gone out with the baby. Bea grabbed the phone and dialled Shani's mobile number. 'Shan,' she said, barely able to contain her excitement, 'you'll never guess what's happened.'

'What is it? Is everything OK?' Shani asked anxiously.

'It's better than OK, I've discovered what A Jersey Kiss is. Hurry up with your shopping and come back here as soon as you can, I've got something to show you.'

Twenty-eight

A New Leaf

Bea was so busy skipping around the hallway she didn't hear Luke knock at the front door. 'Oh.' She stopped instantly as he poked his head around the door. Not caring how idiotic she looked she waved him in.

He laughed. 'You obviously beat Simon then?'

'Not completely.' She didn't care about Simon right now, or the outcome of the court case. 'Better than that.'

He looked puzzled. 'You seem very pleased with yourself about something though. I've got a surprise for you.' He held out an envelope to her, but when she went to take it, he pulled his hand back. 'I know what the Jersey Kiss is that your aunt left to you.'

'Me too,' she giggled. Luke looked stunned. 'Really, I have, but you go first. Tell me what you've found out.' She could barely contain her excitement, but was so touched that Luke had been looking for the mysterious Jersey Kiss she wanted to see what he had to tell her.

'You know the picture I took last autumn?' Bea thought back, remembering and smiled; it had been under their noses the entire time. 'Well, I showed it to my uncle. He's a horticulturist and he'd never seen one before. He double checked and it seems like your aunt has propagated a new strain of Amaryllis Belladonna.'

'I know, the Jersey Lily.' Bea clapped her hands together and squealed.

Luke laughed and nodded. 'He tells me that although it's too late this year for any of the big specialist shows, like Chelsea or Hampton Court, if you were to show it there or maybe at one of the other larger shows you could get it noticed all around the world and make decent money by supplying specialists.'

Bea listened in silence. She hadn't thought that far; he'd obviously done his research.

'Gardeners across the world love discovering new strains of plants and this one is especially pretty. The money you bring in could help you keep this place. I'm sure I'm right.'

Bea stood on tiptoes and took his smiling face in her hands. She kissed him. 'You are.' She held out the envelope she'd received a short while before. 'This came in the post today.' She watched as Luke took the paper out and read it.

'Bloody hell, it's the licence for A Jersey Kiss. This is amazing, Bea. I never thought I could be so excited about a plant.'

Bea laughed, 'Me, neither. Clever Aunt Annabel; so this is the secret that she'd mentioned to me over the years. I never really took much notice, she was always telling me stories about Antonio and I assumed it was something to do with him.' She paused and stared into his eyes, almost overwhelmed by her relief and excitement at their discoveries.

'Bea, this could be the answer to all your worries. I'm so happy for you.' He looked down at her, his mouth breaking into a lazy smile. 'I can't believe I've been wracking my brains trying to come up with a solution to your finances. I would have been able to give it to you months ago if my uncle hadn't been on a world cruise when I first sent him the photo.'

'But I have it now,' she said, painfully aware how in love with him she was. He was so genuinely happy for her. 'Hell, I've just remembered it was your court date yesterday, too. I suppose the fact you're actually standing here right now means you were let off the charges?'

He grinned. 'Yes, thankfully I was. They decided I didn't have a case to answer, although my partner Chris does.' His smile disappeared and a haunted look crossed his face. 'I'm afraid it looks like Tom will do time, too, especially as he was the one who masterminded the fake property deal that Chris used to syphon off funds from our business accounts.'

Bea couldn't help feeling a tinge of sadness at the person she'd thought Tom to be. It was still hard to take in his part in

Luke's investigation. 'I can't believe he tried to implicate you in the case,' she said. 'I feel so bad doubting you at all.'

'Hey, it's not your fault. It's your job to be wary of people being dishonest with money. You have to be careful and it's not like you knew me at all well.'

'I do now though, and I'm sorry.'

'Don't say anything more about it.' He kissed her just as she went to reply, then lifted her up in a bear hug, his muscular arms encircling hers. 'You're incredible. Do you know that?' He kissed her until she was dizzy. 'You did the right thing,' he said lowering her back down and becoming serious once again. 'Why should you have believed me? You're a professional and I could have been feeding you a lie, just like Tom did, but you acted as you should have done. We won't mention it again. Now, about your Jersey Kiss.'

Bea kissed him again. 'That one?' she teased, breathing in the soapy scent of his warm skin.

He tickled her waist. Bea screeched. 'No, the other one. The one that's going to make you a great deal of money if you're clever with it, which I'm sure you're going to be.' He took her by the hand and led her through the kitchen and out into the walled garden. 'That one there.' Luke pointed to the area where the lilies had been the previous autumn.

'I'd love it if you'd help me look into the best way forward with this.'

He nodded, 'I'll do whatever you like.'

Bea, remembering her conversation with Mel, reluctantly changed the subject. 'Did you know Mel and Grant bumped into Leilani at the airport?'

His eyes glistened with amusement. 'So you know what happened then?'

Bea nodded. 'We seem to have been keeping quite a few secrets from each other up until now.'

'We have.' He kissed her neck. 'That's got to change, don't you think?'

Bea happily agreed. 'She's incredibly beautiful,' Bea said, not enjoying stating the obvious, but wanting everything cleared up between them once and for all. 'I don't understand how you

305

would split up from her.' She wasn't sure she wanted to hear his answer but when he didn't say anything, she continued. 'Why didn't you marry Leilani?'

'Because I love someone else.' Luke's expression turned serious. He didn't take his eyes off her.

Bea eyes widened at his blatant admission. She felt bereft and tried to step back from him. He held on to her arms. 'So what are you doing here, then?'

'I wanted to clear the air between us and find a way to help you sort out your problems with Simon.'

Confused, Bea frowned. 'Why?'

'You know why.'

She struggled to get away from him without any luck. 'No, I don't.'

'I would have thought it was obvious.' He looked down at her, his mouth turning up slightly at the sides.

'No, it's not. You've been dating a beautiful model for months. Who, it turns out, didn't dump you at all,' she said, hands on hips. 'She told Mel and Grant the whole story.'

'Oh.' He kicked a small stone off the path with the toe of his boot.

'Yes, oh,' Bea teased. 'But I don't understand what that's got to do with us?'

Damn, thought Bea. He wants me to spell it out to him. She sighed. 'You told Leilani you aren't ready for commitment,' she said, feeling exposed and awkward under his scrutiny, but determined to know everything. 'That's why she's gone, isn't it?'

'Yes, but I meant with her,' he said, not elaborating further.

She couldn't think what to say next and knew that as much as she didn't want to make any more relationship mistakes, this handsome man in front of her was everything she could ever imagine wanting. Bea, unable to say anything else, turned around and picked up a large twig.

After a short silence, Luke stepped up behind her and took her firmly in his arms. 'Bea,' he said, his breath on the back of her neck shooting a million neutrons down her central nervous system, sending it into overdrive. 'I did tell Leilani that, and I

306

didn't lie. I was trying to let her down gently. To be honest our relationship, which has been more of a friendship than anything else for a few years now, had dragged on for months longer than it should have done.'

Bea stood silently, dropped the twig and letting her hands wander up to where his arms crossed around her and gently curled her fingers over the taught muscles. 'I only started seeing her when I thought you were involved with Tom, and then it was really as friends. Childish, I know, but I fell in love with you so quickly, it took me by surprise and I wasn't really sure how to deal with it.' He lowered his voice. 'We haven't slept together for a few years now.' Bea raised her eyebrows disbelievingly, but stopped herself from saying anything. She didn't want to interrupt him, or give him a reason not to tell her everything. 'I couldn't understand why you kept pulling away from me whenever we seemed to be getting close. I know now about Tom and the tipping off business, but then it just messed with my mind. After that night we spent together I hoped everything would be OK.'

'And it wasn't,' she groaned, resenting Tom more than ever for keeping them apart for so long.

'Enough of that. What's past is gone and I think we should start afresh.'

Bea smiled. 'I couldn't agree more.'

He sighed heavily, turning her round to face him. 'Beatrice Porter or Philips, or whatever your name is now, I love you. Surely you must know that?'

Taken back by his unexpected announcement, Bea couldn't hide her smile. 'How could I?' she asked, unable to take in the enormity of his words.

He held her tightly against him. She could barely breathe, but couldn't be any happier. 'I fell in love with you the moment I saw you at the engagement party,' he admitted, 'when you went the wrong way around the palm to see who was talking to you.' He kissed her neck; Bea was relieved he was holding her tightly, so her legs wouldn't give way entirely.

She turned to face the man who she had desperately tried to forget, the same one who now was doing his best to help her to

307

sort out her financial worries and the man who'd stopped her from becoming involved with Tom's arrest the previous morning. She knew she loved him more than she could imagine loving any other man. 'You love me,' she said making certain she had heard correctly.

'I do.' He nodded, kissing her once again. 'Do you think you'd consider marrying me?'

Bea didn't hesitate. 'Yes, I would. I love you, Luke Thornton,' she whispered, enjoying being able to say the words aloud to him.

'And you know I love you.' He took her hand, leading her slowly back towards the house, past the rosemary, its summery scent wafting in the warm air. 'Maybe now you'll take me up on that offer to have dinner on my boat?'

'I think I could do that,' she giggled.

Luke turned to her, thought for a bit and then, taking a piece of the thin green wire from the nearby trellis supporting her honeysuckle, bent it round and fashioned it into a primitive ring. He took her left hand and slipped it on Bea's fourth finger. 'Not the most beautiful of rings, but something to wear until the jewellers open up.'

Bea looked down silently at her grimy hand displaying what to her was the most precious ring.

'So what do you say to my proposal then?' he asked, kissing her fingers one by one.

Bea was barely able to speak. 'Does this mean you'll take me back to the Ecrehous for our honeymoon?' she asked.

Luke smiled down at her, 'If that's what you want, then of course I will,' he whispered, kissing her, just as Bea's honeysuckle fell away from the trellis. Luke put a hand out to catch it immediately before it collapsed on the granite paving. 'I promise you're in safe hands.'

'So it would seem.'

THE END

A Jersey Affair

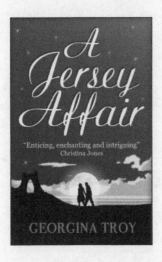

When shoe designer Paige Bingham is jilted she decides to enjoy her honeymoon-for-one in Sorrento. What she doesn't expect is to meet a mysterious entrepreneur, Sebastian Fielding, when she gets there. He helps ease the sting of rejection as he introduces her to the ancient sites he knows and loves. Unfortunately, soon after Paige returns to her island home in Jersey, she discovers that not only is Sebastian's company taking over the struggling store where her business is based, but that her concession is probably surplus to his requirements. How can Paige stop her fledgling business from going under? And what can she do to fight the gossip now that the paparazzi have published their untruths about 'A Jersey Affair'?

A Jersey Dreamboat

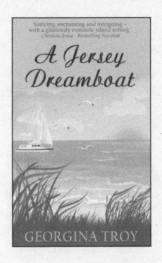

Event planners Izzy and Jess are badly let down when a Jersey socialite hires them for the busiest weeks of the season and then cancels at the last minute, leaving the girls with no bookings and no money.

Feeling despondent, they try a night out to cheer themselves up, and meet the captivating and aristocratic Ed, who invites the two on a luxury yacht cruise to Nice, together with his two brothers. Romance builds through heady days of blue skies and warm seas, but when a last-minute wedding booking is offered, the girls must return to Jersey, and real life has to begin again … or has it?

A Jersey Bombshell

Xavier has returned to the island of Jersey after ten years abroad to help his aging showbiz parents revive their failing Art Deco hotel. This proves to be something of a challenge, especially as his singer father and actress mother are more concerned with staying in the limelight than keeping track of the cash-flow. Xavier isn't going anywhere fast …

Meanwhile, he's stunned to find that the hotel's new receptionist is the girl he fell in love with years earlier in Vietnam, and someone who is tied to Jersey is the last thing she needs.

Romantic Fiction from

Accent Press

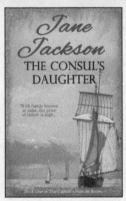

Nominated for the 2016 RNA Awards

Jodi Taylor

The Nothing Girl

Jodi Taylor brings all her comic writing skills to this heart-warming tale of self-discovery.

Known as "The Nothing Girl" because of her severe stutter and chronically low self-confidence, Jenny Dove is only just prevented from ending it all by the sudden appearance of Thomas, a mystical golden horse only she can see. Under his guidance, Jenny unexpectedly acquires a husband – the charming and chaotic Russell Checkland – and for her, nothing will ever be the same again.

With over-protective relatives on one hand and the world's most erratic spouse on the other, Jenny needs to become Someone. And fast!

Fans of Jodi Taylor's best-selling Chronicles of St Mary's series will adore the quirky humour in this new, contemporary novel.

Gillian Villiers

Family Matters

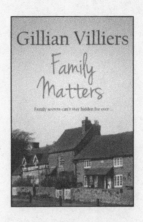

When Hope Calvert's best friend and business partner runs away with most of their money, she has no choice but to close their shop and return to Scotland. The only work she can find is as a carer, which is challenging, but surprisingly fun, and she's pleased to find she's getting more involved in village life. She particularly wonders if this extends to Robbie Mackenzie, the handsome farmer's son, but first she must sort out some long-hidden family secrets

Gillian Villers

As Time Goes By

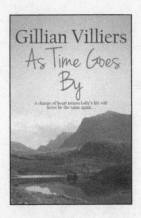

When Lally has to house-sit her grandmother's croft in the wildest part of Scotland with her scatter-brained sister Bel, she fully expects to soon return to her high-powered Edinburgh job. Bel has other plans, though, and Lally quickly finds the people and the place seeping into her soul. Or is it just one person, in the shape of new neighbour Iain? Torn between two worlds, Lally's decision will not only impact on herself, but also on everyone around her.

Kate Glanville

A Perfect Home

Claire appears to have it all - the kind of life you read about in magazines; a beautiful cottage, three gorgeous children, a handsome husband in William and her own flourishing vintage textile business.

But when an interiors magazine sends a good-looking photographer to take pictures of Claire's perfect home, he makes her wonder if the house means more to William than she does.

This is the beautifully observed and poignant love story of a woman who has to find out if home really is where the heart is.

Kate Glanville

Stargazing

Three women, connected by one man: Daniel is father to Seren, husband to Nesta and lover to Frankie. When he leaves Nesta and their beautiful home in the middle of the party to celebrate their fortieth wedding anniversary Seren's world begins to crumble. Only the continuation of the family ideal can make things right. But Nesta isn't so sure. And for Frankie, Daniel offers hope of a safe and secure future. But all three women are carrying secrets that they've kept hidden even from those closest to them. Secrets that might even threaten a life…